Beacon

Leyann Arbor

ISBN: 978-1-5356-1257-9 (paperback)
ISBN: 978-1-5356-1258-6 (hardcover)

Dedication

First and foremost, I would like to thank my husband, Stephen, for all of his support and his unwavering belief in me, even when I failed to believe in myself. He was also the inspiration for more than one of the positive male characters in this story, as well as the inspiration for many of the scenes (he'll surely recognize which ones). I wish to thank my sons for cheering me on when I wanted to give up (which was often) and my daughter, Samantha, for always being my confidante and for showing me what true strength is. I would also like to thank my mother, Sandra, for inspiring the creation of one of my favorite characters in this story, and for her encouragement, my sister, Michelle, for being a sounding board at times, and my second mother, Della, for always being an honest and sincere voice in my world. To both of my grandmothers, Alice and Hallie, I miss you every day. Lastly, to anyone who, like me, has ever struggled to be heard, this story is my voice. Find yours.

Preface

Death usually happens in one of two ways: total, unexpected shock or progressive acceptance.

Either way, it usually ends up being one of the happiest days of a person's existence. In some cases, however, whether because of shock, guilt, confusion, or the inability to let go, people can get *lost*.

Contents

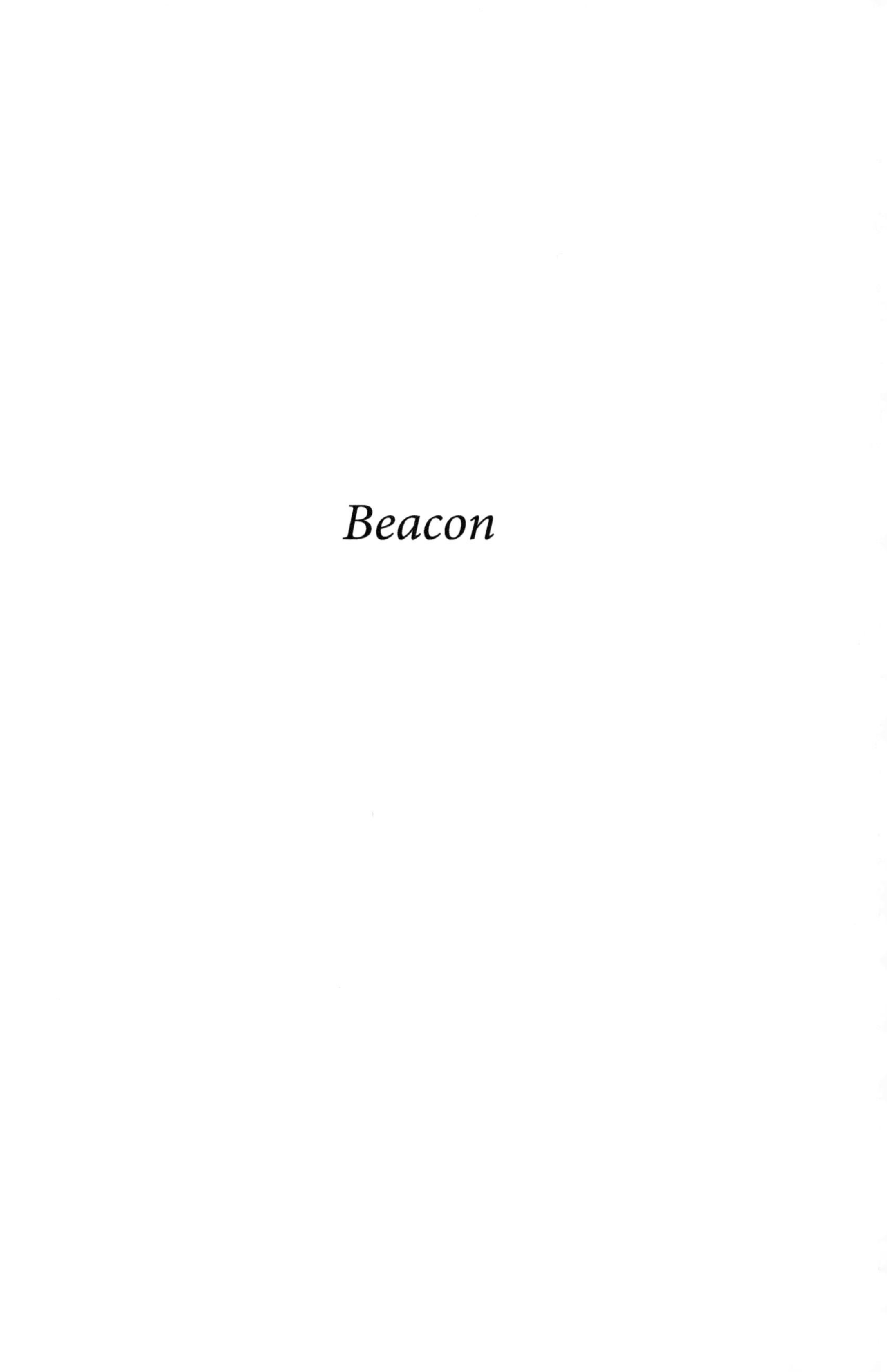

Beacon

1. Raign

When I lived…my home was an apple orchard, surrounded by green, rolling hills and blue skies, and it was where the fragrance of bougainvillea, apple blossoms, and sweet pea filled the air. It was a world without electricity, or even running water.

For most, the world was uncomplicated, but for me and for my family, the world was volatile. Most people's lives were honest and forthright, yet ours were veiled in secrecy. It was a world where 'love thy neighbor' reigned, but for my family, bigotry and hatred proliferated.

Our lives were obscured, our presence masked. We were hidden.

Still, my life was simple until my twelfth birthday.

Our farm was located just outside a small, sleepy town about fifty miles north of New York City. The town was tight-knit and quiet, and the people were gracious, God-fearing, and terrified of me.

Nevertheless, my home was a little slice of Heaven tucked away amidst the vein of a small river. Our quaint little farmhouse sat in the middle of a vast and open field full of apple trees. But the orchard wasn't only the place where I grew up; it was my safe haven. It was my shelter amidst the world's chaos, but most of all, the orchard was where I was accepted for who, and *what,* I was. In fact, it *was* my world, and in my opinion, it was the most beautiful, peaceful place I could have ever imagined living.

Our homestead was my refuge, and the trees were like family to me.

My name is Alyce Raign, or perhaps it *was*. I was born on the orchard in the year 1880. I lived there with my father and my grandmother. I was named for my Grandma Alice, who was my mother's mother, much to her chagrin. Upon my birth, Grandma decided to christen me as "Leesie" instead.

I loved my grandma as much as a person can love another. She was the embodiment of grace and gentility, yet her strength of mind and authoritative presence shone through. The only other soul that came even close to her in my heart, when I was a child, was my father, whom I called "Papa."

Besides the orchard, Grandma and Papa were everything in the world to me, but I had a strong bond with my grandma.

You see, she and I were both…*different.*

I knew when I was a young child that I wasn't like my papa and the other people in town, and for a long time, I believed that they were the ones who were different. But I didn't care. I loved Papa even though he wasn't like Grandma and me, and our differences didn't bother him at all, either. Truthfully, he seemed to be amazed by us and would encourage me by bringing books home from town when I was just a toddler. Then he would watch with pride shining in his bright, steel-blue eyes as I read the books aloud to him, memorizing every single word as I read.

As inquisitive a little child as I was, I was shy and wildly protective of my family, particularly when the word "witch" was whispered in town. And I was wise beyond my years. I knew how to speak, as well as how to read and write in several different languages even before I learned to walk, but Grandma never complained about finding things to teach me. Perhaps she didn't mind because I was like her, or maybe it was because I reminded her of my father. Whatever the reason, she understood me.

My grandma's name was Alice Willow, but that was all I knew about her. That, and that my mama was her daughter. I didn't even know who my mama's father was—or is? That was a question I dared not ask.

Grandma Alice was a beautiful person, inside and out, and she was quite a diminutive woman, standing only about five feet tall. She was roughly the size of a twelve-year-old girl, but she was as beautiful and elegant a woman as I'd ever seen in my life, even in the city.

Grandma had long, waist-length, flowing, strawberry-blonde hair and piercing emerald-green eyes. They were eyes that seemed to peer straight through a person. Her skin was the color of blushed porcelain; it was flawless, save for a few crescent-shaped marks running across her chest, and she had a radiance about her that couldn't be explained. She was tiny, with a slight frame and elegantly long yet delicate limbs. She looked like a china doll.

I learned, though, that underestimating my grandmother because of her size and delicate beauty wasn't something that should be done. She was a powerful being, one who could send shivers of fear through me without uttering a single word. In fact, her intense gaze alone was enough to make me obey. I never crossed Grandma because I was sure that if I did, she could turn me to stone. Although I didn't think she would ever harm me, I didn't want to find out. I wasn't frightened of her, per se, but the respect I had for her was immense. In truth, I was in awe of my grandmother and hoped to be as formidable as she was one day.

Commanding, though, as she was, Grandma had a grace about her that put the image in my mind of a dancer. Even when she was walking, her poise and tranquil splendor spoke volumes. The way she moved was almost like a dance. In my mind, my grandmother was every bit as graceful as any of the ballerinas I'd seen in the city, and she was many times lovelier than any woman alive, myself included.

I could sit for hours on end and simply watch her. The effect she had on me without speaking a single word was hypnotic.

Lovely though she was, she was often sad, introspective, even detached. Sometimes she sat alone for hours, saying not a single word and looking as if her world was about to end. At times, she seemed lost, her mind adrift, somewhere I couldn't reach her. And as much as I loved the orchard, she almost seemed to resent it. Other times I got the feeling that she was trying to distance herself from us altogether—Papa, the orchard and me—but I didn't know why. Still, she was kind, and I knew she loved me dearly. I just wondered what sort of demons haunted her soul.

Grandma was very much her own person and would throw caution to the wind, as Papa always said, by not wearing dresses while working the orchard. Instead, she tailored a pair of Papa's old trousers to fit her and then topped them off with one of his raggedy work shirts and put a big, floppy hat on her head.

I couldn't remember seeing another woman dressed like that in my life, and I often wondered why she did it. It just didn't seem to fit the rest of her personality. I'd often likened her behavior to a ballerina dressing like a vagrant. That was a notion that made me snicker. Of course, it was only out in the field that Grandma wore my father's clothes. And I figured if she thought it was suitable for a woman of her beauty to dress in men's clothing, then who was I to question? And Papa didn't care, either. He thought she was beautiful no matter what she chose to wear.

I hoped to be just like her someday.

My grandmother and I were not like everyone else—I guess that's why we were hidden away. She and I knew things, odd things. We knew intimate details about people in town and even strangers. They were details that no one else knew. They were things that we shouldn't have known. What's more, we saw things about the future or about a person's past. Sometimes we envisioned souls who had passed away years before. That part of the power used to frighten me. Then one day, I saw my grandma help a little girl's ghost get to heaven and back to her Mama. I couldn't do that, and I wondered how Grandma did it. I wondered how she was able to cross the little girl and why anyone would think unkindly of my grandma for helping the little ghost.

I also saw Grandma moving things with only her mind, but she didn't know I caught a glimpse of that. Papa saw it, too, but he just smiled and sighed.

That reaction made me happy.

My mother was Rebecca Raign. She had brown hair, and her eyes were hazel, but that's all I knew about her. Grandma said my mother's eyes were the color of topaz gems, but that description didn't match what I saw in my mind. In dreams, I pictured her eyes as deep, sparkling emerald green, just like Grandma's eyes, and mine.

My mother was Grandma's only child.

My beautiful mother passed away on the night that I was born. I don't even know how she died. I asked Papa about her a few times. I asked what my mama was like, and I always got the same answer from him. He'd say, "Your mama is beautiful, angel, just like you," but that was all. And though the answer was short, I did like the way he'd say *is* instead of *was* while speaking about her. It made her closer, somehow.

I didn't mention my mother to my father very much. The mere mention of the word "mama" seemed to cause him a lot of pain, so I didn't ask. Had I asked, I'm sure he would have told me anything I wanted to know, but the pain in his eyes didn't lie.

Maybe someday…

My mother was painful for my father to talk about; it was still too raw, like an arrow straight through his gentle heart. Therefore, I resigned myself to wait. I would wait as long as it took for him to heal, or at least until it became somewhat bearable for him to endure, if ever that day came.

Papa's name was Asa Raign, and he was the most spectacularly normal human being one could be, compared to Grandma and me, that is. Papa had wavy, sandy-blond hair, and his eyes were light steel blue. They were the color of forget-me-nots in a summer field, the hue of the sky in the mid-afternoon sunshine. His eyes were simply the loveliest, most calming eyes that I had ever remembered seeing. My father was strong, tall, and courageous.

He was almost everything to me.

My father had a kindness about him that ran as deep as his soul and a wonderfully gentle mind to go with it. He was quiet, pensive, and wise for a farmer. What's more, he was an accomplished musician—although the word *musician* didn't do him justice. In short, he was a musical genius.

Papa's family was wealthy, and they lived in the city. I had never met them, and Papa never spoke of them, either. In fact, the only thing my father had to remind him of his family was a small piano that had once belonged to his mother.

It was on that piano my father gave life to his music. I wasn't sure how we had acquired my *other* grandmother's piano, but I overheard once that Papa's mother gave it to him as a remembrance. Whatever the reason, I was grateful.

Papa's music was a gift from Heaven.

The only thing I knew for sure was that my father's mother had inherited our piano from her sister, who had died when Papa was young. Even though I had never met my other grandmother, I couldn't help but be thankful that she gave the piano to my father.

That small piano seemed to come alive under his assessing touch. It was a part of him. As he played, the rich tones of his music breathed and soared through the room, urging everything around it to spring to life. It was at those times when his music came to life that I was perplexed. I couldn't envision how hands that made such divine music could also belong to a farmer or, for that matter, how someone with such a brilliant mind could spend his days working a field.

Still, I loved the orchard, and I was glad that my father loved it, too. Nevertheless, the way that Papa played piano was something that couldn't be taught. It was exquisite. The music came from his soul; it was something that had to be experienced and not just heard. He played with such emotion that sometimes it made me cry; listening to him play would incite feelings within me that can only be described as *bliss*. My heart soared. When Papa played, I felt that we were no longer hidden. His music unchained me, body and soul.

Though my father's hands brought life to his music, they were also deeply scarred. When I was a small child, I used to take his hands into mine and examine them. Every fingernail was worn down, almost to the quick. His palms were marked with deep, long-since-healed cuts running in every direction, and in the middle of his right palm was a diamond-shaped scar that looked like a burn.

I asked him about the scars once. *"Years of farming, angel,"* he whispered.

I remember thinking at the time that it must be a miracle that he was still able to play the piano for us; I prayed he never stopped.

As I listened to my father play, I would often wonder if he could have been an artist or, perhaps, a real musician. But the orchard was his passion, and I loved it as much as he did. I guess in his own way, he was an artist, and his canvas was our trees. Sometimes I'd wonder if he loved the orchard more than he loved me. That was an idea I tried not to dwell on.

Nevertheless, my father spent every sunlit hour working our orchard, and I was pleased when I grew old enough and strong enough to help him. Seeing as I was his only child, and a *girl*, I was grateful he trusted me with something so precious to him.

In truth, I cherished every day of the summer and autumn months, every day that I spent with my father and our trees. But the warm summer evenings were the best time of the year for me.

Those summer nights filled me with wonder. I'd sit on a small, wooden stool just outside of our little farmhouse door as the blazing summer sun sank into the horizon. The brilliant orange light was mesmerizing. It dazzled, reflecting off the bright green canopies of my apple trees. Like a wet painting, the colors bled together, the many shades melding into one. The green and red of the trees fused and blurred, mixing with the burnished fire in the sky. Then everything went a cool shade of midnight blue as darkness eclipsed the sun. Next, the moon awoke from her slumber, sending the stars out to play. I closed my eyes, pretending they shined only for me, contemplating my day as daylight melted into dusk. Finally, the whippoorwill sang in the distance, on my farm, my orchard…my home.

From inside the house, Papa's soft music resonated. He played for hours after a long day of nurturing and loving our trees. And I knew that he played *for* me, but he played *to* her, my mama. The sound of sweet music carried on late into the night. I'd drift off to sleep as the echo of fluid notes filled the air around me with life. My dreams were always so sweet when Papa played.

2. Dream

Many nights as I lay in bed, I was amazed by the beautiful array of colors that flashed through my mind's eye just as I drifted off to sleep. The fusion of colors began as a slow swirling of warm brown. Then they changed from tawny hues to deep sage green and then to a brighter, more vivid shade of green. And, finally, bursting through the mix was a cluster of brilliant yellow starbursts.

Then, *he* appeared.

He was a boy with brilliant hazel eyes, warm chestnut hair, and the most radiant smile that I had ever seen.

I didn't know who the boy was or where he had come from, and frankly, I didn't care. Even though I'd never seen him in my life, somehow I recognized him at once.

I knew I loved him.

The sight of the boy stirred feelings within me I didn't even know existed.

Then a story unfurled around us, and it was always the same.

First, I was out tending the orchard alone. I never tended the farm alone, but in this dream I *was* alone, or so I thought.

In this dream, I was out in the field, picking fresh apples from one of my beautiful trees. Well, not picking as much as laughing while the tree tossed the apples into my basket.

Then it happened…

From atop the largest tree that Papa had lovingly named The Grandfather Tree, the boy floated down from where he perched on the highest bough. To my surprise, he *glowed!* I stood in amazement, staring, captivated by his pure-white light and by the way it reflected off the mass of chestnut-brown hair falling into his hazel eyes.

It was then I noticed that the boy's eyes were a mixture of the same colors that had flashed through my mind just before I fell asleep.

As I stood watching him, the beautiful boy reached into his chest and pulled out a silver rope. I gasped as he turned the rope into a lasso. Then he tossed the rope around my waist and pulled me toward him, almost forcefully, but it didn't hurt. What's more, I never fought him. I could have, but I didn't see a reason to resist.

All of a sudden, the boy reached for me. He caught me in his arms just before I crashed straight into him, and he held me to his chest for a moment. I felt his heart. It was beating fast, and to my surprise, it was in perfect rhythm to my fluttering heartbeat.

The breath caught in my throat. *Our hearts beat as one, but how?*

I peered into his eyes, seeking the answer, but he didn't respond. He only grinned and set me on my feet.

The boy leaned forward and smiled, a tearful, almost mournful smile. He lifted his arm and, while gazing straight into my eyes, grasped my hand. A brilliant orange light shot out from my hand and into the boy's chest. I *saw* the orange flame light encircle his body just before he breathed it into his chest, absorbing it into his soul. I couldn't move; neither could I speak. I could only watch. And though the flame-colored light seemed to startle the boy for a moment, it didn't harm him. It was only a surprise.

After a short pause, the boy steadied himself and reached out for me again. He took a small lock of my red hair into his hand and then ran it through each of his long fingers. His penetrating gaze never left mine.

I stood motionless, gazing at his deep and soulful eyes while also realizing that, through his eyes, I could see his soul. What I saw was that *his* soul was exactly the same color as *my* hair.

The boy stepped back, his gaze never leaving mine, and he smiled. *"I love you, Sita,"* he choked, appearing mournful again.

I frowned. *Who is Sita?*

My question went unanswered.

Just as the thought passed through my mind, a butterfly landed on one of the boy's outstretched fingers. His eyes swept from the butterfly to me and then back again. Again, I frowned at his knowing expression.

"What am I supposed to understand? Who are you?" I asked him directly, using only my mind.

Once again, the boy didn't answer. He tearfully smiled, watching the butterfly as it fluttered away, back up into the depths of The Grandfather Tree, and out of sight.

The angel boy returned my hands to his. *"Dance for me again, like a butterfly,"* he whispered. Then he leaned in and planted feather-soft kisses across my lips.

My heart pounded. I shook my head, and a heated flush rushed over my body, all the way down to my toes.

You are so damned beautiful, much too beautiful for me, I thought.

"Who are you, and why do I love you so?" I asked, peering into his breathtaking eyes; they were full of pain. Then an awful thought pierced my brain. *"Are you dead?"* I asked, recalling the colors of his soul from some distant memory.

I placed my hand over his fluttering heart and felt him flinch. My eyes shot back up to his. *"There's a scar over your heart. Are you dead?"* I asked again. He didn't answer me.

I can't cross him, I thought. *I'm not like Grandma. I can't do such things…*

As soon as that idea skipped through my mind, the boy bashfully snickered, almost as if he had heard my thought—but how? He leaned in, closed his eyes, and kissed the end of my nose, causing my already weakened knees to quake.

Then, out of nowhere, another angel appeared.

This one was a baby, a girl. She was about a year old. She had the same color hair as Grandma, but I noticed that her *eyes* were a glorious shade of light blue, just like Papa. The sight of her eyes took my breath away. She looked up at me and, taking my hand into her tiny fingers, pulled me down to her level. I knelt before her. All the while, her bright, light blue eyes twinkled into mine.

"*Aaleesa,*" she whispered in a sweet, baby voice and then giggled.

The boy stood smiling at the baby and me throughout the entire exchange. Proud tears welled in his sparkling eyes. He was looking at us as if she and I somehow belonged to him.

Just as I stood up, the baby giggled again, ran straight into me, and then disappeared. After she vanished, I awoke. For a few glorious moments, I remembered every detail of my dream, but the images soon disappeared.

I lay in my bed motionless, my eyes shut tight, willing my brain not to rouse. I wanted nothing more than to enjoy my beautiful boy for a few minutes more. And the baby who was just like me and just like Grandma… I longed to keep her little face right in the forefront of my mind. Still, she always disappeared, and she took my boy with her—returning to where? I did not know. They left just before I opened my eyes and as soon as my consciousness returned.

Many mornings just as I awoke, the angels in my dreams slipped my mind until the next time I saw them. Then I remembered that they were mine. I knew them well, and I loved them both—my baby girl and her *papa*.

Still, just before their faces drifted back into my subconscious, I'd wonder, *Will I ever see them in the flesh, the two glowing angels who belong to me?*

And, if the answer was yes, then, the question was when.

3. Orchard

It was a bright and sunny early September afternoon. Papa, Grandma, and I were out tending the orchard. A few of the apples blazed bright red in the sunlight. Those had to be picked first before they fell to the ground and spoiled.

That thought excited me. I loved picking apples and trying not to eat as many as I'd picked that day.

I skipped behind my papa, attempting to mirror his every move. His movements were graceful, effortless. The rippling muscles in his arms and back contracted with each shift of his body.

He was beautiful.

I took a deep breath and sat down in the shade, enthralled by my surroundings.

The air under the canopy was so sweet that day that I could almost taste it. I closed my eyes and sighed just as a cool summer breeze whipped my hair around and into my face, and the scent of sweet apples and wildflowers tickled my nose.

Surely even Heaven itself wasn't any better than spending a sunny day in Papa's orchard… *My* orchard.

I opened my eyes and looked up. The sun was getting high on the horizon, and it was quite hot, but in the shade it was cool, and the gentle breeze felt like Heaven.

I peered around, studying my father's handiwork.

It always amazed me how straight the lines of trees in our orchard grew and how the intricate pattern of rows, cutting straight across and diagonally, reminded me so much of a perfectly made checkerboard.

My eyes swept over the field, studying the way the deep ditches and gullies marked the earth where the trees stood while also allowing fresh water to pool and feed them. I watched as Papa poured water from the river vein that wound a fine line around the back of our little farmhouse into the dug-out holes surrounding the many trunks. He poured water into each of the ditches, quenching the thirst of our beautiful, majestic trees.

Watching my father work was strangely hypnotic to me.

"Leesie."

The sound of my name pulled me from my daydream. I looked up into the delicate face of my grandma. She was smiling down at me. Then she crouched low and pushed a few wild strands of hair away from my eyes.

I met her gaze.

"Where were you?" she murmured.

"Just watching Papa…" I looked over her shoulder at him.

Grandma laughed and then glanced behind her to where he was working. She nodded and sighed. *"Yes, your papa does love the trees, bless him, even though they are dead, soulless things."*

Her words hit me like a blow to the head; they shocked me. My head snapped back, my eyes sweeping up through the many dark green canopies of *MY* trees. The leaves were a mixture of bright green and sage, coupled with sporadic dottings of red, yellow, and green apples. They didn't look dead to me, and I knew they weren't soulless.

I sucked in a long, deep breath of air, sweetened by the apples, my apples, and felt something that I'd never remembered feeling for my beloved grandma before—anger!

"Why would you say that?" I shouted, and it was in a tone of voice that was more demanding than I had meant.

My grandma gave me a knowing look, one that was somehow haunting to me. She cocked her brow, and her penetrating emerald eyes flared into mine.

All of a sudden, I felt wildly protective of a field full of trees. Then I realized why. I'd always considered the orchard to be a part of my father. It was an extension of him, and he, in turn, was an extension of it, and I didn't want death anywhere near either of them. I'd always felt that our trees were more like family to me than just things. I loved them dearly.

I tilted my head. *"Why?"* I whispered with confused tears welling in my eyes.

"For goodness' sake, Leesie, what would you call something that doesn't breathe?" she tersely snapped.

I opened my mouth to retort, but my grandmother stood up before I could question her any further. *"Never mind that, now,"* she muttered, dismissing me, and waved her delicate hand through the air. *"Go fetch a few more bushels. There are more ripe apples than we thought."*

I stood, fisted my hands against my hips, and glared at her. I didn't move a muscle.

Her intense gaze flashed with danger at the sight of my disobedience. *"Go!"* she sternly commanded, her eyes widening. As her eyes flashed, I lost my breath. In the next instant, she turned, her powerful gaze fell, and she gracefully swept away.

I stood motionless for a few moments, attempting to figure out why she would say such a thing. I knew she didn't love the trees, not the way that Papa and I did, but why would she say they were dead? I just didn't understand.

Finally, remembering myself, I obediently ran in the direction of the barn. I ran in between the carefully dug rows, taking great care not to spill any of the dirt that my father had spent so much time digging out.

At the same time, a sense of bewilderment swirled through my mind. *Trees don't breathe? Of course, they breathe! She's wrong! Everything that's alive breathes in some way or another, doesn't it? Why would she say that, and why couldn't she love our orchard? The orchard is a part of Papa, and it's a part of me, and…* I stopped dead in my tracks. *"Oh no, maybe she doesn't really love us,"* I softly mumbled.

That thought stole my breath. I turned and looked behind me, where she was a mere spot in the distance.

Then, shaking that awful thought from my head, I ran farther. Just before I reached the yard, and while traipsing full-speed over a square patch of over-grown weeds about a hundred feet from the house, my foot fell on something peculiar.

Thud! It made a loud noise just as my feet hit it.

I stopped. *Funny,* I thought.

I looked down. The ground didn't look any different. I bent low, looking closer, and ran my hands over the soft dirt. As my hands swept across, I realized I could see that there was a plank of wood where my foot fell. I kicked at the dry ground and weeds covering the plank, and the more I kicked, the bigger the wooden thing became. I grabbed pieces of the earth with my hands, chunked them off, and threw them to both sides of me. With all the hard parts cleared, I stood up, panting. All that remained was loose dirt, and I could plainly see what seemed to be a four-foot-squared wooden door in the middle of the ground.

Feeling brave, I jumped up and down on it, hoping that it wouldn't give way, while at the same time shaking the loosened dirt from the door. As I jumped, two holes about the size of silver dollars, appeared as the dust fell inward. I bent down again and pulled up a piece of weather-worn rope that was tied to the holes to form a handle.

With all my strength, I pulled on the rope, willing it not to break. The door made a loud, cracking sound and whined as I pulled even harder, but it wouldn't budge. I tried again, this time tugging with all my might. Still, it wouldn't move, but I didn't give up. I grabbed the rope with both hands, fiercely twisted, and pulled—hard.

With a final groan, the door finally flew up. Just as the last remaining remnants of dirt fell away, it swung loose while at the same time throwing me backward. I fell hard on my back with the rope still gripped in my hands. I lay still for a moment, catching my breath and trying to feel for any broken bones; there were stars in front of my eyes, and I felt dazed and sore.

A few minutes ticked by…

When I decided that I must be all right, I sat up. The world spun around me for a moment, and a sharp pain jabbed the back of my head. I put my hand to the pain and felt an egg-sized bump forming on the base of my skull. I sat dazed for another minute, almost forgetting what I was doing there.

Finally, my eyes focused and then refocused on the wooden door that lay open before me. There were big grooves cut into the inside of the door, almost as if someone had tried to whittle something into it. The marks were indiscernible, almost like scratches, and ink stains covered both the wood and the old rope.

I scrambled to my feet and squinted down into the dark hole.

It was an old root cellar.

4. Vision

Ilooked down into the old cellar. The steps leading into the ground were worn just as badly as the old door was. In fact, the first step was just a hole in the ground; all of the boards were missing.

I jumped over the hole where the step was missing and onto the second step and then looked down into the dank, moist darkness. It smelled of old, rotting wood and years of rain, and thick sheets of cobwebs threaded the entire area from floor to ceiling. It was a creepy place. Still, I wondered if Papa and Grandma knew it was there. After all, it could be fixed and made useful for the farm.

I jumped from the rickety steps down onto the old dirt floor. I stepped over a broken lantern lying on the bottom by the steps. As my eyes adjusted to the dim light, my sights swept to a row of discarded bushels lined up along the dirt walls, and to the decayed remains of years-old apple cores that were strewn about the floor surrounding them.

As I looked around, the back of my head throbbed, and the world spun around again. I shook my head, trying to focus, and closed my eyes for a moment to steady myself. As I reopened them I noticed something changing in front of me. Actually, it was more of a shimmer, almost like I was staring into a mirage. At first, I thought it was only my imagination at work, or perhaps it was caused by the hit to my head, but then something else happened.

It began with the old rotting bushels…

As I steadied my hazy, throbbing head, the bushels filled with crisp, bright-red apples just as the old, decayed ones disappeared.

I took a step back, shocked by what I was seeing, and pushed my hand to the dirt wall. Only, just as my hand met the dirt, the walls changed from worn dirt and mud to polished wood. Then the lantern lying broken on the ground blazed to life. It hovered upwards, flew across the room, and sat on a small, wooden table that had appeared out of nowhere.

Hmm. That wasn't there a minute ago.

Then the cobwebs disappeared.

I shook my head, attempting to shake the hallucination from my mind. *Surely it must be a dream, or maybe it's something different.*

I'd seen things before, amazing things, things that no one other than my grandma had seen. Still, I'd never experienced anything like that before.

As I stood contemplating my sanity, the old, forgotten cellar door transformed before me. It shifted from an ancient, weathered relic to a new door. Even the rope that was attached to the door went from timeworn, fraying pieces of tattered twine to a bright, new rope. At the same time, the ink stains faded from both the door and the rope, and the grooves etched into the wood melted away, leaving pristine boards in their wake.

I gasped and turned to run. I wanted to get as far away from that place as possible. Only, just as I set foot on the lower step, the old broken stairs repaired, and the missing board at the top of the steps reappeared.

Carefully, cautiously, I set my foot on the bottom step, preparing to bolt. When I felt that the step was sound, I rushed up and out of the hole in the ground, intending to run as far away from that place as I could, but I didn't get far. In fact, I stopped only a few feet from the edge of the lintel before something even more unbelievable caught my attention. I looked around, shocked at the sight before me, and let out a loud gasp.

This was not just an old root cellar. It was the basement of a *house*. It was a house that wasn't standing a few moments before; I could plainly *see* it transforming around me—a *ghost* house.

It was a farmhouse, almost identical to the one we lived in, the one that stood only a hundred or so feet from that spot.

I stood gawking, my mouth gaping, at the walls of the house as they formed in front of my eyes, going from what looked like transparent shadows to solid wallboards within seconds. Then, a parlor, a table, and even a bowl of fruit metamorphosed in front of my eyes. I gaped at the bowl. It was a blue glass bowl, and the fruit looked mouthwatering.

But it's not here! It's not really here! Still, I can see it. Why can I see it?

I wanted to run, but my feet bonded to the ground. I was both too terrified to move and too mesmerized to look away at the same time, so I just stared.

My sights swept down to the old, or rather, to the new cellar. It was in the middle of the front room, about six feet from a large wooden door that appeared out of thin air. Next to the door was a small picture window, framed with sunny yellow curtains. There was a fireplace made of gray stone burning on the wall to my left and a staircase, almost identical to the one that I ran up and down on every day of my life, on the same wall, adjacent to the fireplace. Then a black stove emerged. It sat in the kitchen that hadn't been there a minute before. What's more, the stove was identical to the one we had in our house, except *ours* had deep scratches and scars cut into the sides.

I stood still as a statue, trying to take in every detail of the house as it appeared. It was eerily similar to our little farmhouse.

I did notice one difference between this *ghost house* and ours: In our house, between the kitchen and the staircase, was a bedroom that belonged to Papa. This house had none.

I moved forward and peeked into the kitchen. Yes, there was no bedroom, but the kitchen was much larger than ours. *Hmm… peculiar.*

I stood frozen, my eyes glued to the ghost house, when something else occurred to me: I was *not* the only person in the room, but he didn't seem to be a bit aware of my presence.

Papa stood not three feet from me. Or at least it was the memory of him, but from when? I didn't know. He was looking out the small window next to the wooden door of the house. He couldn't see me.

I stepped closer. He was staring out into the darkness. His brow was deeply furrowed, and his steel-blue eyes darted all around into the pitch-black night.

He was worried. *But why?*

Then a thought crossed my mind. I thought about how strange it was that it was night in the vision but had to be no later than noon when I stepped down into the old cellar.

I moved another pace closer to my father. I wanted to find out what was worrying him, or at least to put his mind at ease.

"Papa?" I called, but he made no move. I was right; he didn't know I was there.

My eyes swept down. He was holding something small in his arms, something I couldn't see. The image grew clearer the longer I concentrated on it. Finally, I saw what it was. It was a tiny baby, swaddled in a blanket.

Just as the baby moved, the blanket fell away from its head, sending a mass of blood-red hair popping out, like flames bursting from a fireplace.

I gasped! The baby was *ME!* My mouth gaped open. I shifted to get a better look.

But how do I see this? And why?

Just then, the baby-me let out a weak cry and wriggled in my father's arms. He put one hand on her head, and then he leaned down and cooed into her…*my* ear. He smiled into her hazy dark-green eyes as she blinked up into his beaming face. Bending slightly, he kissed baby-me on the forehead and closed his eyes.

I could see the love bursting from within, clearly a man enamored with his child. As he held her, he rocked back and forth, his lips still touching her tiny forehead and his mighty hand covering almost the entire surface of her little ginger head. After a moment, Papa pulled back, placed his hand on her pink cheek, and kissed her teeny button nose. Tears brimmed in his eyes—tears of joy.

I stood smiling as I watched him handle baby-me. *"He still kisses me just like that,"* I whispered to myself.

Suddenly, Papa flinched just as a near-deafening gust of wind swept over the little ghost house. It was so intense that the roof shook and the windows ominously rattled.

"It's getting bad out there." He glanced over his shoulder, toward the back of the house, and stepped away from the clattering window. *"Best be getting the baby in the cellar."*

My father put his arms out toward two women who appeared in the room. One was Grandma. She was sitting in a rocking chair, and the other woman was sitting on a small, make-shift bed in the corner of the room.

Papa walked to Grandma with his arms outstretched. She took baby-me into her arms without rising and pulled her to her chest, then rocked in the chair. My father knelt down in front of Grandma. His light-blue eyes were darkened with worry; his hands strummed across the baby's tiny back, and he was saying something.

But I didn't hear any of what he was saying. I didn't hear him because I recognized the *other* woman in the room, the one who was sitting on the small bed.

She was my mama!

I couldn't breathe. She was lovely. All of a sudden, a rush of warm tears fell unbidden down my face. I willed my feet to move the few paces forward toward her, closing the distance between us, the distance that seemed like miles…a hundred miles. It was twelve years' distance. Finally, I stood before her, gazing into the beautiful face of my mother for the first time since my birth.

She was just as Grandma had described yet so much more. She had the same porcelain skin as Grandma, but that was all. In fact, she didn't resemble Grandma much at all. My mama had brown hair and hazel eyes, instead of Grandma's and my emerald-green eyes and ginger hair. Mama wasn't quite as tiny as Grandma, either. Even though she was sitting, I could tell that she was several inches taller.

Mama was sitting on the bed watching Grandma with a rather blank look on her face. It was a look I didn't understand. She seemed sad, almost heartbroken. She looked as if she was in pain. *But why?*

And then it hit me: I must have just been born. She *was* in pain, the pain of childbirth.

I frowned, and a prickling of irritation swept up my spine. *Huh! Birthing. Where babies come from. Why I can do strange things. My life! My mother! All things I don't understand and that my grandma refuses to explain!*

I looked into the lovely hazel eyes of my mother, tears of grief making their way down my cheeks.

"Do you know what we are, Mama? Can you explain everything to me, please?" I asked her, begging for an answer. But of course, she couldn't hear me either.

"Poor Mama," I muttered, reaching for her face, but my hand only touched thin air. It was a strange sensation. I shuddered a bit and jerked my hand away.

While I stood staring at my beautiful Mama, Papa took Grandma and the baby down into the cellar. The cellar door lay open in front of me.

Just then, my father rushed back up into the room, passing straight through me. It was like walking into a big spider's web.

It gave me chills that went straight to my bones, and massive goosebumps erupted all over me.

"COME, REBECCA!" he demanded. *"It's no longer safe for you to be up here. You must go down into the cellar with your mama and the baby right now!"* He held his hand out, gesturing for her to take it, but she pulled away, turning her head away from him.

"No! I'm not going anywhere near HER!" Mama cried.

Her? Grandma? But why is she angry with Grandma? I thought. Mama's words confused me.

"Please, Rebecca!" Papa pleaded. *"You know your mama won't stay down there without you, and the baby needs her mother!"*

He sighed and knelt down before her, his voice drawing softer, cajoling. *"I'm going to shutter the windows upstairs. I'll be right back. Then we'll both go down into the cellar, all right?"* He spoke softly, but there was an undercurrent of panic rising in his tone. *"Please, Princess, it's not safe for you to be up here."*

"I don't care! I'm not going anywhere near her! And you can't make me, Asa!" Mama petulantly snapped, crossing her arms. *"The baby is safe down there with my mother! I'm staying here!"*

She turned her back to Papa. *"Besides, the storm will soon pass."*

Not to be trifled with, my father grabbed my mother's hands and yanked her off the bed. *"I'm not playing these childish GAMES with you anymore!"* He took her around the waist and threw her over his shoulder. Then, with a great deal of force, he stepped toward the open cellar.

Mama kicked and thrashed in his arms. *"Put me down!"* she wailed.

Before my father could react, the window by the door burst, sending shards of glass throughout the room, pelting him in his face and arms. He had large gashes and cuts on his forearms and blood streaks running down his face.

I heard Grandma scream, and she ran up the cellar steps. Tears streamed down her delicate face. Papa heard her, too. He turned and dropped my mother onto the bed, sheer-horror filling his weary eyes.

Without a second glance in my mother's direction, my father leaped toward the cellar, forcing Grandma back down into its depths. Only, his foot caught on the first step, ripping it from its foundation, throwing him forward—down into the darkness.

The roof creaked, and the floorboards whined under the pressure of the fierce wind. It sounded to me as if the *entire* house was coming apart. Before I could think, another horrendous crashing sound burst into the room, and the windows upstairs shattered.

Gaping, I turned just as the staircase swayed, groaned, and then *blew* into pieces.

Even though it must have happened in seconds, the scene seemed to move in slow motion.

I watched in horror.

Papa had lost his footing when it caught on the first step as he pushed Grandma back down into the cellar. He flew through the air, landing on the dirt floor, pinning her underneath him as he fell. Grandma lay unconscious for a few seconds, only jolted back to consciousness by the sound of the house as it came apart.

My grandma was unable to free herself from Papa's hold. She was unable to get to the cellar door. She was unable to get to her daughter before the *tornado* that was ripping the house away slammed the cellar door shut. My grandma was unable to get to my mother before the fierce twirlblast stole her away from *me*…forever.

My mother screamed one last time as she tried to run to the cellar, but it was too late for her.

I wanted to help her. I willed myself to change history, but all I could do was watch as the ghost house exploded around me, sweeping my mother away.

It was unbearable. It was like a scene straight from Hell itself. Every board in the house exploded at once, every window shattered, every piece of furniture blasted apart by the vicious wind. Then the entire house imploded in on itself. Within the span of a few seconds, a once-grand home was reduced to timber.

And the sound… I couldn't believe that a sound, any sound, could be so loud. It was louder than thunder, more deafening than a blast of dynamite. It was as if the house itself shrieked in despair as its life ended.

Through it all—the wind, the explosion, and even through my mother's desperate screams—I heard my grandma crying. She was pleading for my mama's life from deep within the cellar.

But no number of desperate wails or heart-wrenching pleas were going to awaken her from that nightmare. Nothing would bring back what violence had taken from her on the night of my birth… Nothing.

I closed my eyes, praying for the scene to stop, but the hellish vision persisted.

Just as I reopened my eyes, the little, black stove flew across the shattered room, landed atop the cellar door, pinning it closed, and spun like a top from the sheer force of the violent wind.

As the wind finally ceased, Papa's frantic screams resounded from down within the bowels of the shattered house. He was trying in vain to free himself, scratching and clawing at the pinned door like a trapped animal.

"Dear God! Rebecca! Rebecca!" he cried.

Then, as quickly as it all had started, it stopped. The vision evaporated. Like a wisp of smoke, it just disappeared.

I stood there, numb.

It was daylight once again, and I was standing at the edge of the old cellar door, peering down into the cellar of my first *home*.

I grabbed the old door and heaved it shut as hard as I could, sending dirt flying in a cloud around me. The door fell back to earth with a violent crash. I kicked dirt across the old door, hiding it from view, burying it, sending it back into the depths of Hell, sending it away from me!

That didn't stop the pain. My brain reeled with images, horrific images. I clasped my hands over my ears, screeching into the nothingness below, yearning to un-see what I had witnessed. I didn't want to know about it—any of it! I doubled over in pain, my stomach violently retching, sending me to my knees. I gasped, heaving a mixture of both vomit and tears onto the ground in front of me. I put my forehead to the soft earth, desperately trying to breathe, but the air just wouldn't come.

I could only gasp. My middle seized; everything went black.

I'm not sure how long I lay on the ground. My head pounded with every beat of my heart. I kept still. I was afraid that if I moved, even a little, I wouldn't be able to breathe or to think or to *exist* after what I had witnessed.

No wonder they don't talk about her.

Whenever I asked about my mother, Grandma would always say, *"You'll see, child."*

Is this what I was supposed to see!?

I lay motionless on the ground where my mama had died. Tears burned down my cheeks and into my ears. *Help me. Someone, please, help me. I think I'm dying—Paapaa!* I silently bellowed.

Just as that weak thought passed through my mind, I heard footsteps running toward me. Papa was the first to reach me. He fell to his knees, scooping me up into his arms, and cupped his hand under my head. I let out a loud *gasp* of pain as he touched the wound on the back of my head. I tried to push his hand away and groaned in pain.

He sat down on the ground, ever so gently cradling me against his chest. He touched the egg-sized bump on the back of my head, gently probing and feeling my wound, all the while crooning sweet words of encouragement into my ear.

"It's all right, angel, I've got you. I've got you, baby," he murmured, pulling me near, cradling me against his muscular chest.

I inhaled his scent, smelling the pipe tobacco and cinnamon scent of him, and I knew this must mean I could once again *breathe*.

Then I smelled her, my grandma. Her hair whipped across my face, sending the scent of her sweet lilac perfume across my senses. The scent soothed my burning soul and made me feel safe and whole again.

"Leesie, baby?" she whispered into my ear.

With all the might I could muster, I willed my eyes to open. My heavy eyelids fluttered at first and then cracked just enough to look into the worried expressions of my papa and grandma.

An intense pang of guilt swept through me as I remembered my anger from earlier in the day.

Was that today?

It seemed like forever ago before the vision.

How many times had I been angry with Grandma for not telling me about how my mother had died? Now I wished I could take the answer away.

Papa must have rebuilt our house but not on the same spot. I didn't blame him, poor Papa, especially if it meant having to look at that awful cellar every day—the one with his blood stained into the door. The scars on his hands were not from farming!

I burst into sobs.

While that thought raced through my head, Papa stood up with me in his arms and with much care laid my head on his shoulder.

Then something happened.

From over the side of him, Papa grabbed Grandma's hand and pulled her up off the ground. The two of them walked together, hand in hand, with me back to our house, our *second* house, holding one another tight.

5. Town

My twelfth birthday was coming. The *"spirit of the summer,"* as Grandma always said, was growing old and weak. That's what she called the end of the summer season. She'd say the spirit of the summer grew pale, and her days on earth were soon to *pass*. That was why the days became cooler and shorter as summer *passed* into autumn.

I didn't question her too much when she said things like that. It was just her way.

It was the second week of September. The orchard was still a brilliant shade of green, with red, ripe apples dotting the thick sea of dark green leaves—the beginning of the harvest season. I loved that time of year. I loved to help Papa harvest. But mostly, I loved helping him pick apples and eating them!

Apple pie, apple sauce, apple cider. Hmm. Could life get any better?

It was early afternoon. Papa and Grandma went into town earlier in the morning. That was something they rarely did.

We weren't welcome in *that* town.

We used to sell our entire harvest in town, but suspicions about our *peculiar* family had unfairly poisoned many of the townspeople against us, forcing us to travel far into the city, where no one had ever heard of our family.

I didn't understand any of it at all. Our family was just as nice as any other family. Sure, Grandma and I, mostly Grandma, were a little different, but we were harmless.

I hadn't gone into town with them since I was five years old. That was when I started speaking to people about future births…

and *deaths.* That's when things became dangerous for us and when the rumors about us began. That was when whispered names such as "*witches*" and "*demons*" were never far from peoples' lips when discussing our family.

Even when we traveled all the way to the city to sell our harvest, it was quite necessary for Grandma and me to be careful not to talk to or even make eye contact with anyone.

Grandma put my bright-red hair into tight braids. A large bonnet covered all but the ends. The long braids were hidden under an uncomfortable, starched petticoat, and a heavy calico dress over the top carefully concealed every inch of me. Grandma wore something very similar to me.

What's worse, I knew Grandma was even more uncomfortable than I was. She seemed to worry about our trip for days, becoming even quieter and moodier than usual. Then on the day of our trip, she would wring her delicate, porcelain hands, acting nervous and shy, and that was even before she put herself together for our journey.

Even though I understood why she felt uncomfortable, I didn't know why she was always so nervous and self-conscious.

I thought she looked *beautiful.*

Papa felt her embarrassment, too, and tried to help by not looking at her while she was dressed up. My papa was thoughtful like that—although I did catch him stealing a glimpse or two from time to time.

Still, each time we dressed for our trip into the city, I sat thinking about how much I really despised braids, but I never dared complain. After all, it was my fault such torture was needed. I did, however, feel pangs of guilt every time I glanced at Grandma and saw how uncomfortable she was. She looked lovely, and I wished she knew that.

Truthfully, I didn't understand why she and I even went with my father into the city. It seemed to me that it would've been much easier and safer for him to go alone, but we always went.

Just chock it up to something else I don't understand.

It wasn't that I didn't enjoy going into the city; sometimes we had fun. Sometimes we went to the ballet or the opera house, but it had been a long time since we did anything like that.

We did visit the big house during each visit, though. Well, we never went inside, but still, we parked by it.

The *big house* was a mansion, entirely surrounded by a delicate-looking fence, with rose bushes, and big, beautiful maple trees growing along the entire perimeter of the house. An expansive lawn stretched out to the lane in the front. Clear around the back was a vast garden, and off to the side stood a grand barn and a stable for horses.

We visited the big house each time we went into the city although, like I said, we never went inside.

I wonder why?

Instead, Papa pulled the wagon off to the side of the lane, leaving a bushel of apples by the gate. Then he waited for someone to come out to get them. Many times, just as we parked in front of the house, a pretty, *older* woman gazed out the window at us. Each time, the woman stared at me and smiled almost as if she knew me, yet there was a bit of sadness in her eyes as well. Sometimes Grandma nodded just a bit and smiled back at the woman.

Who is she?

Each time we left the apples, it was the same man who took them from my father. The gentleman walked out of the house dressed in an expensive-looking suit. As he came to the gate, he shook Papa's hand and sometimes even embraced him before taking the apples inside. I never saw the man pay for the apples.

I wondered why my father would give them to someone who apparently *could* pay, but I never asked.

Just one more thing to add to my list of the unknown.

After our visit with the mysterious gentleman and the lady in the window, both Grandma and Papa were quiet, and they seemed sad.

I wanted to help them, but I felt much too guilty to bother either of them about it.

Why couldn't they tell me?

When I was little, Papa used to take Grandma and me to the opera house and the ballet while we were in the city, but he hadn't in a very long time. In fact, we hadn't done anything for several years, and things between them seemed rather strained. Besides that, my father seemed distracted by Grandma and often troubled for reasons unknown to me.

I had to wonder if maybe *this* was why things between Grandma and Papa were so hard. Maybe my father was growing resentful of us. I wished to ask him, but I didn't know how. So as always, I said nothing and pretended that my life was beautiful.

At times, it was difficult for us to sell our harvest even in the city, particularly if someone from our town recognized us. We'd have to move to a different vendor, and our apples were all-too-conveniently not needed the next time we tried to sell them.

I don't blame Papa for resenting us…

It was because of this that when I learned about their plans to sell in town, I was a bit bewildered. I wondered why they would even bother going into town at all. Surely no one would as much as talk to them, let alone buy from them, maybe worse.

Nevertheless, my father and grandmother were up with the sun that morning, and it was just peaking over the mountains when they left the farm.

Grandma was dressed up in a brown calico dress. Her bright, strawberry hair pinned back into a neat bun, with a flowered bonnet covering her head.

In the summertime, Grandma's bright, light-strawberry tresses shined and sparkled in the sun. It was beautiful. And how I hated to see her cover such loveliness with that drab bonnet!

As Grandma sat waiting for Papa that morning, she seemed even more uncomfortable than when we traveled. She kept glancing at Papa each time he entered the front room as if expecting him to do something. Once, when she looked away for a moment, I saw him glance back at her, laugh to himself, and then shake his head as if amused.

I didn't know why, but the way he gazed at her reminded me of a man *in love*.

And then it hit me: He seemed happy! In fact, the expression on his face was one that I hadn't seen in a long time…a very long time.

Out in the field, Grandma usually wore a pair of Papa's old trousers and one of his shirts, her hair fastened into a long plait that trailed down to the small of her back.

Maybe Papa was just admiring the way she looks today, I thought to myself as I watched them. *She's probably nervous because she has to blend in with the other folks in town.*

It was perfectly understandable why my father would look at her, though. After all, she was a beautiful woman. But I still hated to see her looking so unsure of herself, and on that day, it seemed much worse than usual.

This was just one of the reasons I was more than a little angry at the idea of them going into that awful town and dealing with such horrible, bigoted people.

Worst of all—the breath caught in my throat—I wouldn't be there to protect them. *I won't be there to keep them safe!* That thought raced through my mind, causing my stomach to belly-flop. I wasn't sure exactly how I could protect them if I were there, but at least I would know they were safe.

Just as they walked out the door, my mind surged, causing my mouth to detach from my brain.

I never shouted at them. After all, obedient little children didn't raise their voices to their parents, not for any reason. But on that morning, I did.

"Why are you going to that horrible town!?" I demanded, fisting my hands against my hips, like Grandma often did, my eyes shooting daggers at her and Papa both.

Grandma stopped short and turned to face me. She cocked her head, her eyes *blazing* into mine. She leered at me as if she didn't understand *who* I was talking to, or perhaps *I* didn't.

She stepped a pace nearer to me, and in return, I stepped a pace back.

Her voice was stern, very stern, when she spoke. *"We must sell what's harvested now, child, or it will spoil! Now, quit being snippy, and get back into the house, right now!"*

She pointed toward the door. When I stood my ground, she took another step toward me, and her eyes blazed again. Then her voice softened almost into a whisper, yet it was unyielding; she leaned nearer to me.

"Your papa may not take a switch to you, young lady, but I will!" Grandma muttered, her intense, green gaze burning straight through me, making my mind swim.

My grandmother had never struck me in my life, and I didn't think she ever would. I wanted to retort, but I held my tongue, just in case. I wasn't foolish enough to challenge her.

My sights swept to where my father stood waiting for Grandma.

I walked backward in the direction of our house, my gaze viciously narrowed on her. A sudden expression of concern drew my attention into Papa's eyes as he glanced toward my grandmother.

I'm right, they are hiding something from me…

I stopped and stood still for a moment. My eyes darted between them, trying to figure out what they weren't telling me. My gaze finally settled on the wagon, where only a single bushel of apples stood in the back.

Hmm, strange.

Just then, Grandma raised her brow and then opened her eyes even wider than before. Her emerald glare *blazed* with a final warning; she took one more menacing step toward me.

She didn't have to say a word; the look she gave me was dangerous enough.

I turned and ran back into the house, slamming the door behind me. Furious tears streaked down my face.

They never tell me anything! They're ashamed of me! I'm an abomination against God and nature! I wish death would've taken me instead of Mama! It would've been better for them! Grandma would be happier! She hates me because I lived! I know she does! I'm disgusting! I'm an inhuman mistake!

The door opened and shut behind me. Even with my back to it, I knew who it was. I didn't need to turn around to know that it was her, my grandma. I smelled her *lilac perfume*. She wore it every day, even with Papa's old clothes.

Huh! Another story I don't know!

I've done it this time, I thought to myself just as she stepped up directly behind me.

I turned to face her and glared into her eyes, expecting punishment for my disobedience.

But that thought was fleeting because, suddenly I knew. Just by the look on her face, I *knew*. For the first time in my life, I knew. Somehow in some way that I didn't understand, she had heard me. Grandma had *heard* what I was just *thinking*.

An unfamiliar wave of fear gripped me. I wasn't afraid of her exactly. It was just that if the horrible people were right, and I thought they probably were, about she and I being *witches*, then she was a much stronger and bigger one than me.

I turned my back away from her. I didn't want to face the truth. And for the first time, I *was* afraid.

"Leesie." Her soft voice cut through my thoughts.

I was frozen in place, too scared to turn back around. I didn't want to see the truth in her eyes, the look that told me I was right, the look that said she *also* wished that my mama, her daughter, had lived instead of me.

Grandma swept clear around and then turned to face me. She pulled my chin up with her index finger until our eyes met.

Good! Turn me to ash! I defiantly thought, petulantly scowling straight into her eyes.

To my surprise, she put her hand to her mouth, laughed to herself, and then shook her head. She seemed amused.

"My goodness. It's like looking into a mirror, Leesie."

She cocked her head; her smile was as bright as the sun shining through the windowpane.

"Do you know what I see when I look at you?" she asked, her perfect smile beaming down at me.

A witch? A mistake? A painful reminder that your only child is dead? Tears stung the back of my eyes, constricting my throat.

I didn't answer her aloud. My lips pursed, my eyes were downtrodden. I was trying not to look at her, but *her* gaze wasn't something to ignore.

My eyes drifted up to hers. She was lovely, stunning even, and she was *me!* Well, a superior form of me, anyway. Then somehow I knew she had heard that thought, too, and I was embarrassed.

I bashfully bit my lip, my conniption forgotten. *"I'm sorry,"* I meekly whispered.

"And what exactly are you sorry for, child?"

For living when she didn't…

I cleared the lump from my throat. *"For making you remember my mama's death again and…"* I stuttered, pained tears choking my voice. *"A-aaand f-f-for looking like you but not being enough like you."*

Hearing my words, Grandma winced and sighed, and her sights dropped to the floor. When she looked back up at me, tears welled in her eyes.

"I remember my daughter every day," she choked. *"I see so much of myself in you, sweetheart…"* She paused and touched my cheek with the back of her hand. *"But Rebecca is a part of you, too, as is your papa. Only, your life is much more valuable to this world than any of ours…even more valuable than Rebecca's life or mine or your papa's. We don't hide you from the world out of shame, baby. We hide you to protect you."*

She looked me in the eyes. *"You, WE, are NOT witches! Hopefully, in time, you will learn to believe that."* She said the last part more to herself than to me. Then she sighed again, and a silent tear dropped to the ground at my feet.

It stunned me. My blood ran cold. I had only seen my grandma cry once before. It was in my vision of the night my mother had died, the night I was born.

All of a sudden, I was overcome with a deep need to hear *her* thoughts just as she heard me at least some of the time.

Grandma grasped my trembling face between her hands, her soft voice cracking as she spoke to me. *"I love you more than my life, more than anyone alive, and just as much as I loved Rebecca."*

My bottom lip quivered.

"And," she said, pulling my face closer to hers, *"your Papa loves you more than…"* She hesitated, and another stream of tears spilled from her eyes. *"He loves you more than his life, more than this farm, or those trees. More than…"* She hesitated again, sweeping her hand through the air. *"It's all for you, my baby. Please believe that."*

Before I could answer, or even think, she pulled me to her bosom, holding me tighter than I'd ever remembered before. In return, I wrapped my arms around her waist, inhaling her sweet, lilac scent at the same time. As she held me, I felt her tears running down the side of my face.

"I love you so much, my baby," she whispered into my ear.

She pulled back, softly kissing my forehead, trailing the back of her hand down my cheek, and gazing into my eyes. *"Please don't ever question my love for you, Leesie,"* she whispered, taking a deep breath.

Then she let go.

Immediately, I felt bereft and achingly alone. *No! Hold me. Talk to me! Please!*

Quickly composing herself, Grandma turned away from me and then glided toward the door. *"Get a bushel, and fetch some apples while we're in town, Lees. There are still a few ripe ones left on the trees. We'll make a pie tonight."*

Wordlessly, gracefully, she *swept* from the room and out the door, leaving me stunned and even more confused than ever before.

I ran to the window, watching as she headed toward the wagon. She had her head in her hands, and she was crying again.

My papa looked lost, standing by the wagon waiting for her; although, she swept past without even looking at him. As she glided by, he gave her another concerned look before climbing into the wagon after her.

Something is happening, and Papa seems just as worried about it as I am.

Fear swept through me like the wind of a blizzard.

•　•　•

I sat on the floor for a long time after Papa and Grandma left for town, a few hours or more, trying to compose my emotions. I was numb, my emotions tattered.

Just like the rope in the old cellar…

With that thought, a deep sigh escaped my lips. I hoped that Grandma couldn't see how worried about her I was. She could only read me when my emotions were running high.

At least I think that's the way it works.

Grandma didn't seem to be able to read me during the vision, or even when I thought about what I saw after the vision was over. She apparently didn't see the vision I had of the night I was born. If she had seen it, surely she would have said something.

Then another thought, a darker thought, crossed my mind. Papa was worried, too. And I knew what worried him. It was the same thing that worried me.

Grandma was crying.

But at the same time, I saw something else in him, as well, something I didn't understand…hopefulness.

Hope for what?

I took a deep breath, lying down on the cold, wooden floor, just thinking. I couldn't imagine what was going on, but whatever it was, I prayed that it didn't happen while I sat there, *alone.*

With that thought, another jolt of anger churned through me.

I sat up, taking a deep gulp of air, quickly quashing my blossoming anger. I wasn't going to give my grandma any more of my thoughts…not any more than was necessary.

Well, at least not today. After all, she has enough to concern herself with.

I thought for a moment, and an idea came to mind. *I'll simply play the obedient child, at least until I figure out what's happening to us. I just hope Grandma doesn't get too suspicious.*

I stood up. *Yes, that's what I'll do!*

I knew I could play along as long as I had to. Grandma always told me that I was truly a child with the mind of a thirty-year-old. But it was what *she* could do that had me worried. I wondered, *calmly*, if reading me like that was something she could always do, or if it was something new.

Will I be able to do it, too?

First things first. Obedient little children do what they are told.

I looked out the window into the clear-blue sky. The sun was getting high on the horizon.

Almost noon. I'd better get to picking those apples like she told me.

Even though I knew she said to fetch the apples only as a distraction to whatever was actually going on, still, I had to obey.

I opened the door and hurried out to the orchard.

I had better be hasty just in case they come home early.

Just as that thought came to mind, I gazed down the empty dirt road leading into our farm, all the while hoping to see the wagon coming into view.

I nervously bit my lip. *I want them home now, right now. Every second they aren't home seems like an eternity to me!*

I took another steadying breath, trying to push everything except picking apples from my mind. Quickly exorcising all thoughts of worry from my mind, I ran to The Grandfather Tree.

Grinning, I lifted one of the bushels high above my head. *"Just a dozen or so…for a pie,"* I hollered, giggling.

Immediately, twelve ripe, red apples fell into my basket.

"Thank you!" I beamed.

And then…

If *he* hadn't fallen from the tree directly above of me, I would've never noticed *the boy* who fell to the ground at my feet.

He let out a loud *"Ow!"* as he hit the ground, shaking my beloved Grandfather Tree as he fell.

The boy sat up, cradling his arm in his hand and rocking back and forth in obvious pain, just as a few apples—MY apples—pelted him in the head. The apples fell, bruised and ruined, on the ground around him.

6. Kristofer Cole

The boy sat very still on the ground beneath the tree, silently staring up at me. He had scrapes on his elbows and his chin, and there were leaves in his hair.

Hmm…

I stared at him.

First, I was struck by his *eyes*. They were warm hazel with dark green around the pupils, a brighter, more vibrant, shade of jade-green flowing through the irises, and yellow stars bursting out of the green.

I couldn't pull my gaze away from them. They were mesmerizing, hypnotic, and somehow *familiar*.

Where have I seen him before?

Then I noticed his hair: warm, chestnut-brown with sparkling amber highlights. Suddenly, I felt groggy.

The clouds soon lifted from my mind just as the strangest thing happened.

All of a sudden, it felt as though someone had lassoed me with an invisible rope around my middle, jerking me forward toward the boy. I had to plant my feet hard on the ground to stop myself from falling right into him.

The boy jumped to his feet and stared back at me, puzzled. He blushed pink on the tips of his ears and took one tentative step toward me.

"Sorry…" he mumbled. *"I-I-I'm sorry if I startled you. I'm Kristofer… Er, Kris… Kris Cole,"* he clarified, wiping his dirty hand on

his trousers and then pushing it out in front of him, offering it to me in a friendly gesture.

Only, I knew enough not to touch *anyone*, so I just smiled politely and stepped a pace back.

In the next instant, my head cleared a bit more, and I remembered that he was hiding up in the canopy of The Grandfather Tree, causing my temper, as well as my protective nature, to flare.

"Why were you in MY tree?" I demanded, and not so politely, my eyes flashing with indignation as well as a bit of fright for what the boy might have seen.

"I was walking by…" stammered the boy, *"and…and I noticed… there was an apple in this tree."* He nodded his head toward MY tree.

I cocked my head. *"Hmm. Apples in an orchard. Well, imagine that!"* I sarcastically replied, trying not to look into his breathtaking eyes again.

I held the bushel out to him. *"Here."* I nodded toward the dozen apples I had collected. *"Here, these are fresh, and not bruised!"* I rolled my eyes.

*As beautiful as this boy is—and he is beautiful, so damned beautiful—*I shook that thought from my head to clear it. *His total disregard for the apples he's spilled annoys me!*

The boy put his hands out, pushing the bushel back toward me.

"No, I think I've taken enough of them…" His ears blushed again, and he flashed an embarrassed lopsided grin.

He peered at the ground where the spoiled apples fell. *"And sorry about that, too. I didn't mean to waste them."*

Oh, wow! He is sorry. Maybe he's not so bad. And his smile… My heart stuttered, my thoughts swimming anew. *His eyes light up when he smiles…*

The boy kicked a rock with his foot, grabbing my attention, and with a sheepish, almost guilty expression on his face, he blushed again, this time going red across the cheeks.

"I was sort of spying on you," he muttered, peering at the ground.

Oh, no! Spying? What did he see? I was panicked and angry.
How dare he come here to spy on me!

A sudden wave of heat swelled in my chest. *"Are you from that town?"* I shouted at him, throwing him a piercing look, narrowing my eyes, and stepping closer to him. *"Come to see the witch, have you?"*

The boy's eyes grew wide, his mouth gaping open for a moment. He tilted his head sideways, clearly studying me.

"You're a witch? Huh. What can you do?" he asked, swinging his hand forward as if to touch me while taking a bold step in my direction.

I gasped, shocked by his audacity.

I set my basket on the ground, stooped down, picked up three of the bruised apples, and threw them at his head—hard.

"You don't have any manners! You're a horrible, horrible boy! You best be careful, Kristofer Cole, or I'll tell my papa that you tried to touch me! And I'll tell him that you were spying on me! He'll thrash you within an inch of your life! He's big and really scary!" I lied.

I wished more than anything right then that I *was* a witch, so I could turn the boy—beautiful as he was, but still, he tried to touch me—into a nice artichoke or maybe a sour kumquat!

The boy threw his arms over his head, the apples bouncing off his scraped forearms.

"I wasn't trying to touch you!" he shouted, glaring at me. He glared at me as if *I* had done something wrong! *"You were about to step backward into that!"*

He pointed toward one of the ditches dug into the ground around the apple tree. *"I didn't want you to fall. Jeez! I was just trying to catch you!"*

He steadied his heaving breath, frowning into my frown. *"And your pa didn't look so scary when I met him and your ma at my house just a while ago today!"*

Clearly exasperated with me, he threw his hands up in the air. *"You sure are jumpy, even for a girl!"*

I didn't know what to think. My mind was sent racing again. *"They went to your house?"* I stumbled over the words. *"But why?"*

As he looked at my confused expression, the boy's frown fell, and his beautiful eyes softened.

He stepped forward again although this time he didn't try to touch me. *"My pa is the new minister in town—his name is Jacob Cole. I guess your parents came to visit him and my ma—she's Molly Cole. They even brought us a bushel of apples."* He eyed the ones on the ground. *"So, you see, I wasn't trying to take anything. I just wanted to meet…you."*

The boy stepped back again, looking me up and down. *"Your pa told me about you."* He paused, blushing on the tips of his ears again. *"He said you are as pretty as a sun-kissed daffodil, just like your mama. Whatever that means."* He shrugged. *"Now that I think of it,"* he said, eyeing me for the second time, cocking his head, and studying me, *"you are beautiful, except I think you look more like a butterfly than a daffodil. Even more when you're not shouting and throwing things at my head."*

As he spoke those words, he blushed red again, trying not to look at me and failing. At the same time, the *lasso* tightened. Again I had to steady myself, but I hardly noticed. Something about his words was familiar.

A butterfly…something about a butterfly. I closed my eyes, trying to remember, but I couldn't. The thought quickly vanished.

"I wanted to see for myself just how pretty you are. I didn't expect you to come out here and start pickin' apples. By the way, how'd you do that, anyway?" he asked, cocking his head again, looking just like a curious puppy.

My mind came to a screeching halt, my eyes growing wide. *"How'd I do what?"* I muttered.

Oh, no! He did see me!

"With the tree. You spoke to it, and then it gave you those apples." He frowned, gesturing toward where the bushel sat on the ground.

"Why would they visit you and your family?" I demanded, completely ignoring his question.

I picked an apple out of the bushel and handed it to the boy, being careful not to touch him, and took another one out for myself.

"I don't understand why they would visit you. I mean, we don't exactly meet, well, anyone actually," I whispered, *"until now."*

I bit my bottom lip, peering down at the ground, waiting for an explanation, and trying to keep from giving one to *him*.

That's when I saw it, a small marble on the ground by the boy's foot, right where he was standing.

The boy noticed it the same time as I did. It must have fallen from his pocket.

I bent down to pick it up at the same time as he did; our hands nearly touched. But the boy stopped short, pulling his hand away.

He stood up and smiled. *"Go ahead and take it. I have loads of marbles and no one to play with me. Maybe you will sometime?"* he offered, winking at me and grinning.

Oh, yes, how I'd love to play with you, I thought, getting lost in his eyes once more.

At the same time, though, the suspicious little witch in me bubbled again.

I shook the wayward thought from my head. *"How do I know they're even at your house? Maybe you just don't want me to tell my papa or yours!"* I squinted at him, crossing my arms.

Huh! Prove it!

"Well…" he began, haughtily pushing his face out toward me and smirking, *"your pa's name is Asa, and your ma's name is Ali. Besides,"* he smirked again, *"our parents didn't just meet. Your Pa and*

mine hugged like old friends when they saw each other first thing this morning, and so did our mothers. Apparently, they're old friends."

The boy thought for a moment, as if he wanted to tell me something but wasn't sure whether or not he could trust me. Finally, he decided to speak. "*Did you know that your ma and mine lived at the orphanage together when they were children? They were like sisters, I guess,*" he muttered, then glancing around us, as if the trees were going to tell on him. "*And our fathers grew up together, too.*"

I almost laughed. *Silly—beautiful—boy.*

The boy paused again, looking a bit guilty. "*Please don't say nothin' about that part, though. I wasn't supposed to hear it. I was listening at the window.*"

His words hit me. I narrowed my eyes, wagging my index finger in his face. "*I don't think you know very much at all!*" I shouted at him. "*For your information, my papa IS Asa, but my GRANDMA is Alice, Alice Willow, not Ali, and she never lived in any orphanage!*"

The boy's brow furrowed, and he cocked his head. "*She's not your ma?*" He seemed confused. "*But she's the same age as my mother and our pas, and my pa introduced them to me as Mr. and Mrs. Raign. That is your last name, isn't it?*" he asked, and it was in a tone that said he thought he was right.

My temper nearly bubbled over! "*I know they're the same age! That doesn't mean anything! And you're wrong about their names. They are NOT Mr. and Mrs. Raign! My grandma's name is Alice Willow!*" I shouted. I was just seething with fury.

Just who is this boy who thinks he knows us?

The boy nervously bit his lip. "*I'm sorry you didn't know about the orphanage, but it's true. I didn't mean to upset you…Leesie.*" He spoke my name for the first time, and for some reason, the way he said it sent shivers up my spine.

I lost my breath.

Kristofer's eyes were soft, sincere. "Your Pa called her 'Ali,' Leesie. I heard him when he helped her out of the wagon, and he did it again as he held her hand while they walked up to our house."

He paused. *"Come to think of it, your ma did keep glancing down at their linked fingers while they were walking. That is sort of strange."*

He sheepishly looked into my eyes. *"And I guess 'Ali' is short for 'Alice.' Maybe?"* He threw me another guilty look, almost as if he pitied me.

"Maybe you don't know much." His tone was reluctant and sad. *"Sorry."*

I was trying *very* hard to steady my feelings, but I wasn't sure it was working.

Kristofer stepped closer. We were nearly nose-to-nose. *"The four of them were friends once, and I guess they still are."*

My thoughts raced anew.

She's not my mother. I know she's not! I saw it myself. I saw my mama die the night I was born—I SAW her! I heard them cry out for her. My mother's grave is right at the edge of the orchard! How could Grandma do such a thing!?

With that thought, a shiver ran through me.

Apparently, she couldn't find her own husband, so she went and took my dead mother's! But I won't let her! Has she tricked my papa into loving her? Has she wielded her power against him? Is this what she was worried about today?

Furious tears welled up in my eyes. *I hope you hear me, Grandma!* I fiercely screamed into my mind, hoping she was listening. *You can't hide from me anymore, and I won't let you steal MY papa!*

Stoically, I picked up the bushel, placing the uneaten apple back onto the pile.

"Go home now, boy," I muttered flatly, dismissing him.

Then I turned and headed back toward the house, my mind racing with unanswered questions, the marble still clutched in my hand.

7. Secrets

I sat at the small table in the kitchen of our farmhouse and just *waited*. I wasn't even trying to steady my thoughts and emotions. In fact, I was mentally daring my grandma to say something to me. I was angry, really angry, and I was determined to find out the truth.

They were going to tell me the truth if I had to force it out of them. For once in my life, I was entirely unafraid of my grandmother, and even though I had no idea what was going to happen when she and Papa came home, I continued to goad her.

She might turn me to ash if I continue to cross her, but I don't care!

Kristofer could be wrong. That thought was the only thing I could think of to comfort me.

"They knew each other when they were younger." I was thinking aloud, attempting to rationalize the situation. *"That means nothing. And so what if Papa held her hand? I've seen him do that before. Kristofer said Papa called her 'Ali.' I never heard him call her that before. Hmm…"*

I sat alone, mulling things over in my mind, and the longer I reflected on our life, the more things occurred to me, odd things, things that just didn't add up.

Like, the fact that Grandma never actually referred to Rebecca as *my* mama. She always referred to her as *her* daughter.

And Papa didn't talk to Grandma much at all, at least not in front of me. He distanced himself from her.

But not today. Today was different; he was different. He was worried. Hmm, what's going on?

Grandma had once told me that Papa was her dearest friend, but they didn't behave as friends.

And when I'd ask Grandma about my mama, she told me nothing. At least Papa was willing to talk about Rebecca. Maybe *he* would tell me.

"I need to talk to him!"

As I sat, contemplating, I unthinkingly turned the marble the boy had given me around in my hands. My mind was so occupied that I hadn't even looked at it until then.

It was quite lovely for a marble. I took a closer look, running it around my palm, thoroughly studying it, and rolling it in between my fingers. The colors swirled and bled together around the center, almost like the colors in the sky blend at dusk, except the colors were different.

The marble was a warm shade of tawny-green with jade and yellow streaks swirling around the middle.

My breath hitched. *Just like Kristofer's eyes.*

And suddenly, I couldn't take my eyes off the lovely little marble.

Without warning, the invisible lasso tugged my middle once again, nearly pulling me off the chair. It shocked me. I didn't understand what it meant.

What's happening to me, and why can't I stop thinking about that boy?

My head throbbed from all the thinking and the knot on the back of my skull. I laid it down on the table. My eyes were heavy, and my mind blurred.

I won't go to sleep. I'll just rest my eyes for a few minutes.

Almost instantly, I drifted off.

Gradually, a vision popped into my mind, and then in the next instant, I was standing in the middle of a stable…*somewhere.*

As I watched, a boy about fifteen-years-old appeared. He was tall and thin with light, sandy-blond hair and piercing, steel-blue eyes. I was struck by his overwhelming beauty. He was brushing a silver-white stallion, taking long, careful strokes as the horse grazed on a bit of hay that was covering the dirt floor of the stable.

"There, there, Butterscotch," the boy crooned, stroking the stallion's shimmering, ginger mane. *"That's a good ol' boy."* He leaned in and planted a gentle kiss on the side of the horse's cheek while also sweeping its forelock out of its soft, tawny eyes.

Out of the blue, a girl about the boy's age ran in. Breathless and panicked, she rushed into the stable and crouched down into one of the empty stalls.

She didn't notice the boy, but he saw her.

The girl was more than beautiful; she looked like a lost, scared angel. Her long, strawberry-blonde hair was the color of the sun at dawn and as straight as a corn husk. She had it pulled back on the sides and neatly woven into a braid hanging down her back, the remaining locks flowing past her small waist. She wore an expensive-looking bright-red blouse, a black skirt, black stockings, and black, lace-up boots. As I looked closer, though, I noticed that she seemed a bit disheveled.

I bit my lip, worried she might get her expensive clothes dirty in the stable.

The young boy grinned almost knowingly and ambled toward her hiding place. *"Hello?"* he hollered, leaning over the door of the stall, and then flashed a crooked smile as he eyed the girl, almost as if he knew her.

The girl crouched deeper, her delicate hands covering her mouth as if masking a scream.

"I'm sorry," she whispered, lowering her hands. *"Please, please don't tell him I'm here! Please, he can't find me here!"*

The boy wrenched open the stall door and knelt down beside her in the straw. He took her small, porcelain hand into his, holding it with tender care. She was trembling. Just as their skin touched, an arc of golden light flashed between their hands, sending the boy tumbling down onto his bottom in the straw.

He stared down at his glowing hand, as did I. The light appeared to be a tiny bolt of lightning. After a moment, the light streaked away from the boy's fingers, ran up the entire length of his arm, and then disappeared into his chest. His breath halted for a few seconds, and he seemed winded but unharmed.

The boy shook his head, seemingly returning from his daze. He leaned forward toward the girl, who was gawking at him.

"Who are you hiding from?" he asked, his dazzling blue eyes full of concern for the girl, concern mixed with a sudden sense of awe.

The girl snapped her hand away. *"Don't you touch me!"* she hissed.

Did she see the light? I wondered.

"I was just trying to be nice!" the boy snapped back. *"Besides, you are hiding in MY barn, you know!"* He made a wide gesture with his hands around the opulent stable.

The girl jumped up, meaning to leave, mumbling a quick word of apology under her breath.

Just as she stood, there was a knock on the stable door.

Her eyes grew wide and fearful again. She crouched back down into the stall just as the boy closed the stall door behind her, safely shutting her inside.

The stable door opened, and another much older young man peered in. He looked to be around twenty years old.

The young man was tall and wiry with slick, black hair, and his beady blue eyes almost disappeared when he smiled, or rather, as he smirked. Dressed in a black suit, a black silk top hat, and crisp, white spats that covered his shiny, black shoes, he was obviously wealthy. There was a sickening air of danger about him.

Just looking at him made my skin crawl.

I stepped a pace closer and looked up into his cold, beady eyes just as a sudden, and disturbing, sense of familiarity rushed through my mind.

I canted my head, thinking for a moment. *How do I know him? Where have I seen him before?*

Even though I couldn't quite place him, I knew he was dangerous. A deep and unexpected feeling of rage swept through me as I stared at him. I wanted nothing more than to shelter the girl, to keep her away from him.

To my surprise, the boy seemed to feel the same frisson of alarm.

Almost instinctively, he moved closer to the stall, placed one hand on the latch, and discreetly secured the stall door shut.

"Have you seen a girl around here? Sneaky, little minx got away from me," the dangerous young man inquired, glancing around the stable with an unmistakable air of entitlement resounding in his deceptively soft voice.

He reminded me of a hunting predator.

"I dare say a man pays good money to free a wayward girl from a life of servitude, and she won't even give that man his proper due." He smirked at the boy.

The boy said nothing.

The dangerous young man stalked closer, to where the boy stood guarding the hidden girl. The man's mien was now aggressive, his thick jaw drawn rigid with barely contained hostility.

Tension crackled through the air.

My heart thumped. *I was right. He is a predator, and that poor girl is his prey!*

The young man's eyes grew cold as he glared at the boy. Threatening as the young man was, the boy seemed unperturbed by him. The boy glared right back though he still said not a word.

The man's jaw quivered with ill-restrained ire. *"I asked you a question, stable boy! Have you seen my girl? This one is a delectable little ginger with green eyes.*" He stalked nearer, leering into the boy's composed eyes. "*I paid good money for that girl, and I don't want her…damaged. If you know what I mean?*" The man winked, and an arrogant smirk stretched across his thin lips.

"*I haven't seen anyone,*" the boy stoically replied, looking the young man squarely in the eye. He stepped even closer to the stall door until he was leaning against it.

"*Fine,*" the young man muttered. Then, without a backward glance, he pulled a five-dollar bill out of his coat pocket and tossed it in the general direction of the boy. "*But if you do happen to see her, you will let me know. My name is Charles Marshal; I'm the new deputy sheriff. My father is a judge; perhaps you've heard of him?*" he asked.

"*Yes, I've heard of him. My name is Asa Raign,*" the boy answered, tightlipped.

Seemingly amused, the man shook his arrogant head and rounded on the boy. "*Asa Raign…Junior, I presume? Yes, our fathers are associates.*" The devil smirked. "*Therefore, being like-minded men of wealth, you and I, if you do happen to find my girl and if you get her back to me unmarked, your father will be greatly rewarded.*" He gestured toward the money lying untouched on the stable floor. "*I suppose that pittance insulted you. I didn't realize who I was speaking to.*" Then, he tipped his top hat and brusquely left, shutting the stable door behind him.

As he left, the girl went to get up, but the boy stopped her. He pushed her back down into the stall, putting one hand up and cautioning her to wait.

The boy hurried across the room and listened at the door.

After just a few seconds, the door reopened, and Charles Marshal looked back in. He had an expectant, even hopeful, expression on his angular face.

"*Just making absolutely certain,*" he drawled with a snide grin and then shut the door for the second time.

When they were sure he was gone, the girl rose and stepped, trembling, out of the stall. She had a blank but terrified look on her face; her emerald eyes brimmed with tears.

The boy gazed at her with a pained look in his eyes. After a few moments, he spoke softly. *"I know who you are,"* he whispered. *"You are Alice Willow. You live at the orphanage. My mother and I take food and clothing to the children. I've noticed you there. My father owns this house. I'm Asa Raign."* He held his hand out toward her.

Alice glanced down at Asa's outstretched hand, but she didn't take it.

"How are you doing that?" Asa pointed straight at her chest.

"How am I doing what?" she screeched.

"That light. You're glowing. It's as if someone is shining a lantern from within you," he whispered. All the while, his eyes never left the spot where the heavenly light glistened through her dress. *"It's beautiful,"* he added, attempting to take her hand again.

"I don't know what you're talking about!" Alice shouted then ran toward the stable door. Before she could get to it, Asa stepped in front of her, putting his hand to it and halting her in her tracks.

"Please don't leave. I want to talk to you just for a minute. Please, Alice," Asa whispered, beseeching and looking into her emerald eyes. He smiled, the same crooked smile that he still had, and placed the palm of his hand against her cheek.

Alice went to pull away but stopped just as the warmth of his skin against her own astounded her senses. She closed her eyes for a moment. His soothing touch calmed her fraying nerves. Then she reopened her eyes, gazing into the steely blue depths of his own, just as a hint of a shy smile crept across her features.

"Please don't call me Alice," she whispered. *"I don't like it. My friend, Molly, she calls me Ali. You may, too, if you want…Asa."*

Asa beamed. *"I'd like that. Thank you…Ali."*

He breathed her name, but it was like a sweet litany on his tongue—a holy benediction. Clearly, he wasn't just in love. He seemed to be worshiping her.

Asa tilted his head and smiled. *"May I ask you something without you running away?"*

Alice bit her lip, looking nervous, but she nodded.

"When I touched your hand in the stall, a flame-colored light shot out. And now, I can't bear to take my eyes off you. Do you know why?"

Alice stammered and stuttered, stumbling away from Asa. *"I… I…don't know what you mean."*

Though Asa frowned, he nodded. He didn't want to scare her away.

He took a handkerchief from his pocket, intending to wipe the tears from her face. He recoiled at the first sight of the large, angry, purple bruise marring one side of her cheekbone and alongside her temple. His eyes flew open with rage. *"What happened to you?"*

Alice's eyes dropped to the ground. *"I…fell,"* she lied.

I woke up *breathless* just as the front door of our house opened and then closed with a thud.

They were home.

What I saw must've been a vision of some sort. Grandma can't see those. At least, I hope she can't! It was a vision of how she and Papa met. Kristofer was right about that. And who was that horrible man?

Grandma walked into the kitchen. I heard the delicate swishing of her skirt on the floor and smelled her sweet perfume.

I lay with my head pressed to the table, pretended to be asleep.

I wasn't angry with her anymore; I was sad.

I'll have to ask her about this, but I don't know when. I don't have the strength to do it now.

Papa walked into the kitchen behind her. I felt his arms envelope my body. Then he picked me up, laid my head on his strong shoulder, and cradled me against him.

I buried my nose against his neck. *Hmm…he smells good.*

Grandma followed him up the stairs to my room. Papa put me down on my bed and took off my shoes. I groaned and rolled over, still pretending to be asleep, but I was never more wide-awake in my life.

Grandma bent down to kiss me, and I smelled her perfume again. I breathed it in.

How I love the smell of her.

"I love you, my baby," she whispered in my ear.

My closed eyes brimmed with pained tears. *I love you, too, so much! Please tell me what's going on.*

She stilled, and I thought she was going to leave, but instead, she lay down beside me on the bed, pulling me close to her, and laid her cheek on the top of my head.

I sighed, feeling her stroke my hair with her soft hand. *I could never stay mad at you,* I thought to her, willing her to hear me, *wondering* if she was listening.

She and I lay together for a long time until I felt her hand slip from my cheek as she drifted off to sleep. Her breath drew soft and shallow.

I closed my eyes but willed myself not to sleep. It had been a long time since she held me like that, too long, and I was going to enjoy every second of it.

After a while, Grandma woke up. Her breath rushed over my ear. She stroked my head and kissed the side of my face.

I opened my eyes. My room was growing dark as daylight slipped out of the sky.

"I hope you'll understand. Please understand, Leesie," she whispered into my ear, imploring me.

After that, she didn't say another word, and I wasn't quite sure if she was asleep or wide-awake like me.

A short time later I heard footsteps in the hall, passing by my room.

It was Papa.

A few moments later, there was a knock at Grandma's bedroom door, then a pause, and my door opened.

The dim light of a single lantern bathed my room in muted light.

Grandma's body tensed, and through the reflection of my window, I saw her close her eyes and pretend to be asleep.

I closed mine, too.

Papa walked into the room. He stopped by the bed, and an eerie silence ensued, stretching out between us like a dense fog. I could almost feel the tension crackling through the air, choking us, or at least choking *me*. I had to wonder if they felt it, too. As much as I wanted to open my eyes, I didn't dare.

After another moment of silence, my father chuckled, thankfully breaking the unbearable tension in the room. He stepped forward, took a blanket off the edge of my bed, and covered both Grandma and me. Then the bed sagged under Papa's weight as he sat down next to us and placed the lamp on my bedside table. He bent over Grandma, kissed the top of my head first, and to my surprise, as well as hers, I'm sure, kissed her head.

I reopened my eyes, staring at him through the reflection in the window, but he didn't notice me. His attention was trained on Grandma, but her eyes were shut tight.

I watched through the reflection of the window as he took the pins out of Grandma's hair. First, he unwound it, handling it gently and with loving care, sifting the silky strands between his long fingers. Then he lifted her hair to his face, inhaling deeply…her scent.

Papa sat next to Grandma and me for another moment, his hands resting on our heads. It seemed as if he didn't want to leave.

"*I love you, Ali,*" my father whispered just as my eyes flew open wide.

I had to force away the gasp forming in my throat. Though Grandma didn't move, I knew she wasn't asleep. She couldn't be!

Papa rose and then placed one knee on the bedside. He stretched all the way over Grandma. His lips brushed across and over her mouth. It wasn't a kiss, per se, but rather a soft caress. Without warning, just as their lips met, he jerked back and stood upright, seemingly startled by something. He shook his head. To my surprise, he sat back down beside Grandma and unbuttoned the first two buttons of her dress. He slid his hand against her bare skin, pressing it against her heart—*her bosom!* At the same time, a few scattered tears dripped down his beautiful face.

"*So bright!*" he choked.

I knew then that he still saw it. Papa still saw Grandma's *light!*

His breath grew quicker and unsteady, almost gasping, and he began to cry.

Oh, Papa! My heart broke for him.

After a few moments, my father wiped his eyes with the backs of his hands. He bent over us again. "*I love you. I love you both so much! I'll never let anyone hurt you. Never again!*"

Finally, he rose from the bed, took the lantern in his hand, and turned to go. He stopped just before reaching the door. He didn't want to leave.

Sadly, he opened the door and left Grandma and me alone in my room.

I wanted to ask Grandma what had happened, but instead I closed my eyes and succumbed to sleep.

8. Escape

I woke up early the next morning and turned over expecting to see Grandma lying next to me, but she was gone. The sun wasn't even up yet.

Where did she go?

I got up, padded to my bedroom door, and cracked it open.

I heard her downstairs; she was talking to Papa.

Funny, talking to each other is something they don't seem to do very much. Well, maybe that'll change now.

I paused and my thoughts returned to the night before.

He loves her. Papa loves her. He SAID it, and Grandma heard him say it. I know she did.

A fresh crop of anxious goosebumps sprang up all over my body.

Hmm. I wonder what they're talking about.

I put my ear to the crack in the door, listening carefully. The sound of Papa's voice could be heard well over Grandma's.

"Do you think this is wise, Ali?" he asked.

"Ali?" I whispered to myself and gasped. *"He just called her 'Ali' again."*

I poked my head just outside the bedroom door to hear them better.

"They've already met, Asa," Grandma replied, and it sounded to me as if she was trying to control her emotions. *"It's out of our hands. Now don't worry. I'll keep a close eye on her. I'll make sure she clearly understands what not to do. After all, it wasn't so very different from the way that you and I met."*

"I think it's best if she just stays away from everyone, like she's been doing until now," Papa grumbled, and he sounded worried.

"Hiding won't help. You of all people should know that! I don't understand what you're thinking," Grandma admonished. *"Molly and Jake are like family. How can we keep them from their goddaughter, especially now that they're so close to us?*

Asa, Molly is like a sister to me. I don't want to lose her again, and Jake has been like a brother to you since the two of you were just boys. Please, we can't keep her hidden, not from them!"

"Well, she's my daughter, not yours, remember? Besides, you're the expert when it comes to hiding," Papa snapped, *"particularly from yourself, not to mention, from me.*

You want Lees to know the rest of her family? Fine! Then tell her everything. Go! Go, right now! Go up and tell her the truth, Ali! But tell her EVERYTHING!"

With that, I heard the clatter of a chair as it scraped across the kitchen floor and then fell over. Grandma came running up the stairs so quickly that she almost caught me spying on her before I had a chance to shut my bedroom door.

I peeked through the crack as she hurried past my room with her head in her hands and then slammed her bedroom door behind her.

I reopened the door just as I heard footsteps coming up the stairs. It was Papa. He walked halfway up the stairs, but then he paused, turned around, and went back down. The last thing I heard was the sound of his bedroom door slamming shut.

I closed my door, walked back to the bed, and lay down.

I'd never heard him talk to her like that before in my life. It made me angry.

I wish they'd tell me what is going on!

I thought about what my grandma said: *Kristofer's parents are my godparents. Why did I not know this before?*

"What's going on?" I mumbled to myself just as my groggy, heavy eyelids fluttered and then closed.

I hadn't realized I'd gone back to sleep until I recognized the stable that I was standing in from the vision I had earlier.

I sighed. *Here we go again…*

I looked around. Alice was standing just a few feet from me, glancing around the stable, absentmindedly stroking the silky ginger mane of the silver-white stallion.

"Asa, where are you?" She took the horse's muzzle between her hands. *"Where is your master, Butterscotch? Where is he? I'm going to accept his proposal. Where is he?"* She pushed her lips to Butterscotch's nose and closed her eyes just as Butterscotch's eyes closed as well; it was as if the horse felt her love.

Just then, the stable door creaked and then opened, and a relieved look covered Alice's small face.

She stepped away from the horse's stall. Her expectant expression turned to fright when she saw *who* had come through the door; it was not who she had *hoped* to see.

"Hello, pet." A silky voice oozed through the air around us as Charles Marshal pushed the door open. His soulless eyes lit up when he noticed Alice's frightened expression. *"Looking for your stable boy, were you?"* he asked, laughing, and his malevolent eyes darkened with hunger.

He stalked forward, reaching out to touch Alice, but she shuddered with obvious revulsion and then stepped out of his grasp.

At the same time, Butterscotch whinnied and stamped on the stall floor. Clearly, he didn't like Charles Marshal, either.

"Where's Asa? Have you done something to my Asa?" Alice demanded.

Charles's eyes flew open with surprise. He tilted his head to the side, studying her. *"Your…Asa? The stable boy? You think he's yours?"* He laughed.

Alice took another step back. *"Asa is mine. He wants to marry me; he asked for my hand today,"* she mumbled, all the while never looking Charles in the eyes.

"Marry you?" Charles spat, throwing his dark head back and raucously laughing. *"Surely you don't believe such nonsense! Even a simpleton such as you couldn't believe that the stable boy is any better than me. Now, do you?"*

He stepped closer, his beady eyes alight with mirth. *"Young Master Raign Junior is a wealthy boy, Alice! What would he want with a filthy little orphaned witch like you?"*

Again, Butterscotch stamped on the ground, his large, ochre eyes flaring with rage.

"Asa loves me!" Alice shrieked.

"Loves you? He doesn't love you!" Charles sneered. *"That boy only wants one thing from you, Alice. It's what all rich men want from pretty, stupid, young girls like you. And once he gets it, he'll cast you aside like yesterday's rubbish!"*

"That's not true!"

Charles backed Alice against one of the stall doors, pinning her with his hips, manically tilting his head from side to side. *"You don't think that what I say is the truth?"*

"No!"

Charles sneered again. *"Well, did you know that the stable boy's mother offered me quite a lot of money to leave you alone? Or rather, she wanted me to sell you to the boy—as a plaything, I'd imagine..."*

Alice took a sharp breath in, as if Charles's words had wounded her; her mouth gaped open, and pained tears welled in her emerald eyes.

"I refused Mrs. Raign's request, of course. After all, you still haven't given ME what I paid for, now, have you?"

He grabbed her by the hair, forcibly jerking her toward him. Simultaneously, Butterscotch thrashed around the stall and reared up as if he were about to break down the stall door.

"I don't believe you! Mrs. Raign wouldn't do such a thing. She's a nice woman!" Alice shrieked as Charles yanked her hair harder.

Charles put his face right up to hers, forcing her to look at him, raucously sneering. *"It's quite...amusing...really."*

"What is amusing?" Alice barely breathed the question.

A wide grin spread across the sharp features of Charles's angular face. *"The way you thought you could get away from me..."*

As he spoke, his cold, calculating eyes bore into Alice's skull; he seemed enraged though oddly pleased with himself at the same time, enjoying her fear.

Alice didn't say a word but cast her sight down, as though willing herself to disappear.

"No matter. Now that I've found you, I'm going to tell you what you are going to do." Charles barely breathed. His eyes were alight with both hunger and excitement; he rocked his hips against Alice as he spoke. *"You are going to come to my house this evening at seven o'clock, sharp!"* he whispered, tightening the grip he had on her hair.

"No!" she shrieked in pain. *"I won't! You can kill me first! I won't go back to your house, not ever again! I'm going to marry Asa!"*

Not to be rebuked, Charles burst into a fit of rage and viciously threw Alice to the ground. Her head collided with the stall door with a sickening crack. Slowly, she sat up, looking dazed, cradling her head in her hands. A steady trickle of blood oozed down the length of her small face. At the same time, Butterscotch reared up again, this time frantically kicking the stall door, attempting to break free.

Startled by Butterscotch's rage, Charles's eyes grew large. He pulled a small pistol from the inside pocket of his overcoat and pointed the barrel of the gun at the horse.

Still bleeding, still half-lying on the ground, Alice rounded on the furious horse, while at the same time, throwing her bloodied hands in the air. *"No. Stop. Now!"* she commanded.

The horse immediately obeyed. It lowered its hooves, backed away from the stall door, and then stood still, his eyes clouded over as if spellbound.

Seeing Alice's command over the animal, Charles gasped while his beady eyes drew wide with sudden excitement. He stowed the weapon, bent down, and pulled Alice's face forward. His hands shook; his lungs heaved with exhilaration. *"I knew you had control of the power... I knew you were lying to me,"* he hissed. Then a triumphant smirk stole over his face while his eyes contracted, becoming hard as stone.

He leaned forward, causing Alice to quake with fear. *"You do anything except what I tell you to do, witch,"* he sneered, *"and I will kill the stable boy!"* His sight swept over Alice's shoulder to where Butterscotch stood. *"You run from me again, and I will kill your friend...er, Molly, isn't it?"* He canted his head, his voice softer. *"And if you don't do what I tell you to do, and I am forced to punish your stable boy for it, I will make damned sure that you. Are. There. To. Witness. His. Death."*

Then Charles ran his finger down Alice's bloody cheek, smearing a crimson streak across her temple with his fingertip. *"Do you understand?"* he asked.

Alice gasped at Charles's threat. Her hand flew up to her mouth, stifling a scream.

Abruptly, Charles rose and turned to leave, though he stopped at the stable door and turned around, his penetrating gaze causing Alice to gasp again.

With a smirk, Charles put his index finger into his mouth, sucking the blood-encrusted tip. *"Remember, seven o'clock, sharp.*

Oh, and if you don't do what I say, I will have no other choice than to burn the orphanage to the ground with all those poor children trapped inside." He cocked his head again in such a way that reminded me of a manic puppet. *"Wouldn't that be a pity?"* he laughed, clearly pleased with himself, and then wrenched open the stable door and left.

I lunged after him. *"You evil bastard! She was going to marry my papa! What did you do!? What did you do to her!?"*

I dropped to my knees, crying.

He did something to her. I know he did something to her…

I peered across the room toward where the young memory of my grandma lay alone on the stable floor. She was sobbing, and blood covered most of her face and hair.

"What did he do to you, and why didn't you marry Papa?" I whispered to her, still weeping. Then I crawled over to where she lay sobbing on the straw-covered ground.

As I watched her, Alice cried into her hands. *"Dear God, I can't let him hurt Asa! I can't let him hurt Asa or Molly or the children! I'd die if he hurt them! Asa, my Asa, I must force you away from me. I won't let him harm you!"*

She raised her sights heavenward. *"Please, Lord, help me. I know I'm an abomination against you. I know I'm a witch, but please, help me,"* she begged, throwing her hands over her face. She then lay on the ground and wept.

After a few moments, the door opened again. Alice bolted upright, an expression of sheer terror showing in her wary eyes.

It was Asa.

Young Alice and I both blew out a breath of relief, but Alice turned away, attempting to wipe the blood from her forehead and face with her hands.

Asa rushed to Alice's side. He sat down on the straw-covered ground and then lifted her up, dragging her into his lap and running his hands over her bleeding head, thoroughly examining her. With one arm wound around her small waist, he pulled her into a poignant embrace.

"What happened, baby?" he whispered, attempting to wipe the blood off her head with his bare hand.

Baby? Gasp!

I thought I was going to faint, but I shook the shock of Papa's endearment from my head and tried to focus on the scene in front of me.

Baby! He called her baby!

"I'm all right, Asa, I just fell," Alice lied again.

Asa pulled her to his chest and held her, touching his lips to her bruised head. He closed his eyes and then breathed in deep—inhaling her sweet scent.

My head swam. *This time, I am going to faint!*

I took a steadying breath and sighed. *Oh well, at least if I faint here, they'll never know.*

Asa opened his lovely, light-blue eyes, seeming a bit intoxicated by her scent. He pulled Alice's chin up, gazing into the dark emerald depths of her eyes.

"I want to take care of you, Ali. I want to protect you from all harm..." He paused for a moment and then leaned nearer, encircling one hand around the nape of Alice's neck, nuzzling her ear. In response to his touch, Alice laid her head on his shoulder and closed her eyes, seeming to *melt* right into him.

"After what happened between you and me earlier today, you must agree to marry me. After all, I've already marked you as...my own." His eyes alight with both hunger and need, he smiled, and the tips of his ears flushed with innocent love. He tipped Alice's chin up. *"It was wonderful for me, by the way. I hope it was the same for you. I'm sorry that Molly came in and ruined our first time together,"* he whispered. All the while the tip of his index finger outlined the contour of her bottom lip. *"Please agree to marry me, so we may do it again, right here, right now."*

Young Asa's eyes grew hooded, darkening with pristine passion. *"I hunger for you, Ali. I yearn to feel your bare skin against my own. I want that again—I need it. The first time was entirely too brief. I want to feel you from the inside again, over and over again...*"

He dragged his nose alongside hers, taking shuddering breaths, and closed his eyes. "*You are so soft and warm, silky and snug. You and I fit together as if we were made for each other. I want to feel the curvature of your spine while I'm in you, to feel you gasp against my shoulder. I need you beneath me, sweetheart. Feeling you, sharing pleasure with you, it was Heaven. Please be my wife, Ali, please marry me,*" he whispered, dragging his full, soft lips against hers.

A kiss!

I gasped at the sight, yet I was perplexed. I didn't understand a word of what Asa said to her. Well, I understood the proposal, but that was all.

Alice jerked away. "*Marry you!*" she shouted, shoving him hard in the chest, startling him. She clambered off his lap and stood, fisting her hands against her hips, and glared at his shocked expression. "*Your mother tried to buy me, Asa, or didn't you know that?*"

"*She didn't try to buy you!*" Asa hollered back, sudden panic and desperation rising in his eyes.

He leaped to his feet. "*Mama just wanted to get you away from that monster Charles Marshal! My God, Ali, he treats you like you are some kind of a—*" He hesitated. "*As if you're a lady of the evening,*" he uneasily mumbled. "*Hell, you should hear some of the things Marshal says about you!*" he spat, wincing as he spoke the words. "*At least I'm nice to you... I love you, and I thought you loved me, too.*"

His voice dropped, and he frowned. "*You made love to me today, right here in this stable. If you don't love me, then why did you give yourself to me?*"

"*Because that is what all rich men want from pretty, stupid, young girls, isn't it, Asa?*" Alice retorted. "*You don't love me. You want to buy me, do as you please, and then cast me aside like yesterday's rubbish!*"

Alice walked a few paces away, turning her back to Asa. *"At least Charles is honest. He doesn't pretend to love me. I know he wants to own me. You're the one who treats me like a… What did you say? A lady of the evening? You and your mother!"*

"I don't do that!" Asa incredulously shouted. He had pained tears streaming down his face.

Alice stepped further away, unable to watch her stable boy cry—to *hurt*. She wrung her delicate hands. *"I thank you, Asa Raign, for being nice to me, but the plain truth is that nice men, like you, are a lot like spending time in church. It's a fine place to visit, but I wouldn't want to live there. Besides, Charles has much more to offer me. He is a man, not…a boy!"* she quickly blurted, administering the final blow.

Before Asa had a chance to respond, Alice swept past him and out the stable door. She left before Asa had an opportunity to see the pain, and the *love,* for him burning in her emerald eyes.

Just as Alice left, my young, teenage papa dissolved into a puddle. He dropped to his knees on the stable floor with his head in his hands and *wept.*

I wanted to help him, but I knew he couldn't see or hear me. I sat next to him, willing him to sense my presence, willing him to stop hurting.

Young Asa and I sat together for what must have been hours until finally he stood up just as darkness swept through the stable. He lit a lantern that was hanging on the wall by one of the stalls. The stable burst into soft, ambient light. Then my poor papa sat back down on the stable floor with his head in his hands and cried again.

It felt as if my heart were bleeding as I watched him. He was more than just hurt. He was destroyed.

I crawled closer, directly behind him. *"She's only doing this because she loves you. She was protecting you and her friend Molly and the children. She loves you all."*

Then a thought came to mind. *"I wonder if she still loves you. I wonder: Does she love you as much as you love her? And how did Rebecca get you away from her?"* I asked both him and myself. *"I just don't understand. If you loved her, then why did you marry Rebecca?"*

I frowned. *"And who is Rebecca's father?"* I whispered to myself.

Just then, the stable doors swung open, and a different young girl flew in. This girl was a beautiful, tall brunette. Her big, hazel eyes were wild with fear and grief. She rushed toward Asa.

"Molly!" Asa cried, leaping to his feet. *"What's wrong?"*

"Molly?" I muttered aloud. *"Molly is Grandma's friend, Kristofer's mother. Yes, Kristofer looks just like her…"*

Molly grabbed Asa by both arms, her expression pleading. She was both crying and screaming at the same time. *"Ali! Ali!"*

Asa grasped each side of Molly's face, forcing her full gaze. *"What happened to Ali?"* Frightened tears welled in his eyes, too.

"He hurt her, Asa!" Molly screamed. *"That monster hurt her! He hurt her as badly as a man can hurt a woman! I don't know how she got away from him! She's covered in blood,"* she whispered. *"I'm afraid she might die! I didn't know who else to come to."*

Asa pulled Molly's face nearer, staring straight into her terrified eyes, both fear and fury rising in his stance. *"How exactly did that monster hurt my Ali?"* he murmured, his voice breathless and winded by fear.

Molly's eyes dropped down and she shook her head. *"Charles Marshal took her, Asa—forcibly."*

Asa understood; a tearless sob escaped his lips, but I didn't understand at all.

I frowned and stepped closer to Asa and Molly. *"What? What does that mean: he took her? He took her…where?"* I looked up at them both, my eyes searching their panic-stricken faces.

Without pause, Asa grabbed the lantern hanging on the stall, blew it out, and then threw it against the stable door, plunging us into darkness. A loud crashing sound reverberated around the stable.

"Get back to Ali, Molly, and I'll be there as soon as I can," he told her. *"I'll fetch my Ma. She used to be a nurse before she got married. Go!"* he hollered. *"She shouldn't be left alone! Dear God, please, please don't let anything happen to Ali, please!"* Asa prayed aloud as he ran.

The scene shifted.

We were now in a small room lit by several lanterns.

The young memory of my father sat next to a little bed in the corner of the room. Alice lay, still as a corpse, beneath a tattered blanket. She was battered, her face bruised, and the dress she wore earlier in the day lay in a bloody heap next to the bed. A sheer cotton slip obscured her delicate frame, her complexion was discolored, and much of her body was wrapped in bandages. Through the gossamer bandages I could plainly see deep scratches and purpled handprints covering her neck and shoulders.

"Somebody strong had her pinned down…" I absent-mindedly whispered.

Asa held Alice's fragile hand, all the while staring, unblinking, at her chest.

Then, a lady I didn't recognize entered the room. I noted that she looked vaguely familiar to me. She was about thirty-five years old, maybe a bit older. Her upswept hair was blonde, and she was quite lovely. She wore an expensive-looking periwinkle blue dress; she appeared to be wealthy. However, her light-blue eyes were clouded with worry and fatigue.

The lady stood next to Asa, placed her hand on his head, and stroked his hair. *"What are you staring at, son?"* she murmured.

"Son?" I mumbled, remembering where I'd seen her before. *"That's the lady from the big house in the city, the one who stares out the window at me. She must be Papa's mother, my other grandmother."*

"*I don't know how, Mama, but I see a light…here,*" Asa explained, placing his hand on Alice's chest, where the light emitted its divine glow. "*The light is usually so bright, but now it's weak and flickering.*"

He leaned down and placed his lips against Alice's chest, as if talking directly *to* the light itself were going to keep her alive. "*Please don't go out,*" he wept. Then, moving her gauzy slip aside with his fingertips, he kissed the delicate skin covering her heart.

Papa's mother seemed both shocked and astonished watching the way her son handled Alice's broken body. She sat beside Alice on the bed and cleared her throat. "*I've heard rumors about this girl, that she can do unusual things, Asa,*" she stammered, her voice wavering with emotion. "*But why can you see a light inside of her?*"

"*Ali saved my life,*" Asa weakly muttered, avoiding his mother's question. His voice cracked. He took an unsteady gulp of air and smoothed his hands over Alice's diminishing light. "*Ali sacrificed herself to save me. She even tried to tell me that she didn't love me to protect me from that monster. Molly said the evil devil told Ali to cooperate or that I would die. That's the only reason she went to his house!*" He balled his fists and placed them against his forehead, unable to stand the fact that Alice had sacrificed herself to protect him.

Papa's mother stroked Alice's hair. "*Thank you, dear girl.*"

She spoke softly, stifling a sob. Then her attention returned to Asa. "*But the light, Asa. Do you know why you see it?*"

When Asa didn't answer the second time, Papa's mother took his face into her hands, pulled it toward her, and forced him to look at her. "*Asa, why?*" she reiterated, and this time her tone was insistent.

Asa seemed nervous. "*I don't know,*" he finally answered. "*I've been able to see the light since the first time I touched Ali's hand. I think she is something holy, like an angel, but I'm just not sure. I pray that I won't have to watch the light leave her. If it goes out, then she will die, and if she dies, then so will I.*" He caressed Alice's breast bone, closed his eyes, and laid his head against her bosom.

Papa's mother gasped at his words. She sat staring at her son for a moment, worry marring her lovely features. It was as if she were seeing him for the first time, or perhaps it was that her son, the boy, was gone, and now her son, the man, lay before her. He lay with the angel who had sacrificed herself to save him.

As Asa lay with his ear pressed against Alice's heart, a single tear fell from his eyes and onto her skin. The tear rolled down the side of her neck and then trickled along her collarbone onto the bed.

"Her heart does sound stronger," Asa whispered, raising his weary head and looking into his mother's pained eyes. *"Mama, is the damage great?"*

Papa's mother stood and then bent down, putting her lips to the top of Asa's head. *"If she lives, it will mend, son."*

Asa solemnly nodded, and with great care shifted Alice over. He lay down next to her on the small bed, curling his body around hers, placing her head under his chin and enfolding her within the contours of his form, protecting her. He held both her tiny porcelain hands within one of his own. *"Please don't leave me, Ali, I love you so much,"* he whispered to her and then closed his eyes.

Papa's mother seemed torn. *"Asa, it isn't proper."* She paused, wringing her hands. *"What I mean to say is: it's not proper for you to sleep with Alice..."* She paused again and then stepped forward and covered her son with a shabby blanket. Wordlessly, she put her weary head in her hands, turned away from Asa and Ali, and left the room in tears.

I blinked twice, and the scene changed again.

The room was bright with daylight, and Alice disappeared from the small bed. Papa's mother sat on it instead.

At first, my grandma's absence from the scene alarmed me, but then I realized that she must be all right. I knew she *had* lived through the attack. After all, I saw her every day.

I breathed a sigh of relief and tried to stop my knees from wobbling.

Just then, young Alice walked into the room. She shut the door behind her, and a look of fright swept through her eyes when she saw Papa's mother sitting on the bed, waiting for her.

I realized *this* vision was quite some time after the last one. Alice seemed well, aside from the look of sheer panic that was on her face as she entered the room. She wrung her hands.

Just like she does now, I thought.

Papa's mother patted the empty spot on the bed beside her.

I could almost hear Alice's heartbeat thumping through the fabric of her dress. Nevertheless, she obediently stepped forward and sat down without looking my much *older* grandmother in the eyes.

"You are, thankfully, looking well, Alice," Papa's mother muttered while taking one of Alice's shaking hands. Then she lifted her index finger and placed it under Alice's chin, urging her gaze.

Their eyes met, and Papa's mother took a deep, shaky breath. *"Please, tell me the truth, Alice,"* she said, her voice cracking with emotion. *"Please, tell me. I must know."* She paused and gulped hard. *"Is my Asa the father of your child? I have asked him, but he will not answer me, and I must know."* She choked back a tear.

Alice turned away, staring blankly ahead. *"No,"* she numbly muttered.

Papa's mother put her hand on Alice's face, turning it toward her again. She seemed taken aback by Alice's reply. *"Are you absolutely sure, dear?"* she asked with a sense of disbelief in her voice as well as in her eyes.

Again, Alice shook her head. *"We never..."* she whispered, staring down at her wringing hands.

"Oh, I'm sorry!" my other grandmother muttered, putting a hand to her chest, seeming both shocked and bemused. *"I assumed because*

of the way that Asa handled you when you were hurt…" She didn't finish the sentence. *"I apologize for that, for my mistake, Alice."*

Alice numbly shook her head. *"No, Mrs. Raign, I'm the one who is sorry. I wish we had, but we didn't get a chance,"* Alice replied. She then stood up, wrung her hands, and turned to face my other grandmother.

"You know, just because I don't have parents and money and a proper last name like you do doesn't mean that I don't have a sense of virtue because I do. Or, at least, I did…" She sobbed, throwing her face into her hands.

I frowned. I didn't understand any of this conversation between my two grandmothers, but I tried to keep up.

"I didn't mean that, child," Papa's mother said, pushing to her feet and hurrying over to where Alice stood sobbing. *"Of course, you have virtue, darling, you still do. That evil boy took what he wanted from you without your consent, Alice. You did nothing wrong. Please believe that, sweetheart."*

She stroked Alice's hair. *"It was the way Asa took care of you. It was the love he showed and the tender way that he held you that made me think the two of you are lovers, that's all."*

Papa's mother grabbed Alice by the hand, pulling her back down onto the bed, and then took her face between her palms. *"Listen to me. You saved my son's life, and I will never be able to repay you for that, but I can try,"* she whispered, taking a deep breath. *"Asa wants to marry you, Alice. Please agree."*

Alice glanced up, and it was with a defeated look in her eyes though she weakly smiled. *"You may repay me, Mrs. Raign, by keeping Asa away from me."*

She stood and stepped away from the bed. *"I don't know how to love Asa properly or how to be his wife or even a mother. Perhaps…if this,"* she said, gesturing toward her middle, *"wouldn't have happened, but not now, not ever."*

She turned to face my other grandmother once again. *"Do you know why, Mrs. Raign, do you know why my last name is Willow?"* She paused for a moment. *"My last name is Willow because my parents, or whoever left me as a baby, didn't leave me with a person. They left me under a willow tree. I wasn't even important enough for them to leave me with anyone who had a soul…who breathed!"* she hollered. *"Those awful people, whoever they were, left me with a soulless thing that didn't even have a pulse or feelings!"*

Oh, Grandma!

Then, in stark contrast, Alice was soft and quiet, her voice merely a whisper, though her self-abhorrence blared. *"I've dreamed of a beautiful, ginger-headed woman who smelled of strawberries and apple blossoms. She was kind; she held me to her bosom and called me 'angel.' I was small, and the woman helped me to fly."* She let out a humorless laugh. *"Literally, with her mind, she made me fly. But I know it was only a silly dream. That woman doesn't exist; if she did, I wouldn't be alone. If she did, I would know that I belonged to someone. So I guess the symbol of the Willow fits me. Like the tree they left me under, I am an inhuman, soulless thing, a thing that doesn't even remember how to breathe anymore."*

I wanted to cry for her, but I felt numb. What's more, I knew that whatever it was that evil man took from her so long ago, Papa was the only one who could give it back.

I paused mid-thought, and my heart sank. *"But he didn't,"* I told myself, realization dawning. *"I know how this story ended: Papa married someone else, and Grandma stayed broken. That's why she doesn't think my trees are alive. She says they don't breathe because she doesn't breathe.*

But maybe she will!" I said aloud, with a hopeful, albeit tearful, smile. *"Papa loves her! Maybe he'll heal her and teach her to breathe again!"* With that thought, my spirits lifted just a bit.

Just then, a man walked into the room, stealing my attention back to the here and now. My heart almost stopped. It was my papa, but it was Papa the way he looked in the present.

No, wait, his eyes are darker, and his hair is darker, too.

Papa's mother wiped her eyes and stood just as the man entered the room.

"Alice," her voice was hoarse. She gestured toward the man. *"This is Asa's father, Asa Senior.*

Dear, this is Alice Willow," she told the man, gesturing toward where young Alice stood before him.

Alice politely curtsied. *"It's a pleasure to meet you, Mr. Raign."*

Mr. Raign made an off-handed motion toward the door as he spoke to his wife. *"Leave us, Margaret,"* he commanded.

Papa's mother went to leave, but she stopped at the threshold. She turned to her husband as if she wished to say something, but she held her tongue. Without another word, she looked Alice in the eyes, warmly smiled, and then, abiding her husband's demand, turned and left the room.

"I shall dispense with the niceties, Miss Willow, and get straight to the point," Asa Senior tersely muttered once his wife was out of sight. *"Firstly, my son is young, and still quite foolish..."*

"I am well-aware of who and what Asa is, sir!" Alice retorted, cutting Mr. Raign off mid-sentence.

Taken aback by Alice's reproachful words, Mr. Raign's dark blue eyes flashed with anger. He took a purposeful step forward, thrusting his index finger into Alice's face, his teeth bared. *"Now, look here, girl! I will not have the likes of you besmirching the good name of Raign in this town!*

I'll have you know that I have lived in this city for my entire life and have never been a party to any scandal. Likewise, I don't intend to let some little harlot like you destroy my son's future.

Furthermore, Miss Willow, I have known the Marshal family for a great number of years, and I am shocked that anyone would attempt to sully their good name. It is one thing to allure the boy with your wiles, but to entice him and then to have the gall to be upset when he takes umbrage at your trickery! And worst still, to accuse a decent young man like Charles of violating you. My Lord, girl. Why, you ought to be horsewhipped!"

Mr. Raign sneered, looked Alice up and down, and then leaned toward her. *"Tell me, did Charles not pay you enough?"*

"I am not for sale, sir!" Alice shouted with angry tears welling in her eyes, *"and I never have been!"*

"Well, that's not what I hear." Mr. Raign growled and glared into her eyes. *"My son has the promise of a brilliant career ahead of him, and that path will not be thwarted, particularly not by a filthy little whore like you. Nevertheless, he is immature, and my wife, love her, does not seem to have his best interests at heart sometimes. Did you know that Asa Junior wishes to become a concert, pianist?! Can you just imagine such a thing?"* A loud guffaw escaped his throat.

Alice put her hands on her hips, stepping forward, and stared him dead in his sights. *"Have you ever even heard Asa play, Mr. Raign?"*

"I don't have time to sit around and listen to my son tinker on a piano, Miss Willow. I am a busy man!"

Alice mirthlessly laughed. *"Well, I have heard Asa play, sir, and so has your wife. Perhaps if you loved Asa as much as she does…"*

"Now, you just hold your tongue, girl! You know nothing about me or about my family. Let me tell you something: pretty girls are a dime a dozen and in your case much less. My son thinks he loves you, but wait and see what he thinks of you then in twenty years or so when your beauty has faded. He'll see you on the street. You'll be standing in front of a house of ill-repute, no doubt, and Junior won't give you a second glance."

"Is that right, Mr. Raign? Hmm. Well, I'd certainly like to know what your wife would have to say about that. How long have you been married? Close to twenty years, perhaps?"

"Why, you filthy, little Jezebel!" Mr. Raign shouted, flying into a rage.

He reached out, grabbed Alice by the top of the arm, and pushed his face into hers. *"Let me advise you of one thing, girl. The Marshals and I have friends in this town, important friends who don't take too kindly to you right now. Therefore, it would be in your best interest to take your bastard child,"* he sneered, *"and leave town. And you won't even think about pinning your shame on my son or Charles Marshal if you know what's good for you."*

From across the room, I heard a man's voice shout, *"Stop it, stop it, that's enough!"* but I couldn't see where it came from. No one else was in the room.

Alice took a quick breath in, gasped, and her eyes flew open wide. *She heard it, too!*

Before I could ponder what had happened, Asa came into the room. He marched up behind his father. *"No one talks to Ali like that, no one, not even you,"* he whispered. And though his tone was soft, his eyes were hard and blazing with fury. *"You take everything you said back now and you will apologize to Ali, too. Now!"*

I'd never seen my Papa so angry in my life—not ever! It was frightening.

Mr. Raign turned to face his son. He glared straight into Asa's eyes. *"I will not take it back, son. Every word is true."*

"It is not true!" Asa shouted.

Mr. Raign shook his head. *"I will not have this, boy! Either you let this piece of rubbish go, or you're dead to me! I will not let you or this common strumpet,"* he said, dismissively gesturing toward Alice, *"ruin my good name in this town, not to mention my dealings with Judge Marshal. You either leave with me right now, or don't come home at all! What say you to that, Junior?"* The words dripped with sarcasm. He shoved his hands into his pockets and then self-assuredly stepped back.

Without a second's pause, Asa marched to the door, then held it open for his father. *"I say goodbye, Father!"*

"No, Asa!" Alice cried. *"I can't let you do this! Not for me, please! I'm not worth it, please!"*

Mr. Raign turned and stalked out the door. *"I'll have George bring your things here!"* he hollered without a backward glance.

Alice walked across the room to a small cracked window, watching as Asa Raign Senior left. Just before Mr. Raign reached his buggy, he stopped and turned around, eyeing Alice, and then he winked and turned to leave once more.

"Pain, I only cause pain. I should have watched you from afar..." Alice murmured under her breath, watching Mr. Raign as he drove away in his expensive buggy.

"What?" Asa asked.

"Everything I have always wanted but couldn't have, I have seen from afar, Asa. Whether it was a nice set of parents or a fine home or..." She hesitated. *"Or a beautiful stable boy who made enchanting music that came from his soul. It has all been from afar. Or, at least, it should have stayed that way,"* she murmured under her breath.

Asa stepped forward and attempted to take Alice's hand. *"I am not afar, Ali. I thank the Lord every day that you chose my stable to hide in. I am right here in front of you, sweetheart. Marry me, marry me, and you will have everything that you've ever wished for."*

Alice pushed Asa's hands away, her eyes cast down. *"I can't marry you. You don't want me. Trust me, Asa, I'm tainted. I'm a demon or a succubus just as the townspeople say. I am evil, and besides, I don't love you."*

Asa gazed into Alice's beautiful emerald eyes, attempting to catch her sights with his own though she quickly looked away. *"You don't love me?"* he asked.

"No."

Asa sighed, placing his hands on Alice's waist. She flinched and stepped back. *"If you are what you say you are, Ali, then, please, tell me this: would a demon have saved my life or Molly's? Would a demon have saved the lives of a whole house full of orphans? Would a succubus nearly die after being violated? And even if you are these things, then believe me, it is already too late for me. I am damned,"* he whispered. *"I see your light, and I am the only person who can. I do believe that means you are mine."*

Asa leaned down, attempting to persuade a kiss from Alice, but she shuddered and pulled her head away.

Truthfully, I had always wondered what it would be like if they were together. I'd even dreamed of it a few times, but seeing it in front of me like that, seeing her so frightened of Papa, was strange.

"Do you love me, Ali?" Asa whispered, his bright, light-blue eyes blossoming with both hope and concern.

Alice shuddered again, her eyes cast down, but she almost imperceptibly nodded. *"Yes, I feel love for you, Asa, but I can't give you what you need, and I can't bear to let you touch me. I couldn't, not after what happened."*

She stepped a pace away, her head hung in shame. *"And besides, I've been untrue to you. Why would you still want me?"* The last part came in a hushed whisper that Asa didn't hear, but I heard it.

Asa frowned, his brow tightly knitted with worry. He stepped forward, attempting to take Alice's hand, but just as before, she pulled away, emotionally barricading herself, protecting her fragile soul from further harm.

"This baby is mine; I know it is!" Asa spat, clearly frustrated. He took a deep breath, controlling his rising temper. *"But even if you won't marry me, I promise to take care of my child. I promise to love both of you, and I'll wait as long as I have to to have you again, Ali. I'll wait forever if need be!"*

"I'm sorry, Asa. I told you, this baby is not yours. If it were, then it would be like me, but it's not. This baby is mortal. She is not like me."

"Which is, what? What exactly are you? I've tried to figure it out, but I don't know!"

Alice stifled a sob. *"I don't know. Something…dark,"* she murmured to herself.

"You're holy, like an angel. I know it, but I don't care what this baby IS! I don't give a damn if she's mortal or otherwise! She is mine!" Asa snapped.

Alice shook her head. *"This is not your child, Asa, I'm sorry,"* she cried as tears streamed down her cheeks.

Giving up, Asa sighed. *"Well, you were right, there was a demon at play here, but it wasn't you, sweetheart. In fact, from what I've heard around town, the demon is in hiding."*

Alice seemed puzzled. Her eyes drifted up toward Asa's, up toward but not *into* his eyes. *"Why would Charles hide? His father is a judge. He has nothing to fear from the law."*

"He's not hiding from the law, sweetheart. He is hiding from me. And wherever he is, he had better stay because if I ever see the evil son of a bitch again, it will be the last day of his miserable life!"

At that moment Asa changed. He was no longer just a boy in love with a pretty young girl; he was a man protecting his *soulmate*.

Funny, I thought to myself, *just last month Grandma took my Romeo and Juliet book away from me because she said it wasn't proper for a girl of my age to read such things. But now, God himself has given me this to look at.*

"How very ironic," I whispered.

From afar, Alice inhaled Asa's scent and closed her eyes. *"Pipe tobacco and cinnamon. I love your smell, Asa. I always know when you're in the room. Even before I see you, I know you're near. I can smell your scent."*

He chuckled. *"I don't smoke a pipe, sweetheart."*

"I know, but that's what you smell like." She didn't open her eyes.

Asa smiled at her comment and then gestured to the small bed.

Alice sat down as Asa knelt before her. "My father was right about something, Ali. It's not safe for you…" He put his hand toward her middle though he didn't touch her. "Either of you…in this town."

Alice glanced up, frowning.

"My mother and I have discussed this. We think it would be best for both you and the baby if you move to a safer place."

Alice started to cry. "You don't want me with you?"

Asa shook his head. It was painfully obvious that he wanted nothing more than to hold her, but he kept his distance. "I want you with me more than anything, but it's not safe for you here in this town."

He heaved a great and tired sigh, suddenly appearing much older than a fifteen-year-old boy. "My family owns a cabin about thirty-five miles from here. I'll take you there. You'll have everything you need, and my mother will help when the baby comes, but until you agree to marry me, it wouldn't be proper for me to live there with you."

Asa's sights dropped, and my dream faded.

9. Dawn of a New Day

The bright morning sunlight shined through my bedroom window, waking me from my dream. I opened my eyes and gazed into the delicate face of my grandma, who was sitting beside me on the bed. She seemed tired and worried, her eyes red-rimmed and puffy, as if she'd been crying…again.

Then I thought about the vision, and my heart ached for her.

She must've been in so much pain. Charles Marshal nearly killed her.

I smiled and took her hand. *"Papa hurt your feelings this morning,"* I whispered, remembering their fight. *"I heard what he said, but what did he mean?"*

"Your papa wouldn't hurt me, Lees," Grandma whispered, all the while sifting her fingers through my hair as she talked. *"Sometimes, grown-ups argue, that's all."*

"But Papa did hurt your feelings when he said that I'm his daughter and not yours. I saw you run past my room, and you were crying."

Her eyes widened, and she sharply inhaled.

I was right, Papa did hurt her.

I sat up and took her hand. *"I'll be your daughter if you want me to. I love you like you are my mother."* I smiled, squeezing her hand.

Please want me, please!

Grandma pulled me to her chest, crying, and rocked me back and forth. *"You're my baby, Lees, and you always have been,"* she choked.

"How did Papa and Rebecca get together?" I hesitantly muttered, figuring that with her guard down she just might give me some answers.

Grandma stopped rocking. She peered down at me with her mouth agape. *"That's a complicated story, baby. I'm not sure you're ready to hear about that, not just yet."*

I couldn't believe what she was saying: I'm not ready for the story? I felt as if I'd grown five years in just a few days after all of the visions.

I leaped out of bed and away from her. *"I'll ask Papa!"* I defiantly hollered. *"He'll tell me everything. You know he will!"*

Before she could react, I scurried downstairs and into the kitchen, where my father sat drinking coffee at the table.

Grandma was right behind me.

I stopped and stood in front of him with an indignant scowl plastered across my face.

Papa put his coffee cup down, and his eyes swept between Grandma's eyes and mine as she stood beside me. What's more, his expression changed from cheerful when he saw me to one of concern as he looked at her in just a few moments.

I moved around the table and sat down in the chair across from him—still scowling.

Papa smirked at Grandma while leaning toward me. *"Did you want to ask me something, angel?"* He was talking to me, but he was looking at her. After a moment, his sights swept back to mine, and he cocked his head in an expectant sort of way.

I glanced over at my grandma and then back to my father. *"Yes, I do."*

But I lost my nerve, so instead I asked the only question I could think to ask. *"What was your mother's name? You don't talk about her, and I've never met her."*

He took my hand. *"My mother's name is Margaret, angel,"* he answered, winking at me, *"and you are a great deal like her."*

"Margaret?" I cocked my head, staring into my father's glorious blue eyes. *"That's my middle name. I was named…for her?"*

He smiled, nodded, and then stood up and crossed the kitchen to the front room. *"Tell me, Lees, what is YOUR mother's name?"* he asked, and without a backward glance at either Grandma or me.

Grandma gasped, jumped up from the table, and rushed into the front room after him.

"*Asa!*" she shouted.

Just as she reached him, glaring, Papa stepped just inside the doorway of his room; he tilted his head to one side, wearing a smug, self-assured grin. "*I'm sorry, but I just couldn't resist that, Ali,*" he told her, still grinning like a school boy. Then he winked at me.

Grandma took a deep breath, and I knew she was bristling with anger. Her eyes flashed at Papa, sending the door to his room slamming shut—hard, right in his face.

"*You missed!*" he hollered, chuckling from the other side of the door.

After a moment, Papa reopened the door and cautiously stepped out, still grinning, and turned to me. He opened his mouth.

Grandma threw him a dangerous look, one that even I had *never* seen. "*DON'T—YOU—DARE!*" She drawled out the words, pointing at him, her hands shaking, her eyes flashing with barely-contained might.

Oh, Papa, please be careful! She'll turn you to ash!

But as I peered at her, I had to wonder, was she angry or *scared*?

Unhindered by Grandma's power, my father stood his ground, goading her, and still grinning.

"*You wouldn't,*" she whispered, her voice wavering. Then she stepped toward Papa; although, she wasn't angry. She was full of fear, her eyes silently pleading.

Pleading for what? What doesn't she want him to tell me? Tell me, Papa!

As my eyes swept between Papa and Grandma, I was struck by the fact that, though she was upset with Papa, he seemed to be enjoying himself.

But then he saw the worry in her eyes. His expression softened, and his riotous grin fell.

He stepped forward and stretched his hands out. To my surprise, she took them without hesitation; he gave them a squeeze. "*You're right, Ali, I won't, not now, but soon. And if you won't, then I will. I'm not allowing you to hide anymore. Not even from us.*"

Papa's eyes were soft. He glanced at Grandma and me and then heaved a deep breath. *"I've changed my mind about the tea today. I think Lees should go; I think you both should. It'll be good for you both to spend time with Molly."*

Papa winked at me.

Once again, I understood nothing about their conversation; I was perplexed. *Why would Papa want to know if I remembered my mother's name?*

"Where are we going?" I asked them, stepping forward and attempting to ignore the throbbing ache in my head.

Grandma turned to me without releasing Papa's hands and smiled, but the smile didn't reach her eyes. She was still worried. *"You and I are invited for tea at the Reverend and Mrs. Cole's house today, so be a good girl and get dressed. Put on something nice."*

She nodded toward the staircase. *"And once you've dressed, come back down here. I need to talk to you."*

She flashed her sweetest smile, but I wasn't convinced. I *knew* that as soon as I left, she and my father were going to argue again. The tension between them arced through the room; it was almost tangible.

My mind swept back to the night before when Papa had touched her. *Perhaps he'll touch her again or kiss her. Hmm…*

Shaking the wayward thought from my mind, I ran upstairs and pretended to go to my room. But instead, I opened and shut the door and then crawled back to the stairs, hunkered down, and hid behind the newel post, eavesdropping.

Hopefully they'll say something that I can understand, or maybe they'll unknowingly answer one of my questions—my face flushed—*or kiss…*

I peeked over the railing at the top of the stairs. Papa stood in front of Grandma; they were nearly touching. She was gazing up at him, stroking his face with the back of her hand. In response to her touch, my father closed his eyes and leaned into her warmth. Then he reopened his big blue eyes and smiled down at her. *"I'm sorry if I upset you, sweetheart. I was only teasing, and you know how I love to tease you, but I can't let this go on any longer."*

Gasp! *He called her "sweetheart"!*

Before I got my racing heart back to a steady rhythm, Papa lifted Grandma's chin with his thumb and index finger, and a look of concern flashed across his eyes. *"Haven't you punished yourself long enough? And what about me, Ali? What about her? I think she knows more than you give her credit for. In fact, I know she does. With your brilliant mind, you're going to tell me you can't see that she's figuring things out?"*

Grandma was silent for a moment, and her eyes clouded over with worry and fatigue, but finally, she answered. *"Yes, I can, Asa, but tell me this,"* she whispered, stifling a sob, *"what if she doesn't forgive me? What if she resents me? Then what do we do? I already had a child who hated me. I couldn't take it if Leesie felt that way, too."*

Her voice sounded so weak and sad that it made me want to cry; it made me want to forget about my questions. I didn't want to know anymore, not if it was going to hurt her.

"I could never hate you," I whispered to myself.

I decided, then and there, not to ask any more questions until she was ready to tell me herself. Or maybe I'd wait until Papa told me; I knew he would, and soon.

He said he would.

With thoughts of Grandma's secrets rushing through my mind, I snuck off to my room and got dressed. I put on a sunny yellow dress that reminded me of happiness, tied a long yellow ribbon around my head, put on my black shoes, and ran downstairs.

Grandma was waiting for me in the kitchen. She had a new dress on; it was one I'd never seen before.

The dress wasn't anything like she usually wore. *Usually,* her blouse was buttoned up to her neck, leaving barely enough room for her to breathe, but this gown was quite revealing. It was made of soft ivory silk accented with shimmering meadow-green ribbons. The ribbons laced up the front from the middle of the bodice to about halfway over her bosoms, beautifully showcasing the single freckle she had midway down the right side of her cleavage. And it wasn't long sleeves like she usually wore, either. In fact, the sleeves were hardly sleeves at all. They were just a loose gathering of fabric ruched at the tops of the arms, reminding me of a peasant blouse I'd seen a milk maid wear in a painting once. The blouse was tucked into a full, dark-green skirt that had a slight sheen running through the fabric, matching the ribbons used to lace up the top. The outfit was lovely and looked expensive.

Grandma's hair wasn't pulled into a bun like was customary when she left the farm. Instead, part of it was in a soft chignon on the back of her head while the rest flowed down to her waist. The style softened her appearance.

As I stood gawking at her, I realized that I'd never seen her look like that before, not ever.

"*It's time,*" she murmured to herself, not realizing I was standing there.

Finally noticing me, she looked up and smiled, a beaming, glowing smile, her emerald eyes shining with what seemed like happiness. It was an odd expression, one that I had never seen before, not from *her*, at least.

"*I see that it fits.*" Papa stepped into the doorway behind me, tilting his head and smiling as I craned my head backward, looking up at him. His assessing gaze swept all the way up and down the entire length of Grandma's slight form, as if drinking her in with his eyes.

I bit my lip and walked across the kitchen and sat next to my grandmother at the table, remembering how Papa had gazed at her in exactly the same way in my visions.

At that moment, I wished that my grandfather Senior was there to see it. After all, it had been more than twenty years since my grandfather had insulted young Alice, saying that Papa wouldn't even look at her when she was older.

But just look at them. Papa loves her just as much now as he did when they were young. Ali and her stable boy. Huh! Take that, Mr. Senior Raign!

Grandma glanced at Papa, and a bashful flush swept across her cheeks. *"Yes, it fits quite nicely… Thank you, Asa,"* she muttered and then bit her bottom lip.

"I've had it for some time. When I saw it, I imagined that the color would play off the emerald sparkle of your eyes quite nicely. And it seems that I was correct," said Papa, grinning at her bashfulness. *"I've been waiting for the right opportunity to give it to you…"*

His beautiful steel-blue eyes drifted between us for a moment before falling on only *her*.

"You both look lovely," he said. He was talking to us both, but his eyes never left her face.

For once, Grandma didn't seem nervous at all. She smiled back— beamed actually. *"Thank you, Asa,"* she whispered and coyly batted her eyelashes at him.

I had to stifle a giggle. *She batted her eyelashes at him! I didn't know she could do that!*

Papa leaned on the door frame for a minute as he and Grandma wordlessly gazed into each other's eyes.

Yep. I grinned. *She still loves him, too.*

After a few minutes, my father turned and went into his room. When he returned to us, he had a white shirt in his hands, but he was naked from the waist up.

Grandma looked up and let out a small gasp, apparently startled by my father's bare chest. Then her full lips parted as she watched him put on his shirt, and it was with a strange expression on her face. She looked almost hungry, as though she was willing herself not to jump up and run into his arms.

I put my hand over my mouth to keep from giggling.

Grandma took an unsteady breath and looked the other way, and I noticed that her hands were shaking.

Papa saw it, too.

He fastened his shirt buttons, grinning from ear to ear. *"I'll be gone most of the day. I thought I'd take a trip out to that old cabin of ours while Leesie and you are visiting with Molly,"* he said.

Grandma's head whipped around, and her eyes grew wide. She stared, unblinking, into Papa's laughing eyes, startled by his words.

In an instant, Papa's expression changed again. His eyes drew hooded; they grew darker, deeper, and his pupils dilated until nearly all the blue was gone. The smoldering look my father was giving to Grandma was almost piercing enough to have come from *her.*

Grandma took another unsteady breath and nodded.

Papa stepped forward. *"I thought maybe we could make a trip out there sometime soon. Show Lees. Would you like that?"* he asked her, inclining his beautiful blond head to the right.

At that moment, it was as if the invisible barrier or fortress that my grandmother had been shielding herself in burst and fell straight to the ground.

"Yes," she breathlessly murmured, blushing pink across the cheeks. *"I'd like that very much, Asa."* Emotional tears welled in her eyes.

Papa knelt down in front of her and took one of her shaking hands. *"You do understand what I'm asking, don't you?"*

Grandma nodded, smiling. Tears ran down her cheeks. *"Yes, I do,"* she whispered.

"Truly, Ali?" He took a halting breath. *"Because there's no going back, not this time."*

My father's wavering voice was full of emotion. He wanted to kiss her. I could tell. He stared at her mouth, his full lips inching nearer, his tongue rimming his upper lip, and neither breathed. Nor did I. They seemed dazed, each set of tearful eyes captivated by the other.

Grandma choked back a tear and shook her head while also breaking the mesmerizing connection between them.

"No, no going back, not ever, I promise," she barely breathed the words.

Papa reached up, wiping her tears with his fingertips. His eyes, too, swam with tears. *"You know, we have some explaining to do."*

"I know. I'm ready," she choked.

Papa leaned nearer, peering straight into her eyes. *"When?"*

She took a halting breath though her gaze never left his. *"Tomorrow?"* she whispered.

"Tomorrow it is, then," my father resolutely nodded, leaned up, kissed her forehead, and then stood up.

All of a sudden, I felt like a voyeur, as if I were interrupting a private moment meant only for the two of them. But just as that thought, or rather, sensation, rushed through me, Papa shook his head and smiled at me, almost as if he *knew* what I was feeling.

"I hope you both have a nice visit with Molly and...the boy." He gave Grandma a peculiar look, one that I didn't understand. *"Have fun,"* he said. Then he turned, crossed the front room, and went out the door, leaving Grandma and me alone.

The invisible lasso pulled again, stronger that time, sending me crashing down underneath the table. I hit the floor with a *thud*.

Grandma let out a bursting laugh and peeked under the table at me. *"What did you do that for?"* she asked, bewildered.

"I slipped," I lied and then clambered back into my seat.

"I want you to do something for me, baby," she said, still laughing.

Before she spoke again, she closed her eyes for a moment and took a deep breath. When she reopened them, she grasped my hand and leaned in close. *"I want you to ask as many questions as you need to, just not today. I'll answer as many questions as you want me to tomorrow, I promise, but you have to tell me some things, too... Deal?"*

"Yes, ma'am," I answered.

Oh no! Grandma does see the visions, and she must hear all of my thoughts, too!

I frowned. *You know, a person could go mad from all of this strangeness, but then again, we've never been a typical family, so I should be used to it by now.* I laughed to myself.

"Something funny?" she asked, raising her brow.

"Yes," I answered, aloud, *but you'll just have to wait until tomorrow to ask,* I whispered to her, mentally.

Grandma cocked her beautiful, sunshine-hued head, her emerald eyes growing wide. She stared at me for a moment. Then she shook her head and patted my hand. *"Here,"* she said, pulling a pair of white gloves from where she had them hidden in her lap beneath the table. *"I want you to put these on and keep them on all day. Do you understand?"*

"Ugh…" I whined. *"Do I have to wear these?"*

"Yes, you do!" Her tone was stern. *"Now be nice, or I'll put your hair into braids!"* she threatened and then playfully smiled.

"And, Lees," she said, staring into my eyes, all playfulness suddenly evaporating from her expression. *"I don't want you to touch anyone, and don't let anyone touch you."* She took a long, deep breath. *"Especially…the boy."*

The lasso pulled again, really hard, sending me crashing down beneath the table.

10. The Link

I t was a bright and sunny morning. The sun was shining, the birds chirping, and I was in heaven, walking hand in hand with my grandma to Mrs. Cole's house.

We're leaving the farm!

Though I was nervous, I knew that Grandma was excited. Her joy was almost palpable; I could feel it!

I gazed up at her as we walked along the dirt road, and I couldn't help but notice the changes in her. She looked different—heck, she was different. And I realized that within the past few days, she had changed, body and soul. She glowed!

To my surprise, Grandma told me about her childhood in the orphanage and her friendship with Kristofer's mother. Molly was her best friend growing up, her only friend until she and Papa met.

She didn't mention her parents or how she came to the orphanage, and I didn't push. After all, I knew that she was abandoned as a baby.

Poor, Grandma. My melancholy bloomed for her. *Why would anybody leave a baby stranded? Especially her? She's beautiful and kind and…different.* My heart lurched. *Oh, maybe that's why…*

While growing up in the orphanage, Grandma was picked on by the other children. They bullied her because she knew things that she shouldn't have known; they called her a witch. But Molly wasn't like the other children. She never cared that Grandma was different—she loved her for the things she could do.

Hmm, I love Molly already, and I haven't even met her yet.

As I listened to my grandmother talk about her life before my father and me, I wondered if she wanted me to know about her childhood, or if she was telling me because she knew that I would ask the next day. But in the end, I guess the reason didn't matter; she was opening up to me, and her walls were coming down.

In the past few days, I saw her cry and laugh more than ever before. She seemed like a different person entirely, a happy person. And I knew why: my papa's love!

"Why haven't I met Papa's mother?" I asked as we walked toward Mrs. Cole's house. *"He said I'm a lot like her. Am I?"*

"Maggie is a beautiful person, Lees, and so are you." Grandma smiled down at me. *"She helped me once when nobody except your papa, Molly, and her husband, Jake, would. I owe my life to Maggie, and I hope you meet her soon."* She squeezed my hand. *"Your papa and I will make that happen."*

"I've seen her in dreams," I hesitantly muttered, looking up at my grandma's beautiful profile.

She stopped walking and closed her eyes for a moment, as if afraid to answer me. She held her breath. *"I know, my baby,"* she barely breathed.

I stared at the ground, shocked. *She knows? Holy cow, that means she sees my visions.*

I peered up at her, but she seemed afraid to look at me.

I screwed my eyes up tight, concentrating hard. *I love you, and nothing you do or have ever done will change that,* I hollered into her mind, hoping that she heard me. Then, I reopened my eyes and, without looking at her, wrapped my arms around her waist, making her gasp, and hugged her as tight as I could.

As I held her, I smelled her perfume. *Hmm, it's wonderful. I'll have to ask her if I can borrow that sometime.*

Grandma wrapped her arms around me, too, laying her cheek atop my head. *"I love you, too, my baby, and I promise, you'll have all the answers you need. There's no going back now."* She said the last part more to herself than to me.

Wow, she heard me!

We started walking.

"Why does Papa call you Ali?" I thought this might be out of line, but I decided to ask, and to my surprise, she answered.

"Your papa and I met when we were just fifteen years old, Lees, and I asked him to call me 'Ali' because Molly did, so he does." She smiled.

"I know that!" I laughed. *"But why does he call you that now? He never did before."*

Grandma stopped walking and turned to face me. *"Your papa used to call me Ali all the time, Lees, and Molly and her husband, Jake, always have, so on the day we went to visit them, they called me Ali. So now, your papa does, too, understand?*

"Just like my name is Alyce, but Papa and you call me Leesie?"

"Exactly," Grandma laughed and then took my face into her hands. *"There are going to be things happening from now on that haven't happened before, or not in a long time, but I don't want you to be frightened or embarrassed, all right?"*

She heaved a deep breath and kissed my forehead. *"Now, no more questions."*

"Just one?" I asked.

Grandma raised her index finger and smiled. *"All right, but just one."*

"Why can't I touch Kristofer?"

"Just don't!" she snapped, her emerald eyes blazing.

Oh, look, I giggled, *there she is. She's still the same.*

I knew I shouldn't tease her, but Papa was right—it was fun.

She must have heard this because she laughed, too, and then took my hand as we made our way down the road.

Molly was waiting for us as we approached her house. She was standing in the yard wearing a flattering, milky-white dress accented with tiny, purple flowers. The dress was bright and cheery, just like my mood. Her mahogany hair was swept up into a neat bun. She looked a lot like the young girl she was in my dream, only older, and she had the same beautiful, chestnut-brown hair and shimmering hazel eyes as Kristofer. In fact, the purple flowers adorning her dress played off the color of her eyes.

Molly was, in a word, lovely.

As we entered the yard, she rushed toward Grandma, throwing her arms around her. Molly was at least five, maybe six inches taller than Grandma and had to bend down to hug her.

"I'm so glad you made it, Ali!" Molly beamed and then turned to me.

"And just look at you!" Her bright hazel eyes twinkled as they swept between Grandma and me. She placed her hands on the tops of my arms, holding me at arms' length and assessing me.

"I'd have thought I was looking at you, Ali." She cocked her head to one side, again, just like Kristofer. *"But I do see Asa in her, too, especially the wavy hair."*

I smiled, pleased that she saw Papa in me.

Molly put her hand out, attempting to touch my face, but I stepped away from her, flinching.

Oh, no, nobody can touch me.

Molly laughed at my reaction and then frowned as she turned to Grandma. *"Really, Ali, did you teach her that?"* She giggled, shaking her head, clearly exasperated. *"Still afraid of what you are, I see."*

She stepped back, fisting her hands against her hips. *"Fine, have it your way. I won't touch you again,"* she muttered. That was when I noticed that when she was exasperated, Molly looked exactly like Kristofer, especially the way the little stars in her eyes flashed.

As I stood studying my grandma's best friend, Grandma approached me and then gestured toward Molly. *"It's all right, sweetie. You may touch Molly. I'm sure you'll be great friends soon."*

But then she frowned and bent low with her back turned away from Molly and Kristofer; she threw me a warning look. *"Keep your gloves on,"* she warned.

As soon as Grandma stepped back, I held out my arms to my new friend, who threw her arms around me, squeezing me to her bosoms.

I like her! I thought as she squealed with delight and squashed my ribs until they were sore.

As comfortable as I was with Molly, I was trying not to look at Kristofer, who stood gawking at me from a few feet away.

Finally, Molly released me from her vise grip and took my hand, walking me toward her son. I held my breath and stared at my shoes.

Why do I find his presence so unnerving?

As we approached, Kristofer smiled, holding out his hand. *"Hello, my name is Kris. It's nice to meet you. For. The. First. Time."* He enunciated each word and then grinned.

Just as his eyes met mine, the lasso pulled again, sending me tumbling to the ground. I fell hard at his feet.

Kristofer stepped back, frowning down at where I was sprawled on the ground, and then offered me his hand. Before I could react, Grandma rushed forward and helped me to my feet herself.

Her eyes grew wide, sweeping between Kristofer and me. *"Oh, dear,"* she mumbled under her breath, wiping the dirt off my dress.

Grandma knows what's happening to me, I thought, eyeing her, knowing that she could hear me.

Hmm, I wonder what would happen if I touched Kristofer's hand?

The thought was intriguing; I was almost inclined to try it.

But, I can't, I thought to myself with a huff though I wanted to; I wanted to see what, if anything, would happen. *She'll strike me down, for sure.*

Grandma glared at me, and her eyes flashed. *Yes, I will!*

Darned witch! I thought loudly on purpose and then giggled.

I was teasing, but Grandma didn't think it was funny. She snatched my hand, mumbled something under her breath about Papa sending me away to a convent, and then tugged me through the door of Molly's house.

Once inside, we sat in the parlor. I looked around. Molly had a lovely home. There was a lush, blue velvet settee by the front window, a pair of big, squashy wing-back chairs in the center of the room, and a dark wood dining table in the corner. To the left was the kitchen and fireplace, and to the right was the staircase with a beautifully crafted balustrade. The house was cozy and quite inviting.

Kristofer sat right next to me on the settee though I was trying my best to avoid him. Unfortunately, he was doing everything he could do to be as close to me as possible. And what's worse, he just sat there next to me, staring, his beautiful hazel eyes nearly burning a hole straight through the side of my head. All the while I tried to avoid his gaze, not to mention his lasso. And poor Grandma was staring at us both. I half expected her to make some excuse for us to leave at any moment.

Molly, on the other hand, was pleased with Kristofer's reaction to me.

"I can't get over it, Ali," she gushed. *"It's as if we were looking at Asa and you. Aren't they just so sweet? I've never seen Kristofer look at anyone like that before."*

Nice for you, but he's gonna get me into trouble! I thought, chewing my bottom lip until it was sore.

As I sat nervously twiddling my gloved fingers, Molly pushed to her feet, grabbing Grandma's hand and tugging her toward the kitchen. *"Who knows, maybe we'll be in-laws someday."*

She whirled around, gawking at Grandma. *"Remember when you predicted that your daughter and my son…"*

She stopped short, putting her hand to her mouth. *"Oops, sorry, Ali,"* she whispered just as Grandma's mouth and eyes popped open.

I cocked my head, glaring at my grandma. *What was that? What did Molly say?* I yelled into her mind.

She glanced at where I sat scowling at her next to Kristofer on the settee, nervously mouthed the word *"tomorrow,"* and disappeared into the kitchen behind Molly.

Tomorrow is going to be a very interesting day! I hollered after her, mentally.

"By the way, thank you for not telling my ma that I snuck off to your farm yesterday," Kristofer drawled, pulling me from my thoughts.

I turned toward him without looking into his eyes. They were too beautiful; the sight of them made my head hurt. Besides that, they caused the strange, invisible lasso to pull me toward him.

"You're welcome, boy," I muttered, still avoiding his eyes, *"although my grandma knows. She knows everything 'cause she's a WITCH!"* I opened my eyes wide, wrinkling my nose and throwing my hands up in front of me like claws, hoping to scare the boy away from me.

Grandma poked her head around the corner, her mouth agape, peering at me as if she couldn't *believe* what I had said.

Our gaze met, and I opened my eyes wider.

Oh, I thought to her, *was I not supposed to tell the boy that? Sorry, you said not to touch him, nothing else.* Then I innocently shrugged and batted my eyes at her.

I knew it wasn't a good idea to goad my grandma like that, but I was enjoying myself so much, I couldn't help it. I thought she might take a switch to me when we got home, but I didn't care.

Besides, Molly knows all of our secrets.

Just as those words swept through my mind, and Grandma's, she rounded the corner. She swept into the parlor and stood in front of me, glaring, her lips pursed and her hands fisting her hips.

"Not all of them!" she sternly hissed.

More than me! I thought, glaring right back.

Her lips pursed even tighter. She pointed at me. *"Be good, or else!"* she said, turning, and then swept back into the kitchen.

Just then, Molly poked her head around the kitchen doorway. *"Kris, why don't you take Leesie outside and show her around. Maybe she'll play marbles with you?"* She gestured toward the front door.

But Kristofer didn't answer his mother; he sat next to me with a baffled expression on his face, eyeing me, apparently trying and failing to figure Grandma and me out.

I sneaked a quick sideways glance into his eyes, grinning. The bewildered expression on his face incited the naughty little witch in me to poke her head up.

Molly wants me to play with the boy—let's play!

I turned to Kristofer. *"Must be kinda strange watching half of a conversation like that, huh?"* I asked, shrugging. *"You see, my grandma—the witch—can read my mind, so I don't even have to talk to her anymore."*

As soon as the words left my lips, I knew I was in trouble, but I didn't really care.

She's keeping things from me, so I'm gonna make her squirm!

Nevertheless, as soon as I heard her rushing into the room, I knew that I'd pushed her too far, and I'd better *run.*

"I'm going to take a switch to you, girl!" Grandma hollered as she came rushing toward me.

No, you won't! I thought at her.

I turned to Kristofer, laughing. *"Come on, boy, let's play marbles!"* I said, still laughing, and running out the front door.

Once outside, I turned to close the door behind me, but the knob flew out of my hand. The door swung open and bounced off the opposing wall with a loud bang.

I stood immobile, my eyes wide, staring into the wrathful face of my grandmother. She was standing inside the house, about five feet from the front door, and I knew she hadn't opened it with her hands.

Grandma stood still, her hands fisted on her hips, glaring at me. She was seething with fury.

Then her gaze passed over me, over my shoulder, and her angry expression melted into one of horror instead. She was frozen with fear—in fact, more than fear. She was petrified, but I didn't understand why.

Surely she wasn't *that* angry with me. After all, I was only teasing—like Papa did.

My stomach sank; I stepped forward, hoping that I hadn't hurt her feelings.

"I'm sorry." This time, I spoke aloud. *"I didn't mean to hurt you. I know you're not a witch. I was teasing you like Papa did this morning."*

She didn't answer.

All of a sudden, a voice came up from behind, one I recognized at once, one that made my skin crawl.

"Hello, pet." The silky voice seeped through the air, surrounding us like a malignant fog, choking me with both fear and an overwhelming sense of rage.

Slowly, I turned, then glared down into the face of my grandma's worst nightmare, *Charles Marshal,* who was standing in the yard.

Grandma rushed toward me, but just before she reached the threshold, I whipped my head around. Then, concentrating hard on what I needed to do, I threw my hands up in front of me and slammed the door closed, locking her in the house.

Once she was safe, I rounded on the devil. I took off my gloves and threw them out into the yard.

I wanted to hurt the bastard; I wanted to hurt him worse than he had hurt her. I thought of nothing except getting him away from her.

With boiling blood, I darted off the porch, my sights trained on the monster, screaming as I ran.

Then…*it* happened.

Kristofer lunged at me, grasped my hand, and forced me to the ground, away from Charles Marshal and into the safety of his arms. I struggled, attempting to free myself from his hold, but before I could react or even think straight, a golden, orange flame light burst from my hand. The beam streaked from my hand and then shot into Kristofer's chest. The force of it sent him reeling backward onto his behind. He gasped, the sudden jolt causing him to lose the grip he had on me.

Charles Marshal stood over us, an expression of sheer delight interspersed with hunger stretched across his angular face. Reaching down, he jerked me up by the collar of my dress and forced me to stand in front of him, his soulless eyes wild with excitement.

I glared up at him.

He had changed since the time of my visions. His once-jet-black hair was now streaked with white, as was the pointed beard covering his chin, reminding me of the many literary illustrations depicting Lucifer that I had seen in books.

Hmm, how apt...

His soulless eyes were hollow, the color flat, reminiscent of a corpse that hadn't yet realized its demise. The skin of his face was sallow and pallid, the thin flesh stretched out over the skull, and twin blade scars etched across both sunken cheeks. What's more, though he had not a wrinkle on his face, he looked ghostly, seedy, even haunted in appearance.

Whereas my father had grown even more handsome with age, the element of time had not been kind to Charles Marshal.

"What. Do. We. Have. Here?" he whispered, his voice breathless with excitement. He eyed me just as I'd seen him eye my grandma so many years before. *"My, my, how enchanting—a set!"* His muddy eyes searched my face as he studied me. He cocked his head to and fro as if I were a foreign object or an exotic animal.

A slow, putrid smirk crept across his thin mouth. *"Her beauty matches your own, Alice. She is exquisite,"* he purred, the words kissing his lips like the sweetest of sugar, while his steely gaze traveled just over my left shoulder.

I looked over my shoulder. Grandma was standing not two feet behind me. Somehow she had opened the door. She was no longer safe—she was within his reach.

Her eyes weren't fearful, though. They were bold and blazing as she stood staring, unblinking, at the devil who had his hands on me.

"Get away from her!" Grandma breathed. Her teeth were clenched, and even though her words were no louder than a whisper, her power crackled through the air around us.

Charles's eyes lit up. He released me and lunged forward, seizing Grandma around the waist and forcing her into his arms.

Without hesitation, I did the only thing I thought to do. It was what my father would have done, had he been there. I jumped between Grandma and the devil, shoved him in the chest, forcing him backward, and threw my hands into his face.

"You touch her again, and I'll turn you to stone!" I spat, my eyes shining with fury.

He won't hurt her again, he won't! I'll kill him! I'll send him straight to Hell!

Grandma grabbed me by the arm, forcing me behind her and shielding me with her body. I struggled, but my feet stuck to the ground. I couldn't move; they bonded to the spot.

What? But how?

Out of the corner of my eyes, I saw Molly struggling from the front porch stoop with *her* feet bonded to the wooden planks.

Charles Marshal stepped toward Grandma, craning his neck around her to get a better view of me, all the while smirking, looking like a man possessed by lust or hate, perhaps by both.

"I heard you lived around here, my dear," he said, his cold eyes sweeping back to Grandma's. Her eyes remained down, her body quaking with fright. *"I'd heard the girl—Rebecca, wasn't it? I heard tell that she'd birthed a child with your stable boy. Is this the child?"* he asked, pointing his chin, gesturing toward me.

I shuddered as his sinful leer sent a potent feeling of disgust through me, clenching my gut.

Grandma wordlessly nodded but didn't look up. Her face was bloodless, and she was trembling.

"Your daughter and the stable boy? My, how that must've stung," Charles snickered, finding pleasure in her pain.

"I thought I might find you here, but never in my life could I have imagined this good fortune!" He gawked at me again. His eyes were blazing with excitement. Then he captured Grandma's face between his hands and forced her reluctant gaze. *"You've been hiding this little prize from me, Alice, you naughty little witch. Lucky for me, though, I've been named sheriff of this town, so I can keep an eye on things now."*

At that moment, my mind reeled with questions. I didn't understand why she was just standing there like that.

Why doesn't she strike him down, or turn him to ash or something? Do something! I screamed into her mind.

And then it happened. I *heard* her speak with her mind. I heard her, and it was as plain as if she had spoken it to me aloud.

"It is not in our nature to hurt anyone, Leesie. I can't. WE mustn't cause harm, not to anything, not even…to him."

My grandma was frozen in place. We both were. What's more, she couldn't move, and she couldn't defend us, and *neither* could I.

My knees began to quake.

The devil stooped down in front of Grandma and then leaned around her, excitedly leering at me.

"You know, my love," he purred in my direction just as my grandma threw her arms out, struggling to shield me. *"You really*

shouldn't threaten the sheriff, especially when he is your grandfather, but I suppose you didn't know that, now did you, pet?"

He threw his hand out, attempting to touch my hair. Before he could touch me, Grandma slapped him across the face—hard, knocking the wicked bastard right to the ground.

Charles's beady eyes drew wide, revealing the secrets tucked away in his dark soul. He leaped to his feet. Just as his boots hit the ground, he retaliated by striking Grandma with his balled-up fist, hitting her on the side of the head and knocking her into me. She and I both collided with the unyielding ground.

My head spun. From the side of us, I heard a livid wail of rage. The sound hadn't come from my grandma; it was Kristofer, whom, until then, I had forgotten. I forgot that he was still lying on the ground a few feet from us.

He streaked forward, colliding with the devil's chest, sending him crashing to the ground. Charles fell flat on his back with Kristofer on top of him. All the while, Kristofer thrashed above him, pinning him to the spot and hitting him with all his might.

Grandma and Molly rushed to Kristofer, tearing him away from the sheriff.

Charles's thin, wiry body lay prostrate on the ground, his lip bloodied, his posh black suit disheveled, and there was an appearance of shock covering his face.

Kristofer flailed his arms as Molly tried to hold him back and out of danger's reach.

"That's what you get for picking on women, you bastard!" he fiercely bellowed.

Finally, Charles Marshal stood just as Reverend Jacob Cole, Kristofer's father, jumped down from his buggy and came running into the yard.

At once, I knew who he was though I didn't know how. I'd never met him in my life.

Mr. Cole glared at the devil standing in front of him. Like the rest of us, he seemed both angered and frightened. He stood in front of Grandma and me with his arms outstretched.

"What are you doing in this town?" he hissed, his sage-green eyes wide and staring as if in disbelief.

The devil sneered, obviously amused by Mr. Cole's reaction.

"I'm the new sheriff, Reverend," he smirked, his eyes dancing with mirth, leering up at the imposing figure of the reverend.

"Get off of my land…Sheriff!" Mr. Cole hissed and then pointed toward the road.

But the sheriff didn't leave. Instead, he stepped a pace closer to Kristofer's pa.

"Being a man of faith, myself, Reverend," the devil began, stretching his hands out toward where Kristofer stood with his mama, still seething. *"I'm going to let this little incident with your boy…slide."*

He glanced at Grandma and me. *"But if I were you, I would be rather careful whom I let my family associate with. After all, you wouldn't want the nice folks of this town to get the wrong impression of you, and you wouldn't want anyone to think that you'd allow wickedness to cross over your threshold, now, would you?"*

"The only way that will happen is if YOU darkened my doorstep, you wicked rascal! Now leave us be!" Mr. Cole shouted.

Charles put his hands up in a conciliatory manner and then bowed toward Mr. Cole. *"Fair enough, Reverend. I'm going,"* he laughed, clearly enjoying himself, and turned to leave.

 He stopped and looked at Grandma once more. *"Where's your daughter, Alice? Rebecca, where is she?"* he demanded.

My breath stuttered, and I peeked around my grandma and the reverend, who were both still shielding me with their bodies.

"She's dead!" I hollered as tears streamed down my face.

The devil bent down toward me. His eyes were wide and curious. He canted his head to one side. *"Was she like you, pet?"* he asked with an odd, mock-sweet tone of voice.

"*No,*" I whispered, so my grandma didn't have to.

The devil shrugged and rose up, eyeing my grandma again.

"Well, no loss, then, right?" he laughed, turned on his heel without a backward glance, and leisurely stalked away.

11. Rebecca

I sat on the front porch stoop of Reverend and Mrs. Cole's house. The adults were inside talking about things they didn't want me to hear—discussing that devil Charles Marshal, no doubt.

I closed my eyes, attempting to hear Grandma's thoughts, but silence ensued. She was closed to me.

Apparently she can control what I hear from her. There must be a window or something that she can open or shut to me.

"I'll have to figure that out," I mumbled to myself.

Just as that thought crossed my mind, I noticed Kristofer, who sat next to me on the stoop. He took my hand and gazed at me as if he'd never seen me before.

With a start, I jumped up and jerked his hand away from mine.

Don't touch the boy! Mustn't touch Kristofer! Grandma's words from earlier in the day echoed through my mind.

"But I did touch him, accidentally, but still, I touched him," I whispered to myself, peering out into the yard, where my gloves lay on the ground.

In the earlier panic, I had nearly forgotten about what had happened to the boy when he tried to stop me from getting to that horrible man—the one who had called himself *my grandfather.*

My heart lurched. *And, the light, what was that light? Can Kristofer see a light shining from within me, just as Papa saw Grandma's light back in the stable?*

I stood up and headed out into the yard with Kristofer trailing right behind me. I stopped just a few feet from the porch and stared down at where my gloves lay on the ground.

"*What's wrong, butterfly?*" Kristofer whispered, taking a few strands of my hair in his hand and running them through his long fingers.

I jerked away. "*Why are you looking at me like that, boy?*" I snapped, and then my heart lurched again.

Oh no! I recognize that look. It's the same one Papa gave to Grandma in every single vision I'd seen of them, and he looked at her like that this morning, too.

"*Just worried about you,*" the boy muttered. Then he stretched his arms out and pointed to my chest. "*That is the warmest, most beautiful thing I have ever seen in my life, and I get the feeling that I'm the only one who can see it.*" He stepped toward me, gazing like a love-struck fool right into my eyes. "*You're glowing just for me, Sita.*"

Sita? Who the Hell is Sita?

I shoved him hard in the chest. "*Get back!*"

"*Fine!*" he angrily snapped, peering at the ground. Or maybe he was hurt.

Jeez, I don't want to hurt him…

"*It's not your fault, really. I'm sorry!*" I cried. "*I think I put a curse on you. Grandma told me not to touch you, and I didn't mean to, really, I didn't! Don't worry, as soon as she's done talking to your parents, I'll ask her take the curse off.*"

Then something horrible occurred to me: What happened today with the light was almost the same thing that I saw in my vision of Alice and young Asa.

Had Grandma cursed Papa? She must have, but I don't think she meant to. Grandma wouldn't. It was an accident, just like when Kristofer touched me.

I hoped Grandma was listening. *Will you take the curse off Papa? Will you take it off him even if he doesn't love you afterward?* I glanced into Kristofer's eyes. *And will you show me how to release Kristofer from the same spell? I don't want to damn his soul.*

"What are you going on about some kind of a curse or something?" Kristofer blurted.

"Don't worry, boy, I'll fix it."

"Whatever 'it' is," he snapped, *"I don't want you to fix it. And I don't think you put any curse on me, either!"*

"Of course, I did—silly boy—*you saw what happened when you touched my hand!"*

Beautiful as he was, the boy exasperated me at times.

"Right!" Kristofer bit out. *"I touched you, so maybe I put a curse on you!"*

"Do you want to go to Hell?" I bellowed, feeling even more exasperated with this lovely, beautiful, brave boy. *"Because if you're cursed with me, you will!"*

"I don't think you know what you're talking about at all!" he snapped back, wagging his finger in my face, scolding me.

He was scolding me—*me*!

I threw my hands up in frustration. *"I sure wish they'd finish talking in there, so we can go home!"*

I was frustrated and scared and angry. And the beautiful boy was looking at me, and—ugh! I wanted to go home. I wanted to go back to my orchard and then never leave again!

"I know you didn't put any curse on me," Kristofer muttered just as I noticed that he and I were sitting on the porch again. I didn't remember leaving the yard.

He leaned into me. *"We just met yesterday, right? So if it was a curse, then you tell me why I've seen this"*—he pointed to my hair—*"and that,"*—he pointed to where he saw my light—*"ever since I can remember, especially in my dreams?"*

Then Kristofer took my hand, and this time I didn't pull away. *"And as far as you sending me to Hell,"* he said, laughing, *"let me ask you something: Are you going to Hell?"*

He canted his head to the right, his bright hazel-green eyes shimmering into mine.

"Definitely," I breathlessly murmured, feeling my heart take flight. The slow, methodical pressure of Kristofer's lasso snaked around my waist.

I heaved a deep breath and looked at the ground, breaking the unsettling (albeit exciting) connection between us, and as a result, my equilibrium steadied.

"Yes, I'm going to Hell. It is a certainty," I hopelessly muttered.

"Well," Kristofer drawled, *"then if it's all the same to you…"* He lifted my chin with his long index finger. *"I'll burn…."*

The lasso snaked around me again. Before I could answer or even think straight, the warmth of his skin against mine, the gaze of his eyes, and his words all caused the invisible lasso to tighten, pulling me straight off the porch. I landed hard on my hands and knees.

Kristofer leaped from the front porch stoop, threw his arms around my waist, and helped me to my feet.

But I just couldn't take it anymore; I just couldn't! It was all too much. I was emotionally spent and physically exhausted due to lack of sleep and the visions.

And Charles Marshal, Charles Marshal is after my grandma again!

I threw my hands over my face, sobbing.

Kristofer pried my hands away from my face. His eyes were soft and nearly bursting with worry. *"Hey, what's wrong, butterfly? Please tell me,"* he cooed.

I pointed toward the house. *"I want to know what's going on in there!"*

Kristofer's eyes grew large. *"Oh, I'm sorry! Why didn't think of this sooner?"* he absent-mindedly muttered. Then he pulled my arm and tugged me around to the back of the house. *"I've listened to Pa and Ma a lot through this window since we moved here, and they haven't caught me yet."*

Through the open window, I heard the adults talking. Kristofer and I crouched low, both sitting beneath it. Mr. Cole was talking to Grandma.

I listened closely.

"*It was a wise plan at the time, Ali, but I think it's outlived its usefulness, and so does Asa,*" Reverend Cole told her.

"*As do I, Jake,*" she replied.

"*What happened, Ali?*" Molly asked. "*One day you were in the city, and the next, you were gone.*"

Grandma was silent, but after a moment, she took a deep breath. "*In the wake of the tornado, Asa and I should have steered clear of the city, but foolishly, I believed the danger had passed. I thought Charles had given up on me. I was mistaken—terribly mistaken.*

On the morning before we fled, Maggie and I were out walking with Leesie. Thank goodness I had her bundled up. She couldn't be seen—even then, I knew that. Out of nowhere, Charles's father approached. He made threats against Asa and me, and he questioned me about Rebecca and about the baby, about Lees. He wanted to know whose baby she was. Maggie told him that Leesie was Rebecca and Asa's child."

She took a rattled breath. "*We moved back to the cabin the next day. I'm sorry we couldn't even say goodbye. Asa rebuilt our house, but I couldn't allow myself to be with him. Had Charles found out about our marriage or about Leesie, he'd have killed them both! I know it!*"

Grandma paused. "*I asked Jake not to tell you about all the particulars, Molly. I was afraid of the danger in which too much information would put you. As we know, Charles and his father have a known proclivity toward violence, and I couldn't have my family endangered because of what I am.*

I'm sorry my decision took you away from your goddaughter. It was never my intention to keep her from you, and I'm sorry it took us away from Kris. Still, I had no choice but to distance myself from everyone."

I heard a quiet sob. *"But I can't deny Asa anymore. I love him so much, and since you've moved here, he won't let me hide. He made that clear to me this morning."*

"Jake officiated your wedding, and I stood beside you as your sister," Molly tearfully muttered. *"You and I carried our children at the same time; Kris and Leesie played together as infants. I mean, my goodness, do you remember when the children were about six months old, and Leesie asked us why Kris couldn't speak to her yet?"*

Molly paused. *"Of course, I figured out the truth, that it was all a ruse to protect your brilliant child. But why did you feel it necessary to keep the truth from her? You are her mother, Ali; Leesie should be told the truth."*

W-w-what?

My mind stood still; I couldn't think. My limbs grew cold and numb. The earth fell away from my feet. I was floating. I felt nothing, and a distant buzzing noise arose from somewhere inside the center of my brain.

Perhaps the sound of shock?

Grandma's voice cracked as she spoke; I leaned nearer to the window, attempting to remain conscious.

"I felt that Asa and Leesie were better off without me. Better a phantom mother than a broken one, especially after the mess I made of Rebecca."

She sighed. *"I told myself there was time to tell Leesie the truth, but before I knew it, that time had passed. Eventually, the lie was knitted into every facet of our lives, and I didn't think we would be able to tell her at all. But then, you moved to town. I'm grateful for that; I want my husband and my child back."*

Mr. Cole blew out a breath. *"I'm glad you feel that way. Seriously, Ali, I don't know how much more of this Asa could have taken. He was in an awful state in the beginning, and I'd hoped it would get better, but it hasn't. He's at the end of his tether."* His voice softened. *"You stole that man's heart years ago, and he needs you now. He needs you as much as you need him, and your daughter needs you both. You are not alone anymore. You have us, and we are your family, too."*

Then Mr. Cole paused. *"Now, as far as Leesie is concerned, she is a bright child. Are you sure she doesn't already know your secret?"*

Grandma stifled a small emotional titter. *"Kris told her when they met yesterday, but I'm not sure she believes it."*

"And, now, Molly just told me…" I mumbled, absent-minded.

Mr. Cole laughed. *"Kris told Leesie that you are her mother because Asa told him to. Well, indirectly. It seems my dearest friend has a bit of a devious side."*

Grandma gasped. *"What do you mean, Jake? Why would Asa do such a thing?*

"Who better to put a bug in a child's ear than another child?" Mr. Cole answered. *"I overheard Asa tell Kris that Leesie is pretty, just like her mama. Kris snuck off to your farm while you and Asa were still here!"* He shook his head. *"I'm going to have to keep an eye on that boy. I don't think Asa was expecting Kris to do that. Did it worry him?"*

Grandma laughed, her bright, bursting laugh. *"Worry him? Asa didn't want Leesie and me to come here today because of it. I wondered what happened. That sneaky man!"*

"Do you still see the kids…getting together?" Molly asked.

"The link was made today, Molly. It is certain," Grandma quietly answered.

Molly giggled. *"I'd forgotten all about your prediction until I saw them together today. I'm sorry I nearly let the cat out of the bag."*

"Now, as far as our sheriff is concerned," Mr. Cole interjected, sighing again. *"I understand how influential a sheriff can be within the community, particularly where it pertains to matters of morality and justice. But I ask you, Ali, who is even more influential than a sheriff?"*

Grandma gasped and then stifled another emotional sob. *"A minister. Of course, a minister, Jake, but I can't let you endanger your family for us. That was why Asa and I stayed away for so long. It was for your protection."*

"You didn't ask, and besides, we're family. That's why we chose to come to this town. We missed you terribly!" Molly choked. Her voice was barely a whisper.

"I just wanted you out of Charles's reach," Grandma sobbed. "Charles knows you're like a sister to me, Molly. I'd die if anything happened to you because of me!"

"Speaking of Rebecca," Reverend Cole interjected, taking a long drag of breath. *"Asa told me what happened with her, Ali, and I must confess that I am the one who told Asa he needed to send Rebecca away from you.*

You are a delicate soul, and I don't think you ever truly saw her for what she was. Rebecca was a spoiled child who was jealous of you and who found a great deal of pleasure in causing you pain. She enjoyed torturing you with thoughts that Asa would one day leave you, something she must've realized was never going to happen. Still, she made you doubt yourself. Asa…never…has…and…never…will see anyone but you. For goodness' sake, Ali, the man waited fifteen years to marry you!"

Mr. Cole took another deep breath. *"Rebecca was such an angry girl. Asa felt that had it not been for the tornado, she might've harmed Leesie on the night she was born. I'm sorry if it's painful for you to hear these things. Asa would never say it to you himself, but he did tell us. I suspect that Rebecca was like her father. And as I recall from experience, as well as by what we have witnessed here today, he, too, enjoyed watching you suffer."*

I heard my poor grandma take a shuddering breath and cry.

"Surely you must see the difference between Rebecca and Leesie, Ali," Molly muttered.

"I do!" Grandma cried. "I see Asa in Leesie, and it terrifies me. She's just like her father—an overprotective fool! She threw herself into *the lion's den today for me, which is what Asa would've done. I shudder when I think about what he'll do when he sees the bruise on my face."*

"Knowing my dearest friend," Mr. Cole replied, *"Asa will try to kill the sheriff tonight. Not that I blame him, but he might end up getting himself killed in the process. Charles Marshal is expecting Asa to act; he wants a fight. Frankly, I think it's a trap. Therefore, we have to keep Asa from being too hasty, which isn't going to be an easy task. With your consent, Ali, I'd prefer to speak to him about this myself."*

"Yes, of course," Grandma whispered.

Mr. Cole sighed. *"I also want you to know, and I'll tell Asa the same thing: I'm going to have a serious talk with my son about Leesie. I won't have him disrespecting her in any way."*

"The link is a powerful thing, Jake," Grandma murmured. *"At best, we can only delay the inevitable. They aren't so very different from Asa and me. Asa and I were a few years older, but don't worry. I know that Kris would never hurt Leesie, and he wouldn't disrespect her, either. The bond for people like us is just too strong. I just hope their journey together will be easier than ours has been."*

"Poor, Grandma," I muttered aloud.

"Why do you keep calling her that?" Kristofer snapped.

"Because that's who she is!"

"She. Is. Your. Ma! Or haven't you been listening?" he yelled under his breath, baring his teeth at me.

"Not. Until. She. Tells. Me. Herself!" I retorted, glaring at the beautiful boy.

Kristofer took my hand while all remnants of frustration fell from his eyes. He was concerned for me. *"Who is Rebecca?"* he whispered.

"She was my sister. She died."

"Oh, I'm sorry."

"I didn't know her. She died the day I was born."

"Oh..."

There was silence in the house for a minute.

"Did Asa ever tell you about the day Leesie was born?" my…*mama* asked. *"What Rebecca said about her?"*

"*No*," Mr. Cole and Molly both answered at once.

Mama went on. *"After Lees was born, Rebecca looked at her and said, 'Oh look, another devil.'"* Her voice cracked. *"Those were the last words she spoke to me. She wouldn't come near Leesie. She didn't want to hold her.*

When the tornado hit, Asa fell into the cellar trying to stop me from getting to them. When he fell, he fell on me. I was dazed, and Rebecca was not in the cellar with us. Asa was crazy with worry. He couldn't get to Rebecca, and he'd hurt me when he fell. He panicked.

The stove had the door pinned shut; we were trapped. Asa clawed at the wood, trying to get us out, trying to get to her. As difficult as Rebecca was, Asa loved her as his own, and he didn't stop. Eventually, he got us out, but it was too late. My baby, my Rebecca, was gone.

Asa and I live with the loss of Rebecca every day of our lives, and what's worse, he feels responsible for not saving her. I'll never forget the look on his face when we found her body beneath the rubble of our old house. The scars on his hands won't let me forget."

She paused. *"Still, her words resonate with me, even today. My first-born daughter once called me a monster for damning Asa's soul to Hell.*

Jake, from the point of view of a minister, do you think I'm a monster for wanting Asa? Do you think he should be with someone human, or at least, someone who is more human than me? I tried to save him from a lifetime with me. I didn't marry him for fifteen years."

I peeked through the window at my mama just as Molly leaned over, wrapped her arms around her, and enfolded her in a tight hug.

Mr. Cole took Mama's hand. *"I think Asa is a lucky man to have two such extraordinary women in his life. And as far as your marriage, you would've married Asa when you were fifteen years old had that devil not attacked you. He and Leesie both need you, Ali. And from the point of view of a reverend, I think that you are more human than most people I know and ever so much kinder and gentler a soul because of what you can do. The Lord certainly has a plan for you and for Leesie. It's your responsibility to follow that path and to teach Lees to do the same.*

Now," he said, taking a handkerchief from his pocket and handing it to her. *"I have to get some papers ready for my sermon on Sunday, 'Love thy neighbor' sounds about right to me. What do you think, Ali?"*

"I think that sounds just perfect, Jake!" My mama beamed.

Mr. Cole rose and left the room, leaving the women in the parlor.

Molly smiled and patted Mama's hand. *"You seemed awfully nervous when you were here with Asa yesterday."*

Mama laughed. *"I wasn't nervous, Molly, I was beside myself. As soon as Asa told me that Jake and you had moved to town, I knew our little ruse was over. Then when we arrived here yesterday, I was anxious and happy and downright terrified, and Asa knew it; he knew it and was enjoying it! I even snapped at Leesie before we left. She sensed that something was amiss, and that terrified me, but she was also thinking awful things about herself, which broke my heart. I lost my composure and broke down. I've never cried in front of Leesie before, and I think it startled her. When we arrived here, and Asa took my hand, I was about to lose it again. If anyone can make me lose my composure, it's that man! And when we got home..."* She paused and shook her head.

"What happened?" Molly asked.

"Leesie was pretending to be asleep at the table in the kitchen, so of course Asa and I took her upstairs. But after she met Kris, I knew she wasn't going to sleep much. And..." She paused again. *"And Asa wanted to reunite with me right then, but I wasn't ready for that yet. He came to my room, but I was with Leesie."*

"Well, Asa is your husband, Ali." Molly took Mama's hand.

My mother shook her head. *"Oh no, it's not that. I want Asa more than anything, but Leesie needs to know the truth first. My goodness. What if she saw something, or what if she heard us?"*

Both women blanched and Mama's ears flushed. *"I can't have Leesie frightened or confused. Just imagine if she thought her father and grandmother were having a love affair!"*

She shuddered and shook her head. *"No, Leesie has to know the whole story, everything, beforehand."*

"And when is that going to be?" Molly asked, kindly stroking Mama's hand.

"Tomorrow," Mama barely whispered, nervously wringing her hands. *"Although after what took place here today, I think it just might be sooner."*

Molly squeezed her hand. *"What is it, what's worrying you, Ali? Surely you're not afraid to give yourself to Asa, not anymore."*

"What if Leesie hates me? What if she doesn't accept me as her mother, ever? All her life, Lees has seen Rebecca as her mother. What if it's too late for me? I know she loves me, but what if she can't accept me as her mother?" Mama put her head into her hands and cried.

Molly threw her arms around my mother, pulling her into an embrace. *"She will accept you because you are her mother!"*

I wanted to come bursting straight through the window and into her arms.

"I have to make her see how much I love her. She's my mama. I have to make her see that I understand," I mumbled under my breath.

Kristofer leaned over and kissed my cheek. *"You are so sweet, Sita,"* he whispered and took my hand.

Just then, Mr. Cole came back into the room with papers in his hand. He sat down next to Molly. *"Ali, tell me about that incredible daughter of yours. Asa said something to me about how the child has begun to have visions. Is this true?"*

"*Yes,*" she tearfully muttered, "*just in the past week. Leesie has seen things before, but nothing like the visions that she's having now.*"

"*But you don't have visions?*" asked Mr. Cole.

"*At times, I know things. I sense them, but no, I don't have visions. I only had them while I was expecting Leesie.*"

My mother beamed, putting her face up toward the heavens. "*Oh, it feels so good to say those words aloud: that she's mine!*"

Then she wiped her eyes and smiled. "*But I do still hear her thoughts,*" she laughed. "*Recently, Leesie has become aware of our mental connection, and, in fact, was teasing me about it today. I tried to be stern with her, but really, all I wanted to do was laugh. That stubborn streak of hers reminds me so much of Asa.*"

"*Amazing!*" Mr. Cole beamed. "*When did you begin to hear Leesie's thoughts? I'm sorry, but Asa never mentioned it.*"

"*Upon conception.*" Mama glanced at Mr. Cole and Molly with a bit of trepidation, as if speaking openly of her gifts brought fear to her heart. "*Just prior to her conception, I saw an image of her soul; she told me I was to conceive her. Then she spoke, not only to me but to Asa, while I carried her. She told him when I was tired or hungry or if I needed anything at all.*"

She laughed. "*And Leesie chose her name, insisted upon it, really; although, changing it a bit was my idea.*"

"*What visions did you have while you were expecting her?*" Mr. Cole asked.

I fell back to the ground, shaken and numb. "*Not only is she my mama, but she's heard me my whole life! My. Whole. Life!*"

My head was filled to the brim, too full of thoughts. I was overwhelmed. I couldn't believe it.

"*I have a mama. I have a…mama.*" Tears welled in my eyes. "*I… have…a…mama!*"

Kristofer pulled my head down until it was lying against his shoulder.

"Kristofer, am I dreaming?"

He chuckled and kissed my head. *"I sure hope not 'cause if you are, then so am I."*

Kristofer sat up, gazed into my eyes, and ran his knuckles down the length of my face, but he didn't smile. In fact, he seemed sad. *"It seems as if I've waited an eternity to have you again, Sita, and now that you're mine, I'm never letting you go."*

From inside the house, Reverend Cole spoke again. His words caught my attention. *"Do you hear every word the child thinks?"*

The breath caught in my throat; I listened intently.

"Well, no," Mama tearfully replied. *"I could, but I don't. I sort of 'close the door,' so to speak, most of the time. After all, little girls need their privacy, Jake."*

She snickered a bit. *"Asa, on the other hand, doesn't quite agree with that. He feels that I should listen to every word, but I know different. I know that little girls, particularly at this age, need time to be alone with only themselves. I won't intrude on her private thoughts."*

Vastly relieved, I stood up, peeked into the window, and gazed at the face of my beautiful mother.

Wow! She's so pretty!

"I hope you know that you both are quite an inspiration." Mr. Cole squeezed Mama's hand and then crouched down in front of her.

"I want you to do something for me, Ali, but before I ask, I have something else to ask you." He paused, finding the right words. *"As your friend, well, as a brother, but more as the minister who married you, I have to ask..."*

"What is it, Jake? You know Asa and I would do anything for you."

Mr. Cole smiled. *"Will you uphold the vows you made to your husband? Will you uphold them without reservation and with the intention of never looking back again? I must know the answer before we go any further with our conversation. And please know I have already asked Asa the same questions."*

Mama's eyes grew wide and tearful. *"Yes, of course, I will. Asa is my husband; Leesie is my daughter; I'm never going to let them go again!"*

"Good." Mr. Cole smiled and squeezed her hand. *"Then Asa and you both agree!"*

He leaned forward. *"Still, you may want to reiterate your vows to one another in private, if for no other reason than to reestablish the bond between you."*

Mama laughed and cried into the handkerchief at the same time. *"Of course, Jake. Now what was it you wanted us to do for you? After how you've helped us, I couldn't deny you much of anything."*

Mr. Cole peered into my mother's eyes for a few seconds, a sudden and startling sense of apprehension blooming in his expression. *"I'm going to ask that you be courageous, Ali. I know how terrified you are of our new sheriff.*

I want the three of you to come to church services on Sunday morning. I want Asa, Leesie, and you to stand united as a family at the head of our congregation, and I want you to take your place in it.

With my help, of course. I'll begin by introducing you as my brother, my sister, and my niece, as you most certainly are to me. I won't ask you to speak unless you wish to, but I will say a few words on your behalves, with your blessings, of course."

"But..." Mama barely breathed. Her voice was small and terrified, and her eyes stretched wide with fright. *"What if Charles is there? Leesie won't be safe around him."*

She took a few ragged breaths. *"And Asa! If we do this, then Charles will know that Asa and I are married and that Leesie is our child!"* She put her head in her hands and shook with fright.

Oh, Mama!

"We take away his power!" shouted Mr. Cole, startling my mother...and me, too.

Mama looked up.

Mr. Cole gestured to the front door. *"If the good people of this town know that you are a part of our family, then how likely is Marshal to try something against you? But if you sit on that farm alone, you don't stand a chance."*

He squeezed her hand. *"I'll talk to Asa, all right?"*

"All right," Mama frightfully muttered; her voice was small and terribly frightened.

All of a sudden, the air in the room seemed to thicken. I could almost see the waves of fear surrounding my mother as she sat… *shaking.*

"Ali," Molly muttered, trying to sound cheerful, *"you never told us about the visions you had while you were expecting Lees."*

Mama took a deep breath as if relieved that Molly had changed the subject to something a bit less frightening.

"I had visions of Lees's face. She studied me. For hours on end sometimes, my baby considered every feature of my face."

She sighed. *"Then, when I was seven months along, she sang to me. Each night as I fell asleep, her voice floated through my mind. I'd been singing to her for months. Then, one day, she sang the same lullaby to me."*

I sat beneath the window listening to the voice of my mother and felt the love in her heart. It was a mother's love. Tears pricked and pooled in my eyes, and a sense of security that I'd never experienced before swathed me in warmth.

I closed my eyes and basked in the warmth of happiness, allowing the love in both our hearts to wash over me.

12. Reunited

Mama and I walked home from Molly's house late that afternoon, hand in hand the whole way again. We were almost home, but neither of us had spoken a single word the entire way. I wasn't sure if she knew what I overheard, but every few seconds she glanced at me as if she wanted to ask me something but was too afraid.

Finally, I could stand it no longer. *"I knew who the sheriff was because I had a dream about him and you,"* I blurted.

My mother stopped walking and then stared down at me with a terrified look on her face. *"What did you see exactly?"* she asked, her soft voice uncharacteristically husky and in a hushed tone.

"I saw when he was mean to you in the stable—when he hit you! And I saw Papa and Molly after he almost killed you. I saw the way Papa took care of you. And that's when I saw my...grandmother." I said the last word slowly, peering straight into her eyes. I had to bite my lip to stop the words from tumbling out of my mouth. I wanted to say much more, but I needed her to tell me who she was first.

Mama put a shaking hand to my face. *"Is that all you saw?"*

If she sees my visions, then why is she asking me what I saw?

"About him, yes," I answered. *"Is there something that you would like to tell me?"* My tone was almost demanding yet tearful at the same time. I frowned at her, my eyes silently beseeching her to say the words I so desperately needed to hear from her.

Please!

"I'm sorry you had to see those things, baby," she choked. *"I was going to tell you about it but not until you were older."*

"Anything else?" I asked.

Please, just tell me! Please!

Seeing where I was going with the conversation, my mother's gaze fell to the ground. *"If I said…tomorrow?"* She cocked her head, looking up. Her eyes were tearful—scared.

Now, please! I pleaded with my mind.

"That man is not your GRANDFATHER!" she blurted.

Jeez, I know that! I thought

"I don't care who he is. Who—are—you?!" I yelled. The tears in my eyes bubbled over, right along with my fraying emotions.

Mama put her hands on both sides of my face, gazing into my eyes. Tears streamed down her cheeks. Her hands trembled, and a single thought ran through her mind: *Please don't hate me; please don't hate me; please, please don't hate me…*

That thought abruptly ceased as she took a deep breath, her face showing with an all-encompassing sense of dread and fear.

"I'm. Your. Mother," she whispered. Then her sights dropped to the ground. She seemed ashamed and frightened, as if she expected me to lash out at her. What's worse, she had a desperate look on her face that I just couldn't stand.

Without pause I threw my arms around her, nearly knocking her to the ground, and sobbed against her shoulder.

In response, she steadied herself and clutched me to her chest, gasping for air, winded by my reaction.

I held her tighter, as if my life depended on it—which, in my mind, it did—all the while blubbering into the front of her dress.

My nose ran, and my breath came in shallow, erratic sobs. *"I…already…knew…who…you…were, Mama,"* I stammered. Then I took a deep breath, stood upright, and gazed into her beautiful shocked face. *"I…just…needed to hear…you say it…to me…yourself."* I hyperventilated and then hiccoughed.

How could I have ever believed that she was anyone except my mother? Looking at her is like seeing myself in a mirror.

Hearing me call her "Mama" took her breath away. She stood stock-still, tears burning down her face, attempting to catch her breath.

"That's the first time you've ever called me that," she mumbled, covering her face with her hands, copiously weeping.

I threw my arms around her, feeling her close—my mama. I needed her to know that I understood why she had to *lie* to me. *"You thought if the bad man saw me as his grandchild, then maybe I'd be safe?"*

She nodded, looked up, and wiped her eyes with her fingertips. *"We had to tell everyone I was your grandmother to protect you from him, Lees."*

She bent down, kissed my head, and held me to her bosom. *"I'm sorry we had to lie to you, my baby."*

"Do you still think I'm safe because he thinks that I'm his granddaughter?" I asked. Though after the way Charles Marshal eyed me, I already knew the answer.

"No." A shock of fright flashed in her emerald eyes.

"Rebecca?" I hesitated, not wanting to hurt her. *"Was she the sheriff's daughter?"*

My mother silently nodded.

As I gazed up into her emerald eyes, I was struck by how tired my mama looked. I threw my arms around her waist, held her tight, attempting to afford her strength through our shared connection, and closed my eyes.

"I love you, Mama. I've always loved you, but today I love you so much more!" I said both into her ear and into her mind at once.

Hearing my heartfelt words, she held on to me as if she never wanted to let me go, and she wept.

I squeezed her tighter.

As I held her, it was as if many years of grief and guilt dissolved from her in the form of tears.

"I love you, too, my baby…my daughter!" she choked between sobs.

As much as I wanted to stand there on that spot and hug her forever, I knew Papa was waiting at home for us—for her—too.

I know everything now, so they can be together and happy!

She must have heard what I was thinking. She let me go of me and took my hand. *"Now, let's get home. I need to talk to your papa."* She laughed although it was a nervous laugh.

Oh, Mama, why are you nervous? Papa loves you, too!

I peeked up at her, grinning. *"Your husband."* I giggled into my hand. *"We need to talk to your husband."*

"Yes!" She beamed. *"My Asa!"*

Just as we walked up the path leading to our farm, Mr. Cole's buggy left the yard. I cocked my head, watching him drive out of sight.

Hmm… He must've left his house right after we did to get here so fast.

My sight drifted to our little farmhouse, where Papa stood on the porch waiting for us.

"I wonder why Mr. Cole didn't give us a ride home," I asked Mama.

"Jake wanted to talk to your papa alone," my mother absently mumbled, her eyes glued to my father. She seemed worried and even more tired than before; her hand quaked as she gazed toward home, toward Papa.

"Oh, Mr. Cole wanted to tell Papa what happened today…with that man."

"Yes, my baby," Mama answered, her voice just a breathless whisper.

"Papa doesn't look angry."

As Mama and I entered the yard, Papa stepped off the porch and headed up the pathway toward us, his arms outstretched. He practically ran!

"There are my beautiful girls!" he hollered, grinning from ear to ear. *"I was beginning to wonder where you were!"*

As my father reached where we were standing, he noticed the angry purple and red welt running all the way up the left side of my mother's face, and his joyful expression faded into an angry scowl. He took her head between his palms, tenderly stroking the wound.

She *flinched.*

"Jake told me about this. Are you all right?" he asked, his voice low, his jaw clenched. He was attempting to stay calm though his hands shook with rage.

"I'm all right, Asa," she murmured, but her words didn't quell his wrath. Papa's chest heaved. His nostrils flared.

"Please, Asa, calm down," she whispered, rubbing his chest, attempting to calm the fury bubbling inside of him.

She stood on her toes. *"Leesie needs you,"* she whispered, laying her hand against his reddening cheek.

When that didn't calm my father, Mama stared him dead in the eyes. *"I...NEED...YOU!"* she breathlessly whispered, and it was in a tone that I had *never* heard from her before.

"Please, Asa," she beseeched.

"I'll kill him for putting his hands on you!" Papa seethed, his eyes flashing.

My mother held her breath, attempting to steady her nerves and regain her composure. With her composure collected, she stretched up onto her toes, brushing her mouth against his.

"I need you. I need you so much," she breathed against his lips, weaving her fingers through his wavy blond hair, tugging on the silken strands. She slanted her lips over his...

And finally, at long, long last, she kissed him—hard!

She kissed him!

Transfixed by their love, I couldn't move.

Her hold was forceful. It was unexpected; it was perfect.

Tears pricked the backs of my eyes.

Papa's body responded at once; he groaned into Mama's open mouth. Then, with one arm wound around her waist, he grasped fistfuls of her hair with his free hand, twisting it in between his long fingers, almost roughly but not enough to hurt.

My parents' connection was fierce, as if twelve years of pent-up loneliness burst, sending their joint senses reeling with uncontained passion.

Initially, I was shocked by the display, but at the same time, a feeling of security rushed through me. It was as if every wish I had ever wished for was granted. In one sublime moment, I had it all.

I have a family and a mother, and best of all, my mother is her!

I giggled.

Hearing my bashful laugh, Mama pushed herself away with great effort, smiling a bit sheepishly at Papa.

"Sorry," she mumbled, *"I got a little carried away."*

My father stepped back, staring into Mama's eyes. He was happy but dazed. He inclined his head to one side, regarding her with a sense of elated confusion.

"You kissed me. Actually, you more than kissed me," he muttered. Then, grasping my mother's hips, he pulled her against his body. *"You kissed me in front of…her,"* he whispered, emphasizing the word "her."

"What, exactly happened at that tea, Ali?"

"Nothing," Mama nervously laughed, putting the back of her hand to the frown forming between my father's bright, steel-blue eyes. *"Since when isn't a respectable married woman permitted to kiss her husband?"*

Tears welled in her eyes. She snaked her arms around his waist, gazing up into his ever-confused expression. *"I told her everything, baby."*

Papa's breath hitched and faltered. His eyes grew wide as if in disbelief. *"You did? You told her everything?"* he mumbled, winded by her sudden honesty. He gasped and choked back a tear.

"Mama told me everything!" I answered him, giggling.

"MAMA?" Papa's head snapped up. He gawked at me as if he couldn't quite believe his ears. *"Leesie, you called her…Mama!"* Tears sparkled in his gentle eyes

"I'm glad you're married!"

Papa's eyes swept between us.

He took my mother's hand and leaned nearer to her. *"I love you, my beautiful wife,"* he choked. He attempted to hold in his tears, but he couldn't. They spilled, and his voice cracked with emotion.

"I love you, too, my sweet, so much," Mama replied, wiping the tears from his face with her fingertips.

Seemingly overcome with love, Papa wrapped one arm around her waist, pulled her in tight, and then held the other hand against the back of her head, holding her cheek to his chest. He sighed and laid his cheek atop her head.

In return, Mama turned her head up, kissed Papa's neck, and wrapped her arms around him.

My parents held each other so tight. It was as if each were trying to pull the other's soul away from its host, attempting to become a single spirit. Neither breathed for a long while.

Finally, though, Mama gazed up at Papa and took a quick tear-filled breath.

"Breathe, baby," she whispered, putting a hand to his chest, her lambent eyes aglow.

Papa took a long, shuddering breath and then bent down. *"Tonight?"* he breathlessly whispered into her ear.

My mother's cheeks pinked, but she smiled and nodded. *"Thank you for still wanting to be my husband, Asa. I am so fortunate to still have you."*

"Your husband is all I've ever wanted to be. I'm the lucky one, sweetheart," he murmured, placing his palms on each side of my mother's face. He then pressed his lips to hers, urgently kissing her.

They're happy! They're really happy!

At that moment, it was as if we were the only people in the world. At that moment, nothing else mattered. At *that* moment…

A shiver ran down my spine.

Something's coming. I don't know what it is or when it will arrive, but I see darkness… coming.

Papa chased the unsettling thought from my mind as he took my hand.

"Let's go home," he declared with a smile so bright that he almost glowed.

The three of us walked, hand in hand *in hand,* back to our house, our family home.

13. *Beneath* His *Clothes*

When we got back to the house, my parents and I sat at the kitchen table together.

During his visit, Reverend Cole brought us a fresh apple pie. Molly had intended to serve it with the tea, but in the bedlam of the afternoon she forgot to serve it…or the tea.

After supper, we sat eating the pie when something occurred to me. *"Mama, you can't see visions, right?"*

"No, baby, I can't."

I thought for a moment. *"Can I show you a vision that I've had?"* I asked, but I already knew that this was something I *could* do.

Without a second thought, I stood up and took both her hands. Then, bending down, I put her forehead to mine and closed my eyes.

The memory of what I wanted her to see filled my mind and hers in an instant. It was the vision of Papa sitting with her at the orphanage on the night she was hurt. I wanted her to see how much he loved her, even then.

I closed my eyes, remembering every detail, for her.

First, we heard the agonizing sound of her rattled breath as she attempted to breathe. She was fighting for her life. Then Papa appeared. He laid against her chest, begging her not to die, pleading with her light.

The sight was even more heart-wrenching for me the second time, knowing that she was watching. I wanted to cry, but I sucked back my roguish emotions and pressed on—for her.

As the vision continued, young Asa talked directly to the light within Alice, begging it not to go out. But the most tender moment was while he cradled her in his arms so gently she didn't even stir, not even when she was in such excruciating pain.

When the vision ended, I tried to stand, but Papa pulled me into his lap.

He put his forehead against mine and closed his eyes.

An image flashed into my head. It was him and my mother. They stood in front of Mr. Cole. Mama held a bouquet of wildflowers in one hand and Papa's hand in the other. They were getting married!

Then the vision shifted. I saw Papa bent over Mama, resting his head against her swollen belly, whispering to it, to me.

The last thing I witnessed was my mother lying on her side. She was almost asleep; her heavy eyelids fluttered, and then a tiny voice echoed through her mind. It was a lullaby, the wee voice drifting into her subconscious as her mind slipped away. The small voice was mine.

When the vision ended, I stood and stepped away from my father, frowning.

How? I glanced at my parents, my feet fixed to the ground. *How did I see that?*

Papa grinned from ear to ear.

No. It couldn't be! It just couldn't!

Mama took me around the waist and sat me next to her in the chair, all the while my mind still raced from one unlikely scenario to another. I couldn't comprehend what had happened and *how*.

Papa sat across from us, smiling and waiting for me to respond, but I couldn't grasp what I saw.

My papa, the one with the NORMAL mind? But it couldn't be, could it?

"*I think she's a bit stunned,*" I heard my mother say with a rather amused *lilt* in her soft voice.

If Mama can't see my visions, then how did they know about them?

I glanced over my shoulder, my eyes darting between my parents—wondering.

"She's putting it together, Asa." Mama laughed.

Papa leaned in, his light, slate-blue eyes twinkling. *"You didn't inherit that particular ability from your mama, angel."* His voice sounded apprehensive, maybe even anxious, but his eyes sparkled with amusement.

"I, I got it…from you?" I muttered, tilting my head to the side. *"Did you see the visions I had, Papa?"*

"Yes, angel." He spoke softly—testing the waters, awaiting my reaction. *"Some of the visions were new to me, but I think most of them you pulled right out of my mind."*

"But did you show them to me?"

He took my hand. *"No, you were searching for answers, so your mind accommodated you by showing you what you needed to know."*

"How?" I was still a bit dumbfounded. *"Was it because Mama accidentally put a curse on you?"*

My father threw his beautiful, blond head back and laughed out loud. *"A curse? You think your mama put a curse on me?"*

My face flushed. *"Yes,"* I murmured, embarrassed, and squirmed in my seat just as Mama gasped and pressed her forehead to the back of mine.

"There was no curse, angel."

I frowned and chewed my lower lip, still unsure.

I don't mean to argue, but I know what I saw. Perhaps he just doesn't realize…

A tiny sob escaped my mother's lips; she was upset.

"But, I saw. I saw…" I mumbled.

Hearing Mama's soft cry and seeing my anxious expression, Papa squeezed my hand tighter. *"Look at me,"* he gently commanded.

Obediently, I complied, looking into his eyes.

"There was no curse—none," he said, emphasizing the last word.

"But I saw what happened when you touched Alice…er…Mama's hand."

Papa shook his head. *"Your mother and I were both born this way, just like you were, Lees."*

He smiled. *"Let me ask you something."* Before he spoke again, he pulled me into his lap, hugging me around the middle. *"Doesn't it make more sense this way? I mean, your mama and I are two halves of a whole, and being such, some things about each of us will tend to bleed into the other, just like those sunsets you watch in the night sky."*

"Do you understand what he's saying?" Mama asked. Her voice sounded uneasy.

"But, Papa, you touched her accidentally. I saw you do it. That's the only reason you're connected."

"No, Lees. I saw a vision, just like the ones you see. I saw that your mother was going to be in the stable, so I was there when she arrived. In fact, I'd been envisioning her in dreams for most of my life, even before I knew who she was."

Oh—my heart lurched—*just like Kristofer!*

Papa gazed at my mother and smiled. *"Your mother and I are soulmates, Lees. Most often, married people or family members are something called kindred spirits, meaning they're kinfolk, baby, like you and me. But actual soulmates rarely live at the same time. When they do, like your mama and me, there's no denying the love between them. It's infinite."*

"It's absolutely…divine," Mama whispered.

Papa leaned over, gazing into Mama's eyes with the same slavish expression as this morning. *"I touched my soulmate's hand, and we've been linked ever since. I see her light, and I'm the only living person who can."*

"Kristofer sees mine…" I dreamily murmured.

I meant to say that only to myself.

Mama gasped and put her face in her hands, shaking her head, mentally trying to stop me from saying it aloud, but it was too late. Papa heard me.

Uh oh, I think I'm in trouble...

My father didn't utter a single word at first. He stared at me but didn't say a word. His brows were tightly knitted, and an uncertain and alarmed expression crept across his face.

"Dear Lord, Leesie!" I heard Mama scold me from her mind. *"I was going to break that particular bit of news to your father...gently!"*

I peeked at her through my lashes, but her hands covered her face. *Sorry,* I mentally whispered, *that sort of...slipped out.*

After a few very long minutes of total silence, my taciturn father finally spoke. *"Lees, go outside for a while, so your mother and I can"*—he glanced her way—*"talk."*

"Yes, sir," I mumbled, eyeing Mama, but she was still hiding.

Is she hiding from me? From Papa? From the world? Did I get her in trouble? Shoot, and they were getting along so well, too.

Slowly, obediently, I got up and scooted across the room with my little black witch tail curled up between my legs. Just before I shut the door, I peeked in. Mama had her head up. She wrung her hands, her eyes on Papa, seemingly considering what she was going to say to him, carefully.

Just as the door shut behind me, I scrunched up my eyes, trying to hear her, but her mind was shut tight. I couldn't hear a thing.

Then I remembered that the kitchen window was open, so I dashed around to the back of the house.

It's still open. Yay! I sat beneath it, just like Kristofer and I had at his house earlier.

"We knew this was going to happen, Asa," Mama anxiously muttered.

"She's twelve, Ali!" Papa angrily snapped. *"I wondered what Jake meant when he told me that he was going to keep an eye on his son!"*

"Kris is twelve, too!" she replied, sounding almost panicked. *"I'm sorry, Asa."*

Papa blew out a breath. His tone softened. *"Why are you sorry? The same thing happened to us; we knew what was to come, and so did Jake and Molly. But, Christ, Ali, our daughter is twelve years old!"*

"Perhaps I should've told her what would happen if she touched Kris."

"From what Jake said, I don't think it would have mattered. Kris was determined to get Lees away from Marshal; he was protecting her."

"Kris tried to protect all of us, and Lees tried to keep me safe."

She paused for a moment. *"Her powers have surfaced, Asa,"* Mama whispered, her voice laced with fright.

"Yes, Jake told me about that, too."

"She shut me in the house. I had to immobilize her. It was terrifying!" Mama cried. *"She's an overprotective fool, just like you!"*

"So it seems, but right now, I'm more concerned about the link with Kris than with her fledgling power."

He paused. *"She's twelve, Ali. What are we going to do?"*

"Kris is twelve, too, and they're both so innocent…"

"The thoughts that boy is having about OUR DAUGHTER— probably at this very moment—ARE NOT INNOCENT, trust me!" Papa pounded his fist on the table, startling me.

But Mama surprised me. She laughed. *"Asa, really, he's just a little boy, and they've only just met. What thoughts could he possibly have?"*

I heard a chair roughly scrape across the floor. *"The same thing I thought about you when I was twelve. When I saw you at the orphanage,"* he softly confessed. *"Trust me, Ali, I know what I'm talking about."*

I stood on my tip toes, peeking through the window.

Mama seemed exasperated. *"Asa, he's twelve!"*

Papa shook his head and agitatedly ran his hands up and down his face. *"Sometimes, Ali, twelve is worse than twenty. Everything is new and exciting to a twelve-year-old boy."* He paused, looking a bit ill. *"Particularly pretty twelve-year-old girls…"*

Mama had her head cocked to one side, eyeing my father as if she was afraid to ask. *"What exactly did you used to think about…me?"*

Papa sat down and raised his brow. Then he shrugged, almost apologetically.

My mother gasped, putting her hand to her mouth and giggling, and a crimson flush rushed across her cheeks. *"Oh, Asa!"* she whispered, considering him for a moment. *"Not Kris, though, not sweet little Kris, surely?"*

Papa raised his eyebrows again and nodded.

Mama stood and then sat on my father's lap. She ran her fingers through his shimmering blond hair. *"Don't worry, my sweet, it will be fine. Leesie will know everything she needs to know about such things."* She kissed his forehead. *"I'll make sure."*

Such things? Huh? What things? Is Papa afraid that Kristofer will try to kiss me?

Papa scowled. *"Why does that not make me feel any better?"*

He laid his head against Mama's chest and then peeked up into her eyes. *"So let me see if I've got this right."* He blew out a breath. *"I have a crazy sheriff wanting to OWN my wife and a RANDY twelve-year-old boy who wants to do Lord-knows-what with my daughter. Is that about right? Do I have a grasp on the situation at hand, sweetheart?"*

"Well, yes, honey, if you want to look at it that way."

"And I'm supposed to do what?" he grumbled, trying to rein in his temper.

"Well, there's nothing we can do about Kris. He's our best friends' son, and besides, he's our godson. Jake will handle Kris accordingly, I'm sure."

She paused, looking frightened. *"But I don't know what to do about Charles. He's dangerous and not just to me. You should've seen the way he gawked at Leesie. He looked hungry."* She choked back a tear and put her head in her hands.

"And until Jake's plan is executed? What am I supposed to do? Am I supposed to sit idly by and let that son of a bitch hurt you again, and possibly our daughter as well?"

Papa stroked the side of my mother's head where the devil had hit her. His eyes were full of rage. *"I should kill the bastard right now!"* he growled.

"Charles will be expecting you to come after him!" Mama sobbed, and I noticed then that she seemed even more tired than before. *"And he doesn't even know we're married yet or that Leesie is ours. I'm afraid of what he'll do when he finds that out.*

Please, let's just go! Please don't do anything to provoke him! I couldn't live without you—not ever again! Please, baby, please, I'm scared!"

"All right, sweetheart, but we'll do as Jake asked first. We'll stand up for ourselves in church on Sunday, but if either you or Leesie is threatened again, we will move. At least for a while, until Marshal is run out of town or until someone kills the bastard!"

I couldn't believe what he was saying. Us, move away from the orchard? *I don't want to live anywhere else! If we move, then when will I see…my boy?*

Papa wiped a few silent tears from Mama's face. Her eyes were red-rimmed, puffy, and purpled with haunted shadows.

"You are dead tired," he whispered. *"When was the last time you've slept, sweetheart?"*

"I don't know, days perhaps. A bit here and there…" Her soft voice trailed off.

Papa pushed her head down onto his chest, tenderly stroking her face, and then laid his cheek atop her head, breathing in her sweet scent. *"My God, but you smell good."* He chuckled. *"Your scent is intoxicating. A man could get drunk just by breathing it in."*

Mama sat up and frowned. *"You know, Leesie was thinking something very similar to that today. She wanted to ask me about borrowing my perfume."* She shook her head. *"I don't wear perfume."*

Papa threw his head back and laughed, and his bright eyes twinkled. *"She thinks you do. In fact, the next time we're in the city, I'll have to buy her some lilac perfume, so she can smell like her mama."*

"No, Asa, I love her sweet scent. Don't do that."

"Sorry, sweetheart. Leesie wants to be just like you in every way, and you smell like lilacs."

He pressed his forehead against hers. *"I understand how she feels, though. I mean, I wouldn't mind if certain parts of my body smelled like you, either."*

He winked and kissed the tip of her nose, causing her to blush. *"But not now. Right now, you need to rest before you drop. Close your eyes,"* he whispered, pushing her head down onto his shoulder.

After a few minutes, Mama was asleep in my father's arms, and I thought he might be asleep, too. He sat very still with his eyes closed.

I ran back around to the front door and opened it slowly. I quietly stepped in, closed the door behind me, and tiptoed across the floor. But just as I crossed halfway through the front room, Papa's voice startled me.

"Come in here, angel. I want to talk to you."

Uh oh! Here goes. I'm in for it now.

My feet dragged as I headed to the kitchen.

Just as I crossed the threshold, he rose up with Mama in his arms. She wasn't moving.

"I'll be right back. Cut us another piece of that pie," he hollered over his shoulder.

I cut two pieces of pie and sat down. Then, looking over, I noticed that Papa didn't have any more coffee, so I ran upstairs to ask him if he wanted me to make him some more. I got as far as the doorway of Mama's room, but I didn't say anything.

He sat beside her on the bed, and he was praying.

I didn't know what to do besides watch.

His head bowed, he held her hands, asking God to protect us from harm, and he prayed for guidance. When he finished, he covered her with a blanket and took the pins out of her hair, just as he had the night before, taking great care not to wake her. He unrolled the part she had in a knot in the back of her head, gently combing his fingers through it until it fell into delicate waves into his hands. Raising the lock to his face, he inhaled and closed his eyes. *"Absolutely intoxicating,"* he whispered. *"We'll have our reunion tomorrow night, my darling wife. I'm aching to make love to you again,"* he mumbled against her lips. Then, moving up, he kissed her forehead, her nose, and lastly, her lips. He then stood and turned to leave.

I stood in the doorway, wanting to disappear or fade into a shadow or something, but I couldn't. Instead, I bashfully stared at my toes.

"Do you want more coffee, Papa?" I mumbled with a shy flush creeping over the bridge of my nose.

My father put his hand out. *"That sounds great, angel,"* he beamed, taking my hand. He softly closed the door and then led us both back downstairs.

He and I sat at the table eating together in silence for a while, though it seemed to me as if he wanted to ask me something. He drank his coffee and stared at me over the brim of the cup.

Finally, he put it down, reached over and touched my face with the palm of his hand. *"Are you happy, baby?"*

I nodded. *"Yes, Papa, very happy."*

A puddle of emotional tears welled in my eyes. I tried to stop them, but they spilled out before I was able to suck them back and away.

"What is it?" He was alarmed by my tears.

I swallowed the lump forming in my throat. *"Well, it's all like some sort of an incredible dream. I've wanted this for as long as I can remember, and now, it's finally happened!"*

"I know you've wanted to have a mother for a very long time." He sweetly smiled.

I shook my head.

"You didn't?"

"No, I didn't want just a mother, Papa. I wanted her to be my mother. I prayed about it every night; I love her so much, and I prayed and dreamed that you would love her, too! And my prayers were finally answered—today!"

Papa slid off the chair and knelt in front of me, gently placing his hands on both of my cheeks. *"Why didn't you tell me how you felt about her?"*

"Why didn't you tell me?" I sniffled, putting my hands on his face, mirroring his actions to me.

"You are absolutely right. I should've!" he chuckled, then pulled my face closer, peering into my eyes.

I couldn't believe how striking his eyes were up close. I bet if I concentrated long enough, I could actually drown in them.

Papa leaned in, releasing me from my daze, and kissed my forehead, but our joint gaze remained. The intensity of his eyes had me captivated; I couldn't look away.

"I want you to know something, sweetheart. I want you to know that your mama and I are going to be together forever now, so you don't have to worry about it anymore. We love each other, and we love you more than anything."

I giggled. *"You're going to kiss a lot from now on, too, aren't you?"*

He threw his beautiful blond head back, heartily laughing. *"Yes, sweetheart, we will! Does that bother you?"*

"Nope, it's fine with me," I said, giggling once more.

Papa returned to his seat. As he and I sat together, I thought about his reaction to my link with Kristofer. I knew he didn't like it; the thought made my heart sink.

But it was my fault, not the boy's; he should be angry with me. After all, I disobeyed Mama by taking my gloves off.

"Please don't be mad at Kristofer!" I blurted.

My father frowned and put down his cup. *"I'm not angry with Kris, Lees. I'm just concerned about you."* He reached over and stroked my cheek. *"You're my little girl, and I want to keep you as long as I can."*

"You sounded angry before when you were talking to Mama," I said, bashfully frowning and biting my lip.

Oops, I really have to stop letting things slip outta my mouth like that. I thought.

"And just…how…did you hear that?"

My face flushed. *"From…the window,"* I mumbled, pointing behind him.

He turned, glancing at the open window behind him, and shook his head. *"We're going to have to be more careful from now on,"* he laughed and then reached for my hand.

"Look at me," he gently commanded, and when I did, I saw that his eyes were gentle yet determined.

"I'm angry with that son of a…" He stopped short, erasing the impending expletive from his lips, taking a deep breath to steady his rising anger.

Oh, it's all right, Papa, I thought. *You may call Charles Marshal a son of a bitch—I do.*

His anger steadied, my father went on, peering into my wide eyes. *"I'm going to do something about that man who hurt your mama today. And if that means we're forced to move, then so be it."* He bent down until our eyes were even. *"But wherever we decide to live, Jake, Molly, and the boy…"* His eyes narrowed, and he pursed his lips—like he swallowed a frog or something. *"They're a part of our lives now, for good, so I don't want you to worry about that."*

He leaned in and kissed my forehead.

I smiled for Papa's benefit, but I was still worried. *What if we're forced to move? And what if the bad man hurts my mama again?* The very thought of Charles Marshal harming my mother was unbearable.

I shuddered, and a burst of fire burned through my middle, scorching my throat. I gasped and closed my eyes. Then out of nowhere, an almost imperceptible cackle resonated from somewhere deep within my mind. It was a wicked sound. The disembodied voice startled me.

"Are you all right, angel?" Papa asked, his brows knitted together.

I steadied the burn in my throat and nodded for Papa's benefit. I listened for the menacing cackle, but the disturbing timbre had gone.

"Yes, Papa," I croaked, picking up my fork. *"I'm just a bit tuckered, I think."*

Jeez, what was that?

"Well, it's been a long day. By the way, how did you like meeting your godparents?" My father smiled, winked, and took another bite of pie.

"I love them. In fact, while we walked, Mama told me all about how she grew up with Molly in the orphanage."

As the last word fell from my lips, another dark thought ran through my mind. *"Papa?"* I asked.

"What is it, baby?"

"Why would anyone leave a child stranded by a tree? Why would anyone do such a vile thing?"

He shook his head and placed the fork on the table.

Apparently he knew the whole story of how my mother came to live at the orphanage. My heart sank.

"Maybe they didn't have a choice, sweetheart." He heaved a grand sigh. *"I've always been inclined to think that perhaps your mama's folks died…"*

"I can't imagine anyone wanting to leave her."

Papa shook his head and patted my hand. *"Neither can I, angel. Neither can I."*

Then he pointed to my plate, sucking back his emotions. *"Now finish your pie. It's getting dark."* His voice cracked a bit, and with those words I knew that my mother's childhood wasn't a subject he liked to discuss.

Poor Mama.

By the time we finished our pie, it was getting dark outside, so I helped Papa light the lanterns and make a fire in the fireplace.

"Papa?" I asked as he stoked the fire. I stood next to him. *"How did you know you loved Mama? Was it as soon as you touched her hand, or was it later?"*

My father froze on the spot and then turned. He stood in front of me, his brow deeply furrowed and his eyes narrowed. *"Your mama and I were older and better able to distinguish the difference between childish feelings and adult feelings,"* he replied with trepidation. He thought for a moment and then nodded to himself.

"Oh, all right…" I said, while thinking to myself.

I'll just ask Mama…

I yawned. *"Papa,"* I said, tilting my head to the side. I didn't want him angry with me, but I needed to tell him what I did.

He frowned. He thought I was going to ask more about love. He seemed uneasy, nearly panic-stricken. I almost laughed!

"Mama told me not to take my gloves off today, but I disobeyed her. That's why the link with Kristofer happened. I'm sorry," I sheepishly murmured, staring down at my fingers.

Papa heaved a sigh of relief. *"She told me about that—how you locked her in the house and went right after that bad man. And then how you jumped right in front of her."* He winked at me.

"Yes."

He laughed, hunkering down until our eyes were even. *"She said you're an overprotective fool—just like me!"*

"You're not angry with me?"

"No, I'm not." He took my hands, his slate-blue eyes dazzling with sudden pride. *"I'm proud of you for protecting and defending her. But just between you and me, you may not want to do anything like that again, or she might just thrash the both of us next time."*

I yawned again.

My father rose, taking me up into his strong arms. *"Now I think it's time you got some sleep, little lady, or tomorrow you'll look as worn out as your mama did earlier."*

Papa kissed my head and then carried me up the steps to my room. As he walked, I snuggled into his chest, my nose against the crook of his neck. I breathed deep.

Hmm, I love my papa.

Just as we came to my bedroom door, he kissed the top of my head, set me down, and then walked past me in the hall, going into Mama's room.

He must be checking on her again.

Once inside, I stood in my room, reflecting on everything that had happened that day. I couldn't believe how different my life was just since yesterday. It was much better, much more complicated, and just plain frightening!

I shuddered at the thought of what had happened with Charles Marshal. Then I changed into my nightgown and flopped down onto my bed. I was so tired I could hardly think.

I drifted off to sleep almost instantly…

As I drifted, a story played out in my mind. It was a familiar dream, one that I'd had many times before, but this time something was different.

From outside my room, I envisioned Mama coming out of hers.

She tiptoed past my door and down the stairs, wearing only a white cotton robe, her hair dancing across her back and trailing in elegant tendrils to her bottom. She stepped onto the landing, holding a lantern aloft in her hand, the soft light guiding her path into the shadowy front room.

But as I looked closer, I also noticed that *she* was glowing!

I stared at her, mesmerized by her light. Then I saw where the light emitted its unnatural glow.

It shined from within!

Just like Papa explained…

All of a sudden, I wanted him to see it, too. I wanted to share her beauty with him, but I couldn't take my eyes away from the resonating light.

She was beauty personified, more than beauty. She was my mother, but as I stood gawking at her, I realized that she was something more—much more. Papa was right; she was an angel.

As my mother swept across the room, the glow bathing her body shifted with her while at the same time altering the radiance of her light. The hue of the sparkling, golden light swirled, and an iridescent halo danced all around her. The ripples of light flowed a fraction of a second slower than the rest of her, leaving a gilded trail in her wake.

It was captivating.

"Papa, you have to see this," I murmured, but my voice choked with emotion.

Just as those nearly silent words left my lips, she whipped her hair around.

The golden light reacted to her movements. It flickered while the cascading light arced in all directions, shooting off the tips of her strawberry hair like lightning flashing through the sky.

Then she turned, and her emerald eyes glistened like gems, darting toward Papa's bedroom.

This must be a vision from Papa's mind; this is the way that he sees her!

My mother ghosted across the room, almost floating, her feet barely touching the ground. Her movements were delicate, demure, and entirely silent.

She moved toward my father's bedroom, and as she progressed, her light caught my eye, but so did her colors. They, too, ebbed and flowed around her.

Just as she reached Papa's bedroom, she stretched her hand out, and as she did, the arm of her robe fell away, exposing her pearlescent skin, making it seem opalescent. Her elegant fingers skimmed over the doorknob, but she pulled them back just before turning the knob.

"I'll make some coffee first."

She blew out a breath and frowned. *"Alice Raign, you are a coward! For goodness' sake, he's your husband!"* She shook her head as if in disgust.

Seemingly unnerved, she turned toward the kitchen, but something caught her eye, halting her. It was the laundry basket in the corner of the room. On top lay the shirt that Papa had worn earlier in the day.

She swept toward it, set the lantern down, and plucked the shirt from the top of the basket, smiling. She held it to her face, took a deep breath, and closed her eyes.

"Hmm…" A soft, satisfied groan escaped her lips, and her sights drifted toward my father's bedroom door once again. She made no move toward it, though. Instead, she took a long, deep breath and slowly slid out of her robe.

The soft glow of the moon shining through the window danced off her naked, opalescent skin. Every curve and contour of her body glistened as if embedded with golden dust, the many gilt shades sending an aura pirouetting around her as she stood there for a moment, silent and bare.

Beautiful. Surely, she's an angel. Papa has to be right about that.

Mama took a deep breath, inhaling Papa's scent, and then slipped the shirt over her glistening skin, covering her nakedness, rolled up the sleeves, and buttoned it up halfway.

The expression on her face as she stood there half-dressed and basking in the moonlight was one of serenity and happiness.

Watching my mother in all her glory, I couldn't help but be grateful for the fact that Charles Marshal couldn't see her the way she actually was—dipped in gold dust and glimmering in the light of a full moon.

As if sensing my thoughts, she whipped her iridescent, jacinthe hair around. It swayed against her bottom, and her gem-like eyes danced in the lamplight.

"Asa, my Asa. I love you so much," she dreamily whispered, her glistening hands sweeping up to the starched collar, lifting it up to her nose. *"Hmm, how I love your scent."*

It was usually at this moment that my dream ended, but this time, the vision went on.

I watched, fascinated…

My mother reopened her eyes and glanced toward Papa's bedroom door once more, biting her lip as if in contemplation. After a moment, she let out a nervous titter and shook her head. *"I just don't have the nerve,"* she bashfully murmured.

"Why not?" a voice from the very back corner of the room asked.

She and I both gasped at the same time.

Mama took a rapid gulp of air, gasped for the second time, and then lost her breath entirely as she spun around and saw Papa. He was sitting in the back of the room dressed in a pair of brown trousers—nothing else—and watching her.

She hadn't noticed he was there, and neither had I.

Her mouth gaped open for a beat. She was trying to catch her breath, her radiant porcelain hand clutched against her heaving chest. She was startled though her eyes betrayed a different emotion. They never left Papa's—not for a second—and they were bold. However, despite the boldness of her gaze, her skin flushed. I knew that even though the moon and lantern light was dim, my father noticed the rosy hue. He saw it through the light shining from within her.

Papa stood, but his eyes never left hers, and he smiled. *"You're flushed."* His voice was hoarse, his bright eyes sparkling with amusement.

"I know, I can feel it," she breathed, her sights cast down with embarrassment or perhaps something else, something that I couldn't name. All I knew was that her eyes blazed with an unnamed emotion as she waited with bated breath for my father to act on what he'd seen.

He strode across the floor, his long strides eating the inches between them. With each step taken, her breath drew shallower. Her eyelids nervously fluttered.

When finally he reached her, Papa put one hand out, his fingertips skimming the hem of his shirt. *"You know,"* he muttered, slyly grinning, clearly relishing every second of that unexpected moment—unexpected by *her*, at least. *"I've always found you alluring in my clothes, but this shirt is especially fetching on you."* His eyes dazzled into hers. *"Although, I must say, what you had under that robe was especially...nice."* He chuckled, running his fingers up and down the buttons.

My mother wrinkled up her nose and timidly buried her head in her hands. *"I didn't see you."*

"I saw you." Papa's voice was gentle, soothing, and in his eyes a sudden sense of not only love but awe and gratitude bloomed.

He put his hands on her hips, persuading her toward him, and then tenderly clasped her chin between his index finger and thumb, tipping her chin up and smiling into her beautiful, bashful eyes. His gaze was soft, loving.

She self-consciously smiled, bit her lower lip, and shook her head. *"What you saw, Asa... I didn't want the first time that you saw me unclothed again to be like this,"* she barely whispered, placing both hands flat against his chest.

I gasped again. Mama's glowing light reflected off Papa's bare chest, causing his skin to shine almost as hers did!

He leaned down, gazing at her directly, their collective sights both sparkling and burning at once. *"No, sweetheart, it was perfect. I missed the sight of your bare skin, Ali, and I have to say, you are even lovelier than I remembered."*

As my father stood gazing at the woman of his heart, his penetrating steel-blue eyes twinkled and glowed. At the same time, her golden light refracted off them, making them appear to shimmer and dance.

And suddenly, I was reminded of the sun setting over the ocean. *Absolutely brilliant!*

Mama sighed just as the sunset in Papa's eyes moved up and down the entire length of her slight form, drinking in her beauty.

After a moment, he chuckled, breaking the mesmerizing connection between them. *"Yes, I definitely preferred the view before you put on my shirt."*

He inclined his head. *"Why, exactly, did you do that?"*

My mother's emerald eyes blazed again; her breath stuttered.

Oh, Mama, are you nervous? What's wrong?

She bashfully smiled. *"The same reason I have always worn your clothes, Asa: because you wore them, my love."*

She took another steadying breath, placing a shaking hand to his face. *"When I wear your clothes, I imagine your naked skin beneath them, which evokes many fond memories for me. And I smell your scent on them."* She put her face to his bare chest, breathing deeply. *"I wish to have your scent on me, as well as mine on you."* Her lips caressed his chest; she dragged them against his bare skin, gently kissing him.

Papa closed his eyes as my mother touched him. He took long, deliberate breaths, and quivering gasps rose from beneath his chest. His taut nipples puckered against her assessing tongue, and a sudden crop of goose pimples sprang up, covering his skin in tiny bumps. The hair on his arms stood up as if at attention.

"You also believed that by wearing my old clothes I wouldn't find you attractive, didn't you?" he asked and then opened his eyes.

Mama froze and peeked up into his eyes, frightfully putting her hand to her mouth and nodding, her brilliant eyes falling downtrodden again.

Papa held her face between his palms, gently forcing her gaze. *"How in your mind could you possibly conceive such a notion as that, Ali? Don't you know by now that you could never be anything except beautiful and sensual to me, no matter what you wear? Truthfully, I found the bashful way you behaved toward me to be, if anything, even more alluring."* He wrapped his arms around her waist, pulling her close.

Tears welled in her eyes; she stifled a soft sob against his chest.

Oh, Mama! When will you understand just how beautiful you are?

After a moment, my mother raised her head, and her eyes blazed with that look again!

What is it with that look? I wondered.

Her body quivered, and with her hands against his bare chest, she swirled Papa's blond curls with her fingertips. *"I've wanted to touch you for so long; I've dreamed of it for so long. I couldn't stand the fact that you were no longer mine...to touch,"* she whispered, licking her lips—as if hungering for the taste of his skin.

He pulled her chin up. His eyes were blazing with love and something else, something I didn't quite understand. It was the same look that Mama had given to him. *"I have always been yours. Even when we were apart, I was yours!"*

"Oh, Asa!" she croaked, throwing her arms around his middle.

Papa shuddered, his chest fiercely rising and falling with each labored breath. I wasn't sure if he was upset or happy. It was hard to tell.

After a moment, he pulled Mama's chin up. Papa's eyes glistened like aquamarines, Mama's like emeralds. *"I want to touch you right now. I want to feel you everywhere. I want to run my tongue over every surface of your shimmering skin, to breathe in your sweet lilac scent. I need to be inside you, beside you, always. I want to love you, Ali, my beautiful Ali...*" His choked voice trailed off.

He blew out a deep breath and stared into her wide eyes. His gaze was fierce, focused. *"But the way I'm feeling right now, I might be a little uncontrolled. I'll need you to tell me if it's too overwhelming for you. I'll need you to tell me to stop before I scare you."*

He pressed his forehead to hers and blew out another breath. *"All right? Promise?"*

Without hesitating a bit, my mother reached up, pulling Papa's face down to hers. She grasped his ears, and I thought she was going to kiss him, but she shocked me. Instead of giving him a kiss, she stuck out her tongue and outlined his lips with the tip, taking small enticing licks—tempting him, softly moaning against his mouth.

Papa didn't move, but after a moment suspended in time, they both opened their eyes.

"You would never hurt me, and you've never scared me, not ever, but I promise," she whispered.

Papa nodded and then hastily grasped her, snaking his arm around her waist and forcibly pulling her into his arms.

I gasped; the ferocity of his need for her startled me. And Mama gasped, too, but she didn't struggle. In fact, she succumbed to his will quite eagerly and with equal enthusiasm.

Before I could process what I was witnessing, Papa swept my mother up into his arms and carried her across the room toward his bedroom, all the while fiercely kissing her and groaning into her open mouth, as if it held the sweetest of nectar within it.

Just before they reached the bedroom, he set her on her feet, his eyes burning into hers. With their gaze still locked, he slipped his hand under the hem of her shirt, caressing her bare backside with his fingertips.

In response, she groaned and lunged forward, grabbing fistfuls of his hair, tugging hard—roughly pulling his mouth down to hers.

Papa shifted, but their connection remained. He ran his hands up and down the contours of her waist. His hands slid down her to her thighs, exploring and touching every inch of her body, and then he slowly, at a snail's pace, made his way to the front.

Mama gasped as his adroit fingers reached between her legs. Remembering and exploring, his gentle hands skimmed over the scant patch of strawberry-blonde hair.

She threw her head back. *"Dear! Lord! In! Heaven!"* she cried out. Her eyes rolled, and her spine stiffened as a tremor ran through her body.

But to her surprise—and mine—Papa abruptly stopped and pulled his hand away.

Momentarily confused, my mother cocked her head, panting and quivering from the aftershocks of Papa's touch. Then she opened her mouth to speak, but my father put a single finger to her lips. He, too, was panting. They both were.

His usually light eyes drew dark, provocative, and more intense than I've ever seen them, the blue nearly eclipsed by the black.

For a beat, neither uttered a word. Still, their silent connection spoke volumes.

"I love you, Mrs. Raign." Finally, Papa breathlessly whispered.

Mama's eyes welled, and she sucked back a sob. *"I love you, Mr. Raign!"* she tearfully vowed.

My parents stood motionless, each quietly gazing into the face of their soulmate, one linked spirit nearly losing itself in the eyes of the other. Their connection was almost palpable, like a charged aura surging around them. The unspoken promise between them was raw, inviolate; it was perfect.

It was my father who broke the mesmerizing bond between them. His steel-blue gaze gradually wandered to the front of his shirt, the one that my mother was so coyly wearing.

He grinned, almost bashfully, and tenderly smiled. *"After so long, are you sure you're ready for this? You seemed rather nervous and unsure when you came down the stairs. We can wait if you want to… get to know one another again. Maybe court for a while."*

He snickered and eyed the shirt. *"You can wear my clothes for a spell longer…"* His tone was amused though I noticed an underlying bit of trepidation and concern as well.

He's anxious. Oh, Papa, but why?

For a moment, Mama said nothing. Then she sighed, smoothing her hands down the front of the shirt, deliberately finding the buttons and gently undoing each one of them in turn. Just as the last button gave way and the shirt hung open before my father, her eyes returned to his.

My mother smiled coyly while Papa's eyes drifted up and down the entire length of the open shirt that was almost falling off her tiny frame.

His eyes were wide yet blazing with fire, his mouth partly agape, and a sharp hissing sound whistled between his teeth as he sharply inhaled.

"I don't need your clothes anymore, my sweet," she breathlessly muttered. *"I only need what lies…beneath them."*

Wordlessly, she took Papa by the hand, leading him toward his… their…room.

"What are you doing?" he asked, canting his head to the side.

She laughed, her gem-like emerald eyes sparkling. *"Well, I'm giving you your shirt back, of course,"* she replied and then pulled him into the room.

Just as they crossed the threshold, she shrugged off Papa's shirt, letting it fall to the floor, exposing her naked body to him.

Finally, my beautiful mother shut the door while neither touching it nor pulling her gaze away from my father's radiant smile.

14. Birthday

I woke up the next morning to the smell of coffee and something burning in the kitchen. I got right up and ran downstairs only to find Papa dressed in my mother's apron and scorching his hands on the hot stove.

He cursed as he touched the much-burned *thing* he was removing from the oven.

I sent a towel over to him mentally.

He caught it in his hands and whirled around, his face beaming. *"Good morning, angel!"* he shouted, tossing the charred and smoldering whatever-it-was onto the table. *"Happy birthday!"* He beamed. *"I tried to make…breakfast."* He gestured to the charred something, frowning as it bubbled and smoked.

"What was that supposed to be, Papa?" I asked, stifling a snicker.

"Never mind that," he muttered, dismissively waving his hand in the air. Then he lifted me into his strong arms, holding me securely to his chest.

I threw my arms around his neck and closed my eyes. *Hmm. Papa even smells good when he's burning things. He smells of pipe tobacco and cinnamon.* I closed my eyes again, inhaling deeper. *And…lilac perfume?*

My eyes flew open. I leaned back, eyeing him, puzzled. *Could that dream I've had over and over, so many times…be real?*

I thought for a moment, remembering that I was able to see Mama's light and feeling even more perplexed.

"Angel?" The sound of my father's voice brought him back to my attention.

He put me down, sheepishly smiling. *"Will you try to salvage breakfast?"* he asked, gesturing toward the table. *"And I'll wake your mama."*

He kissed me on the lips and then hurried out of the kitchen to get her.

"Papa, give me her apr..." I ran after him. I meant to ask for her apron, but I didn't get the whole word out.

He didn't go upstairs. He went into *his* bedroom to get her.

I stood in the front room, which was just adjacent to Papa's bedroom, my mouth gaping open, my eyes wide and staring.

Mama was lying in *his* bed. She was still asleep, and the shirt he wore the day before—the shirt from my dream—lay on the floor by the bed. I stared at her—shocked. From the sight of her bare shoulders as she lay sleeping, it looked like she had nothing on.

Just then, Papa leaned down to plant a soft kiss on her bare shoulder and then her forehead and finally her lips.

My mother's eyes fluttered open just as his mouth touched hers. She yawned and slowly sat up, letting the bed sheet fall away from her skin. The thin material pooled around her waist. Just as the sheet fell, he swept her hair away from her chest. It trailed in graceful waves straight down her back, while at the same time exposing all of her body to him.

I gasped, standing immobile, just staring. I'd seen her without her clothes on hundreds of times in my life, but not in front of Papa! *Never* in front of Papa!

I stared at the ground biting my lip, and a hot flush rushed up and down the entire length of my body.

In front of Papa she seemed so exposed, so *naked*. All of a sudden, I felt naked, too.

Just as that thought trampled through my confounded mind, he crawled over her, lying on the bed between her outstretched legs. He ran his hands over her bare skin, tenderly caressing it.

My mother closed her eyes, contentedly sighing as he inched forward, hugging her around the waist and laying his head directly over her heart—against her bare breasts! At the same time, she gently tangled her hands into his hair, holding him close to her heart. Then she swept her hands down and softly caressed his back.

Their breath was heavy; I could hear it all the way into the front room.

"Thank you for last night, sweetheart," he tenderly muttered, nuzzling her puckering breasts with the tip of his nose. He deeply sighed—a happy sigh.

"No, thank you, my baby. It was just…" She paused for a moment just as he gazed up into her eyes. *"There aren't words, Asa…"* she breathlessly, almost tearfully, whispered in reply. She put the back of her hand to his cheek and joyfully shuddered. *"It was everything…"*

Huh? What was everything?

I glanced over at the laundry basket in the corner. Mama's robe was lying on top, and right next to it on the floor was the spent lamp—just like in my dream.

"Adults are just too complicated!" I muttered to myself. I shook the confusing images from my mind and headed back to the kitchen.

My mind was still reeling as I took one look at the *biscuits* Papa had tried to make, but there was no salvaging them.

Out of the corner of my eye, I saw him dart over to where the laundry basket sat. Then he grabbed Mama's robe and ran back to his room with it.

I stood in the kitchen, remembering the vision again.

I have had that dream for so long; I can't even be sure exactly when it began. I must've plucked that right out of Papa's mind, too, especially the part about her light. I'll have to tell him about that.

Just then, I felt Mama come up from behind. She wrapped her arms around me and held me close. *"Happy birthday, my sweet daughter!"* she said, and kissed me on both cheeks.

I turned to give her a proper hug. She and I were almost the same height, so I didn't have to reach up like I did with Papa.

Funny. I didn't notice I grew…not until just now.

She kissed me on the lips again and held me to her bosom.

I smelled her lilac perfume. *Wait, and something else: pipe tobacco and cinnamon.*

I frowned, and my mind wandered back to the sight of my parents a few moments before. Then I took a step back and away from them and gave them each a baffled look.

"What exactly did you two do last night while I was sleeping?" I nervously stammered, curiously glancing from one of my parents to the other. *"I had a vision last night…"*

I walked past them out of the kitchen and stood in the middle of the front room. I pointed to Papa's bedroom. *"About…that shirt."*

My face flushed. *"Was it true?*

I'm not upset," I quickly murmured when I saw the concern on my father's face. *"I just don't understand.*

And, why were you naked, Mama?" I bashfully stammered and stared at the ground, suddenly remembering how Papa had touched her in my dream and again just a few moments before.

Papa put his hands over his face, shaking his head, while Mama just stood there, laughing at him. *"I told you she'd have questions, Asa."*

He glanced down at her, frowning, and shook his head again. *"She's still too young, Ali. She won't need to know anything like that…"*

"Until the boy tells her? Or worse, shows her?" she cut him off.

She stepped closer to him and peered, with a bit of amused concern, up into his frowny face. *"Come on, honey. I understand that most women are kept in the dark about such things until their wedding night, but I don't want that for our daughter. You've never been one to believe that upon marriage a man buys ownership to a woman's body, and I don't want our daughter to think that way, either,"* she whispered, attempting to soothe him with a rub to his chest.

She held his face between her palms. *"And why don't you think that way?"* she asked. *"You don't think that way because your mother taught you otherwise and because she explained the facts of life to you when you were young. Besides, Lees would have known long ago about such things if we'd have raised anything besides trees."* She looked into his eyes with emotional tears welling up in her own.

She took a stuttering breath. *"I won't have our daughter feeling fearful of our love or ashamed of herself, her blossoming body, or of her own feelings, Asa. It's my privilege, as her mother…"* She paused. *"Preparing our daughter for becoming a woman is my duty. Lees is asking questions; it's time for me to give her all the answers she needs."*

With my mother's heartfelt words spoken, a sudden expression of understanding bloomed in my father's shining light-blue eyes. He nodded, put his palm flat against her cheek, and smiled down into her eyes.

Mama, too, nodded, smiled tearfully at me, and took me by the hand. Without another word she led me back to the kitchen.

She and I sat down, and she held both my hands while taking a deep and steadying breath. *"All right, I told you yesterday that you could ask me anything today, so ask."*

It seemed to me like this was something she'd been preparing to discuss with me for some time.

I opened my mouth to speak, but before I could utter a sound, Papa walked back into the kitchen. He took Mama's apron off, handed it to her, nervously said something about chopping firewood, and then quickly went outside. I watched as he practically ran out the door.

"Is he angry with me about something?" I asked, thinking about the vision I plucked from his brain.

"No, baby. Your papa's not prepared for the fact that you are rapidly becoming a young lady," she said, squeezing my hands.

"But you are prepared?" I hesitantly asked.

"Yes, I am," she definitively answered, looking straight at me, and then handed me a piece of left-over cornbread from the day before.

As I nibbled, she began to explain…

She and I sat for over an hour, and she answered every one of my questions without pause. Her openness with me gave me a sense of profound joy that I had never felt before.

The day before, I knew in my *mind* that she was my mother. But on that day, on my twelfth birthday, after she shared her thoughts with me and after the way she made me understand about her and Papa, I felt like her daughter in my heart.

With that thought, a blissful shiver ran through my body.

I giggled to myself, recalling what she had told me about her night with my father.

When I thought about it, what they did together the night before wasn't too bad, but I couldn't imagine why anyone would want to.

Even if Kristofer and I do get married someday, I still won't want to do that! I bashfully giggled to myself again.

My mother's bursting laugh pulled me from my daydream. She must've heard my thoughts and was finding them to be quite amusing.

She leaned over and kissed my forehead. *"You'll have to make sure to tell your papa what you think about that,"* she said, laughing brightly, and then winked. *"Trust me, it'll make his day!"*

Then she patted my hand. *"Any more questions?"*

"Just…one," I said and fearfully frowned.

"What is it, my baby?" she asked, sensing the tension in my voice.

"Today is my birthday." I paused. *"But it's also the date that… Rebecca…died."*

As my words tumbled out, a flash of pain crossed her eyes.

I gulped hard, and my sight dropped to the tabletop. *"How do you stand it?"* I mumbled, not wanting to look back into her eyes, not wanting to see her pain. *"How do you pretend to be happy for me every year?"*

She took a gulp of air, and I could tell that she was trying very hard not to cry. *"Leesie, honey,"* she whispered softly. *"I do celebrate your birthday with you every year. I'm so thankful that we have you, and so is your papa."*

She paused, choosing her words carefully. *"Still, I also mourn the death of Rebecca, but that's not something I can let myself dwell upon. If I did, I'd go mad."*

She leaned over, put our heads together, and held mine against hers. *"I try to view this day, your day, as a celebration of you, not as a loss of her."*

A tear fell from her cheeks and landed on the table between us.

I raised my head, gazing into the lovely emerald eyes of my mother, the eyes that exactly mirrored my own, and wondered how my sister could ever cause her pain.

"Why, Mama? Why was Rebecca so hateful to you? I overheard what Mr. Cole said about her. Why?"

She sat up and wiped the tears away from her eyes with her delicate hands. *"Rebecca never forgave me for the fact that she didn't have…a father. Well, she didn't have a father that shared her blood, at least."*

She looked the other away as if ashamed. *"She didn't want your papa to marry me. She felt that I didn't deserve a decent man like him. And for a long time, neither did I."* She took a steadying breath, attempting to steal herself away from the hurtful memories of the past. *"But that's over now."*

A deep chill ran down my spine, as if a shock of icy water were pressing against my soul. All of a sudden, I was putting things together in my mind. Things that didn't seem to fit, but I knew must be the same. Then I recalled what I'd seen happen between my parents.

"Mama?" I barely whispered. *"What you told me about you and Papa?"* I paused, sucking back an impending sob of fear. *"Is that how you got…me? Is that how Papa and you made me?"*

She softly gasped, and then she nodded.

I glanced away from her. I couldn't bear to look at her while I asked the next question. *"And, Rebecca? What about her?"* My mouth went dry as fear choked my throat.

"That's complicated, Lees…" Her soft voice trailed off as if she didn't know what to say to me.

My mind was baffled, and a sudden darkness gripped my chest.

"YOU and THAT man?" I yelled, appalled by the thought.

I jumped up from the chair, causing it to fall over behind me and stood, glaring at my mother in disbelief.

She couldn't! She wouldn't! Not with that horrible man!

Gradually, though, a notion crept into my head, one that caused the icy water in my soul to solidify into a glacier. The ice then turned to heat as my blood began to boil. Fire steadily swelled up in my chest, melting the ice and turning it into a molten rage. Angry tears rushed and pooled in my eyes.

Slowly, I turned, lifted the chair back up, and sat down, my body seething with fury.

"That's how Charles Marshal hurt my mama. That's what he did. That's how he hurt her," I mumbled to myself, shaking my head, attempting to rid my brain of the sudden horrifying images streaking through it—almost as if I remembered the attack.

But how could I remember? I wasn't even born yet…

"Leesie, baby…" Mama murmured, trying to take my hand, but I wrenched it away and stared, unseeing, into her startled eyes.

But what's the difference? I didn't know what to think. I didn't know what to do.

I threw my hands up over my face. *"I don't understand... I don't understand..."* I whispered that phrase over and over again, rocking back and forth in my chair, violently shaking.

My mother knew in an instant what I had understood.

As she reached for me, a dark shadow swept through me, grabbing hold of my mind. I tried to shake it off, but it cackled and dug deeper—deeper within the depths of my consciousness. I attempted to take a breath, but the fire in my chest was too intense. It scorched my throat as I tried to pull air into my heaving lungs. It was as if the blistering darkness had ripped a cavern into my chest, choking me and suffocating my light.

My core blazed into an inferno.

My head was filled with thoughts of that man touching my sweet mama. The ghastly images streaked through my mind.

I wanted to cause him pain! I longed to send him into a hole deeper than the one I was falling into. My very being ached to see him suffer—to die!

I attempted to take another breath, but all I could do was gasp.

Without warning, I heard a loud pop, and then something unseen exploded in a violent burst around us, throwing slivers of jagged debris into my face.

My head spun, and pain more intense than I ever imagined possible took up the entire area of my body, leaving me writhing in agony. Every fiber of my being was alight with despair.

I pictured that man hurting and touching my mother—just like Papa did.

But he doesn't hurt her. Papa wouldn't, would he? Is that why he was worried? Is that why he thought she might be scared? But she said he never hurt her! She said it!

With that thought, I plummeted into the fiery pit within myself. The darkness pulled me down, deeper down, drowning me in its dank clutches.

"Absinthe..." the darkness whispered into my mind.

And then all the lights went out.

Only, just before the shadow consumed me, Mama reached out, grabbing a firm hold of me with her light, pressing her forehead against my own. Her tears oozed down my cheeks.

Then she was in my head, in my very consciousness, trying to calm my mind, her gentle might affording me a trifle of breath.

In response to my mother's power, the shade lifted just a bit, allowing her sweet, sinless soul to take me away, if only for a moment.

I breathed, and a soothing wave of cold air seemed to pass straight through me as she held our heads together and continued to cry. With her gentle breeze came a feeling of serenity.

I took another long, quick breath, and the fissure in my soul closed up just a bit. Her softness sent the sweltering heat away from me, away from my burning essence.

Then her soothing voice filled my mind. It was a soft hum, a lullaby from my past, one that she sang to me when I was a baby.

With her arms wrapped around me, holding me close to her bosom, her fresh lilac-infused breeze swept all remaining remnants of the oppressive heat and the dusky shadow away from my soul. The fresh breeze afforded me tranquility.

The breeze shifted, turning into a calming wind, further easing the fire, lifting me out of the bottomless cavern.

Finally, the wind ceased, and she sent a rush of warmth through me.

In my mind, I envisioned a golden beam, radiating from her consciousness to mine.

Just like my dream.

The light was a living piece of her soul, and it felt as if she were sending a fragment of her own essence into me. I sighed just as our joined consciousness parted, and a deep sense of calm washed over me.

When it was over, Mama returned to her chair. She tearfully gazed down into my weary eyes.

I was sitting on the floor.

A massive coat of goosebumps rushed over my body. My mind was exhausted from our ordeal, but I *had* to know the truth.

"Mama? Does Papa hurt you like that man did?"

I was terribly afraid to hear the answer, especially considering she had promised never to lie to me again. But before she uttered even a single word, my weary head spun and my stomach twisted. Suddenly nauseous, I put my head in my hands, painfully sobbing.

The chair she sat in scraped across the floor. Then she swept through the kitchen. I heard the gentle swish of her robe as she moved across the wooden floor. After a moment, she sat beside me, touching my face, and gently stroked my cheeks with a wet cloth. As she touched me, a stinging sensation I hadn't noticed until that moment ran across my face and forehead, causing me to flinch and look up.

I looked into the weary eyes of my mother, and with a feeling of shock, realized that she had cuts on her face, too. I glanced down at her hands; they, too, were injured. Still, she continued to fuss over me. There was blood on the cloth she was using, and most of it seemed to be *hers*.

Then I saw the reason for our wounds: Papa's coffee cup lay shattered to pieces on the table.

"Did I do that? Did my anger, my fire, cause that?" I weakly muttered.

Mama stroked my cheek with her injured hand. *"You didn't mean to, my baby. It was an accident,"* she whispered back, trying to reassure me, but there was fear in her eyes. She pushed my head down onto her shoulder. We both sat on the kitchen floor together, clinging to each other and weeping.

She hadn't answered my question. But at that moment, I didn't care. I hurt her.

I hurt my mama! That was a thought too painful to bear.

I caused her harm, but how?

My mind spun anew, and I dissolved into a puddle in her arms.

Just then, Papa walked through the door into the kitchen with a shy smile on his face. His smile soon turned to a look of panic when he saw us lying on the floor clutching each other and sobbing.

Suddenly terrified, he hurried to us. He lifted Mama first and then me back into our seats. He crouched down in the space between our chairs, placing one gentle hand on each of our wounded faces, staring horrorstruck at us and smoothing his fingers over our many injuries.

"What happened?" he whispered.

Mama shook her head. *"That doesn't matter right now."* She closed her eyes for a moment, trying to halt her tears. *"Leesie wants to know the difference, Asa. She knows what Charles did to me, and she's afraid that you harm me while we're intimate. She doesn't understand…the difference."*

Papa's eyes widened; he understood. Wordlessly, he stretched up to Mama, tenderly kissed her forehead and took her hand, careful not to touch any of the various cuts covering her hands and face. Then he stood up, lifted her out of the chair she was sitting in, sat down, and returned her to his lap. Papa hugged her close for a moment, attempting to soothe her fraying emotions.

As I watched the soothing, peaceful way he handled my mother, my fears began to lessen.

He could never hurt her. He loves her. He loves both of us too much to cause us harm. There must be a difference, but what is it?

Just as that thought crossed my mind, Papa scooted my chair over to theirs, so it was sitting directly in front of them. He wiped the tears from my eyes with his fingertips and placed his palm flat against my face. *"Tell me, angel."* He spoke softly. *"Does that hurt?*

Does my palm against your cheek cause you pain? If I touched you as I am now, would it hurt you? Does it scare you?"

I felt his warm hand on my cheek. "No," I whispered, confused. *"Why would that hurt or scare me? I like it when you do that, Papa. It makes me feel loved and cherished."*

He removed his hand from my face. Then, holding it up in front of him, he harshly slapped his hands together.

I flinched.

"Now," he asked. *"If I were to hit you on the cheek just like I did my hand, would that hurt you? Would that scare you?"*

I nodded. *"Yes, it would…"* My eyes widened.

He smiled and pressed his warm hand against my cheek for the second time. *"That, is the difference, my love,"* he whispered. *"You see, baby, two different people can perform a nearly identical act, but one is kind and loving while the other is cruel and violent. One is meant to be a joyful expression of love while the other is intended only to harm, scare, and intimidate. But the acts themselves can be almost identical."* He hugged Mama tight. *"Do you understand?"*

I paused for a moment, thinking about his words, and about what I had witnessed of their love earlier that morning.

"You would never hurt her?" I asked.

Oh, yes, I see…

Mama put her soft hand to my worried face. *"In that vision of yours, my baby, did I seem frightened to you?"*

I reflected for a moment on the vision; then my mind swept back to what I had witnessed of my parents earlier that morning.

In both instances, she was happy. She was joyful!

"No, you seemed…happy," I beamed. Then I leaped from my chair and threw my arms around them both, planted a hard, wet kiss on Papa's cheek, and closed my eyes in veneration.

Thank you, Lord! Thank you for giving Mama and me such a gentle soul as my papa!

My father wrapped his arm around my waist and pulled me onto his lap next to my mother.

As he held her, Mama put her lips to his ear. *"Thank you for making her understand, baby. I didn't know what to tell her."* Then she laid her head down on his shoulder, contentedly sighing as she held his hand.

I sat staring at her hand. It was so small compared to his. I knew that he could crush it if he wanted to. He could crush it to dust. But he never would. My heart melted as I watched them—her tiny hand entwined with his, his free hand gently tangled in her hair.

I knew then that *someday* Kristofer and I would be just like them.

Hmm. Maybe what happened between them wouldn't be so bad to try with Kristofer after all...

Then, remembering my dream, I got up from Papa's lap and stood in front of them, breaking their mesmerizing gaze.

"Mama," I said slowly, hesitantly. *"I have something to show you."*

She sat up, eyeing me curiously. *"What is it, my baby?"*

I stood in silent contemplation for a moment, trying to decide how best to express what I wanted to say.

"That vision," I began, nervously biting my lower lip. *"The one I had last night. I've been having it for a long time."*

"So have I, angel. So have I," Papa chimed in and then nuzzled Mama's neck. *"And it finally came true..."*

"Yes, but last night was different."

"How so?" He appeared intrigued.

I looked into his beautiful pale, steel-blue eyes. *"It was different this time because this time, I got to see her as you do! I got to see her light!"*

I took Mama's hand. *"Would you like to see what you look like to Papa?"*

Mama stared at me, seemingly dazed, saying nothing. She only nodded.

Without a beat, I reached over and took both sides of her head in my hands. I leaned in, placing my head on hers. My forehead stung a bit, but I didn't care. My mama needed to see the vision.

We both closed our eyes, and I sent images into her mind from mine. The vision unfolded, and her breath stuttered as she beheld herself in an entirely foreign way—the way of her light.

I looked deeper, remembering every moment in perfect detail… for her.

When I saw the vision the night before, I didn't think it was possible for her to be any lovelier, but it was even more breathtaking the second time.

Seeing her own divine glow, her shallow breath hitched as her robe dropped and as she saw her skin shimmering in the moonlight. Then she laughed, witnessing herself being surprised by Papa.

The last memory was of my mother, placing her bare hands on my father's chest. Her resonating light reflected off his skin, making him appear to glisten as she did.

I stopped at that moment, much too shy to go on any further.

When it was over, she sat up and gazed into my eyes. *"Do you have any conception of how much I love you? And how lucky I am to have you as…my daughter?"*

Her words were like sweet music in my head. My heart sang!

Then she turned to my father and put a hand to his face. *"I had no idea,"* she softly muttered.

Papa's eyes welled. *"Now do you see why I can't pull my eyes away from your beauty? Your light shines bright, sweetheart, and it shines only for me…"*

All of a sudden, a thought pulled Papa's attention away from us. He stood, placed Mama back into her seat, and ran out of the room. He returned a few moments later with his hands hidden behind his back, his face beaming.

"I have something for you both, a gift to celebrate the day that our beautiful baby girl was born, Ali." His eyes swept over us. *"Hold out your hands."*

Mama and I eagerly complied.

He dropped something shiny into each of our outstretched palms.

I looked down. It was a lovely charm in the shape of a silver crescent moon. The charm had two shining emeralds at the very top, and it hung from a delicate silver chain.

I held it up to the light coming through the kitchen window. The charm caught the sun, sparkling and glimmering, sending prisms of light cascading off the walls around us.

I glanced at Mama. She had one, too, only, hers was gold and in the shape of a sunburst.

Because her light is golden. And Papa can't see my light; he doesn't know my colors. That's why my charm is silver. But why the sun and the moon?

Hmm. I'll have to ask Kristofer what color I am. The thought of my boy sent a joyful shiver through my body.

I jumped up, nearly leaping into my father's arms, hugging him as tight as I possibly could just as Mama threw her arms around him and kissed his lips at the same time as me.

Papa beamed the widest smile I'd ever seen, but his delighted smile swiftly turned to disbelief. He gaped at the two of us. Then the surprise turned to astonishment and then…to fright. He dropped down in the chair, looking us up and down.

Mama and I peered at him, confused.

"Ali," he said, after a minute. *"Stand right next to Leesie."*

She obeyed, standing next to me.

She and I looked at one other, both gasping at the same time. Her mouth hung slack, and she was considering me with alarm.

I was the same height as her. She and I were eye to eye.

"What happened?" I asked, but for a moment, I didn't recognize my own voice. For a moment, I thought Mama had spoken. But it wasn't her. It was *me*. In just a few minutes' time, my voice had changed. It was softer, older, just like hers.

"She grew at least three years older in just a few minutes!" Papa exclaimed, gesturing toward me. *"But, how?"*

"Well," Mama stammered. *"Not in a few minutes, maybe a week. I noticed her growth spurt the last few days, Asa."* She gave him a reluctant smile. *"Perhaps she's going through puberty; that's all. She is twelve, honey. I grew a bit when I was twelve although it took me all summer to grow a few inches. Still, Lees has grown more now, but she probably won't again for a while, maybe not anymore at all."*

"I've heard of children sprouting up overnight, but not in just a few minutes, Ali. This is ridiculous! Look at her, she looks like a woman!"

I wanted to shrink down and crawl under the table. He sounded almost angry.

Angry with me?

Papa threw his head down onto the table, making a loud thudding sound and groaning low in his throat.

"I'm sorry, Papa, I didn't mean to grow," I barely whispered in my new softer voice.

He raised his head, forced a smile, and then held his hands out to me. There was still worry in his eyes.

Without pause, I took his hands. *"Maybe it's because…I'm different. I'm sorry I'm so abnormal."*

Papa's expression softened. He put his palm flat against my cheek and tenderly smiled. *"I just don't want you to grow up too quickly, angel. That's all. I love you just the way you are. You are not abnormal!"*

Mama smiled. *"Baby,"* she said to me. *"Go get dressed. Wear something pretty. The Coles are coming for supper tonight to celebrate your birthday with us."*

My father stiffened and then frowned and let go of my hands.
"*The...boy...is coming here...today?*" he incredulously spat.

Mama nodded and bit her lip.

His mouth gaped open for a moment and it seemed as if he wanted to say something, but he quickly shut it again. He groaned and pointed at me, his eyes darting between my new body and my mother's wide eyes.

Wordlessly, my father threw his head back down onto the table again. His forehead made another loud thudding sound as it connected with the hardwood.

15. Butterflies

I ran out of my bedroom and down the stairs. My parents were in the kitchen. They were talking—discussing me.

I stopped by the open kitchen doorway and peeked in.

Papa was stroking the cuts on my mother's face. *"How exactly did this happen, Ali?"*

"I don't know. It seemed like some sort of an emotional burst," Mama whispered then shuddered. *"It happened right after she realized what Charles did to me."* She choked back a sob and shook her head. *"It was my worst nightmare realized, Asa. I never wanted her to know about that—about my shame!"* She put her head in her hands, sobbing.

Oh, no, Mama!

Papa shifted forward in his chair and pulled her into his lap. He cradled her against his chest. *"It's not your shame, Ali. He hurt you. It wasn't your fault."*

"I went to him that night! I chose to go! I'll never forgive myself for being unfaithful to you, and I'll never understand why you chose to be with me despite what I did. You deserve so much better." Guilt overshadowed my mother's eyes. She peeked up, and her sights darted between my father's face and her wringing hands.

"Shut your mouth!" Papa spat. He clenched her wrists, gripping them between his fists. His eyes flared with sudden anger; his jaw was tight and pulsing with tension. Then he pulled her closer, staring her dead in the eyes. All the while, her whole body quaked with dry sobs. *"I swear to God almighty, Ali, if you ever say anything like that again, I will take you over my knee, and I won't give a damn about*

your fear of pain! How can you possibly think about last night, not to mention that little girl upstairs, and still say those words to me? How?"

After a moment, he paused, taking deep breaths and closed his eyes. Pained tears dripped down his cheeks.

He pressed his forehead to hers, apparently attempting to settle himself. *"I'm sorry,"* he whispered. *"I never want to hurt you, but it shatters me to hear you speak of my love for you in such a frivolous manner, as if it's something you don't deserve. You have never been unfaithful to me—not ever. Our love is perfect. You are everything to me. I need you desperately. Don't you know that? Didn't I prove that to you last night? I thought we were past all that ugliness."*

He reopened his brilliant eyes and stared into hers. *"You and I are linked souls. Someday, I'll make that connection soul-deep. I swear, I will. I'll make it holy. Then you can tell me just how undeserving you are!"*

Releasing her wrists, he took her face between his palms; his eyes blazed with strength. *"You did not have an affair with that monster, Ali. The man ra—"*

"No! Stop! Please!" Mama recoiled and pressed her fingers to his lips. She let out a shuddering gasp. Obviously winded by his words, she buried her face against his shoulder. *"Please, don't! I'm sorry! I'm so sorry!"*

Soul-deep? Holy? What does that mean? And what didn't she want him to say?

Papa crushed her to his heaving chest and then kissed her head several times in rapid succession, attempting to soothe away the sting of his threat. *"No, don't be sorry. Just don't say that again. Please, Ali, I can't take it. It tears me apart to hear you devalue yourself, and our love, in such a way. Now tell me what happened with Lees. Please, tell me."*

After a moment's pause, Mama sat up and ditched the tears in her eyes away with her fingertips. *"It was frightening. I felt the rage running straight through Lees's body. And what's worse, she had no control over it.*

I'm worried about you doing something hasty, but when it comes to protecting me, I think she's worse than even you! I'm afraid she might end up getting herself hurt, or worse…shattering!

I had to blend with her, Asa. I had to pull her from wherever it was her mind sent her! It was a distant, dark place—almost like dwelling amidst a shadow. It was like nothing I've ever experienced. I mean, I've crossed all types before. But this, this was something different. I've never been frightened of spirits—even mentally disturbed ones—but this shadow or whatever it was frightened even me!"

Oh, wow! Mama felt it, too.

Papa seemed astounded. *"You blended with her?"*

He paused for a moment, staring down at the table, his eyes fixed and unmoving. *"A shadow? Why does that seem familiar?"* he distractedly mumbled under his breath.

Mama ran her fingers through his hair. *"What seems familiar?"* she whispered.

He shook his head, his brow tightly knitted, staring down at the table again and thinking. *"I don't know. Just déjà vu, I guess…"*

Papa shook the thought from his mind. *"Now tell me about when you blended with Lees."*

"I always knew I could blend with her although I've never tried it, not before today, simply because there was no need." She looked him dead in the eyes. *"But today, today was absolutely necessary. I had to get whatever that shadow was away from her—and quickly. Her very existence was in jeopardy; I'm sure of it."*

Blending? What's blending? I thought, and then I remembered feeling Mama's essence pulling me from the dark place. *Oh, something else only she and I can do…*

"Perhaps it was simply her emotions coming to the surface," Papa offered.

"*I'm not sure. Whatever it was, I pray that it never returns though I fear it will. Unless I can teach Leesie to control her emotions, the darkness will return.*"

"*Poor girl. Her only desire in this world is to be just like you in every way.*" He paused. "*And though she is the image of you on the outside, on the inside, she is me, through and through.*"

Mama tearfully smiled and put the back of her hand to his face. "*I love that she's like you, my sweet. Especially the fierce way that she loves. She loves just like you do—completely, sometimes irrationally. And she's passionate about things, like you are.*"

She softly laughed. "*Our daughter is a force to be reckoned with; that's for sure! She set me in the mind of an erupting volcano today!*" She glanced down at her injured hands. "*I believe I'm still stronger right now, but very soon, I may not be. I mean, I can't do what she did today. I have to find a way to tame her power, Asa.*"

Papa interjected. "*You mean, you and I have to find a way to tame her, not just her power. And in light of what happened with the boy yesterday, we might have to take a firmer hand with her from now on.*" He wiped a few scattered tears from her eyes. "*Don't worry, sweetheart. Leesie loves us, and she respects us. And you incite a certain amount of fear into her, as well. That's definitely helpful!*"

He laughed and then tipped his head to one side, searching my mother's face. "*So tell me. If Lees is a volcano, then what does that make…you?*"

He sat back in his seat, his arms crossed, eyeing her inquiringly.

My mother let out a small, tear-filled laugh and weakly smiled. "*I'm not sure. What force of nature is stronger than a volcano?*"

Papa reached out and grasped her hand. "*A mother's love?*"

"*Definitely,*" she whispered, trying to hold back more tears.

A few moments later, my father took a deep breath and kissed Mama's hand. "*You know, I've noticed something—especially today.*

I've noticed that you and Leesie seem to be mirrored images of one another—opposites. On the inside, at least."

He thought for a second. *"In fact, even the colors of your light are contrary."* He lifted the sunburst charm off her chest, smoothing his fingers over it.

Mama seemed taken aback. *"You think Leesie and I are… opposites?"*

"Polar opposites, actually. You said it yourself, Ali. Leesie is explosive while you are tranquil. She's strong and forceful, akin to an erupting volcano, while you are more akin to the wind. Still active, still a force to be reckoned with, only instead of raw, explosive power, you are calm tranquility. Nevertheless, you are still a powerful force. Lees is just a bit more volatile than you are. The two of you are fire and air, sweetie."

He paused, his eyes sweeping down to her charm once again. *"The two of you are the sun and the moon—le soleil et la lune. Still, as unstable as Leesie's capricious personality is, one look into your placid eyes, and her fire is put out."*

Mama frowned and glanced down at where the charm lay close to her heart. *"But if what you say is true, Asa, considering her explosive, volatile power, shouldn't Lees be the sun, and I the moon?"*

He thought for a moment, scratching his stubbly chin with his long index finger. *"Well, the sun is almighty. It is raw, static power. In essence, the sun is the center of our solar system. It is the axis of absolute control. What's more, everything revolves around the sun. It gives life. Alternately, the moon is a bit more enigmatic. In fact, the term 'lunatic' originated from the word 'luna,' meaning 'moon.' The moon is powerful. It sets the tide, at times causing violent and volatile shifts within the ocean's current. At first glance, it may seem harmless, but, in reality, it is a mysterious and inexplicable power, much like a sleeping volcano. Lees and you truly are le soleil et la lune. Besides that, the Lord himself chose to brand you both as such."*

His eyes twinkled wickedly. *"And how I loved kissing that sweet beauty mark of yours last night, my beautiful wife…"*

"I am calm, and Leesie is volatile. We are opposites, the sun and the moon…" Mama's voice trailed off as if attempting to take it all in.

"Yes, Lees is volatile, yet she is calmed by you, sweetheart. But then again, I guess one could say the same about me." Papa kissed Mama's hand, bringing her attention back to him. *"Take yesterday, for instance. I was ready to kill that bastard!"* He shuddered with anger. *"But with a single gaze into those lovely, serene eyes and a mere taste of your sweet, fragrant lips, my heart was inflamed, but my wrath was calmed. Now that's what I call absolute control."*

"I don't control you, Asa. I never have. You know that!"

He nodded. *"Yes, I do know it, but just think about it. Lees is fire, and you are air, but which is the more powerful element?"*

Mama frowned.

Papa leaned in closer. *"Fire can neither live nor breathe without air. Just think about that,"* he whispered. Then their lips met.

Before yesterday, seeing my parents kissing would have captivated my attention. But as I sat eavesdropping on them for the third time in less than a day, I couldn't keep my father's words out of my mind. I looked down and ran my fingers over the charm that hung around my neck, his words ominously echoing through my mind.

"We're…opposites?" I muttered under my breath. Then I stood, stepped through the kitchen doorway, and softly cleared my throat. *"Mama?"*

My mother stopped kissing Papa and peeked into my eyes. She sheepishly grinned, wiping his lips with her thumb. *"You're not dressed yet?"*

I shyly shrugged. *"My clothes don't fit anymore. None of them do."* I shook my head and pointed to my chest *"Here."* I flashed a guilty look toward Papa and then gestured to my changed body. *"Here, too."* I bit my lip. *"And they're also too short. I didn't even bother trying them on. They're all just too small…"*

Papa threw his forehead back down onto the table, making a thudding noise again. Again, I wanted to disappear. My face turned a bright shade of puce.

Mama sympathetically smiled and held her hand out to me. *"Well, I guess you'll just have to wear one of mine. I'm sure you'll fit just beautifully into any one of them."*

She eyed me for a moment, quickly assessing my new figure, and then nodded. *"Yes, I believe we're just about the same size now."*

My father groaned at the same time, begrudgingly releasing her from his lap.

With my hand in hers, she pulled me up the stairs and into her former bedroom. Once inside, she opened her wardrobe for me and swept her hand across the row of dresses inside. *"It's your day, my baby,"* she brightly declared. *"Choose anything you like."*

She pointed toward the full-length mirror sitting in the corner of the room. *"Use the mirror to see how you like the dress you've chosen. Underlings are in the bottom drawer as are several pairs of stockings. Take what you like."*

She kissed my lips. *"I'll be right back. I'd better check on your papa—to make sure he hasn't given himself a concussion!"* she laughed, leaving the room and shutting the door behind her. I knew the real reason she left was to give me privacy.

Just as the door closed, I took a deep breath and wandered around the bed to my mother's full-length mirror and then stood right in front of it, frowning. It looked ominous and foreboding as if it were going to show me a lie.

Breathe. Just breathe…

I tilted my head and thought for a moment. After all, it was still me, just an older me.

"A different me," I fretfully whispered.

I heaved another deep breath and slipped my too-short nightgown over my head. Then, with my eyes closed, I stepped out of my tight underthings. I stood still for a few minutes, my eyes shut tight—afraid to look.

Why did this happen so fast? Why can't I just be normal? And what was that dark shadow, the one that frightened Mama? Is she right? Will the darkness return? And if it's not a spirit, then what is it?

My heart fluttered, and my breath hastened. *Be calm. For heaven's sake, just look!* I silently scolded myself. *What's there to be afraid of? It's just my own body.*

I paused for a moment, allowing my senses to take over, silently feeling the many new sensations of my changed body. First, my legs were sore. In fact, they felt fatigued as if I had just run a few miles—or climbed a dozen trees. And, second, my chest ached but not from the inside. I mindlessly swept my hands over the skin of my new breasts, apprehensively fingering the odd mounds that weren't there earlier in the day. They were tender, almost as if the surrounding flesh was being stretched. And my back ached, too.

I wonder if this is normal. Should I ask Mama?

The thought of showing her my body sent a warm flush rushing across my skin. *Why am I embarrassed? I never have been before. Not in front of her…*

Finally, I took a deep, cleansing breath and slowly opened my eyes. I stood silently staring for a moment, in awe of the stranger reflecting back at me. I inclined my head to the right, my eyes drifting up and down, silently assessing.

The stranger was much too tall to be me. Her face was longer and thinner than mine, and her body, though a bit smaller, looked more like it should belong to my mother than to me.

I swiveled to the side.

The girl's torso was long, and her waist curved inward, giving her an elegant hourglass shape. *"She's me. She's really me,"* I distractedly muttered, spinning around, taking in all the changes in me, and viewing myself from every angle.

The image of my mother's body danced through my mind, reminding of how lovely she had looked bathed in the moonlight and how all of a sudden my own body seemed to echo hers.

"I even have a bosom!" I giggled to myself.

Then my eyes swept down to the sparse patch of fire-red hair that, within an hour's time, had abruptly sprouted up between my legs. I cocked my head to and fro. *Hmm…the color is darker than Mama's. Then again, so is the hair on my head—much darker.*

I bashfully bit my lip. *I can get used to this, I guess…*

Although, with that thought, another more worrying notion crept into my head. *I wonder what Kristofer will think of me now. What if he doesn't like me anymore?* I thought darkly just as Mama cracked open the door and peeked in. Startled, I wrapped my arms around my new chest and turned away from her.

"Oh, I'm sorry, sweetie. I thought you'd be dressed by now. I'll leave you alone…"

I spun back around, dropped my hands, and stretched one out toward her before she could close the door. Even though I felt a slight flush creeping across my skin, I desperately wanted her with me. *I need her with me. She's my mama, and I have questions…*

"No, Mama, please, don't go…"

She reached for my hand as I walked forward, closing the door behind her.

I tugged her back to the mirror. She stood behind me, running her fingers down the length of my waist-long bright-red hair. *"What do you think?"* she asked, gently petting my head, and then smiled at my reflection.

I frowned. *"I'm not sure yet. It's all so sudden,"* I whispered, glancing into her reflection in the mirror.

"I'm sore." I paused, and my sight dropped. I bashfully bit my lip. *"My legs, my back, and…"* My eyes flit back to hers. *"And, my, my bosoms."*

My mother nodded and kissed the back of my head. *"Just growing pains, my baby. We'll draw you a warm bath this evening. It will soothe the pain."*

"Why did this happen so quickly? I don't understand. This doesn't happen to normal people. What makes us so…different?"

With that, she swept across the room to the wardrobe without answering my question. She opened the wardrobe doors. She took out a lavender dress and then held it up in front of her, considering it for a moment. *"Yes, this one will look lovely on you, sweetie."* Then she opened the bottom drawer, grabbed a pair of bloomers, stockings, and a small corset, and returned to where I was standing. She held the dress up in front of me.

I smiled. She was right, the dress was lovely. But besides the dress, what I noticed was the reflection of our beautiful necklaces. They sparkled in the reflection of the mirror as she stood behind me. Papa was right. They *were* opposite in every way, even the color. Each pendant twinkled as the sunlight bounced off of it. They were equally beautiful, one just as lovely as the other and each the perfect complement to its match.

Just like Mama and me.

As I stood before the mirror considering my father's words, and while gazing into the eyes of my mother, a question came to mind. *Being opposing parallels of the same power, are she and I destined to be allies or rivals?*

I bit my lip and peeked at her. That was a question that I had no interest in answering.

I hope my powers never surpass yours, Mama, I thought, all the while hoping she wasn't listening. *"I could never challenge you. I hope someday to be your equal but never your superior. I want us to balance one another, not to oppose each other."*

A chill ran down my spine.

"Mama, what are we?" A frightened tear slid down my face.

She wiped my tear with her hand. *"We are people, Lees,"* she adamantly whispered. *"We're just a bit different from most. That is all."* She smiled at my reflection in the mirror although I noticed her eyes, too, were tearful. She shook her head. *"I don't know what you would call us, but we were put here to love and to help the lost souls of this world. And your papa, and others like him—Kristofer, for instance, and Jake, Molly, and your Grandma Maggie—were put here to help us do just that and to enrich our lives by loving us."*

Hearing her speak my grandmother's name again brought a flutter of joy to my heart. As she spoke, Mama helped me into the underlings and corset, and then she pulled the dress over my head and fastened up the buttons running down the back.

I stood back, admiring the stranger in the mirror. The dress fit perfectly. It was so lovely; I couldn't believe that it was me in the dress.

I bashfully, appreciatively smiled at her reflection in the mirror but frowned at my image. *It looks so funny to me that we're the same height.*

Hearing my thought, she laughed. *"You may be equal in height, young lady, but I am still stronger!"* She kissed my head. *"Remember that!"*

"I hope it stays that way forever," I answered back.

Mama didn't say a word. She suddenly seemed pensive, even distracted.

Why? What did I do?

After that, I finished dressing in relative and somewhat uncomfortable silence. My mother seemed to be as deeply lost in thought as I was. She seemed worried and quiet—too quiet.

Oh, Mama, please don't stop talking to me!

She and I still didn't speak at all while she fixed my hair.

I watched her in the mirror. First, she put part of my wavy red hair up in the back, much like she had done with her own hair the day before. Next, she twirled a long curl around her fingers. Then she pulled the long curl over my left shoulder, laying it down on the front of my dress.

When she was done, she stood back and smiled. *"There. All done!"* she brightly exclaimed.

She speaks! Yay! She's not angry with me!

I bit my lip and turned to my reflection, staring at the stranger who stood frowning in front of me and attempting to admire myself in the mirror, but the image still seemed wrong. It looked foreign, and it felt uncomfortable.

"I don't look twelve," I mumbled. *"I look more like fifteen. I look like you did when you met Papa."* I blushed a little.

"You are twelve, Lees," she softly assured, turning me to face her. She placed her hand over my heart. *"Just remember who you are… inside."*

My frown deepened. *"Kristofer looks twelve."*

"He'll catch up, baby," she said and then kissed my forehead.

With that, she swept around me to her bureau, opened the top drawer, took out a book, and then handed it to me with a knowing glint int her eyes. It was the *Romeo and Juliet* book she had taken from me a few weeks prior. *"Here,"* she said, her eyes glowing. *"I think you've earned this back."*

I flashed a timid smile and handed it back to her. *"Thank you, but I don't need it. I had the whole thing memorized before you took it away from me,"* I giggled.

Mama sneered at me, playfully swatting my behind with the book, and sternly pointed. *"You are entirely incorrigible!"* she brightly declared, laughing, her emerald eyes twinkling.

My Mama's so beautiful!

Just then, Papa opened the door, chuckling from the doorway *"It's been my experience that most beautiful little red-headed witches are incorrigible! And I should know, I have two!"* His eyes twinkled playfully as he eyed my mother. Then his gaze swept from her to me and then back again, quickly glancing between us. I noticed tears welling in his eyes. He shook his head. *"My God, she looks just like you, Ali,"* he said to Mama. *"You're absolutely stunning, Lees."* He held his arms out to me.

I ran to him, hugging him around his neck. *"Does this mean you won't be hitting your head on the table anymore?"*

Papa grinned and Mama laughed.

He released me and peered down into my eyes. *"I'll probably do that until the day you get married, and then I'll just have to learn to cope with it…somehow."* He choked back a tear and kissed my forehead. He snaked his arm around Mama's waist, holding us both to his chest. *"Overprotective fool?"* he mumbled into her ear.

She stretched up on her toes, kissed him, and wiped away a few scant tears from his eyes. *"You love us, and you protect us, my beautiful husband. That's not a job for a fool."*

He gazed down at her.

"Are you still angry with me?" she meekly muttered.

"No." He kissed the tip of her nose.

"Do you still want to punish me?" Her voice was small, hesitant, and almost fearful.

Papa blew out a deep, emotional breath and held her tighter. *"No, baby."* Taking her face between his palms, he gazed down into her tear-filled eyes. *"I'd never punish you. Throw you over my knee and give you a good swat on the behind—yes. Punish you, hurt you—no. What I want is to take it all away from you, but I can't. That's what hurts the most."*

Mama buried her face into his chest.

"*Papa?*" I said, suddenly remembering that I wanted to ask him something.

He looked down at me. "*What is it, angel?*" His eyes were tearful.

"*Why were you playing the piano in the middle of the night last night?*" He frowned. "*I wasn't.*"

"*I heard it most of the night! Quit teasing me, Papa!*" I giggled. "*It's all right. I love when you play all night!*"

A sudden look of comprehension fell over his face; he eyed my mama. "*Ali,*" he began, and a sly grin crept across his face. "*Why would Leesie hear piano music in the middle of the night—in—her—head?*" He emphasized the last three words and then raised his brow.

Mama glanced down at the ground for a moment, and then, gradually, her eyes met his. "*I love the way you play. Sometimes, I let your music run through my mind…all night.*"

I gasped. "*Mama! I was listening to your mind?*" Wow!

She bashfully nodded just as my father caught her around the waist and then crushed her to his chest. "*God, I've missed you, woman!*" he breathlessly whispered. "*Did you really miss my…music… that much?*"

She closed her eyes and held him tighter. "*You have no idea. You are everything to me, too. And you're right. Our love is perfect. I'm so sorry I ever thought otherwise.*"

"*Uh huh. I knew you played…to…my mama!*" I grinned at them both, but I don't think they heard me.

Papa kissed my mother's forehead. "*Just out of curiosity, why do you like the piano so much?*" he asked, canting his head to one side.

She bashfully smiled. "*I love it, Asa, because you play the piano in exactly the same way as you play…me.*" She heaved a quivering sigh. "*Slowly, deliberately, with feeling. You put everything you have into it. When you play either the piano or me, you captivate me entirely.*" She coyly shrugged. "*What can I say? I am a slave to your talented hands, my love.*"

Huh? Papa plays...her? What does that mean?

I glanced at my mother. She was gazing up into Papa's eyes; they were both breathless. *And there's that LOOK again!*

Papa threw his head back, laughing. *"I like that answer!"* Then he leaned down. *"Anytime you want, my love, anytime you want, I'll play,"* he whispered, flashing the same sweet, crooked smile he had as a boy.

Finally, he released my mother and glanced down at her clothing. She was still wearing her robe. *"You're not even dressed yet?"* he asked, laughing.

Without another word, he walked around her to her wardrobe, opened it, and went through each one of her dresses one by one until he found what he was searching for. He pulled the dress from the cupboard. *"Hmm...yes,"* he appreciatively muttered, studying it for a moment.

It was a pale, shimmering-green dress with intricately sewn lace and pearls running down the front and back. The neckline was fashioned into a low-cut square shape, and the bodice was form-fitted. The sleeves were made of cream-colored silk that came down just past the elbows and were accentuated by a delicate row of soft ivory lace.

Even though the dress was quite understated, it didn't need much adornment. It was gorgeous the way it was. And I got the feeling from the way my mother glanced between the dress and Papa that *this* was yet another gift from him.

"This one," Papa murmured low in his throat, still considering it. *"This one, I like."* He winked at her and ran the index finger of his free hand up and down the front of her robe. *"And you haven't worn it in quite some time."* He stepped closer and swept his hand down the back of her head, raking her lovely strawberry hair with his long fingers. *"And please, Mrs. Raign, don't tie your hair up, all right?"*

Mama serenely smiled and put her hand out to take the dress from him but stopped, eyeing the wardrobe just as he went to close it. Something inside had caught his eye. Then I, too, saw what it was. It was the same white shirt that my mother had worn the night before—Papa's shirt. It was hanging in the very back of her wardrobe as if…hidden.

Papa chuckled slyly and pulled it forward just enough so she could see it.

I giggled at my mother's deep blush; her eyes were cast down. She reminded me of a child who had just been caught with her hand in the cookie jar.

"*A souvenir?*" Papa asked, apparently enjoying her reaction.

"*Yes,*" she barely breathed. "*That one I'm keeping.*"

Then Mama snatched the dress from Papa's hands and swept from the room and down the stairs, giggling like a schoolgirl the whole way.

Papa's eyes gleamed with excitement. He let the shirt fall back into the wardrobe and darted downstairs after her—laughing.

It feels so good to laugh! Our house is happy!

That joyful thought was broken by a knock at the door, though.

For a moment, my heart faltered, and a sense of fear gripped my chest. I stood on the landing listening as Papa opened the door. However, I had to note that he was still laughing.

All at once, my tension eased: It was Jacob Cole.

I hunkered down by the newel post, so I could see them.

"*You're early, brother,*" Papa told him, glancing around Mr. Cole for the rest of the family.

Brother? Papa called Mr. Cole "brother." My heart lurched again, that time with pleasure.

Mr. Cole stepped in and took my father's proffered hand. "*I wanted to speak to you before we got together tonight,*" he replied and then surprised me by pulling Papa into a huge bear hug. "*Regarding church services tomorrow.*"

After a moment, Papa pulled back, solemnly shaking his head. *"Actually, Jake, I'm glad you came early…"* He hesitated as if searching for the right words. *"I believe we'll have to cancel our plans to attend church in the morning. It seems there have been a few changes in Leesie. Under the circumstances, I don't feel it wise to parade her around town."*

Mr. Cole's eyebrows shot up in surprise. *"Changes? What sort of changes?"*

Oh no! Papa is going to show me off to Kristofer's father!

That horrifying thought burned through my brain. Before I could think of a nice place to hide or figure out how to disappear, Papa hollered up the stairs to me.

"Lees? Come down here for a minute, and say hello to Reverend Cole."

"Damn it!" I cursed under my breath, hoping that Mama's mind window was shut.

Resigned to my humiliation, I took a deep breath, stood up on shaky legs, and slowly scuffled down the stairs. All the while, the butterflies in my stomach fluttered—in fact, they had almost gnawed away at my stomach by the time I reached the bottom step.

Reverend Cole looked up toward me as I came into view. Just as he caught sight of me—of the foreign girl in front of him—he lumbered back a few steps, apparently shocked by my abnormality. His mouth hung open, and his eyes were as wide as saucers. His head whipped around; he gaped between my father and me with a hundred unanswered questions blaring in his eyes, none of which I had a prayer of answering for him. All the while, I swept gracefully toward him, looking just like the mirrored image of my mother.

As I approached I heard a loud gasp from behind the reverend. Kristofer stepped around his father, gaping at me. Then his gape slowly melted into an expression of disbelief and distress. He frowned and shook his head back and forth, scrutinizing my much-matured frame, his mouth hanging open in shock and what seemed to be horror.

The butterflies in my stomach turned into violent hornets, and I feared that I was about to faint or vomit or both. So I just ran!

Mama came out of her room just in time to witness Kristofer's reaction to me. I heard her behind me, but I couldn't stop. I flew past Papa, Mr. Cole, and the boy and went right out the door. I didn't stop running until I passed the orchard, but I twisted my ankle just as I came to the tree line. *"Damned shoes!"* I cried out with all my might, leering up at the clear, blue sky above me. I felt as if it were mocking me with its simplicity, its normalcy.

I raised my head in defiance, pain, and pure hatred for what I was. I raised my head straight into the air, cursing the wind and God and myself and everything else that had caused me to be so damned abnormal!

"You're a witch! You're a witch and a freak and an abomination!" I screamed at myself.

My sore ankle finally gave way, buckling under me and sending me hard onto the dirt. Hot tears screamed down my face.

After a few moments, I lifted my head and glanced around. That's when I noticed that I'd run to the very edge of the orchard. I was sitting right in front of Rebecca's grave.

Without a care in the world, I picked up a rock and threw it as hard as I could at her tombstone. Then I sprang up, wrathfully advancing on it. My ankle protested the weight, but I stood my ground. *"I hate you!"* I screamed at her. *"You had everything! You had everything and you gave it all away! YOU got to be normal! YOU didn't have to HIDE! Mama loved you SO much! How could you be so MEAN to her...to ME?"*

Without warning, something fierce overcame me. I don't know if it was instigated by anger or grief, but its force overtook me with a level of intensity of which I had no idea I was capable. I threw my hands up in front of me, wailing into the air. It was a howl that came from the pit of my core. Then the shadow returned, and with it came an inner sense of fury.

Truthfully, the level of my hopelessness should have been frightening. And it would have been if not for the fact that Kristofer's reaction to me had sent my soul into a cold, dark hole from whence I never wished to escape.

I wailed again, throwing my fists into the air, my every muscle clenched, my soul screeching in agony. *"WHHHHYYYY!"* My head spun with the force of it all. I squeezed my eyes shut, trying to regain my equilibrium, but I felt as though my head might burst.

The heat streaked down from my temples to my neck and then exploded from my fingertips.

I gasped.

The air was taken from me. I couldn't think, let alone *breathe*. I stood motionless and numb, staring helplessly at the flames bursting from my fingers. As I watched, the flames flew up into the air and began to swirl. The flaming twirlblast spun in a violent cyclone above my head, sending shards of brilliant colors into the sky.

The blasts of light began with a vivid surge of golden citrine which erupted into dazzling amaranthine and then deep vermillion red. Then a gush of bright cerulean blue streaks seeped through. The dark blue burst into sparkling azure which faded to a nearly transparent albicant white. Just before I thought the flame was surely going to explode and take me with it straight to Hell, it burst into a pure beam of radiant diamond light.

I flinched, expecting to be burned, but the light wasn't hot; it was soothing. In fact, the light reminded me of how pure love might appear to the naked eye if it could be perceived by mere mortal sight.

The ray shone not only from my fingertips, but the warm light blazed from my chest and then radiated and *burst* forth from my soul itself.

I teetered on one foot, gaping at the magnificent beam that seemed to be illuminating from within me. *Me!*

As I stood gawking, a small form appeared. At first, it was indistinct, almost like looking at a mirage, but then it took shape, and the tiny silhouette of a person emerged. I wasn't sure exactly what it was, or *who*. But then, someone stepped, or rather, hovered, forward. The outlined form reminded me of a jellyfish, moving as if it were more gliding than walking. As it floated toward me, I reached out to touch *her*.

It was a girl.

She stretched her hand out to meet mine, and we touched fingertips. I grabbed hold of her hand, and she smiled although her smile was forlorn, her hazel eyes dark with regret.

Just as she stepped up to me, her translucent appearance faded, and her form steadied, becoming as clear as my own. Simultaneously, the swirling whirlwind stemming from her soul slowly eased until it was absorbed into the pure-white beam shining from within me.

My sister Rebecca smiled.

"Hello, little sister," she tearfully choked, beaming a bright, lovely smile—my mother's smile—while tears ran down her face. *"You are the image of our beautiful mama."*

I couldn't speak. I wanted to say something, anything, but my mind was blank.

Before I could compose myself, Rebecca's expression changed again from bright and shining back to weary. She looked down at the headstone that lay in ruin beside us. Apparently as a result of my rage, it had shattered and was reduced to nothing but a pile of broken pieces. An image of the broken coffee cup from earlier in the day ran through my head.

Sensing my distress, Rebecca stroked my cheek with the back of her hand.

Oh, also just like Mama.

She smiled. *"Don't worry, Leesie,"* she whispered. *"You'll learn to control your power. You always have."*

My sister pulled my chin up until our eyes met, and hers were filled with tears. *"I'm so sorry for the pain I have caused. I was a spoiled, unruly child. I regret everything I put my family through."* Her eyes dropped. *"Especially the way I hurt our mother."* She put her hands in front of her face and wept. *"I didn't understand how to love. She tried to show me. She loved me so much, but I was angry, and I wanted her to hurt as badly as I did. Even though I understood that how I was born wasn't my fault…or hers.*

"Asa wished that I was his child. Sometimes, I'd catch him studying me, trying to see a spark of himself in me, trying to make himself believe that just maybe I was…his. But I wasn't, and he knew it. So did Mama." Her hazel eyes hardened, looking as if they were nearly set in stone. She let out a small, humorless laugh. *"How could I be his? Look at me!"*

She shook her head, and the hard-edged appearance of her eyes solidified into disgust. *"Mousy brown hair and moss-colored eyes, not vivid green, not icy blue…"* Then she let out another cynical snicker. *"I'm nothing like our mother. I am nothing like Asa. They are beautiful."* Her eyes returned to mine. *"You are beautiful. You are the mirrored image—the perfect one."*

"I think you're beautiful," I whispered, attempting to take her hand. She pulled away, and a sudden and disturbing chill ran down my spine. *"And as a matter of fact, I happen to be quite partial to brown hair and hazel eyes."*

Rebecca ignored my comment and went on with her story. *"Asa convinced Mama to send me to a finishing school when I was fourteen. When I returned, they were married, and she was expecting you. That was when we moved here, to the orchard."*

Rebecca's head dropped down. *"Asa was the only real father I ever had, and I tormented him for it. And then you came, and he looked at you with such love. It was the love that I wanted. I was jealous. That jealousy destroyed me. It almost ended their marriage."* She looked up; the tears in her hazel eyes glistened like tiny stars. *"But thanks to you, little sister, Mama and Asa are whole again."*

She clasped my hands. *"Please tell Mama that I love her and that I'm sorry. She asked nothing of me, and that's exactly what I gave to her. I guess that must be why I can't cross over. It is my penance,"* she whispered.

"You're stuck here? You're a ghost?"

She nodded and dropped her hands to her sides, her eyes downtrodden and hopeless.

"Mama can cross you into heaven. She will! She loves you! She loves you just as much as she loves…me." I reached out to take her hand, but she pulled away again.

"I've taken enough from her." Then she raised her sights up to mine, her whole body quaking with dry sobs. *"But will you give her something…from me?"*

"Of course, I will! Anything! You're my sister! I'd do anything for you!" As I said those words, a steady stream of tears ran down my face and dripped onto the front of Mama's dress.

Rebecca stepped forward and took my head into her hands. She pushed my forehead against her own. An image flashed into my mind, and then another and another, all forming a fantastic story within my brain. My sprained ankle ached from under me, and so did my head, but I didn't care. I was utterly astounded by what I was seeing and by what my sister was helping me to *realize*. When the vision was over, she looked into my eyes. *"Thank you"* is all she said. Then she turned to leave.

The tornado, derived from her lost soul, swirled above us once again, threatening to take her away—but to where? She was lost. Where would it take her?

"Wait!" I shouted, holding my hands out to her. *"If you won't let Mama help you, then let me!"*

Rebecca stopped and turned to face me with a sense of disbelief in her eyes. Just as she turned, the cyclone ceased and evaporated into the air above her. She smiled and nodded and then reached out to stroke my face once more before we had to say our goodbyes—our final goodbye.

I precariously hobbled toward her, took both her hands into mine, and peered into her lovely hazel eyes for the last time.

Instantly and without even thinking twice, I sent the radiant, white beam of light out toward my sister. The light—my own power—obeyed my command straight away. This time, the light formed what appeared to be a tunnel that arose from within me and then quickly branched out toward my sister. The light enveloped her completely, bathing her in a soft blanket of glorious serenity and peacefulness. It was the peace that can only be found in Heaven.

She took one step across, passing straight through me and into the blissful happiness that had eluded her for so many years. She paused for a moment and blew a *kiss* in the direction of our house. *"I love you, little sister,"* she whispered to me and then disappeared into my light.

Just as she crossed, my ankle throbbed and gave way, sending me tumbling to the ground. I fell back down in front of her grave; a puddle of tears ran onto the dry earth in front of her shattered tombstone.

All the resentment I had felt for my sister only moments before was now replaced with love, compassion, and a deep-seeded sense of joy because she was finally at peace.

I raised my head and glanced toward our little farmhouse in the distance, but instead of *it* my eyes fell upon my mother—our mother—who was standing a few yards from me.

The kiss Rebecca blew was for Mama.

Mama ambled forward, disoriented and stunned, as if at any moment she might drop to the ground. She reached out for me as she walked, almost ran, closer.

I stood, trying not to fall down again.

Then she came quicker, stumbling as she walked, her gate confused and staggering, nothing like the poised and fluid, dance-like way she usually moved. When she reached me, she pushed me back down onto the ground and held me close to her heart. We both sat in front of my sister's broken grave, painfully sobbing. I held my mama with all my strength as she mourned for her lost daughter… *again*. I knew it was the first time that she had ever let herself grieve in such a way.

Just as that thought passed through my mind, she went limp in my arms. I stroked her hair as she clutched me, holding onto me for dear life. It was frightening, but I knew I was the only one who could do that for her. This was something that not even *Papa* could do for her. I also knew she would do no less for me.

In the distance, Papa and Mr. Cole ran toward us. Then my sights drifted to Kristofer, who was already standing at the edge of the orchard.

He must've followed Mama. He witnessed what I did for Rebecca. A renewed sense of dread swept over me.

Wordlessly, Kristofer stepped closer. He paused.

Is he scared of me? Does he think I'm a witch?

I looked into the eyes of my soulmate, praying for understanding and acceptance. As he stood gazing at me, a single teardrop fell from his beautiful eyes. He slowly shook his head back and forth and smiled—a glorious, heart-wrenching smile.

My pulse skipped a beat while my blurry mind was held captive by his gaze and by the many thoughts of my parents' night together that were running amok through my hazy thoughts.

He plays her like the piano... Oh, yes, I see. That realization brought a warm flush across my already overheated skin.

As I sat staring, Kristofer deeply sighed and balled up his fist. Then his eyes flared with power, locking mine into focus. I couldn't look away. For a second, there was no one else in the world but him—only him. *Only us...*

He clutched his fist against his heart and then mouthed the words: "*I—love—you.*"

With our joint gaze locked, my heart fluttered anew, and within the span of that most perfect moment in time, my world unexpectedly spun on a whole new axis.

"*I—love—you—too,*" I mouthed the words back to him.

Just then, Papa and Mr. Cole sprinted past Kristofer on their way to Mama and me, wrenching my brain from its lovestruck daze. Papa's eyes were wide with fear. Before they reached us, I put my hands up, gesturing for them to stop.

I have to talk to Mama now before I forget any of what Rebecca showed me!

My father seemed to understand, or perhaps he saw the vision, too. I gave him a questioning look.

He nodded, telling me that he *had* seen it.

Without pause, he took Mr. Cole and Kristofer by their arms and turned them around, giving Mama and me a few minutes of privacy while still being close enough just in case she fell completely apart.

I won't let that happen.

I took a deep, cleansing breath. "*Mama?*" I whispered into her ear. "*Rebecca wants you to know where you came from. She showed it to me.*"

I paused for a response.

She raised her head, gazing at me with disbelief. As our eyes met, I wiped the tears from her cheeks.

I thought for a moment and took a deep breath. *"Your parents' names were Matthew and Alyce Clay, but your mama's family called her Lusita, which means 'bringer of light.' Your parents were just seventeen years old when they died."*

I took her face between my hands and peered into her eyes, knowing that I could only *tell* her so much. I was going to have to *show* her most of it.

"Your mother was just like…us," I whispered.

She shook her head and closed her eyes, attempting to take it all in.

I continued. *"Matthew and Lusita Clay were well known to many of the Indian tribes for miles around. One in particular was a small band of The Abenaki Tribe, and Lusita thought of them as home. Despite her white heritage, she was born into their tribe; she thought of them as her family. In truth, the Abenaki became her adopted family after the death of her own parents when she was a young girl. And in return, they revered her as a divine being."*

I wrinkled my brow, trying to remember more. *"It wasn't clear how your parents died, but you were not quite two years old when it happened."*

Mama put her head in her hands, weeping.

I leaned in and softly stroked her head. *"The Abenakis were the ones who took care of you after the death of your parents, and they desperately wanted to keep you, but it wasn't safe. It wasn't safe for them or you.*

And there's something else," I whispered just as she raised her head. *"You would only speak with your mind at first. So your Indian family called you 'Shysie,' which means 'silent little one.' Nevertheless, fearing that you'd be hunted if seen with them, they were forced to give you to someone who they knew would protect you until you were found."*

She frowned; confusion flooded her eyes. *"Who?"*

"According to legend, the ancient willow tree is a sacred and protective being. She looked after you until someone from the orphanage came across you, but even then, you weren't alone. The chief's own son stayed with you until you were found. He told the woman who found you that your name was Alice, just like your mother."

I stopped.

Mama put her shaking hands out and held my face between her palms. *"Rebecca showed you all of this?"*

I leaned closer, and my sight darted to where Kristofer stood in the distance. *"Rebecca showed me some of the stories…"*

I smiled, placing my palm flat against her cheek. *"But most of it I-I remember…"*

Baffled, she frowned, canting her head, clearly at a loss.

So I must make her understand, I thought.

"I remember your mother, Mama. I remember her because, Lusita. Was. Me." Just as those words fell from my lips, my eyes filled with emotional tears, and my sight blurred. Through the blurry haze in my eyes, I gazed into the rapturous emerald eyes of my mother. *"I was Alyce Clay. I was Lusita, Mama. And you were my baby daughter—Alice Clay—not Willow!"* I began to sob. *"We called you Ali, just like Papa does now, just as Molly always has!"* Emotionally spent, I collapsed into her arms, sobbing. I felt her trying to catch her breath but not succeeding very well. She gasped, clutching me to her heart.

I looked up. *"And Mama…"* I softly whispered through the sobs rising from my throat. *"Kristofer was your father. He was Matthew Clay."* My sight fluttered to where my beautiful boy stood, watching us. *"He had a pet name for your mother. He called her 'Sita.'"*

Just then, my father, Mr. Cole, and Kristofer hurried toward us again. Papa didn't seem so fearful anymore. He dropped to his knees and scooped both Mama and me into his lap at once. He peeked down into my eyes and with an expression of utter amazement whispered, *"Lusita."*

"Oh!" I croaked, remembering something else from Rebecca's vision. I gazed up into the canopies of our majestic apple trees. *"The trees aren't dead, Mama!"*

"No?" She tilted her head.

I pushed my lips against her ear. *"They do breathe!"* I conspiratorially whispered. *"They breathe through their leaves!"* Then I touched her face. *"Besides, I know you weren't really talking about the trees anyway. You were talking about yourself."* I tilted my head, studying her, considering my mama and all that she had endured. *"Can you breathe now? Are you alive again?"*

Her beautiful emerald eyes drifted between my father and me. *"Thanks to the two of you, I am alive, and I can breathe, too!"* She put one hand on each of our faces. *"Except when you do something to take my breath away!"*

She kissed each of our lips in turn and then pulled back. She gazed at Papa for a moment, and a sense of wonder bloomed in her eyes. *"Leesie was my mother, Asa. In her lifetime before this one…"* She turned to me. *"No wonder you're always trying to protect me!"*

Papa squeezed us both. *"I know. I saw the whole thing!"*

I contentedly sighed, leaning into my mother, placing my head against her heart, and listening to the steady rhythm of her heartbeat. *"I like it better this way. I love being your daughter."*

She kissed my forehead. *"So do I, my baby. I absolutely adore being your mother,"* she whispered softly.

"Why don't we all get back to the house," Mr. Cole tearfully declared, lifting me off Papa's lap. Then my father raised Mama as we headed back through the orchard.

As they walked, Kristofer reached out and held my hand.

In the distance, I saw Molly standing on the porch. She was there to celebrate my birthday.

I sighed. *It's my birthday, but I feel like I'm sharing it with my mother. In a way, she's been reborn in the past few days. Like a caterpillar, she's transformed into a beautiful butterfly.* I proudly mused, glancing down at Kristofer as he walked next to his papa.

As if feeling my gaze, his eyes lifted. He smiled brightly, his lovely hazel eyes twinkling and glistening in the sunlight. *"Happy birthday, butterfly,"* he whispered, blowing me a sweet kiss. *"I love you,"* he silently mouthed.

I giggled to myself, thinking about Mama. *Maybe we're not as different as Papa thinks…*

16. Beacon

By the time we all got back to our house from the orchard, Molly was busying herself in the kitchen preparing supper, and I was eager. In the confusion of the morning, my parents and I hadn't eaten much, and my stomach was violently protesting.

Molly seemed anxious as we came into the house, though. She was standing just outside the doorway with a half-peeled carrot in her hand, glancing nervously between us all.

Papa came in first, holding Mama in his arms. He set her down on the fireplace hearth.

Molly flung the carrot behind her in the general direction of the basin and rushed toward my mother. She looked horrified. *"What happened to you, Ali? I saw you out in the field. What happened?"* she tearfully cried. *"Did that monster come here to hurt you?"* She crouched down, putting her hands on either side of Mama's face while her eyes darted between Papa and Mr. Cole. *"Is she all right? Jake? Asa? Please, what happened?"*

With much care, Mr. Cole set me down on my feet. *"Thank you, Mr. Cole,"* I said to him and then turned to Molly. *"It's all right, Mrs. Cole, I'll explain,"* I muttered, politely answering for my father and the Reverend.

I hobbled over to the hearth, sitting next to my mother and putting my head on her shoulder. Molly took my free hand. *"Call me Molly, baby,"* she tearfully muttered and pulled me into a warm hug. *"What happened to her?"* she whispered into my ear. She pulled back, eyeing me, looking me up and down. *"And what in heaven's holy name has happened to you, child?"* I felt her trying to stifle a sob as she ran her fingertips over the cuts on my face.

Just then, Papa stood next to Mama. He took her by the hands, pulled her up off the hearth, and placed her on his lap as he sat down. She seemed a bit dazed.

I leaned over. *"Are you all right, Mama?"*

Molly gasped and threw her hand over her mouth. Then she smiled. *"You called her Mama!"* She touched my face and turned, half-crying, half-laughing, to Mr. Cole. *"I guess we did help,"* she said to him. *"And from the look of things…they're together now, too?"* She eyed me hopefully, sneaking a quick glance toward where my entwined parents sat beside us.

"You have no idea just how 'together' they are!" I boisterously announced, staring Molly dead in the eyes, and then giggled into my hand.

My mother sat straight up, peering at me for a moment, her mouth gaping. *"Out of the mouths of babes,"* she wearily tittered.

Papa wasn't amused; he blanched. *"I knew you shouldn't have told her about such things,"* he curtly whispered to Mama under his breath and then glowered toward where Kristofer sat a few feet from us.

I smiled at Molly. *"It's all right. She and I had an intense experience out in the orchard."* I put my hand on my mother's head as she leaned against Papa's chest. *"But I think she's all right."*

At least, I hope she's is. Please be all right, Mama.

My mother nodded and ran the back of her hand down my face. She then stretched her other hand out to Molly. *"Leesie crossed Rebecca. She crossed her over. I wasn't even aware that Rebecca was lost."* She paused and closed her eyes, clearly in pain.

Molly tearfully gasped and squeezed my mother's hand.

"How did I not know she wasn't at peace, Molly? Why did she never show herself to me? She's my own child. How could I not know? I've been out in the field hundreds of times since her death, and I've never

sensed a thing!" my mother scolded herself, seeming guilt-ridden and confused.

I laid my head on her shoulder. *"Rebecca didn't want you to see her, Mama. She didn't mean to burden you. She felt that, under the circumstances, she'd taken enough from you during her short life. She felt that perhaps being lost was her penance."*

"She told you that?" Mama choked.

I nodded. *"She said she loves you and Papa, and she's sorry for everything she put you both through. She knows that the two of you are together now. She's happy for you."*

"Amazing!" Reverend Cole declared from across the room.

Molly took a big, relieved breath and smiled. *"Well, at least Rebecca is at peace now. And now Ali can be, too."* Then she cocked her head and turned her attention back to me. *"Tell me, was this your first crossing, baby?"* she asked.

I took a sharp intake of breath, winded by Molly's knowledge and her almost nonchalant attitude toward our powers. *"Yes, ma'am,"* I mumbled.

Wow, Molly and Mr. Cole really do know everything about us!

At the same time, Kristofer scoffed under his breath from where he sat a few feet from us and shook his head. *"Not your first crossing!"* he silently mouthed to me.

Overcome with grief, Mama melted into a puddle in my father's arms. *"I miss her so, Asa!"* she wept as Papa held her and cried with her. She peeked up into his gentle, steel-blue eyes. *"I know she was difficult at times, but she was my baby, my little girl."*

"Rebecca was our baby, just as Lees is our baby, sweetheart." My father shook his head. *"And I still say, I think she was my daughter— my own blood. I don't know why, I just feel it in my heart. I always have."* He cried, holding Mama tighter.

With those words from my father, my heart broke for him. Rebecca wasn't his child. She told me that herself. Nevertheless, that was one bit of information I had no intention of sharing with my parents.

Rebecca is at peace now, so Papa doesn't need to know the truth—although if he saw the vision, then he already knows what Rebecca said. She said she wasn't his.

A pained tear dripped down my cheek as I thought about my half-sister.

"Speaking of babes, Leesie, what happened to you?" Molly interjected, attempting to bring a new subject to light. *"I just saw you yesterday. You look as if you've aged at least three or four years just since then."*

I shrugged just as Mama grasped my hand. *"I'm not sure, Mrs. Cole…um, Molly,"* I answered her. However, my thoughts stayed with my mother, who was still copiously weeping in Papa's arms.

Are you all right? I mentally asked her, hoping her window was open.

Mama sniffled and gazed into my eyes. *"I will be, my baby,"* she mentally replied.

My breath stuttered, and I flinched. The sound of her voice in my head was still shocking to me. Shocking as it was, though, it also gave me a sense of great peace and comfort. In truth, it was through that shared link between our minds that I finally realized that she truly was my mother.

"Seeing Rebecca again stung quite a lot. I had no idea she was lost." Tears welled in her eyes again, but she faintly smiled. *"You saved her, sweetie!"* she proudly declared into my mind, baring her very soul to me. *"And you succeeded in your first crossing. I'm so very proud of my girl!"* She took a long, exaggerated breath, and her intense eyes bored straight into my mind. *"Therefore, I think it's time for your instruction to begin. I think you're ready."*

Huh? Instruction? What do you mean? I hesitantly asked, and a sudden, puzzling sense of fear gripped me.

Mama kindly smiled and pulled back the intensity of her emerald gaze. *"You've succeeded in your first crossing, you hear me in your mind, and your papa tells me that you were able to levitate a kitchen towel this morning. Is that correct?"* She smirked, her eyes glistening. *"And let's not forget about the door that you slammed in my face yesterday!"*

Yes, ma'am, I mentally whispered and bashfully bit my lip.

Jeez, let's not bring that up again! I thought to myself.

She proudly nodded. *"I'll start by showing you how to open and close your mind window—we'll go from there."*

I saved Rebecca for you—for you and Papa. You know that, don't you? I silently asked, and a torrent of emotional tears fell from my eyes.

All the while Molly continued to talk beside us. Although my mother was trying to listen to us both, I knew our silent conversation had her captivated.

Mama frowned. *"I know why you did it, Lees, and I also know why you went after Charles. But you have to remember one thing: I am your mother. It is my duty to protect you. Not the other way around!"* she sternly scolded, her powerful eyes flashing with righteous parental indignation.

I narrowed my eyes at her. *I'll never let that awful man hurt you again!*

She drew closer; her mind gripped mine. She scowled. *"You! Will! Mind! Your! Ps and Qs, miss!"* she dangerously hissed.

No, I won't! Not if that man tries to hurt you again! I petulantly huffed and then dropped my gaze away from hers, my mind sent reeling from the intensity of her mental hold on me.

I was once her mother! How can she expect me to stand idly by and do nothing? Not likely!

Mama exasperatedly sighed, giving up—for now.

My pique fell as well. I bit my lip and timidly took her hand—feigning submission. *"Since you're going to teach me, there's something I'd like to do for you,"* I sweetly muttered.

Mama gazed at me and resignedly laughed. *"What is it, my stubborn baby?"*

"When I do remember everything about my other lifetime, I'll show it to you, all right? I'll show you everything."

She tearfully nodded. *"I love you,"* she whispered into my head.

"I love you, too," I mouthed to her.

Finally, she let her attention return to Molly, who was still chattering about their childhood. Smiling, she took Molly's hand and listened intently.

I gazed at my beautiful mother and sighed. *She's my mama. She really is my mama!* Somehow I still couldn't quite wrap my head around that fact. I was afraid that it was just another one of my dreams, a dream from which I would soon awaken.

Then I would be half an orphan again…motherless…lost.

I shook my head, willing that awful thought to leave me alone. *No, she's here; she's mine, and I'll protect her at all costs.*

I smiled and stared at my mother as she continued to chat with Molly. I was glad she was feeling better. Her grief frightened me. In fact, any display of weakness from her scared me.

But I'd do it again if I had to, for her. I'd do anything to protect and defend her and my papa! My eyes swept to where Kristofer sat silently gazing at me. *And for him, I'd die. Simple.*

As I sat thinking about my beautiful boy, sudden images of my mother as a baby flashed into my mind. The memories were few and sporadic. I closed my eyes, wrinkled my brow, and desperately tried to remember more. *Gah!* It was so frustrating! The memories just wouldn't come. I screwed my eyes up tighter, concentrating hard. As my mind focused, someone sat down beside me and took my hand. I knew without looking that it was Kristofer. He smelled of jasmine and lavender. I inhaled deeply. *Hmm…* The sensation of his warm hand holding mine seemed so natural, so *right*.

Then another image flashed through my head. It was the picture of myself *with* Kristofer. We were holding each other…and kissing. I tasted his sweet lips and felt his arms encircle my waist. Slowly, he unfastened the buttons on the back of my dress, peeling it away from my shoulders, down my arms, letting it pool at my feet…

I gasped, and my eyes flew open in shock; my sights darted to his. *Was that a vision or just a thought?* I gazed into his beautiful face. His lips parted, and his bright, hazel eyes blazed with a *familiar* expression. My breath stuttered. Suddenly, it came to me—the look. Kristofer was looking at me the same way that Mama looked at Papa.

Oh, that's what that look means…

With that little epiphany, the air in my lungs evaporated, and the invisible lasso tugged hard, furtively persuading me toward him.

Without pause, Kristofer leaned forward, grinning. *"My…Sita,"* he whispered, blinking as he said it. His eyes twinkled like topaz gems mixed with starlight and clear jade water, and they sparkled like the sun casting off gentle ocean waves—soft loving waves. *Waves to drown in. Hmm. What a nice way to die.*

He snickered and stroked my face with the back of his hand. As his skin brushed mine, the lasso jerked again, this time harder, sending me reeling forward, right into his waiting arms. He caught me around the middle and held me with both arms. *"Are you all right, Sita?"* he whispered, his beautiful hazel eyes boring into mine, making me dizzy.

Mama quickly inhaled and threw her hands up over her mouth.

At the same time, Molly turned to Kristofer. *"What? What did you call Leesie, Kris?"*

My mother jumped to her feet, abruptly grabbing both Kristofer and me by the hand and hauling us toward the kitchen. I hobbled as quickly and obediently as my sprained ankle would allow. As she pulled, I turned and glanced toward the hearth. I was afraid to know what my father's reaction was going to be. To my relief, he was still sitting on the hearth, frowning at us with a confused expression on his face.

I heaved a sigh. *Good. He didn't hear what Kristofer called me.* Molly trailed behind us.

The four of us sat at the table, silently at first. Molly had a bewildered look on her face. *"Why did you call Leesie? What was it? 'Sita?'"* she asked Kristofer.

"There's something we have to tell you. Well, there's something that I have to say to you, Molly," Mama replied, anxiously wringing her hands. *"It's about Kristofer and Leesie."* She glanced at me as if she didn't know how to begin.

Before either she or I uttered a word, Kristofer spoke. *"I'm the man here; I'll tell you, Ma,"* he mumbled and sheepishly glanced her way.

"You know because you heard me tell my mama, right?" I turned to him.

He shook his head. *"No,"* he answered, frowning. *"I know because I remember it, too."* He chewed his top lip for a moment. *"In fact, I've recognized the truth since the day I fell out of the tree. I've been waiting for you to remember."*

He smiled at me and then turned to his mother. *"Ma,"* Kristofer muttered, timidly glancing between his mother, my mother, and me. He took a deep breath. *"In our life before this one, Leesie and I were married. And…Mrs. Raign was…our daughter. We were killed when she was just a baby. This was why she had to grow up in the orphanage with you."*

The words tumbled out in a rush. Then he turned back to me and took my hand. *"And 'Sita' was a name that I used to call…my wife. It was short for 'Lusita.'"*

Molly gasped and gaped at us, her eyes darting between Kristofer and me. *"What? What? What?"*

Tears pooled in Kristofer's eyes; he leaned in toward me and took my other hand. *"Alyce Lusita Clay was her name. She was my Sita. She was my sweet, funny, frustrating wife."*

Huh? Frustrating?

Kristofer's eyes welled. *"Sita was pure perfection and all I've ever needed from a woman. She still is flawless. Sita has always been my mate, and she always will be—always."* He paused. *"Or rather, I am her mate."*

He looked into Molly's wide eyes. *"My name was Matthew—Matthew Stephen Clay."*

Molly sat staring down at the table, unseeing, her expression one of both shock and astonishment.

My eyes swept back to Kristofer. Just as our joint sights met, his eyes flashed with intensity. I had the impression that he was staring straight past my eyes and into the depths of my soul—learning my secrets, silently searching my very essence for every hidden thought that I had ever had.

But how can that be? Kristofer isn't like Mama and me.

A shudder ran through my body, and I knew then that our love was limitless and timeless. The lasso tugged again, and that time, I didn't fight it.

"I am my beloved's, and my beloved…is mine," Kristofer whispered, shifting his head, moving forward—asking, requesting permission.

Permission for what? What does he want?

He licked his lips. *"I am but a humble servant at your regal feet, Goddess,"* he whispered, beseeching.

Oh, he wants permission to kiss me…

Almost imperceptibly, I nodded.

He reached out, clutched my hands, and ever so slightly, moved nearer in his seat.

I inhaled, drawing closer, my breath shallow and erratic. My body tingled, and it felt as though I could at any moment suffocate in his proximity or simply drown in his beautiful, chartreuse eyes.

Our joint lips drew nearer, only inches apart. I closed my eyes. His breath was on my skin, in my hair. The heat of his breath flamed through my blood, all the way to the depths of my soul. The quiet puff reached into every cell; it plundered, diving into each crevice of my being. The hot blood pooled below my waist, and beads of sweat rushed to the surface of my skin. In response to the heat, my labored breath stuttered, and I gasped as the air between us crackled with static energy though it didn't startle me. If anything, the primal connection emboldened me. I leaned forward, closing the gap between us.

I could almost *taste* him…

Just before we touched, the two ear piercing gasps of our respective mothers pulled us apart. They gaped at us, their collective eyes wide and disbelieving.

Kristofer and I cautiously peeked at them.

Molly sat stunned, glancing from Kristofer to me and then to Mama. *"Ali?"* she squeaked, finally finding her voice.

Mama warily nodded.

Molly looked as if she were about to faint. She eyed Kristofer. *"How in heaven's name do you know all of this, Kristofer Jacob? And… were you just about to kiss Leesie?"* She took his face into her hands, incredulously glaring.

Kristofer's eyes trained on his mother's eyes. He was carefully assessing her reaction. *"I told you, Ma, I remember my last life. I remember…my wife."* His vision swept to each one of us in turn before finally concentrating on me alone. *"I remember…everything,"* he emphatically whispered. *"And yes, I wanted to kiss her. I still do."*

Molly stared at us for a moment, unable to articulate her feelings. *"Tell me everything!"* she blurted and then winced at her own words.

She stopped and bit her lip, clearly contemplating whether or not she wanted to know, but finally, she nodded. *"All right, I'm ready."*

She opened her eyes; her sight swept between Kristofer and me.

Kristofer began talking without even waiting for me, and once he did, it seemed like he couldn't stop himself. I was surprised at how much he remembered about my life, but I was saddened by the fact that I didn't seem to recall much at all. Every once in a while, he turned to me as if *waiting* for me to chime in with a memory of my own, but I had none, so he continued without me.

"One time," he excitedly babbled, *"my Sita crossed an entire village of people!"* He gazed at me with awe in his eyes. *"You amaze me."* His eyes were full of love and devotion for me.

For me! Or for Lusita, at least. Hmm, I wonder if he wants me…or her… Suddenly, I felt uneasy. A warm, troubled blush rushed across my skin, and the green-eyed little witch in me bubbled with jealousy.

Molly regarded me for a moment. *"How did you cross so many, Lees?"* she asked, seemingly astonished and quite possibly in shock from our revelations.

I timidly glanced at Kristofer before answering his mother. *"I don't know. I don't exactly remember that."*

Kristofer frowned as I self-consciously looked away. *"You don't remember?"* he incredulously asked. *"There was a deadly outbreak of smallpox in the village neighboring your own, remember? All but one man and one woman died…"*

I thought carefully for a moment, trying to see a vision or something, but again, *nothing*. I shook my head.

"Two hundred eighty-seven souls…" Kristofer drawled, sensing my frustration. *"They were disoriented and confused. They didn't realize what had happened to them. You crossed them…all."*

I shook my head again, frowning.

"They were happy to see your light, Sita. They were drawn to it! Just like I am!" Kristofer's face beamed.

My light? I thought for a moment. *"Oh yes, my light. Kristofer?"* I bashfully muttered, recalling what I wanted to ask him. *"What color is…my light?"*

Kristofer's grin widened. He leaned in and put his hand under my chin. *"But you've already seen it, love, out in the orchard when you crossed Rebecca."*

Oh, the diamond light…

As if hearing that thought, Kristofer nodded. *"Yes, you remember, don't you? Your light, love, is the brightest, purest white that I have ever seen. It's even brighter than the moonlight reflecting off the falling snow. It's more radiant than a thousand stars each bursting at once. It's…"* He lifted the crescent moon charm off my skin. *"It's just like this."* He fingered the charm Papa gave me. *"But many times more brilliant."*

I leaned past him and looked into the front room, where my father sat talking with Mr. Cole. *How did he know? Can Papa see my light, too?*

Mama answered my question; she whispered the answer into my mind. *"Your papa saw your light once, baby, just for a few seconds. It was the minute you were born. He was the first to hold you, and that's when he saw your light."*

Suddenly my necklace had even more meaning. I jumped up, forgetting about the pain in my sprained ankle, and half-ran, half-wobbled to where my father sat. Without pause, I threw my arms around his neck, curled up small in his lap just like I did when I was little, and sobbed into his chest. *"Thank you! Thank you! Thank you for the lovely necklace, and thank you for knowing what color my light is!"*

Papa cuddled me in his lap as I continued to sob, his piercing blue eyes penetrating mine as he smiled. He wiped my tears with his fingertips.

"That's why Mama's charm is gold and mine is silver!" I happily declared through tears and then a hiccough.

He chuckled and lifted the charm up so I could see it, his bright blue eyes dancing straight into mine. *"This, angel, is not silver…"* He chuckled again, focusing on the pendant. *"This—is—platinum! Just—like—you!"* He kissed my nose, and his beautiful eyes bored into mine, seeming to absorb my happiness. They were full of love and a great deal of pride.

Pride for me?

I looked down at the charm and then back up into the gorgeous, rapt eyes of my father. *"It must've been expensive,"* I bashfully muttered, biting my lower lip, and a sudden sense of guilt gripped my chest, making it hard to breathe.

My father's expression fell; he took my face between his hands. *"Yes, the necklace was costly. But you, you, Leesie, are priceless!"* he tearfully choked, pressing his lips to my forehead. He kissed me then, just like he did when I was a baby.

I hugged him around his neck—holding him close for a minute and taking a deep breath, every fiber of my being absorbed in his love for me. *Hmm, he so smells good. He smells of pipe tobacco and cinnamon mingled with just a touch of Mama's lilac scent; it's simply heavenly.*

I sat up and peeked into his wonderful eyes again, but he wasn't looking at me. He was gazing into the kitchen…at Mama. And she was staring at us both. What's more, there were tears in her eyes, too. But this time, they were tears of pure, unadulterated joy, melting away her sorrows.

I beamed at her and then kissed Papa's cheek and hobbled back into the kitchen, where I sat beside her in the same chair with my head pressed against hers. As she and I sat head to head, the same thought kept repeating in her mind. *"Two-hundred-eighty-seven people…at the same time…"* She absentmindedly shook her head. *"How did you cross two-hundred-eighty-seven…at the same time? The power that would take is staggering. What are you capable of doing now? Maybe I'm not stronger…"* She peeped at me through the corner of her eye and frowned. *"I wonder,"* she thought. *"But, how would we test something like this?"*

Obviously, you forgot to close the window, I timidly whispered into her mind. *But it's all right. We don't need a test. I don't choose to be stronger than you.* I took an unsteady breath.

Then something occurred to me. I sat straight up and gaped at her. *"I should've asked Rebecca what we are,"* I said to her, suddenly kicking myself for the lost opportunity. *"I didn't even think about asking her any questions, and now it's too late."* I put my head in my hands. *"I'm sorry, I was so overwhelmed!"*

But before my mother could answer, Kristofer burst out laughing from beside us. *"Sheesh! Do I have to tell you everything?"* he asked, still laughing. He sorrowfully shook his head. *"Poor, butterfly. She doesn't even remember what she is,"* he teased in a mocking sing-song tone of voice.

I glanced at Mama and then back to him.

He smirked.

Usually, I found Kristofer to be quite irresistible, but he was being a bit aggravating just then. *Imagine, him knowing more about my life than I do! Huh, infuriating boy!*

I jerked my hand away from him as he began talking in a manner in which I found to be just a little too maddening!

Mama snickered and gently patted the side of my head.

"According to Abenaki legend," Kristofer began, still smirking at me. *"You are often called 'the Jyoti,' which means light. In the English translation, you are known by just one word."* He stretched across the table. *"Do you remember…now?"* he singsonged again.

I didn't even have to think about the answer. I just knew! I turned in the chair and beamed into the beautiful face of my mother. *"Beacon! That's what we're called. We are Beacon, Mama!"* I proudly proclaimed as my heart flipped, fluttered, and nearly jumped out of my throat!

The annoying—beautiful—boy sitting beside me snickered wildly. *"I knew if I irritated you enough, you'd remember for me!"* he howled with laughter.

Mama gasped and her beautiful emerald eyes grew wide and full of wonder. *"Beacon, that's right,"* she softly muttered, barely containing her emotions. *"That's what we are. We are a Beacon for the lost souls of the world!"*

A warm rush of happiness washed over me, and I knew that my mama felt it, too. We clung to each other, laughing and crying at the same time. *"There's a name for us!"* she blissfully repeated in my mind, taking my face between her palms, her eyes swimming with tears. *"We're not witches; we're…Beacon!"*

My mother grabbed Kristofer and pulled him from his seat. She hugged him tight. *"Thank you, baby!"* she gushed just as I hugged him, too.

"You're welcome, Mrs. Raign," he said, his voice muffled.

All of a sudden, Mama froze. Then she stopped crushing Kristofer and peered into his eyes. *"What did you call me when I was a baby? Do you remember?"* she almost fearfully asked and then expectantly tilted her head, her big eyes wide and curious.

I nearly lost my breath again. Suddenly, she looked so young, just like the images I had of her as a baby.

Kristofer blushed. *"I used to call you Ali, just like my Ma does. Funny thing, huh?"* he shyly muttered.

She laughed. *"Then you may call me Ali now."* She hugged him again, and I was so happy that I wanted to hug myself!

"We're not witches," I muttered. *"We're not demons. We're… Beacon!"*

Papa chuckled from the doorway. *"I never thought you were witches or demons or anything except maybe some sort of holy angels who I am blessed enough to be able to call my own."* He smiled. *"All I know is, whatever the two of you are, first and foremost, you are mine."* He put his hand on his heart. *"Mine,"* he said again, this time glancing toward Kristofer.

My mother pushed up from the table and ran to him. As she rushed toward him, Papa bent down, caught her around the waist, and lifted her up until they were face to face. She pressed her forehead and nose up against his. *"Yes, my love,"* she whispered. *"We are yours, forever yours."*

"So," I interrupted, entirely ignorant to the tender moment my parents were attempting to share. *"If you never believed we were witches, Papa..."* I asked, mindlessly scooting toward them. *"Then why do you call us witches?"*

Without pause, my father set Mama on her feet and turned her around—his front to her back. He draped his arms around her shoulders, securely locking their bodies together, and laid his chin atop her head. He smiled into my confused eyes. *"When your mama and I were kids, angel, she was terribly frightened of the word 'witch.' Understand, she'd been called that for most of her life, and the very mention of the word terrified her."* He winked at me. *"So I began calling her my beautiful little red-headed...witch. And before long, the word lost its frightening value. In essence, she grew to think of it as a term of endearment instead of as an insult, which it's not. There are plenty of witches and seers in this world. This is why I call you that, as well. You see, Lees, words only have a negative meaning if we give it to them."*

Mama turned around, wrapped her arms around his waist, pressed her cheek against his chest, and squeezed him tight. She curved her head upward and gazed into his eyes.

I giggled into my hand. *They are so beautiful together. How did I never see the love between them?* I thought for a moment about the visions that I'd had of them. *Actually, I guess I did see it.*

Kristofer squeezed my hand, pulling me from my thoughts. He leaned in until his lips were almost touching my ear. *"There's something else I remember, Lees, but I didn't want to say it in front of Ali and my Ma."* He gestured toward Mama. *"Is she listening right now?"*

I glanced toward where she stood in Papa's embrace and shook my head. *"No, we're alone. What is it?"*

Kristofer's eyes fell to the table for a moment. He took a deep breath, evidently afraid to speak the words. *"You and I have rarely ever lived past seventeen years old, and we've never lived past twenty-five. Not ever."*

My breath hitched, and my mind blurred with fear, but then a strange sense of calm washed over me. I turned and glanced at my parents. Then my gaze swept back to my love's startled eye, and I knew then that things had to be different for us. We couldn't die young.

We will survive. I squeezed Kristofer's hand. *We have to live this time…for them.* I glanced at our parents again. *And we have to live… for her.* "Whoever she is…" I murmured, remembering the face of our baby from some distant dream. *Her name is Aaleesa. We have to live for Aaleesa—for our daughter. I won't leave my baby without a mama…not again.* And I was determined to make it true.

Kristofer nodded. *"I'll never let anything happen to you, Sita. Not ever again!"* he passionately avowed, heaving a deep sigh. Though he attempted a smile, he still seemed quite upset.

Kristofer let go of my hand, reached into his pocket, and then placed a small package in front of me. He seemed nervous. *"Happy birthday,"* he bashfully muttered, blushing on the tips of his ears.

It was a small square box. I took it into my hands, my face beaming with joy. *"I love it!"*

"Open it! You don't even know what it is yet!" He laughed.

"I love it, whatever it is. I love it because it's from you," I muttered, quickly unwrapping the brown paper package. My fingers trembled with excitement as I lifted the lid of the box. Inside was a pair of small combs. They had butterflies on the edges, and the colors were the same as my marble, the same as my dream. Most important, they were the same as my true love's eyes—my Kristofer's eyes. I picked them up, handling them with loving care. I handled them as if they were made of the most precious gold and gems in the world. I gazed at them just as a rush of something warm swept through my body. My heart was inflamed.

I peered into the wondrous hazel eyes of my soulmate as a sudden question sprang to mind. I tried to steady my pounding heart, as well as my breath, so I could speak. I leaned in. *"Kristofer?"* I softly murmured so my papa couldn't hear. *"What do you remember about us?"* I paused. *"Not about our lives, but about us together?"*

A vivid image of my parents the night before frolicked through my brain, rousing a deep-seated feeling of longing. Suddenly, everything that Mama had explained to me earlier in the day didn't seem entirely unnecessary anymore.

My heart skipped as Kristofer's eyes bore into mine. He smoothed the side of my hair with his long fingers, placing a few strands of the short tuft that never grew longer that my chin behind my ear. His soft touch sent shivers through my body. He leaned in closer to me, his pulse violently beating through the hand that I was holding. To my surprise, his eyes fell; he seemed crestfallen. *"I can't tell you that, Lees,"* he whispered. *"Our love is something that you have to remember for yourself. I won't rush those memories. They're too special, too amazing to explain. You need to see those things for yourself."*

He sighed. *"I hope you don't remember them until you and I are old enough to be married again. I hope you remain ignorant until we can be in love like that again. Believe me, I wish I didn't have to see them.*

It's painful to remember you like that and to know that I have to wait so long. I won't force that kind of pain onto you. I will endure it for us both."

His eyes welled. *"A few days ago, I was just a boy—an ordinary kid. But now, I remember being married to you. I remember falling asleep with you in my arms; I remember everything about you."*

He took my face into his hands. *"I'm in love with you, Sita. I am now, I always have been, and I always will be desperately in love with you."*

He paused, and another tear fell. *"You and I died together, and I know that someday we will live together. I also know that we will be married eventually, and then the memories I have of you…of everything will be real again."*

He looked me dead in the eyes. *"And baby, I was only startled by the way you've changed because now you look very much like you did when we met in our other life. And as soon as you remember everything, I promise to remember it with you."* He kissed the end of my nose just as a torrent of tears rushed down his cheeks.

It broke my heart to see my beautiful boy in pain, and I tried not to cry, but the tears came just the same. I sucked in a deep breath, willing myself to stop, but soon I felt painful sobs rippling through me. *Don't cry… Mustn't cry… Don't cry!* I screamed into my head, but my mutinous eyes overflowed anyway.

Kristofer reached for me. He leaned forward, laying his sweet-smelling head on my shoulder, gently stroking my hair. All the while, I wept. I screwed my eyes up tight, trying desperately to stop, but the tears ran freely; I was helpless to stop them.

Suddenly noticing us, Molly let out a gasp and hurried to me, followed by both my parents and Mr. Cole. Molly knelt down beside me, eyeing the butterfly combs in my hand. *"Oh my, Leesie loves your gift so much, Kris, it made her cry."* She petted my head.

I lifted my head from where it rested atop Kristofer's and weakly smiled.

Mama sat beside me. She pulled me into her arms, and her powerful voice rang out clearly from the depths of my mind. *"I know it hurts, my baby, but Kris is right. You don't want those memories. Not just yet."* She caressed my head and sighed. *"Your papa and I have memories like that. They are wonderful yet painful at once. Believe me, you don't want memories like that—ones you can't act upon."* Her eyes swept to Kris. *"I'm sorry that Kris has to endure such memories, especially knowing the two of you must wait years to be together."*

I want to remember now! I want to be married to him…now! I snapped into her mind. *"I want him like you want Papa,"* I added in a faint whisper.

Mama blinked a few times. The expression on her face was something of bewildered disbelief. It was as if she hadn't heard me correctly. Then, slowly, she lifted my chin with only her index finger, and her mighty eyes blared into mine.

She spoke into my mind once again, and though her tone was calm, the power behind her Beacon might raged. *"Alyce Margaret, you are twelve. You are not married to that boy. You are a child—my child. And he is a child, regardless of what memories his mind holds. You—will—behave!"* She almost imperceptibly shook her head. *"I won't tolerate any inappropriate behavior from either of you, and neither will his parents!"* Her mighty eyes darted to Papa. *"And rest assured, your father will forbid you to see Kris at all if you push him too far, which isn't going to be far…at all!"*

She leaned in closer still, and our foreheads nearly touched, which sent my head swimming with the expansive power of her mind. *"Do you understand me, child?"* she whispered aloud.

I numbly nodded. It was all I could do. Her penetrating emerald glare had me even more captivated than usual. I could hardly think, let alone respond. She was powerful, even more so than I had ever realized. I was absolutely spellbound. *Papa was right.* My groggy mind slurred with the thought. *Her stare almost puts me into a trance. She's not even blinking!*

As soon as that thought crossed my hazy mind, she broke the spell, her eyes drawing soft again. She leaned in, sweetly kissed my forehead, and then sat back in her seat.

Wow. I blow things up, and she hypnotizes. But which is stronger—the explosive force or one that can restrain the explosive force?

Mama snickered. *"I guess we'll just have to wait and see, now, won't we?"*

Just then, Molly took my hand. *"Lees,"* she said, gushing. *"Kris sold his entire marble collection to get you those combs."* She reached over and ruffled the top of Kristofer's head. *"He saw them at the trading post and just had to get them for you."*

"You sold them all?"

Kristofer nodded, and the tips of his ears flushed.

"You can have the one you gave me back—that is, if you want it," I whispered, putting my hand on top his.

He shook his head. *"No. That one's yours. The colors match your soul."* He ran his long fingers through the length of my hair. *"Just like this color matches…mine."*

I wanted to kiss him so bad at that moment that I could hardly stand it. His beautiful eyes had me utterly captivated. *Very much like Mama's eyes did before.* I glanced away before letting myself get too absorbed in his gaze. I peeked at where my mother had returned to Papa by the doorway. They were holding each other and kissing…again!

As I stared at them a sudden vision popped into my brain. It was an image of my mother. She was being held but not by Papa. It was that monster…Charles Marshal! He had one arm wound around her, and with his free hand he was tearing at her dress.

Mama was screaming, trying to get out of his clutches, but he was just too powerful for her.

My eyes swept around to our surroundings. We were in our kitchen, standing just where she and my father stood holding each other only a moment before.

As my sights cast an eye over the ground, I wanted to scream, but my throat choked with fear. Papa laid face-down on the floor with his nose submerged in a puddle of his own blood.

My attention shifted back to Mama and the devil. I watched in horror as Charles Marshal snatched a fistful of her hair and threw her on the tabletop.

"Asa! No! Asa! Asa!" she screeched.

With a triumphant howl of laughter, the devil grabbed at my mother's breasts. He squeezed and shoved his vile head down. He licked her throat, and his spindly hands ran over her chest and then down the contours of her waist. He was touching her—all over her body. He pawed her as if she were his to do with as he pleased—*his* instead of Papa's!

I tried to stand. I wanted to fight him, but I couldn't move. My body was frozen with fear and rage. *Let go of my mama!* I screamed with my mind, but the sheriff persisted. He threw his head back and laughed again, this time tearing at her clothes, putting his filthy hands up her skirt, and whispering foul words into her ear.

My mother screeched in pain as his hand disappeared up her skirt. He was plundering her body. He was touching her, touching her just like my papa did!

Papa! Get up! Get up! Please don't be dead!

As my mother fought, I tried to move forward toward either them or my father, but again I could barely twitch a muscle. All I could do was watch in horror as Charles Marshal grabbed my mother by the neck and forced her to kiss him. He shoved his vile tongue down her throat. Then he bit her lip, sending blood oozing and then dripping off both the devil's chin and hers.

"You had to know that I was coming for you, witch!" he growled. *"You shouldn't have run from me, Alice. Now your stable boy is dead!"* A sickening guffaw escaped his blood-encrusted mouth. *"Your sweet little quim is mine!"* Then with one hand around her neck, he released the buttons of his trousers with his free hand. Charles shoved down his pants, then crawled over her laughing as my beautiful, innocent mother screamed.

I screwed my eyes up tight. I knew what was about to happen but couldn't bear to watch. As I stood shaking, I realized that the sounds had disappeared. I reopened my eyes. The vision of the monster vanished just as my picture-perfect life returned.

My eyes darted to Papa. He and my mother were still in each other's arms.

He didn't see it, and Mama can't see visions unless I show them to her.

The fury I felt that morning returned with a vengeance, but my thoughts remained calm. I didn't want to alarm my mother. *"I have to stop him. I don't have a choice. I have to hurt him before he hurts them,"* I quietly muttered, my sights sweeping back to my mother— my lovely, innocent mother. *"Charles Marshal won't foresee me coming. I so look forward to the expression on his face when he realizes that he is about to die…by my hand."*

I deeply sighed, and a terrifying realization suddenly dawned. *This is the darkness that I felt coming, but it won't come. It won't come because I'm coming for it…first.*

Just then, our family joined hands around the table as Reverend Cole said grace, asking the Lord to bless our lovely meal.

A meal that would quite possibly be…my last.

17. The Burning

It was just before dawn when I noiselessly stole down the stairs of our little farmhouse. Thankfully, with my recent growth spurt, I had also developed my mother's gentle *sashay*. This made it easy for me to glide down the stairs undetected by my parents, who lay sleeping not twenty feet from the front door.

Just as my feet hit the landing, I peeked around, making sure that I was alone.

Dim sunlight shone through the kitchen curtains, giving me just enough light to see where I was going and what I needed to find.

Gliding through the deserted front room, I passed my parents' bedroom door and then headed into the kitchen. I hurried to my mother's china cabinet, grabbed a paring knife from the bottom drawer, and carefully slipped it up one of the sleeves of my dress. Then I turned and rushed into the front room although I stopped directly in front of my parents' bedroom door and noiselessly peeked in.

In the pale morning light, I could just make out their silhouetted forms as they lay pressed together. They were skin to skin, holding one another tight. My father lay on his back with Mama's head resting on his bare chest, his hand tenderly caressing her head, mindlessly stroking her hair in his sleep. Mama's hair was arranged like a beautiful sun-colored fan across the entire length of his torso; her soft tresses glistened in the dim morning light, her arms securely wrapped around his waist.

I smiled to myself, wondering if the beautiful sight before me would be the last memory that I would have.

Just then, my mother peacefully sighed and pulled the single blanket that covered them from her naked shoulders. She kissed Papa's chest and buried her face beneath his chin.

A sudden jolt of fear gripped me as I watched them dreaming in each other's arms. I thought about what my death would do to them.

Will they survive? Is this really something that I should be doing?

That thought gave me pause for a moment, but just as quickly, I envisioned my mother being harmed by that madman for a second time, just as she had been violated and nearly killed the first time years before.

Would she survive another assault? And my papa, Charles planned to kill him!

All my doubts vanished at that point.

If Charles Marshal kills me, I thought, blowing each of them what might be one last farewell kiss, *they could have another child.*

I glided across the room to the front door and quietly opened it. *After what Mama told me yesterday, perhaps she's already expecting again.* I closed the door behind me. *I know she's a bit older now, nearly forty-three, but she looks much younger than other women her age—a lot younger, at least a decade younger—and so does Papa. Besides, I've seen women in the city who were even older than Mama, and they had babies.* That thought made me smile. *Maybe this time Papa will have a son. He'd like that…but people like Mama and me—Beacons—only give birth to daughters for some reason.*

Hmm. How did I know that? I paused for a moment, thinking. *Oh well, he wouldn't mind having another girl.*

Then I remembered my boy, and tears stung my eyes. I would never know what it was like to hold him or to kiss him, or… This thought was too painful to bear. I would never marry him.

I envisioned my love for Kristofer being cut painfully short—like a severed rope. I would never have him. I choked back a sob. And I would never have our baby daughter either—our Aaleesa. She would cease to exist, her angelic existence forever absent from the face of the physical world. They both might be lost to me forever. But my parents' lives were well worth *any* sacrifice I had to make.

I ditched the emotional tears away and pressed on.

It was early autumn and quite chilly that time of day, and that morning was no exception. I stared down as I walked through the yard, counting my steps and trying to remember everything about my home. Dew gathered on my shoes as I passed over a patch of tall grass.

Just as I made my way up to the path that led to our home, I stopped and glanced back for a moment—any longer than that and I would have lost my nerve. I'd have run back home to the temporary safety of my parents' arms.

Finally reaching the end of the yard, I stood still for a beat, considering my plan: The knife up my sleeve was securely in place and concealed. I'd walk to Charles Marshal's door and knock, and as soon as I saw his foul, vile eyes, I'd plunge the knife directly into his black, soulless heart. I would send him to a place where he could never harm my mama and papa again!

I'm gonna send you straight to Hell, you wicked monster, even if I have to take you there myself!

Then I ran. With all my might, I ran!

Nobody knew how fast I was, and perhaps nobody ever would. That talent of mine was one that my mama did not possess; she didn't even know about it, for that matter.

I was fast, faster than fast. I was a locomotive in lace-up shoes.

It was quite liberating, really, sprinting along like a panther between the trees, the wind blowing my hair back and the air rushing through my ears. It was exhilarating, freeing even, rushing around the other farms on the outskirts of town, holding my breath and taking the curves that wound around the copse at full speed, without even hesitating for a moment.

Just as I flew past a tall line of fir trees, I sprang, without faltering, over a sizeable creek. It must've been at least fifty feet across, but I didn't even get my shoes damp.

That was exhilarating.

Despite the fear in my heart, finally letting off some steam made my spirit soar. Therefore, I decided to take the circuitous route. After all, it'd been five years since I explored the town, and if this were to be my last day on Earth, well, I intended to see some of it.

Just before I reached *that* town, I skirted a peaceful-looking little farm surrounded by a lovely white picket fence. I lowered my head, sprinted faster, and leaped over the fence. I cleared it without pause and then landed like a cougar, silently and without missing a step.

My sights focused ahead. The town was growing nearer in the distance—presumably innocent and benign.

Oh, how appearances can be deceiving, I thought, spotting the picturesque little bridge leading toward the many quaint buildings in *that* town, the one in which we weren't welcome.

I took a long gulp of air to steady my nerves, my lungs burning in protest.

More from the cold than the speed, though.

As I ran, I thought again about the fact that I had never told anyone about my talent—about how swift I was—not even my mother. I could probably outrun any man on earth, possibly any panther.

I looked down, entranced by my own power. My feet barely hit the ground. It was fascinating; I was featherlike, simply floating along at a rapid, carefree pace. The wind whistled through my hair, carrying it far behind me as I streaked closer to my fate.

My feet barely reverberated off the wood as they fell upon the planks of the bridge leading into town. It wasn't a thump like the sound shoes would make while walking, or even a clopping sound, like hooves, but rather an eerie whoosh as I breezed over the timber.

Once across the bridge, I didn't stop. I darted straight through the silent, sleeping little town. There was a certain uneasy quiescence surrounding the empty street, but I knew otherwise. I knew what sort of people dwelled there.

Finally, I came to rest directly in front of the sheriff's house. *How ironic.* I scanned the street. *The sheriff's house is across the street from both the church and the graveyard.*

I stroked the weapon as it slid down from my sleeve to my hand—ready for the fray—and crept across the porch. I peeked into the sheriff's front room window. The devil's lair appeared to be empty and still, but I knew he was there somewhere, probably sleeping, perhaps even dreaming about my mother. My stomach twisted at the thought of him putting his hands on her, sending bile into my throat; the very thought choked the breath from my already burning lungs.

And he intends to kill Papa. I have to stop him!

I lumbered across the porch to the shabby white door of my adversary's house, raised my fist to knock, and slowly slid the knife handle into my palm. I held the weapon in front of me, ready to strike. With any luck, only a single deathblow would be necessary, but whatever happened, I was determined to stop him.

I would not run.

My head spun. I didn't breathe. I closed my eyes and said a silent prayer. It was a prayer for my parents, for Kristofer, and for forgiveness…forgiveness for what I was about to do.

With my eyes still shut, I let out a quick huff of air mixed with panic-stricken tears. *"Just do it! End this!"* I scolded myself out loud as my balled fist moved forward.

"No. You. Won't!" A voice from behind me urgently hissed.

Then, before I could even think, let alone react, a faceless person grabbed my knife-wielding wrist. He wrathfully shook the blade from my hand and with the other hand cupped my mouth to prevent a scream.

My eyes flew open in alarm. I tried to fight, but he was too strong. He pulled me up by my waist, tossed me over his shoulder, and carried me away from the sheriff's house. I was upside down. All I could see of the stranger was his bottom, the back of his legs, and his dusty black boots as we crossed the street.

The unknown man kicked open the church house door, set me on my feet, and then shoved me inside. I hit the wooden planks of the church house floor—hard. My body collided with one of the pews. I landed on my hands and knees, paralyzed with fear.

Then the unknown soul jerked me up again, this time setting me back down onto my feet in front of him. I stared down at his dusty boots with a sense of rising panic. *Who is he? Is it Charles Marshal?*

My knees wobbled with fear, but finally I looked up and then gawked, wide-eyed, into the livid face of Jacob Cole.

"In the name of all that is holy, what do you think you're doing, girl?" He wanted to curse at me; I could feel it. He wished to flay my behind. I'd seen that look in Mama's eyes before. He was barely containing himself.

I stood frozen beneath him, glancing up every few seconds into his terrifying eyes. I hadn't realized until that very second just how tall and muscular he was. He was several inches taller and quite a lot more substantial than my father was. Papa wasn't a small man; my mother barely came up to the middle of his chest, and my father was powerfully built due to years of farming, but the irate minister who stood glaring down at me was a great deal larger than even he.

Reverend Cole's sage-green eyes blared down at me, his leonine face still as marble. Beads of perspiration dripped off his angular nose. It struck me that as angry as he was, the good reverend still seemed like a living seraph to me. There was only purity, only innocence in his wrathful leer.

I searched the boundaries of my mind for an explanation. *Should I tell him of my clandestine plan? Should I trust him? And what about Charles's illicit plan to destroy my family? What should I say?*

Reverend Cole bent down until his angelic face was parallel to my own. Stony-faced, he glared into my horrified eyes. I attempted to look away. My eyes drifted up to the mass of wavy brown hair on his head. Just as my sights wandered, he moved closer, his breath puffing heavily and almost viciously into my face, reminding me of a weary horse.

Mr. Cole's giant hands shook as he pressed them down onto each one of my small shoulders, his mammoth strength nearly buckling my knees. He took a large, steadying breath, clearly attempting to behave a bit more peacefully. *"What were you going to do, child?"* he asked as forced peace swept through his burdened eyes.

I wasn't at all sure that I could speak, but I cleared my throat and tried. *"I was going to kill him—the sheriff,"* I meekly sobbed.

He shook his head and wiped the sweat from his brow with his hand. *"Why?"* he gasped just as both sweat and panic-stricken *tears* ran down the length of his face.

Suddenly, the floodgates broke, and uncontrollable sobs came gushing out from my fear-constricted throat. *"Charles Marshal was planning to hurt my mama again!"* I cried out loud, shrieking in agony at the thought. *"I had a vision last night! He had a plan to come to our house! He was going to hurt her again! He was going to kill…"* I couldn't finish the words; they were too vile. The image hurt my head.

Then my sprained ankle from the night before gave way, sending me crashing down to the floor. I hadn't felt any pain at all until then, but I seemed to have re-injured it while being forced into the church, and it was now angrily throbbing.

I peeked up at the reverend. His serene eyes were full of terrified tears as he stared down at me. Then he picked me up with absolutely no effort at all, just like the night before in the orchard, and carried me to where his buggy stood behind the church.

He spoke not a word as we headed away from the devil's sanctuary, going toward the safety of *his* home. In return, I sat beside him, unmoving and terrified for my parents.

I glanced back at the town as it grew smaller and smaller in the distance. I wondered when the devil would strike and wished that Mr. Cole hadn't prevented me from stopping him.

• • •

The sun was up by the time we arrived at the Coles' house. Molly gave Mr. Cole and me both a look of distress as her husband carried me through the door, and an obvious tremor of fright passed through her body as she peered into our tear-stained faces.

Mr. Cole ambled to a soft chair sitting in the parlor and put me down. Then he took Molly's shaking hand and led her into the kitchen with him, explaining to her what I did…and what I had *planned*.

I felt both shamed by the fact that Molly seemed so distressed and angered by the fact that my plan had been foiled by Mr. Cole. *Maybe if I just sneak out the door and run back into town…* I eyed the front door with a sense of frightened yearning, but the painful gasps and horrified cries resounding from the kitchen stopped me flat.

It was Molly. Clearly, she was horrified by my actions, but her reaction didn't make sense. She had been there the first time that Charles Marshal hurt my mama. Surely, she understood why I would want to stop him.

Just as that thought crossed my mind, Molly hurried from the kitchen. She flung herself around me and wept and then put her hands on each side of my face, surprisingly roughly. All the while the same anger that I had seen in her husband's eyes in the church arose in her eyes. Her hazel eyes bore into mine; large drops fell from them; she shook me as she spoke. *"What were you thinking? What do you think would happen to your mother if she lost another child? Did you even think about that? Huh?"* she shouted at the top of her lungs, shaking me violently. *"What of that? What of it, girl! I should whip you myself!"* She yanked me up by my wrist and stood me in front of her, prepared to punish me herself.

Mr. Cole hurried to her, seized me from her clutches, and then set me back down into the chair. He placed his hands on both sides of Molly's face, stroking her tenderly and nodding as she protested his action. *"I know, sweetheart,"* he spoke softly. *"Believe me, my first inclination was to do the same thing, but…"* He held her shaking body to his chest. *"Leesie is not our child to discipline. I'm certain that Asa will deal with her harshly enough."*

Molly turned her head up and looked into her husband's equally teary eyes. *"She's our godchild, Jake. It is our place to watch over her, just as Asa and Ali would do for our son."* She blew out a shaky breath. *"But I guess you're right."*

She turned, glared at me, and pointed a finger. *"You stay in that chair until your papa comes for you! Do you understand me?"*

"Y-yes, ma'am," I sheepishly mumbled, staring at my shoes. The way she reprimanded me reminded me of my mother.

I shuddered and nodded, trying not to think about what Papa was going to do to me. I gripped my legs in an attempt to stop my knees from knocking together.

Molly walked with her husband out to where his buggy stood. I watched from the chair that I was forbidden to leave, looking through the window. Reverend Cole kissed Molly, jumped up into his buggy, and drove out of the yard on his way to retrieve my parents.

Soon they'll know what I did. That thought brought massive shivers of terror to my mind. Never in my life had I feared my father…not at all. But I certainly feared him that day. *And he doesn't even know what I did yet.* "But soon, he will," I whispered to myself as my heart nearly leaped from my throat and my mind reeled from one horrifying scenario to another—all involving me, my bottom, and Papa's belt!

Papa had never whipped or even swatted me in my life. Sure, there were threats—idle threats—from both of my parents, but nothing ever came of them—not ever.

My body quaked with fright at the thought of what horrific punishment awaited me, sending vast shudders through my core and making the chair I was sitting in vibrate.

Molly walked back into the house just as Kristofer made his way down the stairs. *"What are you doing here?"* He yawned and then glanced around for my parents. *"Where are Ali and your pa?"*

At the same time, Molly pointed a sharp finger at me, giving me the same furious look that she did before. *"You just sit there and don't utter a word, not one word, or I'll take a strap to you! Do you hear me, Alyce!"* she yelled. The harshness of her voice startled me, making me jump in my seat, though she sounded as if she were trying not to cry.

Kristofer let out a gasp of shock when he heard what his mother said to me. He gaped at her. *"What happened?"*

Molly took a deep breath and smoothed down the front of her dress. Then she turned to Kristofer. *"I want you to go into the kitchen, sweetie, and eat your breakfast. Then I want you to go back up to your room. Mr. and Mrs. Raign will be here shortly to take Leesie home. Your pa has gone to get them."* She smiled serenely and held her hand out to him. *"It's just a good thing you forgot your catechism book at the church. Otherwise, your pa wouldn't have been there to bring Leesie"*—she glanced my way and her voice cracked—*"home."*

Huh? Kristofer sent his father to the church this morning?

But that thought was fleeting. All of a sudden I didn't feel quite so terrified. *Mama,* I thought to myself. *My saving grace. She'll never let Papa touch me.*

I wrinkled up my nose and opened my mind to her, hoping she'd be awake. I didn't hear anything at first, but then, clear as a bell, I heard *piano* music playing in my mind.

She's either still asleep…or playin' with my papa. I snickered to myself.

I screwed my eyes closed and as hard as I could yelled *Mama!* into my mind.

There was a pause, and then the music stopped… *"Leesie?"* I heard her soft voice in my head. *"I'm sorry, baby, we thought you were still sleeping. Are you hungry? I thought I'd make some hotcakes this morning. Would you like that?"*

"No, Mama," I meekly muttered. *"I'm not home."*

Her mind drew blank for a moment; then it was full of chaotic and jumbled thoughts. I couldn't keep up. There were just too many thoughts. Finally, after what seemed like a small eternity, she spoke. *"What do you mean you're NOT home!?"* Both anger and panic swelled in her mixed-up mind. *"Where are you?"*

Never in my life had I left the orchard without my parents, so I understood her fright.

"I'm, I'm at Mr. and Mrs. Cole's house. Mr. Cole is on his way now to get you and Papa. I'm fine. He should be there in just a few minutes…"

Another pause ensued, and then her mind exploded. *"DID YOU SNEAK OUT OF THE HOUSE TO SEE KRIS!?"*

I tried to answer, but she cut me off. *"NEVER MIND! JAKE'S HERE!"*

The window slammed shut.

Mama, please, I can explain, I mentally pleaded, but she didn't answer. *Mama…please!*

Still…nothing!

I sat within the confines of the chair that was holding me prisoner, violently shaking. *My salvation is gone—I'm doomed! She was my only chance.*

I hugged myself around the middle—willing myself not to fall apart. *Reverend Cole is there with them. He's telling them what I did.*

My head swam and I broke into a cold sweat. *Mama,* I desperately called once again. *Please, I can explain…* She didn't answer me. I frantically listened for the sound of her window, but it was shut tight.

I sat shaking, my imagination running amok. I knew they were getting closer every second. I could almost see them running out the door on their way to me—on their way to punish me.

I peeked at the clock sitting on the fireplace mantel. It had already been almost an hour since Mr. Cole left to get my parents, and our farm was only a short wagon ride away.

I stared, unblinking, out the parlor window, my knees trembling with fright…and *waited.*

My eyes were fixed on the yard just outside the house. I couldn't get them to move anywhere else. I knew they'd be there any minute.

What's going to happen?

Every once in a while, Molly peeked at me from the kitchen door. I glanced at her once; she didn't look angry anymore. She looked *terrified,* just like me.

I was hardly breathing. My gaze held only the yard. Any second the sound of hooves would come…any second. Tick tock, tick tock, thump, thump, thump, thump—both the clock and my heart echoed in my head, reminding me of my fate and counting down the seconds until the demise of my backside.

Just then, my head spun again, and I closed my eyes. My heart felt like it was in my mouth. I didn't remember ever being so afraid.

Mama, I weakly called, trying one last time to reach her, making one last desperate plea.

All of a sudden, a soft hand touched the side of my face, causing me to jump out of the chair and almost out of my skin.

It was Molly.

She sat on the arm of the chair and pulled me into a tight embrace. She stroked my hair. I pressed my cheek against her chest. Her heart was pounding almost as urgently as mine was. I took a shuddering breath, sobbing into the front of her dress.

"*Shh…*" She pulled my face up until our eyes met. "*What did you see last night?*" she whispered, and thankfully it was in her usual kind voice. "*Tell me exactly what you saw, Lees.*"

I frantically hyperventilated and could barely speak. My explanation came out in almost unintelligible stutters and sobs. "*I. Saw. Him. Hurting. My. Mama. Again. Only. It was. At our house. This time! And he was going to…*" I buried my head back into her dress, distraughtly bawling.

Molly hugged me tighter. "*He was going to what, baby?*"

"*Kill my papa!*" I bawled into the fabric of her dress.

She held me tighter, mindlessly rocking. As she held me, I peeked around her. Kristofer was standing in the kitchen doorway. He was crying. Our eyes met only for a moment before his mother jumped from the arm of my chair and rushed to the window.

My blood ran cold, and my eyes drew wide with fright. "*Maybe Papa will be so glad to see me unharmed that he won't be angry,*" I whispered to myself. "*Yes, maybe…*"

I closed my eyes, saying a silent prayer for my *gentle* Papa.

The sound of hooves fell like a boulder straight through my brain. My heart sank. I mindlessly stood and peeped around Molly just as Mr. Cole's buggy came to a halt outside the window, followed by Papa's wagon. I held my breath, gaping at the horrified face of my mother and the terrifying *glare* of my father.

Oh no, Papa's mad! Papa's really mad! I wanted to run. I wanted to hide. My sights darted around—all around. *But where to hide? Where?*

I couldn't move. My feet were fixed to the floor. My body was numb. I couldn't move. I couldn't think. All I could do was watch. Everything seemed to be happening in slow motion.

Papa burst from the wagon even before it stood still and then rushed toward the front door. His boots reverberated off the front porch stoop as he leaped forward. He wrenched open the front door. His face was distorted, twisted up with fury, his familiar gentle steel-blue eyes squeezed up tight, and he was looking daggers at me.

"*P-p-pa-pa…*" I tried to mumble, but the word just wouldn't come out. My breath was gone. It was crippled by fear, not even allowing a single whisper to push its way through my quivering lips.

In the next instant, he unbuckled his belt, violently tearing it from the loops of his trousers. Our sights met, and his eyes constricted. No longer were they bright and gentle. Fear had reduced them to harsh, dark slits. Then his teeth clenched, and he flew toward me.

I stood paralyzed as he charged at me. It was surreal, as if I were watching the scene unfold from somewhere outside my body. I wanted to run, but my mind blurred again although I plainly saw the expression on his face. It wasn't one of fury but grief.

With that sight, my throat further constricted, and I wanted to burst out sobbing. I wanted to cry, not out of fright for what my father was going to do to me, but out of sorrow—sorrow for what I was putting him through.

I thought about how upset Mr. and Mrs. Cole seemed earlier… I was *wrong*. Papa's expression was something between mad, frantic, and utterly, hysterically insane.

Then, for some reason I didn't understand, I stared down at his boots as they moved toward me. *One step, two steps, three, four…*

My eyes swept back up to his face. It was screwed up in sheer agony. He was gnashing his teeth. Just as he took his fifth step across the parlor, he heaved his entire seething body forward, grabbing me and tossing me clear over the chair. I landed hard, flat on my back.

The force knocked the wind out of my lungs. Papa glared down at me and reached for my head, first seizing fistfuls of my hair, and then lifted me up and threw me against the wall behind me. I flew through the air. Like a ragdoll, my limp body connected with plaster and wood, my lungs burned by the force of the blow. I screamed and fell to the ground, but he wasn't stopping.

Papa bent over me and twisted my hair between his fingers. He threw his livid face into mine. His breath hit me on the side of my head. *"I have never taken a belt to you before because you've never given me cause. Well, you've done that today. I'm going to whip you within an inch of your life!"* he viciously hissed.

Every muscle in my body twitched with terror. My lungs huffed, gasping and trying to breathe. My quaking knees buckled and gave way, but my father's grasp on my hair didn't permit me to fall to his feet. I writhed, shrieking in pain, my scalp fiercely protesting the hold he had on my hair. I willed both my ankle and my knees to support my weight as I attempted to stand, but I was weak and injured, and through my peripheral vision I saw his belt dangling from the hand he had twisted in my hair.

Then from somewhere behind Papa, my mother shrieked. *"Asa!"* she cried. She ran to him, took his hands out of my hair and threw her body in front of me in a protective stance. She had one arm stretched out toward his chest, pushing him away as forcefully as she could while with the other she grabbed my hand and led me around him. *"Please, Asa, please!"* She was sobbing. *"Let her explain, please, baby!"*

I couldn't look at him. I stared at my shoes.

My body was so exhausted that I felt as if I were going to drop unconscious at their feet at any moment, but I stood my ground next to Mama…*my saving grace.*

But Papa didn't give in. He took one large step toward us, grasped me by the wrist, and jerked me away from her. *"She can explain after I take my belt to her bare behind!"* he spat through clenched teeth.

Without another word to my mother, my father turned to Mr. Cole, suddenly calmer, resolved, maybe. *"May I use your barn, Jake, please?"* he whispered numbly. He didn't wait for a reply. He pulled me behind him through the parlor and out the door. I limped as fast as I could to keep up with his frenzied gate. He dragged me out the front door and down the porch stoop, his belt grasped in the same hand as my wrist. I could feel the stiffened leather almost cutting into my skin due to the powerful grip that he had on us both.

Mama ran behind us as we headed through the yard. I could hear the sound of her weeping.

Papa stopped at the barn door and pushed it open, but it was jerked from his hands and slammed shut mentally by my mother. He turned, glaring at her; she was in tears. *"I have to do this, Ali. Please go inside!"* Papa was crying, too. I could hear him. His breath was harsh, and uneven sobs emanated from his chest as he spoke to her.

Still, I couldn't look at him.

"Not. While. You. Are. Raging! I've been hurt by rage before, Asa. I won't allow you strike at her—not right now!" she cried, putting her hands to her face, weeping, and then she threw herself into my arms. She clutched me to her chest. *"You could've died! He could've harmed you! What were you thinking?"* she sobbed, clinging to me for dear life.

Papa let go of my wrist and pulled Mama to his chest, all the while sobbing with her, and dragged us all to the ground.

I lay in the arms of both my parents for what seemed like an eternity, unsure of my fate, but I didn't care about that. Mama was still whimpering. I pressed my ear against her chest, listening to the rapid fluttering of her heart. She was terrified, and so was my papa. He would have to be to *strike* at me in such a way.

"We have to move," he mumbled to Mama, or maybe it was to himself. *"I have to take you away from here. I can't lose you. I can't lose either one of you. I'd die. I couldn't go on without you…"* With those

agonizing words, my father sobbed and folded both Mama and me into his arms.

After a while, he wiped his eyes and looked up. He took my face between his palms. *"I'm sorry for what I did, but I still have to punish you. I must,"* he whispered, sorrowfully shaking his head. He seemed lost yet determined. *"I don't know how yet, but your mama's right. I can't do it now, not in this state of mind."* Tears fell from his chin as he put his lips to my forehead. Without another word, he stood, lifted me to his chest, and carried me back into the house.

•   •   •

My parents decided to attend church in a last-ditch effort to gain some support for our family from the rest of the town. I sat half-listening to Mr. Cole as he tried over and over again to convince Papa that his plan just might work. In the end, he succeeded in persuading him. I, incidentally, stayed at the Coles' house with Molly, a fact that I didn't mind at all, except that Kristofer attended church along with his father and my parents. That must have been my father's idea, I concluded.

Although I wasn't exactly thrilled to be left behind, I wasn't in any position to argue with my parents just then, either. So, I obediently said nothing and stayed firmly planted in the seat that I wasn't permitted to leave. All in all, considering what had occurred with my father, I was thankful to be able to *sit* anywhere at all.

I sat quietly waiting for my parents to come back from church. Even though I didn't want to admit it, I was having a rather nice time with Molly. *"Do you know what Reverend Cole's sermon is going to be about today?"* I asked her.

Molly peeked up from her Bible. *"The seven deadly sins, baby,"* she answered, smiling kindly at me.

"And just how long does church service last?" I asked her. I was worried; I wanted them home!

She peeped up over the top of her Bible again and smiled. *"They should be back pretty soon."*

I bit my lip, thinking about how upset she was with me earlier. *"I was just tryin' to protect my mama!"*

Molly closed the Bible and sighed. *"You could've gotten yourself killed, Lees,"* she sternly retorted and then frowned as only a mother can.

I shook my head and sucked back a sob. *"It would've been worth it to protect my mother!"* I put my head in my hands. *"I just found her! Papa just found her! I can't lose her again—I won't lose her again! I'll fight anyone who tries to harm her or Papa!"* I almost unintelligibly mumbled through my fingers.

Molly rushed to my side. She sat beside me in the overlarge chair and held me to her chest. *"I know, baby. I'd protect her myself. In fact, I tried to get her away from that madman a long time ago. So did your papa, your Uncle Jake, and your Grandma Maggie. And believe me, I would do anything I had to do to keep her out of his clutches now—any of us would…"* Her tearful voice trailed off, and she cupped my face between her hands. Our eyes met. *"Still, you can't go around putting yourself into danger. That's just not helpful. Your parents lost one child already, and it nearly destroyed them. Losing you would kill them."*

She heaved a deep sigh and stroked my hair. Her eyes were soft. *"And, Lees, your papa was scared today—that's all. He was just scared. Are you worried that he's going to punish you when they return?"*

I shook my head. *"I don't really care about that right now. Besides, Papa didn't really hurt me. He just knocked the wind outta me is all. He can punish me if he wants to. I don't really care."*

"How can you not care about that?" Molly's eyes drew wide.

I stared her straight in her pretty hazel eyes. *"All I care about is protecting my family."*

She blew out an exasperated breath and closed her eyes for a moment, apparently to steady the tumultuous emotions that were brewing inside of her. Then she opened them, and the mother stare returned. *"You are a child, Leesie—not an adult! It is our duty as your parents and godparents to protect you. Not the other way around! You must behave! Anything less is going to get you a whipping from your father!"*

I crossed my arms over my chest and looked the other way. *"I don't care. Mama needs me."*

"Your mama is much stronger than she used to be!" Molly retorted.

My sights swept back to hers. She was incredulously glaring at me. *"Something has happened to me within the past few days, Molly. I'm not sure what, but I've grown up. And not just physically. I'm not the same person I was before. I'm not a child anymore. I know things that I just shouldn't know. And I can do things that shouldn't be possible—but still, I can do them."*

I paused and shook my head, trying to figure things out. *"I'm as strong as Mama is now—maybe even stronger! Therefore, I have just as much responsibility to protect her as she does me. Papa can whip me all he likes."* I glared right back at her. *"I won't stop until Charles Marshal is no longer a threat to her!"*

Molly's face fell, and she practically sagged with exhaustion. *"Then I fear that you're going to get yourself hurt, either by your father's terrified hand or by that madman's."*

"So be it," I muttered. *"Better me than her. If my fate is sealed by protecting my parents, then that's just the way it has to be."*

Stoically, wordlessly, Molly rose and returned to her seat on the chesterfield couch. She picked up her Bible and opened it.

"By the way," I whispered to her, changing the subject. I didn't want her upset with me. *"Why is Reverend Cole preaching about the seven deadly sins this week? I thought he said his sermon was going to be 'love thy neighbor?'"*

She put the Bible down onto her lap and sighed again—a tired sigh, and her eyes welled with tears. *"Well, it was, but he felt that the seven deadly sins might get his point about your parents and you across better. In the sermon, he is going to explain that there should've been nine deadly sins instead of only seven."*

I gave her a confused look. *"Why nine?"*

"It is your Uncle Jake's opinion that prejudice and ignorance should have been included on the list of deadly sins. Then he'll introduce your folks and talk about what nice people they are. Nice and misunderstood."

"I sure hope his plan works." I smiled into Molly's tearful eyes. *"I rather like having a family."*

She stifled a sob and nodded. Then she smiled, and I knew she wasn't angry with me anymore. *"So do I, sweet girl. And no matter what, we are your family!"*

All of a sudden, I heard the sound of a wagon coming up to the house. I jumped up, forgetting that I was forbidden to move from the spot, and hobbled to the door. *"That must be Papa and Mama!"* I grinned, relieved. *"I hope everything went well. Because if it didn't…"* I gave Molly a grave look. *"We'll be moving."*

I couldn't stand to think about that.

I limped, full-speed, toward the door, happy to feel that my ankle was a bit better, expecting to see my parents standing outside, waiting for me.

"Oh, Lees!" Molly hollered just before I reached for the doorknob.

I turned, grinning.

"When you get outside, give your papa a big hug and tell him that you're sorry." Then she paused for a moment, and her face fell serious again. *"And if that doesn't work—cry! Men hate it when we cry."*

"You think I should use my 'feminine wiles' on Papa?" I giggled.

Molly nodded. *"It's better than finding yourself over a barrel in my barn with your bloomers down around your ankles,"* she frightfully muttered and then shuddered at the thought.

I uneasily bit my lip. *"Right. Good idea,"* I mumbled and then turned the knob.

I ran straight out the door and right into…the sheriff.

He was standing on the porch. In my eagerness to get to my parents, I bounced off his chest. It was *his* wagon I heard. My parents weren't back. *Thank goodness!*

Charles Marshal grabbed me, eyeing me like I was some sort of a prize…one that he wished to either win or *kill*. It was hard to tell. *"Well, well,"* he hissed through clenched teeth. *"What happened to you?"* He grasped my face, jerked it up, and pulled it from side-to-side, studying me. *"You've done some growing in the past few days."* His mouth twisted with disgust. *"Your father's little prize, now, aren't you!"* he viciously spat.

I said nothing. *Must not panic, must not panic, must not panic…* That was my mantra, grounding me. A level head would keep me safe—that, and my powers. *Yes, my powers. Steady, steady…* I took a deep breath and balled up my fist, and with all my might, I struck him in his awful mouth.

The sheriff lost his hold on me for just a second. He stumbled back, his eyes drawing wide and insane with rage. *"Why, you little bastard witch!"* he spat just as a trickle of blood oozed down into his pointed beard.

Then, the devil charged. He clasped his hands like a vise grip around my neck and threw me against the house. I hit the wooden siding hard, my already sore lungs nearly bursting with pain. He threw his pointed face into mine. His hot, ragged breath blew against my cheek. *"You know, girl,"* he spat at me, his jaw tense. *"You should be nicer to me. After all, as sheriff, I could take your…mother."* He said the last word as if it were an expletive. *"I could take her into my custody should I feel that what she can do is a danger to my town's safety. And I think I just might!"* He plunged his fingers into my throat, constricting my airway tighter, and then lifted me off the ground by my neck.

My mind blurred from lack of air while his vile words resounded in my head.

"I bet if I had her, your mother!" He hissed the word again as if it were dirty. *"I bet you would do anything I told you to do—anything at all."* He thrust his face forward, stuck out his tongue, and licked the entire length of my face—tasting me!

I shuddered with disgust, and my stomach twisted, but I knew I had to keep my wits about me. I steadied my emotions. *Don't react; don't react. It's what he wants.*

Charles set me on the ground, his bony hips pinning me against the house, a wicked gleam shining in his cold eyes. *"You don't even taste good,"* he sneered, and then spat on the wooden planks of the porch. *"Your mother, on the other hand, is a rare and exotic delicacy."* He closed his eyes and took a deep breath, as if actually breathing in the memory of her flavor. *"Alice is pleasing to the palate—sweet and soft. I simply can't wait to taste her again, her entire body, particularly where that enticing sunburst birthmark lies…"*

The devil leaned back, eager for my reaction.

I shoved my face into his. *"You touch my mama, and I WILL kill you."*

He stood chuckling at me, his eyes alight with amusement, apparently surprised by my lack of fear. *"Don't I terrify you? Like I do…your mother?"* He manically cocked his head, studying me as if I were some sort of an anomaly.

I smirked with defiance as a sudden memory of my past life, or rather, death emerged. *"My mother—bless her—is a gentle soul. Her patience is a trait that, unfortunately for you, I DO NOT POSSESS!"*

Go ahead, you evil bastard, do something. Do something, so I can blow you up just like I did Papa's coffee cup!

The devil lumbered back, apparently thrown by my words, and a flash of fright crossed over his face, as if he were staring into the face of a ghost—which, in a way, he was.

Quickly regaining his composure, he thrust toward me and jerked my face upward, pinning me tighter against his body. I could feel him, hard and excited, against my belly. *"I suppose you think that your father will save her…and you?"* he silkily drawled, squeezing my throat. *"You know, I could kill you right now. I yearn to watch the light leave your eyes, witch."*

Bile rose in my throat, but I stood my ground, even though his fingernails were biting into the sides of my neck, and I could smell the cloying stench of liquor on his breath. *"I could say the same to you."* My voice was hoarse, yet strong. *"Has it yet occurred to you that you are toying with the wrong witch? Has it occurred to you that I just might destroy you?"*

He chuckled.

I looked dead in his sights. *"You come near my mother, and this time, you won't be hiding from a ghost. This time, you'll be hiding from a real. Live. Witch!"*

A slow grimace swept across my face. I leisurely inclined my head again—playing with his cowardice, making quite certain he clearly understood my meaning. *"You remember that ghost, don't you? The one who looked a great deal like…my mother?"*

He gasped and released me, jumping back as if my flesh had seared his hands. He cocked his head again, his chest heaving with a sense of fright, and a sudden bloom of uncertainty streaked across his lifeless eyes.

I stood up on my toes—entirely fearless. *"You lay one hand on my mother, you evil bastard, and this time, you'll be hiding from me,"* I whispered in a sweet little-girl voice. *"Just like you did before. Just like the last time you laid eyes on me."*

Charles's eyes grew wide with comprehension, and he took another step away, almost stumbling backward off the stoop.

I pushed forward, gaining the upper hand. *"Tell me, Charlie, do you know who I am?"*

The devil's face drew white as a sheet.

"You see…pet," I sardonically laughed—giving him back his own vile words while inching closer. *"I was there that night. I saw how you maimed her, how you scarred her, all because she didn't love you. I saw it all. I saw it with my own eyes. So you can wipe that horrid smile right off your face. I know what you are. You are nothing but a liar and a coward. Isn't that right…Deputy?"*

A half-horrified, half-amazed look fell over the monster's face as if he were trying to comprehend what I was revealing to him, his beady, soulless eyes darting back and forth between mine.

Yes, you understand…

I placed my face dangerously close, glaring into his cold, soulless eyes and almost pushing him off the porch. *"But, I avenged her, didn't I?"* I whispered, pushing closer still. *"I remember the worry on your face. I remember the fear in your eyes, when you thought I was about to take your life. I remember…your pain. How could you ever forget that first time we met, Charlie?"*

I shook my head. *"No, you don't fool me. You remember the pain I showed you."* I stepped closer—until our eyes were mere inches apart and he had to grab hold of the porch railing to keep from falling down the steps. *"I told you I'd be back for you. After all, a ghost can't kill,"* I whispered.

Without another word, I concentrated hard, envisioning his plans for my mother. I let the fury seep deep inside, straight to the core of my being, and heaved a deep breath. I held it for a second and then released all the power I could muster. I let it go—right into his revolting face, sending both flames and my hands into the air, straight toward him.

The sheriff's eyes grew wide for a moment as if he were sensing his own demise. But before he could react, my power exploded, sending him soaring twenty feet or more into the air, finally crashing headfirst into a tree in the Coles' yard. At the same time, three large clay flowerpots burst from the front porch, launching debris into the air and shooting flowers as high as the house.

I looked down at my hands; they were glowing with bright blue sparks. I tried to catch my breath, but as I pulled air into my burning lungs, my head spun around, and fatigue swept through me in vast waves, sending my already blurry mind into a fog.

"Steady, steady," I mumbled to myself, glaring at the evil monster who was now scrambling to his feet, attempting to right himself.

I leaned over, panting, my palms against my knees. Thankfully, after a few moments, my mind stabilized, and I stood upright—ready for another battle if need be though I doubted he would instigate another attack.

As I stood watching the undermined sheriff, I had to laugh at the irony of the situation: Charles Marshal came to hunt and became the hunted.

Finally, the devil stood upright, his revolting face twisted up in pain. He wiped a steady stream of blood from his head. But then, a sinful, malicious, almost lustful, gaze fell over it. He stalked closer to me, trying to catch his breath while clapping his hands, viciously smirking. He was applauding my attack.

Still, I stood my ground.

He stepped up to where I stood scowling at him and threw his foul face into mine. *"There is one difference between now and when we last met, witch!"* His vile eyes bore straight into mine.

I didn't falter; I glared right back. *"You don't scare me!"*

He smirked at my audacity. *"The last time we met, you were a ghost. But this time…"* He hissed, grabbed my hair, pulled a fistful of it out, and then shoved it into his coat pocket. *"I can hurt you."*

I screeched in pain and clutched the side of my head.

He shoved his face deeper into mine, pushing our noses together, and wickedly laughed. Then he wound his fingers around my neck again. *"At least this time I know what I'm up against and who to kill first."*

I was unable to attack. My power was spent. My mind blurred.

"Your. Mother. Was. A. Ten. Cent. Whore. I bought her evenhandedly. She is mine," he whispered in my ear.

My mouth popped open, and I gaped at him. I wanted to kill him!

Seeing my shock, he triumphantly smirked though his evil smile quickly turned to pain just as my father seized him by the neck from behind. Papa punched him in the mouth, sending him reeling to the ground and away from me.

The devil went to get up, but I dove at him with all of my strength. I pounced on top of his chest, clawing and scratching. Blood burst and then streamed from his nose as I grabbed hold of it, viciously twisting, feeling it shatter under my hands. I screeched and hissed at him like an animal. I wanted to tear every inch of skin from his head with my bare hands.

From somewhere beside me Papa yelled; his arms encircled my waist. He pulled me off the sheriff and threw me to the ground. My already aching body made contact with the gravel. I skidded facedown into it. The force took my breath away, and I knocked my head against the porch of Jacob and Molly's house.

My father pointed at me, frantic tears and panic showing in his wide eyes. *"STAY THERE!"* he screamed at me.

Understanding his defeat, the sheriff stood. He threw both his hands into the air as if in surrender. Then he slowly lowered his hands while pointing at Papa. *"You best mind yourself, stable boy,"* he silkily drawled, taking a handkerchief from his coat pocket and wiping the blood from his broken nose.

"YOU PUT YOUR HANDS ON MY DAUGHTER! I'M GONNA KILL YOU, YOU SON OF A BITCH!" my father roared, his hands twisting into claws as if prepared for the kill.

"You come one step closer to me, stable boy," the sheriff sneered, *"and I'll see you hanged."* He gawked at me *"All of you. The reverend and his family, too."* He smirked and then shrugged. *"Well, everyone but my Alice, of course,"* he raucously laughed and then winked at me.

"NOT IF YOU'RE DEAD!" I screamed, holding onto the porch banister. I pulled myself to my feet.

Papa stopped dead in his tracks. He turned, stony-faced, scowling at me, and threw me a look that I had hoped *never* to see. It was frightening. He GLARED at me as if he were actually *considering* beating me unconscious.

I shut my mouth and sat down on the stoop.

Just then, Mr. Cole rode up the path leading to his house. He jumped from his horse and ran toward Papa and Charles Marshal. He took one look at me and gasped in horror. I knew my face was bleeding. I could smell and taste the blood as it ran into my mouth, but I wasn't sure where the blood was coming from. Every inch of me seemed to hurt.

Mr. Cole tied his horse to the railing and charged at the sheriff, but my father stopped him. He put one hand to Mr. Cole's heaving chest. *"No. Let him be, Jake,"* he muttered.

The devil grinned. *"Now, that's a wise decision, stable boy!"* he laughed, walking backward, taunting Papa.

Just before climbing into his wagon, he stopped and tipped his dusty, weed-covered hat. His soulless eyes twinkled with malicious delight. *"I will have them. Both of them. After all, a man simply can't break up such an enticing set, now, can he? I just hope your daughter is as sweet a piece of calico as my Alice was."* He threw his head back and wickedly laughed. *"And if you were wondering how I found Alice…"* He chuckled, clearly enjoying my father's helpless position.

"My father was told where to find her by none other than Mr. Raign, Senior." He smirked at my father's shocked expression. *"Follow the reverend—that's what he was told..."*

Laughing, the devil jumped up on his wagon and rode away.

Mr. Cole turned to Papa and indignantly gestured toward the sheriff.

Papa shook his head. *"You were right. It was a trap, Jake. There's no way he would've come here otherwise."* Papa surveyed the yard, shaking his head. *"I knew it wouldn't work. It was a good try, my friend, but we must go."*

Just then, the door of the house burst open, and Molly came rushing out, shrieking. She clasped my hand and tugged me into the house. *"I'm so sorry, Lees!"* she screeched. *"I didn't know what was going on! I thought you were having an argument with your papa!"* She hurriedly got a wet towel and wiped the blood off my face and hands, but she withdrew her hand in horror when she peeked at my neck.

"What?" I asked her.

"You have big purple hand prints around your neck."

"I'm all right," I croaked, but I could feel where the sheriff had squeezed my neck. My throat was swollen and stung when I tried to speak.

Papa walked into the house. He stood glaring at me, looking at me with the same angry stare as before, and pointing. *"DON'T YOU EVER DO ANYTHING LIKE THAT AGAIN!"* His teeth were clenched, his eyes wild. *"Your mother is right!"* he spat. *"You are an overprotective fool, and so help me, I'm gonna beat it right outta you, girl!"*

His words impaled me like a knife through my chest...

"My mother? Mama? Where's Mama?" I frantically looked around. *"Papa?"* I screamed. *"Where's Mama?"*

"She's still at the church with Kris... Why?" Seeing my sudden panic, his face melted into an expression of confusion instead of anger.

"THE SHERIFF, PAPA!" I yelled as tears poured unbidden from my eyes. *"He said he was going to take her into his custody! He said she was a danger to the town. And if he has her, then he can get me to do anything he wants! And he CAN, Papa! HE CAN!"*

Instantly, I knew what I had to do. My eyes swept past my father to the opened door that wasn't but five feet from him.

I know what I have to do. I have to save her.

My father saw it in my eyes, too. *"You stay right there,"* he said, pointing at me, his voice calm but forceful. *"You can't get by me, anyway, angel."* He raised his palms as if talking to a cornered animal.

I tried to take a breath, but I was too numb, too resigned to my own fate.

"There's something you don't know about me," I whispered, shaking my head, tears burning down my face, my throat constricting with fear. *"Something no one knows."*

"What is it?" he, too, barely uttered, eyeing me carefully, ready to catch me if I tried to get past him.

"I'm…really…fast," I whispered. Then I bolted straight past his outstretched arms and right out the door.

"ALYCE RAIGN!" Papa bellowed.

Obediently, I stopped and turned to him. I stood about fifty feet from the house. My ankle throbbed a bit but thankfully held my weight.

"You come back here right now!" he commanded, blue eyes blazing.

My father was forcing himself to remain calm, but he was terrified, his face writ large with horror. *"You come here, and I swear, I swear not to punish you for anything you've done here today."* He took one bold step off the porch—toward me. *"But you run from me now, and as God as my witness, I'll turn you over and beat your behind black and blue! Do you understand me, girl?"*

I flinched and nodded, and my heart sank with grief. *"Yes, sir. I understand."* Then I turned and ran full-speed toward town—toward my mama.

I could hardly see as I ran. Tears and blood blinded me; instinct and fear drove me forward, propelling me toward my mother's danger. My fatigued eyes stung and tried to close, but I forced them to stay open by sheer will alone. *I don't want to be faster than Papa! I don't want to be stronger or bigger than Mama! I don't want to be braver than anyone! And especially, I don't want to disobey my papa! But I have no choice! I can't let that horrible man hurt my mother! I just can't!*

As I got closer to town, I concentrated hard, feeling for Mama's mind, silently praying that it was open to me—thankfully, it was. *Stay with Kristofer!* I thought with every fiber of my being.

Nothing came back at first, and then… *"Why?"* she answered back to me with her mind, seemingly confused by my anxious tone. Without pause, I sent images as I ran closer to where she was. Until that moment, I wasn't aware that I could send her visions in that way, but fright had seemed to awaken the hidden talents within me. Now, I was strong.

At that moment, I was a fully grown Beacon soul.

I'm almost there, I frantically whispered into her head.

A few moments later, I came flying into town. I sprinted toward the little white church just as she and Kristofer came down the steps. My mother was trying not to react, but she was clearly shaken. Kristofer stalked down the steps in front of her, protectively holding her hand behind him and scanning the nearly deserted street.

Suddenly, my mother froze. She was blankly staring across the dirt road at something, or rather, *someone*.

I looked where she was looking. It was the sheriff standing in front of the jailhouse, his soulless gaze trained straight on her, his eyes alight with lust and *longing*. A putrid grin stretched across his bloodied face, and he wasn't alone. Three other men were with him, all making their way toward the church—toward my sweet mother. She looked panic-stricken.

I stopped in my tracks right in the middle of the road and turned toward the devil, momentarily thrown by the clear intensity of the sheriff's desire for my mother. Still, I was ready to stand my ground and prepared to fight, to the death if necessary. *It's all right, Mama. I'm here,* I whispered into her mind.

She turned, spotting me standing in the middle of the road, all the while my eyes darted between her and the sheriff. *I can't let him hurt you.*

"No! Leesie, no!" she frantically screamed out loud.

"*Hey!*" I yelled at the men who were walking toward my mother, but they didn't stop.

I turned to the sheriff, glaring him dead in his cold eyes. "*Take me! Leave her alone, and I won't fight you!*"

The sheriff leered at me and smiled, a slow carnivorous smile, and then amusedly laughed. He looked like a wild animal that had just found its prey…*prey* that wouldn't run.

I stepped one more pace across the road, ready to sacrifice myself for my mother, but just as I stepped forward, someone caught me around the waist, whirling me around.

It was Papa.

My sights swept to the church just as Mr. Cole ran toward the church house steps, the reins of two horses in his hands, his arms stretched wide, shielding Mama. And Kristofer was right behind him—both protecting her from the men.

The sheriff's men stopped at the church steps just as Reverend Cole tied the horses to the railing. "*Is there a problem, gentlemen?*" Mr. Cole determinedly inquired.

"*We don't have a problem with you, Reverend,*" one of the men told him. "*We just want the witch.*" The man gestured toward my mother.

Kristofer's stance drew taller, dominating, and his eyes blared with determination. He threw his body in front of Mama.

"I assure you, gentlemen," Mr. Cole tightly stated, slowly shaking his head and pushing Mama deeper behind him and Kristofer. *"There is no witch here."* Mr. Cole eyed Papa and me from across the road. *"Therefore, if you want to take Mrs. Raign, then you'll have to come through me. And I dare say I don't think the good people of this town will take too kindly to anyone who hurts their minister."*

"Or their minister's son!" Kristofer shouted from behind his pa.

Papa and I slowly stalked toward the church, his hand clutching mine, neither of us taking our eyes off the sheriff.

Finally, thankfully, the sheriff's men backed away.

Reverend Cole reached around Kristofer, took Mama by the hand, and led her toward Papa's wagon that was sitting in front of the church where they had left it, all the while still shielding her between himself and Kristofer. He cautiously lifted my mother up into the front seat. Then just as we approached, Papa raised me up into it as well and sat me next to her.

Mr. Cole turned to my father and sighed; he placed a hand on Papa's shoulder. *"Leave now, my friend. Kris and I won't be long behind you."*

Papa nodded and quickly jumped up into the wagon next to us. As we started down the street, I looked back. Mr. Cole and Kristofer were still standing in the middle of the road, glaring at the sheriff, still protecting us and giving us extra time to get away.

• • •

Papa rushed us back to the farm. He was frantic. He dragged Mama and me into the house. *"Just get what we need. We have plenty at the cabin."*

Mama took my hand and then silently pulled me up to my room.

"What are we doing?" I tearfully screeched.

Please say we're not moving away…

"Running! AGAIN!" she cried, turned, and then ran back downstairs.

I moved around my room, grabbing my things and trying not cry. I felt numb. It was as if I was trying and failing to wake up from a bad dream. All of a sudden, my head spun, and I almost passed out. Then I saw a clear picture in my mind of the same three men and the devil, coming up to our farm. They had Mr. Cole's horses in their possession and a look of cold-blooded murder in their eyes.

"They're coming!"

My parents rushed back into my room.

"I see them, too!" Papa frantically cried and then grabbed me around the waist and threw me over his shoulder. Without another word, he darted down the stairs and out the door with Mama and me in tow.

"It's too late!" I screeched. *"They're coming for us!"*

Papa stopped in the yard; his eyes swept the ground. He was frantically searching for something. Then he set me down and knelt before me. Panic-stricken, he peered into my eyes, and with tears streaming down his face. *"Where is it, Lees?"* he sobbed, his eyes beseeching. He put his palm to my cheek. *"Where is the old cellar?"* He was terrified for us. He thought we were going to die. I could see it in his eyes. *"It's been so long, I just don't remember where it is,"* he desperately whispered, reaching out, clutching Mama's hand.

Without pause, I darted out into the yard and found the cellar door with no problem at all, my parents trailing right behind me—still clutching hands.

The old cellar door creaked and protested as my father pulled the age-worn rope, but finally it rose. Once it was open, he lowered us into it. Then he jumped in himself and slammed the old door shut, sending dirt and debris raining down on to our heads. Just as the door slammed, the sound of hooves coming up the path resounded above us, along with the voices of the men who meant us harm.

Mama closed her eyes for a moment. Then, concentrating on her power, she mentally covered the cellar door with loose dirt to hide us, darkening our shelter. The dirt fell through the cracks, dusting our heads with a fine powder. As the dirt fell through, the slats and holes in the door reappeared, allowing the sunlight through, but the door lay hidden beneath the loose soil.

From above us, we heard the voices of the sheriff and his men. They were searching for us.

In my mind, I got a mental picture of Mr. Cole and Kristofer, both in the distance, powerless to help us. All they could do was watch from atop a nearby hill as the wicked men scoured the orchard, searching for us.

Papa saw the vision, too. He turned to me, looking frightened.

"They know we're all right, Papa. They know we're down here. Kristofer can see my light through the cracks." I took his hand, trying to reassure him.

The men drew nearer, their voices louder. *"They couldn't have gotten far!"* the devil screamed at them. *"Find them! And when you do, kill the man, but I want the witches for myself!"* he laughed. *"And be mindful of the young one. Her anger causes things to explode!"*

With those vile words, my father threw his arms around both Mama and me and dragged us to the very corner of the cellar.

I was afraid to breathe. I was afraid that my heartbeat was too loud. I willed it to stop beating to save my family, but it just wouldn't stop pounding! Every inch of my body shook with anger and fear. Both my mind and my heart were racing, and I could feel cold fury building in the pit of my stomach.

I glanced down at my hands, where faint, blue flames were forming around my fingertips. My body shook as I tried to pull back the massive explosion building inside of me. Like a volcano, I was ready to erupt. I breathed in and out deeply, trying to get a hold of the power I so desperately wanted to unleash. At the same time, I wondered if I was capable of stopping the evil men with my *own* raw force.

What should I do? Perhaps I can end this right now! My thoughts were frantic. I wanted to end it then or to have them take *me* and leave.

Mama's mind broke through mine. *"You'll do nothing. Because if you die, then I will!"* She squeezed my hand, begging me with her eyes—her beautiful eyes that were full of both panic and love.

All right, I whispered mentally.

I heaved another deep breath, attempting to subdue the fire. My head fell back onto Papa's chest. I closed my eyes, allowing the explosive force pulsing through me to wane and then to cease altogether.

The three of us stood motionless, silently listening as the men ransacked our precious little house, but we could do nothing to stop them.

My father held my mother and me to his chest, all the while deep sobs echoed from the inside of him.

Mama held my head to hers. She closed her eyes. *"Be still. Please, be still, my baby. I need you,"* she whispered into my mind.

And then, the devil gave one final despicable order to the other men. I wanted to scream. I wanted to go tearing out of the cellar and blow them as far as I could get their mangled dead bodies to fly. I wanted to strike them down, one by one, until only the devil and I remained. Then I would be free to rip him to shreds and send his vile soul to Hell where it belonged!

But all I could do was listen through the cracks of our hiding place as our home *burned.*

My knees buckled and gave way, sending me to the cellar floor. My weakened body twitched with pain.

I tried to contain the fire that was consuming me, but it was too intense. The flames burned through my brain, making me shake, allowing the darkness to tear through my light. My head lulled against my father's chest and rolled back. I was helpless and burning with rage.

And just when I thought the pain could get no worse, I heard a chorus of screams in the distance. It was the agonizing sound of dozens of souls crying out in pain at once.

I knew then what had come to pass. It happened in an instant, yet the pain seemed to go on forever. The flames seared through my head, sending me first to my hands and knees and then to my back on the ground. I rolled around the dirt floor in anguish, realizing that there was nothing I could do for my cherished friends.

My beloved orchard was in flames.

The screams and moans of my majestic trees seared through my brain like a white-hot poker, winding me. Just before I blacked out, Papa's hand clasped over my mouth as the screams in my head moved down to my throat. He dragged me into his arms just as I collapsed, sobbing, blinded by the pain of my trees. I cupped my hands over my ears just as the individual voices of each one of my glorious trees cried out for me—into my head—begging for my help. But I was powerless to stop their suffering.

Then, in an instant, the torturous screams ceased.

I knew; without a doubt, I just knew. Our orchard was no more. It was *dead,* and like it, so was my soul. My sights turned to ash; my world lost all color. Only charred blackness remained.

The earth stopped spinning, and everything faded to black.

18. The Aftermath

We stayed hidden in the old cellar throughout the night. It was dark and dank. The smell of smoke permeated the small cracks of the cellar door, causing us to choke, but at least we were safe—for the moment.

Papa and I saw Reverend Cole and Kristofer in our minds. They were watching over us from afar, standing silent witness to the atrocities taking place above us. Thankfully, though, they didn't need to intervene on our behalves. Our shelter was well hidden from the monsters who hunted us.

We stayed huddled together the entire night, Papa, Mama, and me.

Just as the sun came up the next morning, the men began to leave. They were drunk with power and whiskey. The sheriff hooted and hollered obscenities, describing to his men in detail what he planned to do to my mother and me if ever he found us.

"I've got some of the girl's hair!" Charles Marshal sneered. *"Let me tell you, that one's a spitfire! Although, her mother, My Alice, is my type. She's genteel, soft, and womanly. Not that I won't find a certain amount of delight in possessing the girl, especially in the presence of her father, the stable boy. But it's been far too long since I've had my fill of Alice! Even if I have to keep her in irons. I'll chain her to my bedpost indefinitely if I have to. She's never getting away from me again! Believe me, boys, I'm gonna take endless amounts of pleasure in having that sweet little quim!"*

The other three men roared in agreement.

"But that little one..." The sheriff's chuckling voice drew low, almost fearful. *"She threw me what must've been twenty-five feet*

headlong straight into a tree. And with nothin' but her mind! Exploded three flower pots, too. Blew 'em right into the air.

Boom!" He clapped his hands, causing me to jump. *"Told me she'd kill me herself if I ever touched her mama…"* He chuckled low in his throat. *"I'm gonna do more than touch her mama! Her mama is mine! And once I've got Alice in my possession, the young witch will do anything I please. Bet she'd even fuck me if I tell her to."* The devil growled. *"Perhaps after I've fucked the girl into submission, I'll order her to kill her father to save her mother."* He paused. *"Yes, now wouldn't that be something to behold…"*

The men stopped walking. They were standing directly above us. *"You know, for being such fine deputies…"* The sheriff's words were drunkenly slurred. *"When I do find the witches, I'll let you fine gentlemen share what's left of the girl after her father is dead."*

He paused for a moment. *"In fact, I don't fancy her at all. You may have her for yourselves. The three of you may fuck that little cherry till she's stone cold. Think of it as a gift for your loyalty. Just make sure to leave enough to bury—or burn. After all, even a witch needs a proper Christian funeral. We'll bury her right next to the rotting corpse of her…"* He snorted. *"Father!"*

I gasped, nearly out loud. *What does that mean? I don't understand…*

One of the men spoke up, pulling me from my horrified thoughts. *"You really hate the man—the husband—don't you, sheriff?"*

Charles anger exploded. *"The stable boy is NOT her husband! Alice belongs to ME!"*

The sheriff paced above us. I closed my eyes and said a silent prayer that he wouldn't step on the dirt-covered cellar door. *"I should've killed Asa Raign, Junior when I had the chance—years ago. Then, the little bastard witch would never have existed, and Alice would be with ME!"* He growled. *"My Alice is exquisite, and anything that perfect must belong to me—and only to ME!"*

The same man spoke: *"But will you give us just a taste o' her, too? She sure is purty!"*

"No, no," the sheriff slurred, reining in his anger. He sounded almost wistful. *"That one is all mine, and I'll be keeping her. Sure, she rebuffs me now, but after her child and the stable boy are dust, she'll be broken, and then she won't fight me a bit. After that, I'll have her right where I want her. Absolute obedience! Then the real fun'll begin!"*

Charles paused for a moment. *"You see, boys, it's all about finding your opponents' weaknesses."* He paused again. *"Find the weakness, and the battle is all but over."*

"So did you find 'em, Sheriff? Their weaknesses?" another one of the men asked.

Charles amusedly snickered. *"I certainly did."*

"But couldn't we just have a taste o' the girl's mama? Just a taste? I reckon she's 'bout the purtiest woman I've ever laid eyes on, Sheriff!" inquired the same man.

"No!" The devil roared with anger, and I knew by the sudden sounds of scuffling that he had attacked his man. *"I told you! Alice is mine! Only mine! And any man who comes near her will end up dead, just like her stable boy is going to be dead when I get a hold of him!"*

I gasped and lost my breath. *He wants to own Mama. He wants to break her, and he wants to kill Papa!*

With those loathsome words, my father dragged Mama and me into the shadows, squeezing us so tightly into the dark corner of the cellar that even if the horrible men found the door and peeked in, there was a good chance they might not have perceived our presence.

Papa stood like a sentinel, guarding us with his body, his arms stretched backward in an attempt to shield us from harm. I knew that the only way those men would get to Mama and me was if they killed *him*. He was like stone, unyielding and unmoving; he didn't even appear to be breathing. His head was tilted slightly upward, his eyes fixed on the sounds coming from just above us.

At any moment, they would find us. I knew that was what he was thinking. That's what we all were thinking.

He knows our weaknesses. I racked my brain, trying to think. *What can they be? What are our weaknesses?*

I glanced between my parents. *Mama's weakness is her fear, I think…* I paused, still thinking. *And her love for Papa.* My eyes darted to my father, our protector. *Papa's weakness is us. We'll be the death of him.*

With that horrible thought, I screwed my eyes shut. *He would die for us. I know he would!* Tears stung my eyes.

Suddenly overcome, I threw myself into my mother's arms—silently weeping. I listened to her mind as it lay open to me. She was praying, reciting *the Lord's Prayer* over and over again in her head. I held her hands and joined her. After a moment, she let one of my hands go. She knelt up behind Papa and slipped her arm around his middle, resting her head on his back. She closed her eyes and silently sobbed.

All of a sudden, several visions flashed into her terrified mind—startling me. They were memories, recollections of her first ordeal with that evil man. She tried to stop them, but the memories broke through anyway. It was as if the visions had a mind of their own, and their greatest pleasure was tormenting her.

I shuddered and put my free hand on the back of her head, gently stroking her hair as she cried, attempting to soothe the images away, but it didn't work. The visions were relentless.

Sobbing, I took a rasping breath, thankful that my father couldn't see into her mind at the moment. The memories were horrific. I was certain that if he saw them, he would try to kill the sheriff. Instead, he stood still as a mortar in front of us, ignorant of the atrocities running through the mind of his love.

My mother had never told Papa what happened when the sheriff brutally violated her—she couldn't. The acts of the sheriff were too vile, too despicable. In essence, he didn't just harm her; he mutilated her. And from the brief, yet violent, memories that flashed into her mind, I understood why she kept it a secret. Her pain wasn't a secret to me, though. I saw it all. After all, like I told the sheriff, I was there when it happened.

Being a ghost at the time didn't diminish the pain of watching my child suffer.

My eyes swept up to the cellar door. Unbeknownst to the monster, he was standing only a few feet above us, planning another attack, one that he didn't intend on letting Papa and I survive. And he wanted to own my mother. He wanted her in irons—literally and metaphorically speaking. He wanted her in his possession for the rest of her life, a life that I knew would be short without *us*.

I knelt next to Mama and laid my head on her shoulder. Her mind was becoming increasingly panic-stricken the longer the vile men stood over us. Soon, the memories turned into terror-induced hallucinations as her mind envisioned the atrocities the sheriff had planned for us. She was beginning to weaken. I could feel her light growing dimmer. I wished to help her, but I didn't know how, and Papa could neither see nor hear what was going on in her head. Still, I feared that if something wasn't done to soothe her straightaway, she would lose her mind and quite possibly her light.

I have to do something. I have to help her.

Finally, the boisterous guffaws and obscenities of the lawless monsters above us moved away from our hiding place. I could still hear them, but their vulgar words were getting softer as they finally walked away.

Mama's clutch on my hand loosened just a bit, and she sighed. Then she laid her cheek against Papa's back and spoke a prayer of thanks although her painful sobs continued.

My father, on the other hand, didn't move a muscle. He stood like a sentry in front of us, defending us at all costs to himself. I wrapped my arm around his middle, just like Mama had hers, and stood on my toes until my lips were at his ear. I needed him to hear what I had to say to him. I let go of my mother's hand and placed my palm flat on the side of my father's face. His cheeks were soaked with tears, and coarse stubble covered his chin. *"I'm sorry, Papa. I'm sorry for disobeying you."*

He took a jagged breath as he heard my words.

"Please, forgive me. I love you no matter what you have to do to me," I sobbed into the back of his shoulder, feeling hot tears running around the hand that I had on his face.

He turned to us, wrapped us into his arms, and then pulled us to the ground with him, still protecting us—always.

We sat in silence. Mama had her head laying in Papa's lap as he mindlessly stroked her hair. Her blank eyes stared ahead while I watched her. I knew what she was thinking. Even though she tried to block me from it, I still knew.

My father wasn't able to see into her mind. He didn't know about the horrible images she was envisioning. I wasn't sure if he could help her even if he wanted to, but I decided to ask. *"Papa,"* I whispered so that Mama couldn't hear. *"Can you help her? She's hurting, remembering the attack. And she's also imagining the things that the sheriff is planning to do to us. Please, she's hurting so much that it's frightening!"*

Tears streamed down my face as I looked into the beautifully tormented face of my mother. Her mind was blurred, and the panic in her eyes was worsening by the second.

My worried gaze swept back to Papa's teary eyes. *"She tried to block the images from me, but her mind has weakened from fright, so I was able to break through."* I drew closer. *"She's scared for us, Papa. She's scared that you and I are going to be killed."*

Papa leaned over until his lips were touching the side of Mama's face. He kissed her cheek, which grabbed her attention. Then he sat her up and lifted her into his arms, cradling her against his chest.

"*Please stop, sweetheart,*" he gently crooned, stroking her hair. "*I won't let anyone hurt Leesie or you, I promise.*"

My mother shuddered and sobbed. "*I can't get those horrible images out of my head, Asa,*" she whimpered against his chest while voraciously bawling into her hands. "*The things he wants those other men to do to Leesie…my baby! And he wants you dead. I always knew Charles would come after my family someday!*"

What? What things? What did that awful man mean? I don't understand… Her desperate cry sent a rush of terror through my veins.

Papa paused and then took her face into his hands. He smiled down into her weary eyes. "*Would you like me to take you away? Would you like me to blend with you? It'll help ease your mind. Will you allow me to do that for you, sweetheart?*"

Huh? Blend? They mentioned that yesterday while they were talking. But what does it mean?

Mama hesitated for a moment, and her eyes swept to me. "*I never got a chance to explain blending to Leesie.*" She ran the back of her hand down Papa's cheek. "*I'll be all right. Thank you, baby,*" she whispered, her eyes full of tears.

Papa shook his head. "*No, Ali, you're not all right. You need this. I won't allow you to go on hurting yourself like this. The thoughts you're having are dangerous for you.*" He placed his hand over her heart. "*It's a threat to your light.*" Then he glanced at me. "*I'll explain it to our daughter.*"

Turning to me, he took my hand. He seemed nervous yet determined. "*Lees,*" he began. "*I'm going to do something with your mama right now…*" He paused, finding the right words. "*It's called blending. It's something that is usually done between her and me while making love.*" He sighed, and I knew he was uncomfortable. "*But it can be done without, as well.*"

I frowned as he went on.

"Essentially, I'm going to bring together my soul with hers. And by doing so, I'll have the ability to take her away from the disquieting visions. I'll take her mind somewhere blissful." He gazed into my eyes, becoming less formal with his explanation. *"It'll make her feel good. She'll be happy. Do you understand?"*

"But how will you do it? Is it anything like Mama described to me yesterday?" I asked, feeling a shy flush creep across my face. My eyes swept around the small space of our hiding place, and I wondered where I should go to give them privacy.

Jeez, I hope they don't take their clothes off again… I nervously bit my lip. *"Do you want me to turn around and close my eyes?"*

Papa smiled and chuckled at my innocence. *"Nothing like that, Lees. I'll show you."*

His attention shifted back to my mother. He gently took one of her hands in his, kissed it, and placed it over his heart. Then he placed his hand over her heart.

Mama breathed in deeply. She seemed a bit anxious at first, but she succumbed to his touch without hesitation. She relaxed and pressed her body up against his until her torso lay against his chest.

Papa glanced over his shoulder toward me. He took Mama's free hand, laced their fingers together, and laid his head atop hers. *"I don't want you to be frightened of this, Lees, or embarrassed. It's a wonderful experience and perfectly natural for us."*

He paused. *"I'm going to let my soul intermingle with your mama's soul for a while. It's pleasurable for us both, but it will appear to you as if we're simply kissing. You won't see anything else. It's all done in the mind and, of course, in the spirit. Our souls will combine and fuse together. During this connection I'll lead both her mind and her spirit higher and higher every moment. Exactly what level we're able to attain will be up to her, but I'll be able to set her free from the horrible thoughts in her head. Likewise, I'll extend her consciousness as far as she needs me to—until her soul reaches a state of ecstasy or euphoria.*

Then when I bring her back down, that elated sensation will stay with her for a while, but more importantly, the awful thoughts and images will be gone, all right?"

"Oh, all right, Papa."

With that, he kissed the top of her head. *"Ali?"* he whispered.

My mother raised her head. She looked at him and weakly smiled. Her eyes were only partly open and unfocused.

"All right, baby, kiss me," Papa whispered.

She stretched her head up and placed her lips against his. I expected them to close their eyes, but they didn't. Instead, Papa gazed, unblinking, straight *into* hers.

Mama's emerald eyes sparkled and seemed to reach *into* his. At first it seemed like she was putting Papa into a trance, but soon her eyes, as well as her body responded with desire as *his* gaze overtook hers. She gasped against his lips and then melted into his arms while surrendering herself to him from tip to toe and allowing his spirit to enter and take hold of hers. What's more, she didn't hesitate for a moment. Her body shuddered with a pleasure that shone on her face as well as in her eyes. She shivered and trembled, and electrified goosebumps erupted over every inch of her radiant soul.

Then the quality of their kiss shifted and intensified while their gaze turned from the trance-like state at the beginning to a look of blissful happiness.

Curiously, I tiptoed into my mother's mind.

As Papa pushed her consciousness up and beyond the confines of her mind, he unlaced his fingers from hers, placed his shaking hand onto her back, and pushed her closer to his body.

Still, they never blinked.

Mama moved against him, almost like a dance, and she clutched his hand.

I studied them.

Hmm. Papa was right. If not for the peculiar stare, I'd think they were just kissing—rather intense kissing but kissing just the same. Still, I'm glad he told me what they were sharing; it's lovely. And I'm also glad I can peek into Mama's mind.

As I looked closer, their joint breath went from deep and steady to heavy and almost gasping. Then Papa spoke without removing his mouth from hers. *"How high, baby?"* he whispered.

My mother took in a few intense breaths before answering. *"Take me as far as you can. All the way, please!"* she moaned.

With her words spoken, Papa forced his head down until their foreheads were pressed together, their breath coming in perfect unison, both inhaling and exhaling at precisely the same moment.

I tried to listen to my mother's mind again, but it was blurred. I could, however, clearly *hear* their hearts beat in rhythm with one another. I couldn't determine which thundering beat belonged to whom.

As Papa pulled my mother higher and higher into nirvana, their eyes glimmered with a look of sheer delight. It appeared to be a sort of joyous frenzy as he took her beyond the boundaries of her imagination, ascending her mind and her soul as well as his own to paradise.

After a while, though, they seemed to hit a plateau. There they lingered, each barely breathing, barely moving as the minutes ticked by, their lips molded against one another, their joined souls sharing equally in nirvana.

I screwed my eyes up tight, attempting to see into Mama's mind again. Her consciousness was consumed by Papa. He seemed to be pushing her essence to a level previously unattained.

"More, sweetheart?" he asked, his voice strained.

My mother quivered in response, and her eyes flickered. Before she was able to answer, her body shook from the intensity of his love. She pulled her mouth away from his, breaking the seal between them. *"Enough!"* she gasped, and her eyes rolled upward.

With the detachment of their lips, Papa took gentle guardianship of my mother's fragile soul, carefully guiding its descent back down to Earth. Her pleasurable confinement released, she fell into a breathless heap on his chest.

Papa was out of breath, too. He put his strong arms around Mama and pulled her into his lap. *"Is that better, sweetheart?"* he whispered, breathless.

My mother didn't answer. She simply nodded a little and serenely smiled as he held his lips to her forehead.

After a few minutes and after he caught his breath, my father turned, looked at me, and smiled. *"See, angel, nothin' to it."*

"How come you can do that to her, Papa?" I asked. She appeared to be sleeping; he stroked her hair. *"Can a normal person do that? Or is it because Mama is abnormal?"*

Like me…

Papa patted the ground next to him while at the same time taking my waist and pulling me closer. *"No, angel. So-called 'normal people' can't do that. It's because you and your mama are…"* He thought for a moment. *"Beacon. That's the word, right, Lees?"*

I nodded and smiled, pleased that he had remembered the name.

"Because I'm her soulmate, blending is just one of the ways that I look after your mother. It releases her mind from any worries she may have," he answered. *"You see, baby, with the two of you, any serious emotional despair can be quite dangerous. Like your light, your souls, too, are pure. And something so delicate needs to be tended to quite carefully. You are wondrous beings, but even with all the power you wield, you are actually quite fragile."*

Papa pulled my chin up and stared into my eyes. *"Your mama did something similar with you yesterday. Because of what you are, you're able to comfort one another in a way not unlike what you saw me do for her. There are some differences, though.*"

I frowned, thinking. The memory of what occurred when I realized the truth about the sheriff flashed into my head. I looked back into Papa's eyes. "*When I exploded the coffee cup, it felt as though I was falling into a dark, sorrowful place.*" Then I glanced down at my sleeping mother. "*She 'blended' with me to comfort my mind?*"

Papa nodded. "*Of course, it's different between the two of you than it is for your mama and me. She only calms and comforts you with it. It's exactly like any other kind of affection she gives to you, versus the kind that she and I share with one another.*"

"*Yes, it is,*" I mumbled, blushing. "*Can I blend with her like she did with me?*"

"*Yes, baby, you can. Your mama just didn't get a chance to explain that to you.*"

I bit my lip and thought about what the sheriff said to those other men and how it had upset my mother. "*Papa? What the sheriff said to those other men…what he told them to do to me. What did it mean?*"

My father's face fell, and his eyes hardened into stony shards. His hands shook with obvious ire. He took my face between his palms, and his eyes welled with pained tears. "*Marshal wanted those other men to hurt you,*" he whispered, his voice was soft—too soft.

Oh, no!

I gulped hard. "*Like he hurt Mama when she was a girl?*" I squeaked, barely recognizing my faltering voice.

He sucked back a sob and nodded and then pulled me into his lap next to her, crushing us both to his chest. His heart was beating fast. Clearly, he was terrified. "*I won't let them touch you, either of you,*" he mumbled, and his voice choked with fright and tears. "*And neither will Jake…*"

And Kristofer. He won't let them hurt either of us. He loves us both.

Just then the thought of *my* soulmate entered my mind. His beautiful face danced and skipped through my brain, thankfully chasing the horrific thoughts of the other men away. At the same time, the naughty little witch in me purred with curiosity. *"Papa?"* I asked, intrigued by my wayward thoughts. *"Can Mama also blend with you?"*

Before he could answer, I heard the stern voice of my mother ringing out through my head. *"Don't you even think about trying it with Kris!"* She opened her eyes, and they illuminated into mine. Her eyes were no longer murky. Their power had returned full-force and blazed straight through my mind. *"You leave that boy's mind alone! It's already filled with enough improper images of you as it is!"* She pointed one willowy finger straight at me.

I nodded angelically while in the back of my mind, the disobedient little witch in me made plans to try that fascinating new talent out on *my* soulmate. *Hmm…*

Mama put her hand to her mouth and gasped. *"You will listen to me, young lady!"*

Papa silently glanced between us, his expression bewildered, although it melted into anger as the realization of my silent exchange with my mother dawned on him. He took hold of my wrists and glared down at me. *"You will not!"* he firmly commanded.

A deep sense of dread crept into my mind as I stared back into the eyes of my father. I began to panic, remembering the day before and what he had vowed to do to me if I disobeyed—just before I *had* disobeyed him.

Papa sat my mother and me on the ground next to him and stood up and stalked a few paces away from us. He ran his hands up and down the length of his face. He took in a rattled breath. When he turned back around, his eyes weren't soft like they usually were—like they were just moments before. They were cross, boring into mine with such intensity that I couldn't look at him for more than a few seconds.

Suddenly, I was frightened of him.

He ran his long fingers along the belt that he'd nearly used on me the day before, glaring down into my terrified eyes.

Mama, sensing danger, stood up.

He didn't look at her while he spoke to me. *"That reminds me,"* he murmured. He was attempting to remain calm, but his fingers still skimmed the belt. *"You and I have some business to attend to when we get to the cabin, Alyce. I need to teach you how to obey."*

My blood ran cold, and my heart nearly leaped out of my throat. Papa never called me by my given name—not ever. He had only ever used it once the day before and again just now.

My knees wobbled, but I sucked back the fear and took a large step forward. I slipped my tiny hand into his and then cautiously peeked up into his eyes. They were no longer gentle but were instead icy shards impaling me to the spot. My breath stuttered. *"I'm sorry, Papa,"* I stammered. *"I was just teasing Mama like you do. I didn't mean to worry you. I know you're still fretting about what those men did. I promise to obey you from now on."* I wrapped my arms around his middle and squeezed my eyes shut, praying for my kind, gentle papa to return to me.

My father's strong, substantial arms wrapped around me; his fingers caressed my head and face. Then he deeply sighed—an emotional, shuddering sigh.

I peeked up at him again. His beautiful, steel-blue eyes shined with love as he looked at me. I breathed a sigh of relief. *Oh, good! He's back!*

His lovely steel-blue eyes shined into mine. Then he crouched down, gazing into my eyes, his full of weary tears. *"What do you say you and I deal with this little matter when we get to the cabin? Huh, angel? Does that sound like a good idea to you? Because it sounds good to me."*

He stroked the many cuts and bruises on my face. *"And, I'm sorry, too, about your injuries. I didn't mean to hurt you. I hope you know that."* He stretched up and kissed my forehead.

I nodded, relishing in his gentle touch. *"It was an accident and entirely my fault, Papa. I know you were just scared and trying to protect me."*

With that, he sorrowfully sighed again and glanced up toward the cellar door. *"Speaking of the cabin, I think it's about time we make our way out of here. The sheriff and his men have gone."*

With those words from my father, I felt as though someone had pushed me into a bottomless cavern. I could only imagine what awaited us outside the security of our shelter. I wished to stay in our tiny hiding place. Then we would never have to face the horror of what lay just above us.

Just then my mother stepped forward and put her hands on Papa's broad shoulders. *"What, Asa?"* she asked, puzzled by his sudden anger.

"Not now, sweetheart," he rasped *"That's a story Leesie and I can tell you about later when we get to our new home."*

I shivered at the very thought of us needing a *new* home.

Abruptly, the cellar door flew open, and Mr. Cole and Kristofer peered down at us. Smoke and ash rained down on our heads as did the bright morning sunlight. *"Is everyone all right?"* Mr. Cole hollered. His eyes fell on me, and he let out a loud gasp. *"Leesie? You're a sight!"* He held his hands out to me. *"Kris!"* he called back. *"Get the canteen out of the buggy. Leesie needs to wash those cuts soon, or she'll get sick!"*

Kristofer obediently ran.

Papa put his hands around my waist and then lifted me up to Mr. Cole.

I stepped up onto solid ground and peered at the charred wasteland that until the day before had been our beautiful home.

Our sweet, little farmhouse was destroyed. All that remained of it was a pile of blackened debris, with only the stone chimney sticking up amidst a massive pile of burned wood and ash.

Slowly, I turned to my orchard. I was afraid to see it *dead*, but I knew that I had to see it if I was truly going to believe that it was really gone. I screwed my eyes shut for a moment, emotionally stealing myself for the shock that I knew was about to come. First, I threw my mind out toward the field. I hoped to feel something—anything, any sort of life force, but there was nothing but blaring silence. The ground was desolate and still. Every soul, every seed was taken from me.

I peeked open my eyes and gasped, and my mind blurred with shock. My once-regal field full of living trees was in one night reduced to nothing but row after row of smoldering stumps.

I squeezed my eyes shut, trying to feel something—anything. I wished to feel some sort of life force, no matter how insignificant, beaming out from the field. But there was nothing. The connection was gone. I was empty.

My knees buckled, and I fell hard onto the cold morning ground. My head flew back, and I bellowed. I shouted screams of anguish for my murdered loved ones and roars of hatred for the monsters who took them away from me.

They were innocent! They were innocent and pure, and they were murdered because of me and what I am!

I wanted to die with them. I was in too much misery to go on living. All hope was gone. It burned along with our home; it died alongside my orchard. I couldn't even cry.

Then I was falling, plummeting through the depths of my hopelessness, my very essence in a freefall. I had nothing inside. There was no light and no world, just darkness—cold, still darkness.

I wailed aloud, and my soul splintered. It was ripping apart inside me—tearing me to shreds from the inside out. I was outside my body, barely breathing and only half-alive. I was inhuman. My heart beat, but it was the beat of a ghost heart, one that ceased to live. No longer could I feel anything, nothing but pain. My loss was too great. I heard myself scream just as white-hot pain shot daggers through my head. Then the pain moved from my head to my heart. It grabbed hold of my splintering spirit and pulled it inward into the depths of nothingness, urging me to implode into oblivion, devoid of life, of light…

But there was light—glorious, golden light that within a matter of seconds reached into my soul, tearing me away from the despondency of my grief.

It was Mama—my savior. I felt her touch. It was warm and kind, almost like sinking into a warm bath on a cold night. Through my grief I felt her soft hand as she placed it over first my heart and then over her own. She pressed her forehead against mine. The sensation of her breath against my face comforted and calmed me.

I sighed and rejoined my body.

Then something I didn't expect touched me. It was Kristofer. He stroked my face, and his sweet breath washed over me.

Greedily responding to him, my damaged essence absorbed the scent of his breath, the warmth of his skin, the very quintessence of his being into my own.

My mother led my soul away, allowing me to drift with her through a glowing, golden beam I could have never imagined on my own. The beam was warm, radiant even, without being hot. I threw my head back, basking in the flame, feeling relaxed and safe again. As I soaked up the glorious light, a cool breeze scented with wildflowers and apple blossoms swept around me.

It was the scent of my orchard!

I opened my mind's eye, and I knew we were in Heaven. It was *my* Heaven, at least.

Mama's light set me down directly under an enormous apple tree. I gazed up into the massive canopy. The tree was three times as large as any of ours. It was even larger than The Grandfather Tree. But just as that thought crossed my mind, his life force pulsed through me.

Wait, holy cow!

As I looked closer I realized that it *was* my beloved Grandfather Tree, or it was his spirit, at least.

My breath hitched, and I wanted to sob. I reached out and stroked his bark, feeling his precious energy coursing straight through me. I closed my eyes, basking in his sweet existence. Flesh to wood, blood to blood, soul to soul, our connection returned.

I opened my eyes, and an involuntary sob escaped my lips. I looked around. There were dozens of trees, each larger and more spectacular than the next, all gleaming with life—sweet, sparkling life. They all sparkled and glowed just like Mama...like *I* did. And not only did they sparkle, but these glorious living beings *breathed*. Their trunks rose and fell, each one independently inhaling and exhaling.

I turned to my Mama just as she also realized what she was seeing. She threw her beautiful, glowing head back and laughed; tears of amazement fell from her eyes. But I couldn't take my eyes off the trees.

As I sat gawking at the many souls surrounding me, my mother breathed a warm, lilac-scented puff of air into my face. I felt her essence, her soul. It was a part of me. It was as if we were no longer two different people but one soul split into two.

My breath faltered, and I gasped as a sense of both joy and wonder filled me up until I felt as if I might burst with pleasure. I gazed at my beautiful mother and smiled. This vision was a gift. It was a gift of love, a gift from her. I closed my eyes and breathed in the sweet scent of my apple trees mixed with Mama's lovely fragrance, knowing that the treasured visions were nothing less than an expression of pure love from her spirit to mine. I also knew that I could never repay her for showing me, *proving* to me, that my trees were not only alive but that they breathed.

Sadly, I realized I couldn't remain at that level of ecstasy much longer, and as much as I wanted to linger, I simply couldn't hold on. It was time to go home. *Hmm. Home?*

My body shivered just as Mama placed her lips to my ear. *"All right, my baby, are you ready to go back?"* she whispered.

Reluctantly, I nodded. But first, my gaze swept into the beautiful canopies of my friends.

I reached out just before Mama detached her soul. I placed my palm flat against the trunk of The Grandfather Tree. He shuddered and swayed into me, purring. He felt my touch, my *love,* and I felt his. Then the wonderful living, thinking being wrapped one of his branches around me and pulled me into a tender embrace, and his love pulsed through me. I gazed up into his glorious branches and on his urging put my hand out toward him. He dropped a single apple into my palm. I clutched the apple to my chest, never wanting to part with it.

Finally, sadly, he uncoiled his mighty branches from my body, and I closed my eyes. Just before my mind was swept away, the wondrous creature sent one last vision flashing through my head.

At that singularly *perfect* moment, I knew without a doubt that my dear orchard would one day *live* again.

Swiftly, the trees vanished, and my mother separated her soul from mine. Then the firm ground pushed against my back, and Kristofer's hand returned to my face.

Mama kissed my forehead and laid my head into my boy's lap.

Kristofer touched a wet rag to my face, cleaning my wounds. His adept fingers ran along the cuts and bruises on my face without causing me any discomfort at all although the sensation of water on my sore hands made me flinch.

I opened my eyes and smiled up into his ravishing eyes just as he picked something small off my sore palm. I jerked and tried to sit up, but he cupped my head. He didn't want me to rise too quickly.

Slowly, I sat up, gazing into his brilliant eyes as he caressed my face. Then he opened his hand and placed four apple seeds back into my palm. I looked down at them. My head spun, and my brain felt fuzzy. I tried to focus on Kristofer and the gift that my beloved friend gave to me, but in my giddy condition it was difficult. I smiled through the fog in my brain and placed the seeds in my shoe.

I sat staring at Kristofer, trying to concentrate on the beautiful eyes of my boy as both my mind and spirit continued to come down from the atmosphere of euphoria. As I looked at him, I realized that in my slightly altered state, I could see his aura. It was breathtaking. It was as if an emerald-green light basked him in color, and blood red flames shot out from all sides. Then bursting from his middle, a fiery, incandescent, diamond-hued beam erupted from within him.

They are the colors of me, but why can I see them?

Kristofer leaned forward, his brilliant hazel eyes sparkling into mine. *"I know why you see. Don't you?"* he inquired, tipping his head like a curious puppy. He stroked my face with the back of his hand. *"I've always loved you, Sita, and I always will love you—forever."*

The sweet words of my soulmate brought a warm flutter to my heart. For a fleeting moment, I considered trying to *blend* with him, but I thought I'd better not get myself into any more trouble.

"I love you, too, and I wish I could show you something, but I can't. Not just yet."

Kristofer jerked away. He pulled his eyebrows together and glared at me. *"Do you love me? Do you, really?"*

"Of course, I do. Of course, I love you," I nodded, trying to figure out what on *Earth* was wrong with him.

Pursing his lips, he heaved an exasperated breath, and his eyes bored into mine—very much like Mama's eyes flashed when she was angry with me. It was kind of spooky. *"Well, if you love me so much, then don't ever put yourself into danger again! You know, I was really mad at your pa yesterday!"*

I glanced at the ground. *"Because he was going to spank me with his belt?"* Oh Jeez! I'm glad he didn't see Papa spank me! The thought of my boy witnessing something like that was just too mortifying to consider.

Kristofer threw his face into mine. *"NO! I was mad at him because he didn't whip your behind! You DESERVED it!"* He pushed his purpled face closer to mine. *"If you ever do anything like that again, I swear to God almighty, Alyce Margaret Cole, I will take you over my knee, and I will use a belt on you MYSELF!"* Then his face turned puce, and he stalked away from me in a huff.

Huh? Cole? I didn't know what to think. *Why did he call me 'Alyce Cole'?*

Great! Now everyone's angry with me. Well, everyone except for Mama. I glanced over at her. She and Papa were standing still, peering between the orchard and the ruins of our home. I went to them. They were both crying.

Wordlessly, each took one of my hands as I cried with them. Papa bent down and kissed the top of my head. *"I'm sorry about the orchard, angel, but things could've been a lot worse. We're alive. That's all that matters now."* He snaked both his arms around Mama and me, holding us tight. After holding me a moment in his embrace, he pulled my chin up and stroked the many wounds covering my skin. He sighed then took my mother by the hand and walked a few yards away.

I stood anxiously watching my parents, the proverbial witch-tail tucked up securely between my legs.

Every few seconds Mama threw me a shocked expression.

He's telling her what I did…

All of a sudden, Papa became emotional, and I knew that he was recalling what I did to the sheriff and how I had acquired my injuries. He put his head into his hands and cried. Tears welled in my mother's eyes, too. She pulled his head down and laid it on her shoulder. She stroked his hair and wept with him, but her touch didn't soothe him; he cried harder. Clearly, he was unable to deal with the fact that he had hurt me. Finally, she took his head, pressed it to hers, gained eye contact, and placed her hand over his heart. Papa did the same; his body immediately responded to the blend. Where his body was rigid and taut just moments before, it relaxed at her touch and his facial expressions softened. She held him for several minutes until it was clear to her that his mind was peaceful.

My parents are amazing! I've simply got to try that with my boy!

Just then, Kristofer came up beside me. *"What's she doing to him?"* he asked, canting his head like a puppy again. He took my hand.

"She's doing the same thing to him that she did to me," I explained. *"She's taking the hurtful things that he was thinking away from him and comforting his mind. He can do it for her, too. I saw it. Only, there was a lot of kissing involved then. Only soulmates can do it. Well, and Beacons can do it for each other, too."* I glanced sideways at Kristofer, carefully watching his reaction. *"Papa said the way he did it for Mama was almost like…making love."*

Kristofer's brow twitched up, and a wicked grin swept across his breathtaking mouth. *"I'll have to remember that,"* he muttered and then winked at me.

My heart jerked as if it was about to burst right through my chest and leap into Kristofer's arms. *Yes! Let's try it! Let's try it NOW!*

Just then, Mr. Cole cleared his throat, startling me and wrenching my brain from the sudden erotic thoughts. *"I think we should probably be on our way."* He gestured to where his buggy lay hidden amidst the dense wood.

My head darted toward Mr. Cole.

Kristofer chuckled under his breath. Then he stretched up on his toes, planting a soft kiss on my cheek. *"Patience, love,"* he murmured.

At the same time, Papa turned to Mr. Cole with a question. *"Jake?"* he asked, looking puzzled. *"How'd you get the team back?*

Those men let them loose last night before they burned my wagon. I heard all four horses run past us."

Mr. Cole grinned. *"You know, those horses of mine are pretty smart!"* He chuckled. *"Kris and I were about to leave our hiding place up on the hill this morning when the funniest thing happened."* He glanced between my mother and me. *"Both of my horses came running straight up to us. It was the darnedest thing, almost as if someone had guided them to where we were. Kris and I fetched my buggy just before we let you all out of the cellar."*

He looked at Mama just as she smiled and then turned away.

"I haven't found yours yet, my friend." He patted Papa on the back. *"But when I do, I'll be sure to get them to you right away."*

My mother turned, and her skirt swished over the ground as she sashayed to where Mr. Cole stood smirking at her. With a devious smile creeping over her face, she patted his arm. *"You won't have to worry about searching for our horses, Jake. They're already waiting for us at the cabin."*

Papa's eyes flew open wide, and an astounded look swept across his beaming face. He chuckled to himself and then threw his arms out and caught my mother around the waist. Breathless, he pulled her close. *"What else don't I know about you?"* he whispered into her ear, clearly amused by yet another ability of hers—one that he obviously knew nothing about.

Mama smiled and batted her eyes. *"Well, I guess you'll just have to learn me better, now won't you, Asa?"*

Papa took her by the hand and led her to Mr. Cole's buggy. When they reached it, he drew her into his arms. He put both hands on either side of her hips, making sure her body was pressed against his, and then sighed and pulled her into a tighter embrace. *"You know,"* he said. *"We've lost our home and the orchard, but as long as I have you and Leesie, I know that all is well."* Then he pulled back, suddenly emotional. *"We've been through this before—the loss of our home, but at least this time our family remains intact."*

Mama wrapped her arms around him. *"I feel the same way, baby."* Then she let go and gazed up into his eyes; she stroked his face with the back of her hand. *"What do you need, Asa? I know the words of those men disturbed you. What can I do to help?"*

Papa pressed his forehead against hers. *"I thought you were safe. I thought we had moved far enough away. I should've never let my guard down. That won't happen again. I'll move you to the end of the earth if I have to."*

My mother stroked my father's face, her eyes full of regret. *"You could've had a normal life without me…a rich life. You should've been a doctor or a musician, not a farmer. As it is, you were a wunderkind. You should've had so much more than life in hiding. You had your pick of any woman in the city. Debutantes and socialites pined for you…"*

"Shut your mouth!" Papa hissed, heatedly pushing a single finger to her lips, halting her incriminating words. *"Yes, debutantes sought after me! Many women sought after me!"* He ran his hands up and down his face, frustrated. *"All manner of women pursued me, yet I wanted perfection. I wanted you!"* His face drew nearer. *"I told you before. You are my life, Ali. Both Lees and you are! I won't have any of that self-deprecating nonsense! I happen to love my life and my family, and I wouldn't change it if I could! I would rather be a simple farmer with you than a wealthy businessman or doctor married to one of those uppity socialites any day!"* He took a steadying breath. *"Besides, as the sole beneficiary of my grandfather Adam Winchester Cain's fortune, I am a wealthy man."*

"But you graduated from Princeton, head of your class. And how old were you when you began to play?"

He pushed his finger to her lip, halting her again. *"I was two when I discovered the piano. And as far as my college education goes, I had to do something while I waited for you marry me."*

"*Still, you gave up so much. You wanted to be a doctor. You should be performing on a vast stage in a symphony orchestra, not hidden away on a farm or in the middle of the woods…*" Mama's eyes fell; she stared down at her wringing hands.

Pained tears welled in Papa's eyes. He leaned down, laying his head against my mother's shoulder. "*The only thing I need is to keep Leesie and you safe. If I lost either of you…*" He couldn't finish the sentence. He looked up, gazed into my mother's eyes, and stroked her cheek. "*You are simple perfection and all that I have ever wanted. Hell, why do you think Charles Marshal wants you? He's drawn to you, too… obsessively. He doesn't know that you are divine, but he can feel it.*" He shook his head. "*I don't know why he can feel your light, but I know he can. That's what tempts him. And he won't stop searching for you until he has you or until he's dead.*"

Papa paused. He took in a terrified, shuddering breath and laid his forehead against Mama's. "*I am yours, Ali Raign. You chose me, and I am thankful for that choice every day of my life.*"

"*I am thankful, too. I just can't stand to see you tormented like this. What can I do?*" she tearfully whispered, caressing the back of his head as he cried.

"*I need you, sweetheart. When we get to the cabin. I simply need the comfort of your love. That is all. I want for nothing more. I could've lost you. We nearly lost our daughter.*" He closed his eyes for a moment, seemingly exorcising that thought from his mind. "*What that son of a bitch said about Leesie—that despicable word on his lips—I just can't keep it out of my mind. I wouldn't want to live without you and Lees, not for a moment. I need you desperately, both of you.*" He blew out a breath. "*I'll be all right, sweetheart.*" Then he stood straight up, stroking Mama's soot- and tear-stained face; he looked desperately tired. "*I just need to get you and Leesie to a safe place. I need to be with my family. I need you by my side, and I need to feel your silky, sweet-smelling body next to mine.*"

He tearfully laughed, looking her up and down, suddenly realizing how filthy they were. *"We're quite dirty you know, from our…ordeal. Fortunately, this will give us a valid excuse to take a swim in the creek this afternoon."* He grinned and cocked his soot-stained brow. *"Can I possibly entice you to bathe with me later, my beautiful wife?"*

My mother closed her eyes, taking shallow breaths as Papa ran his hands up and down each side of her waist. *"I'd like nothing more, my husband,"* she breathed, touching his cheek. Then she stretched up on her toes and kissed his lips.

In response to her intimate touch, he leaned down and wrapped himself around her, enveloping her within his own. When finally he released her, he lifted her up into Mr. Cole's buggy. She didn't take her eyes off him.

As beautiful as the display was, it was also a bit startling for me. Then I realized why: The way they gazed into each other's eyes was like it was while they were blending. It was as if they were actually merging themselves together with *only* their eyes.

I blushed and bashfully looked the other away, but at the same time, my mind was sent reeling. *Papa went to college, and he inherited his grandfather's fortune. That's how he's able to take care of Mama and me like he does.* I thought for a moment. *Hmm. Adam Winchester Cain… He must've been my Grandmother Margaret's father. But why didn't he leave his fortune to her?* I stared at the ground, my eyes focused on a rather unremarkable rock, but I didn't see it. My mind was too occupied with thoughts.

Since I was a child, I knew my father was brilliant. I always felt that there was something wrong with him spending his days digging drudges and using the sweat of his brow to work a field. Although I had loved the orchard, deep down it just seemed wrong for him. *He had wanted to be a doctor, yet he gave that up…for us.* My heart sank. *Another piece of the puzzle. No wonder my grandfather, Asa Senior, dislikes Mama so much…*

After a moment, Papa startled me out of my musings. He lifted first me and then Kristofer into the buggy.

I sat next to my mother, thinking about the intimate moment my parents had shared. But at the same time, I was deeply disturbed by her words of regret and by the knowledge of what my father had given up for us. *Mama wishes that Papa had a normal life. He wanted to be a doctor.* I sighed, and my heart stung.

Then I sat thinking about my boy and bit my lip. The butterflies in my stomach returned. *Maybe Kristofer shouldn't be with me. Maybe he would be better off with a normal woman…*

That feeling was so overwhelming it frightened me.

Sensing something amiss, Mama took my hand. *"What is it, my baby?"* she whispered into my mind.

"I remember being like you and Papa," I answered back, biting my lip again. *"I don't remember exactly, but I do remember feeling that way for Kristofer. I felt the way you just felt for him. Only, it was before, when we were married…"*

I turned away from her, gazing, unseeing, across the vast meadow skirting our broken little farmhouse. *I wonder if Kristofer would tell me the truth about us. After all, I do remember a little about us now. Maybe he would tell me if he ever had any doubts,* I silently pondered, but I wasn't alone. Mama was in my head.

"Don't you dare ask him something like that!" she yelled at me in my head; her voice was frantic. *"Leesie Raign, Kris and you are children! It doesn't matter what you remember about your other life. You're just going to have to wait until you're older before we allow you to have any kind of relationship with him! Your papa and I didn't get married until we were thirty years old. For heaven's sake, how would you like to wait until then?"*

I shuddered at the very concept. The idea of waiting even a few more years to be with my love was horrible enough, but to wait until we were thirty? That was a notion too painful to even consider. Still, the idea of saving Kristofer from a life of hiding niggled at the back of my head.

No, ma'am, I muttered, chastened.

Mama sighed with exasperation and pushed my head down onto her shoulder. *Thank you for showing me the trees,* I thought to her with a yawn.

She squeezed my hand. *"You're welcome, my baby. You know, I'd do anything for you. I'd even give up my life for you, as would your Papa. We love you more than anything. Your father and I have a rare type of love, and you were created from that."*

She paused and sighed. *"I know you thought you were doing the right thing by protecting us yesterday, but you were wrong. You almost got yourself killed. You and I are powerful beings, Lees, but even our powers can't compete with the sort of evil that Charles possesses inside of himself. He would hurt you without even thinking twice about it. And if he ever did, the very idea would kill your papa and me. Do you understand?"*

"But the very idea of him hurting you kills me inside," I whispered. *"I believed that Charles Marshal was about to come to the house with the intentions of harming you and Papa both. I couldn't allow that to happen. I couldn't allow it any more than you'd allow him to hurt Papa or me. I have just as much responsibility to protect you as you have to protect me."*

My mother peeked down at me with a frightened expression. *"Were you really able to throw him with only your powers?"* she whispered aloud.

"Yes. Clear across the yard."

"Did you tell Charles that you would kill him if he touched me?" Her eyes widened with fright and disbelief, as if she couldn't image how I could not fear Charles Marshal.

I looked straight into her eyes. *"Yes. And I wanted to kill him right then, but Papa came along. Charles Marshal is a bully and a coward. I don't fear him."*

Sudden wrath mixed with fright flared in her eyes. *"You are just like your father, an overprotective fool! What am I going to do with you?"*

"At least now Charles Marshal understands who I am," I barely breathed.

"Yes, of course, Charles knows who you are. Jake explained everything in church yesterday."

That's not exactly what I meant...

"What then?" she asked, having heard my thought.

"Never mind. Just tired..."

My mother seemed unnerved by the absence of fear in my eyes, the fear she felt for that evil monster—the fear I lacked. She shook her head, mentally reflecting on my words for a moment, and then closed her eyes in silent contemplation. *"Your powers are getting much stronger now, baby. You need to work on not losing control of your emotions. Even though I understand how much pain losing the orchard caused you, it can be damaging for you to lose control. You nearly shattered, Lees. And seriously, if your soul were to shatter, I'm not sure that I could save you, and if I couldn't, then I would shatter, too."* With those words, a tear rolled down her cheek and onto mine. She seemed so tired.

"I'm sorry you can't understand," I whispered.

Before she could answer, Papa came back around. *"We're getting ready to leave."* He smiled at me. *"I hope you like the cabin, angel. Your mama and I have wanted to show it to you for a long time. I know it's not the orchard, but I hope you can be happy there."* He reached over Kristofer, kissed me, and then hopped up into the front seat next Mr. Cole.

I hope this means Papa isn't angry with me anymore.

Mama broke through my mind. *"Angry about what? What is going on with the two of you? One minute he seems angry with you, and the next, he isn't. What happened?"*

I glanced the other way while I answered her. *"I defied him,"* I whispered, still not looking in her direction. The words hurt. In fact, the very idea of defying my father hurt. I closed my eyes in pain, and salty tears burned the cuts on my cheeks and lips as they rolled past.

Obviously, Papa didn't tell her about when I ran away from him...

"How did you defy him?" she questioned. *"Please, Leesie, I don't want to keep barging into your thoughts. I'd rather you told me yourself."*

I shook my head and scrunched up my eyes, determined not to let myself think about it again. I didn't want her to know what I did and especially not what that horrible man had *called* her.

Mama grabbed my face. *"All right then. If that's the way you want it!"*

I knew I couldn't resist her stare; it was powerful, much too powerful for me to fight. It seemed to penetrate directly into my soul. *Another Beacon thing, no doubt...*

"Yes, something like that," she answered aloud, laughing. *"Now, tell me. Right now!"* This time, she asked more forcefully and not with her mind. She put her arms out, wanting to hold me. I knew at once what it meant, but in my state of sadness, grief, and plain exhaustion, I couldn't deny her request. I succumbed without another word. I laid my weary head against her heart. My mother cradled me against her chest and stroked my hair, being careful not to touch any of my various injuries. *"Show me, please,"* she whispered, softer that time. She wanted me to show her what happened between Papa and me, and between Charles and me as well.

I stretched my hand up and placed it on the side of her head. Then I closed my eyes and showed her almost everything that had happened although I changed a few details of my encounter with the sheriff, like when I *revealed* myself to him.

By the time I got to the end, I was so exhausted that I drifted off to sleep in her arms. I listened to the steady rhythm of her heartbeat. My over-tired mind fell away with Kristofer sitting beside me, his warm body pressed against mine. *As much as I love being in my mother's embrace, I can't help but wish his arms were around me...*

• • •

I awoke with a start just as Reverend Cole's buggy stopped.

I sat up and looked around—toward our new home in the middle of the woods... Reluctantly, I peeked up into a mass of fir trees surrounding us. The trees were so big that I couldn't even see the sun. The trunks of the trees jutted up at least fifty feet toward the sky.

I probably couldn't climb these trees if I tried, I thought to myself, sadly reminiscing about all the blissfully happy summer days I'd spent sitting atop my dear Grandfather Tree.

I glanced toward the cabin. It was an unremarkable house, quaint and small but inviting at the same time, made of log and cut timber with a pretty front porch, much like our farmhouse. There was even a nice little wooden swing hanging from one of the front porch beams.

Hmm. Not bad, I guess...

I peered around—still unsure. The yard was nice and big. There was a huge stack of firewood piled up and covering one whole side of the house. On the other side it was bare, save for a dilapidated barn in the distance and a small outhouse toward the back. Then I noticed our horses, which were standing in front of one of the side windows and grazing on a patch of tall grass.

Papa saw them, too. He chuckled, lifted Mama from the buggy, and gave her a squeeze. *"You are truly an amazing woman!"* he laughed.

I scooted next to my parents—still feeling uneasy about my new…*home.* They each took one of my hands, but Mama pulled me with her as she started to walk away. *"Walk with me a while,"* she said and tugged me away from Papa.

I let go of his hand and frowned though he smiled and winked at me.

Mama led me past the house and out toward the back, excitedly pulling me along.

Where is she going?

In the distance, there was a break in the trees, where a large untouched pasture full of wildflowers lay. It was beautiful, but I still didn't understand her excitement. Just as that confused thought filled my mind, I saw it. Directly in the middle of the vast clearing, shooting up toward the sky and bursting with life, stood one colossal oak tree.

It was breathtaking.

"I bet I could climb that!"

Mama laughed. *"I knew you'd like it. Just don't break anything!"*

"All right, Mama. I promise!" I laughed, pulling her behind me.

As she and I neared the tree, the surrounding ground grew less and less indistinct. That's when I noticed something growing on the ground. I gasped. It was strawberries, a great big field full of strawberries. I was thrilled! There must have been at least two acres of nothing but strawberries, meadow grass, and wildflowers, except for the one beautiful oak tree shooting up right in the middle.

I halted and gazed up at the oak tree, mesmerized by the sight and by a sudden sense of familiarity. I inclined my head, still studying…*her.* That thought startled me.

Why do I remember the tree?

She stood like a sentinel in the distance. The regal tree's aura seemed to pull me nearer.

"What do you think?" Mama asked as she pushed the short tuft of hair hanging in my face out of my eyes, pulling me from the tree's captivation.

"Glorious!" I beamed, but I still felt puzzled.

She leaned over my shoulder. *"Your papa and I have planned to bring you here for a long time, sweetie."* She took a deep breath and made a wide gesture around us with her hands. *"This was our first home. In fact, it was my first home, ever."* Her eyes welled with unshed tears. *"I know nothing can replace the orchard for you, honey, but I hope this place might help to mend your heart a little."* Wrapping her arms around me, she hugged me tight.

I peeked into her eyes, unsure of myself. I'd never told my parents about my talent before—about my connection to the trees.

Well, it's now or never.

My eyes swept back to the oak tree. Just as my vision settled on her glorious canopy, the tree's life force surged straight through to my soul, as if urging me to tell Mama my secret—our secret. I heaved a deep breath and almost imperceptibly nodded. My heart fluttered with apprehension. *"I felt them,"* I softly mumbled. *"I felt them…die."* A wave of fear swept through me as I spoke. I didn't think my mother would understand. *After all, talking to trees and sensing what they feel is strange, even for us.*

Thankfully, Mama wasn't shocked or even startled by my revelation. She placed her head against mine while rocking back and forth. *"I know, my baby. I saw it in your mind last night. I don't know how exactly, but that seems to be one of your gifts—communicating with trees. You loved the trees in the orchard as if they were people. They were family to you. Maybe because of your papa, I'm not sure."* She squeezed me tighter. *"Who knows, maybe we'll all get back there someday."* She laughed. *"And thanks to your love for them, I know now that they still are alive and that they do breathe."*

Mama pulled me down to the ground with her. We sat atop a patch of grass and wildflowers growing between the many rows of strawberry plants. I laid my head on her shoulder and cried. It felt as if a part of my heart were ripping from my chest. Even though I saw the orchard alive in my mind, it still wasn't the same as having my trees with me every day.

The Grandfather Tree. He was the center of my orchard—the heart; all the other trees were sown from his seed. Will he live again someday? Will they all live again? That was something that I just didn't know.

Mama squeezed me tight, rocking with me in her arms, holding me for a long while—letting me grieve. She held me in her arms until I was too exhausted to cry anymore.

19. Memories

As Mama and I sat in the strawberry field, I watched as the first of the massive oak tree's leaves began to fall. The sight swept my mind away from that place; my thoughts took me back to my orchard. In my mind, I was sitting under The Grandfather Tree. His apples blazed red amongst a sea of sage green leaves, the sweet smell of autumn growing faintly in the distant wind…

An abrupt sob escaped my lips. I covered my face with my hands and wept. The very thought of my beautiful orchard made my heart sting with pain.

Mama stroked my hair as I began to cry again. *"What is it, my baby?"* she asked.

"My trees…" I choked, mindlessly picking at a blade of grass with my fingers. *"We were just beginning to harvest, but now I'll never harvest them again. They're gone. Maybe not forever but for now, they're gone."*

I laid my head on her lap, mourning for my friends, the sense of loss tearing at my already wounded spirit.

"I know, my baby."

As I cried, a soft breeze blew the sweet scent of autumn into the air above us. I raised my head, looking around at the lovely stretch of the earth entirely covered in strawberries. It felt so strange to me that it was once a place my parents had called home. That they even secretly owned the land and the cabin and I knew nothing about it was strange to me. I peered around, imagining them living there without *me*.

I envisioned them at the cabin with Rebecca and shook my head. That notion was just too peculiar. Although I had grown to love my sister after that day in the orchard, the life the three of them had shared without *me* seemed unnatural and uncomfortable.

It was only a short time my parents had lived here together without me, though. My mother conceived me the same night she and Papa married at the cabin, and they moved to the orchard just a few months before I was born. Then, after the tornado destroyed our first farmhouse and my sister, the three of us lived in the cabin together for an entire year.

I wished that I could remember living here with them, but I was too young at the time.

A sudden thought came to mind. I sat up and looked out toward the oak tree once again. *Perhaps that's how I remember the tree—from when I was a baby.*

"Noooooo…" The wind swept through my hair, sending a soft voice resounding from where the old oak stood in the distance.

Out of the blue, I recognized the voice. *"Pamela?"* I dreamily muttered, stunned by the unexpected realization. *That's right. The oak tree. Her name is…Pamela.*

"What, baby? Did you say something?" Mama inquired and pulled me into an embrace.

Still reeling, I shook my head and closed my eyes, attempting to remember more about my old friend—my friend *Pamela.*

As I lay in her arms thinking, my mother stroked my face. She was humming softly. *Hmm, how I love the sound of her voice.* The beauty of it seemed to wash the pangs of misery from my soul.

I peeped open my eyes and looked out at the old oak. Mama's voice wasn't the only thing that washed away my grief. The knowledge that I still had at least one friend was immeasurably comforting, too. *I wish I could remember more about her…*

Just as that thought crossed my mind, Mama's hum melted into a tender melody. I smiled and closed my eyes—absorbed in the ambient tones. Her voice was dulcet and gentle, just like the rest of her. Her stare wasn't the only thing that could hypnotize me. Her beautiful voice could as well.

I giggled to myself. Her voice had the same effect on Papa. I'd seen it with my own eyes. Her sweet voice was as pleasing and harmonious to *his* soul as his piano playing was to *hers*. It was so melodic, in fact, that if I closed my eyes, I could almost see it floating through the sky, dipping and rising with the air currents.

Her tender melodies could surely mesmerize any living being, be they mortal or immortal, human or spirit. She could turn the most aggressive ghost into a mellow apparition and could send even an angel's pure soul soaring to heaven with nothing but the sweet melodies flowing from her lyrical throat. My father, being merely a *human* man, was entirely at the mercy of her inebriating powers.

My mother had the ability to reduce Papa to a gushing puddle with just one look or with just one song; she could throw him completely off balance with the faintest hum or the slightest sigh. All she had to do was purr in his direction, and he was under her spell and without control of his faculties. Add to that her hypnotic gaze, and he was in her command.

Luckily, though, my mother didn't use her Beacon wiles on Papa. The plain truth was that she didn't have to. He was in her control without them, which was *his* choice. She wouldn't dream of using her abilities or her body to take charge of him. She loved and respected him too much to use manipulations or seductions of *any* sort. In truth, she didn't wish to use her powers at all unless necessary. My father didn't simply *love* my mother; he *worshiped* her. As a matter of fact, so did I. Therefore, any influence she possessed over him was surely self-induced and greatly *enjoyed*.

Mama's a lady in every sense of the word. She's genteel, composed, courteous, and refined. She'd never even dream of doing anything vulgar or improper... I smiled, and my thoughts of her trailed off with the breeze.

Mama ebbed and swayed with me. The sweet song in her heart reverberated into my soul. It soothed and comforted me, flowing through me like the tide coming in and out of the bay. I sighed, retreating within myself, fading further and further into the most gorgeous sleep I'd had in quite a while.

The cabin may not be my orchard, I thought, letting my mind drift and float on both the sweet sound of her voice paired with thoughts of Pamela. *But, at least we're safe here. She's safe here.*

As I lay in her arms, falling into a deep and comforting sleep, her sweet song faded. It faltered and declined until all at once it diminished. She sighed and lay down beside me. Then just as she fell away, my mind drifted into hers. I had concerns about her well-being. I didn't want her to have nightmares. I peeked deeper. Her head wasn't filled with horrible images anymore. Thank goodness, Papa had put a stop to those. Instead, she was dreaming about Papa and me and about our life together.

I was thankful that they could be happy...and together. That was the one thing that was the utmost of importance to me: their happiness. I knew they each had sacrificed so much for me and for my safety.

I closed my eyes and delved deeper into her dream. She was dreaming of my father, but I wasn't sure how long ago it was. They were *together*, but oddly, I was there, too. *Hmm...* I saw myself, about five years old. *But my parents weren't together when I was that age. They were apart until recently.* Or so I *thought.* I decided to look some more...

Mama's mind shifted. In the next dream, I was about seven years old. That dream didn't carry the same tone as the first one. In fact, the entire feel of it had changed to something a bit different, something not quite as pleasant. I concentrated on the vision. My parents were fighting. Mama was crying and pleading with Papa. He was angry. He seemed devastated by something, *something* that I couldn't understand.

My mother's mind blurred. Then the dream collapsed and slipped out of her consciousness, and though I tried to catch every last glimpse of it, it was too late. She awoke with a start and sat bolt upright, looking around, a bit disoriented at first by our location.

"Are you all right, Mama?" I whispered to her while also sitting up.

She smiled. *"Yes, sweetie, I'm just fine. I didn't realize I fell asleep. I guess we're both more tired than we thought."* She touched my face and her eyes fluttered. Then her body sagged with fatigue; she sank back down into the grass, her eyes flickering, the lids drooping, threatening to settle her back into a deep sleep at any moment.

I bent down to her ear. *"Mama?"* I softly called to her, not wanting to jar her awake.

With much difficulty, her heavy eyes opened, and she smiled though her eyes were clouded from fatigue.

"Mama," I stammered, thinking about the profound love she had with my father and the powerful connection I felt for Kristofer. All of a sudden, a crippling fear overcame me as I realized I wouldn't be seeing much of him. The thought jarred me to the core, sending forceful waves of pain down my spine. Tears poured from my eyes like torrential rains, my grief driven by a fear so intense that I could hardly breathe.

What if he stops loving me? What if we can't be together, ever?

Mama sat up, seemingly panicked by my tears. She put her hands to my face. *"What's wrong?"*

I couldn't answer her. The only thing I could think about was my boy. My beautiful boy, who was only a few yards away from me. My heart ached as I thought of how I felt for him and about his sweet words. I wanted to be older. I wanted to *marry* him. I wanted to kiss him. I wanted to kiss *him* the way that Mama kissed Papa. I wished he didn't have to be so far away from me. I wanted him near me… forever.

"Mama?" I stammered.

"What?" she shrieked with distress. *"Either tell me, or I'll open your mind window to me!"*

"How'd you do it?" I asked, my brow furrowed. *"How could you stand to be around Papa? How could you stand to love him, knowing that he was your soulmate, your true love, but not allow yourself be with him?"*

Her worried expression melted into one of shock. She seemed a bit taken aback by my question. Her eyes drew wide, and it seemed as if she didn't quite know what to say or how to *explain*.

"Papa and you weren't together for twelve years after I was born, right?"

She stammered a bit. *"Well, yes and no, Lees."*

"What do you mean…yes and no?"

She took my hand and sighed. *"There were times, Leesie, when your father and I were together. It was never out in the open, and we never let you know it, but he and I were together…to a certain degree."*

She frowned back into my frown.

"To a certain…degree?" I shook my head. *"What does that mean?"*

She sighed, seemingly defeated. *"It means that we were only together some of the time, mostly at night, when you weren't awake,"* she stammered, glancing away from me while she said it.

Her answer startled me. The breath caught in my throat. *Oh, I see…* My wits were scattered. *"But why would the two of you do that to each other? I mean, if you loved each other, then why not just be together? You've been married the entire time! What would possess the two of you do that to yourselves, and to me?"*

Teary-eyed, Mama spoke softly. *"It wasn't your Papa's fault, sweetie."* Her voice cracked. *"It was mine. I was terrified of…"* She paused for a moment. *"Well, of just about everything at the time, including my guilt. But mostly, I was terrified of loving your papa and having either one of you hurt or taken from me because of that love."*

She clutched my hand. *"Your father wanted everyone to know about our family. He didn't care that we were different—he still doesn't. In fact, had he gotten his way, we would have never been apart. He wanted to go right up to his parents' house and introduce us to his father as his family. That was something that would've infuriated your grandfather and would've also made Charles aware of our marriage and of you!"*

She wiped some tears from her eyes. *"That's one of the reasons I've always been so nervous about going to the city. I always knew that at any given time, your papa might choose to tell our secrets. This, incidentally, is also why I've always insisted on going to the city with him."*

I gave her another confused look.

"Because I felt that if he were to go alone, there was more of a chance he might pay his father a visit. But he never did. And as far as Charles is concerned, it wouldn't have mattered, anyway. He would've hunted us no matter what we did."

More tears rolled down her face. *"My fears got in the way of our happiness, Lees, and I'll always regret that."*

She paused and then looked at me as if she feared the words in her mind. *"Because of my fears, your papa and I were secret lovers, so to speak. We were married but still secret until five years ago. What happened then was almost the end of us. I feared I'd lost him forever..."*

I sat straight up, gaping at her. *"Why? What did you do?"*

"I hurt him horribly. I cut him to the quick." Another tear fell.

Just then the wind shifted, sending the sweet smell of pipe tobacco and cinnamon into the air around us. Mama and I both turned as one. Papa was standing behind us, appearing rather shocked and worried at the same time.

My mother smiled. *"Hello, stable boy,"* she softly purred and winked and then patted the ground next to us. *"Won't you join us?"* She held her hand up to him.

Papa was white as a sheet, his eyebrows pulled together in the middle of his forehead. He stood blinking for a few seconds, but finally, he took Mama's hand and sat beside her.

She leaned in toward him until her eyes reflected off his. *"Can we please talk about this now? It's been five years, Asa. I think it's about time. It was one horrendous night that we both regret. In truth, had I listened to you, not to mention my heart, in the first place, then you wouldn't have felt so overwhelmed, and that night could've ended in joy instead of pain."*

"I'm the one who hurt you, sweetheart," Papa muttered. *"And I'm so sorry. I always will be."* He placed his palm flat against her cheek.

Mama closed her eyes for a moment, relishing in his touch. Then she turned to me and took a deep breath. *"You were seven years old, baby,"* she began. *"We were coming home from a trip to the city. You were asleep in the back of the wagon, so your papa and I were discussing our relationship quite freely."*

I reached out and grabbed hold of my father's hand. He smiled and gave it a squeeze. He didn't realize what I was about to do.

I pretended to listen to my mother, but I was actually searching his mind for the exact memory that she was relaying to us. Images flashed before my eyes. I looked deeper and deeper into his psyche until finally the image of him and Mama in the wagon flashed before my mind's eye. I concentrated on their conversation. Papa was talking:

"I don't understand why we have to keep up this charade, Ali," he said, glancing at her. *"It's not like we're apart. I mean, what would it hurt to let our daughter…"* He raised his voice shortly, before regaining composure. *"What will it hurt to let our daughter know that*

you are her mother? Not her grandmother! I can't stand lying to her anymore. I think we should just stop pretending."

Mama shook her head. *"No, Asa, we can't!"* She began to cry. *"If anyone finds out that I'm her mother, then Charles may find out as well. Then you both will be in danger! I can't lose either of you! I just can't! For heaven's sake, your father is in business with his father. They're friends! How can you even consider telling him! How?"*

She turned to him, her eyes wide and beseeching. *"I don't mind your mother knowing the truth because I know we can trust her. After all, she did give us the orchard as a wedding gift. And I'll be forever grateful to her for all she's done for me. Not to mention that she's the one who thought quickly enough to save us from harm in the first place when Leesie was just a baby. But we can't tell your father! Not ever! It's just not safe. And if we tell Leesie, then she'd have to remember not to tell anyone else, and she is just too young to have that kind of responsibility set in her lap!"*

My father stopped the wagon. He put on the brake and set the reins down beside him. He leaned over, kissed Mama on the lips, and gazed into her troubled eyes. Bright blue interspersed with brilliant green, their collective sights shined in the sunlight.

"You are my wife." Papa's voice was strong, determined. *"You are the mother of our child, and I don't care who knows it. I don't care what my father thinks! I do not care what that bastard who hurt you does! I am sick and tired of pretending. Therefore, I'm not going to be stopped! I'm not going to be deterred! I'm not going to be fearful or worried! We are a family, damn it! We are going to live in our house…together! We are going to live our lives together! And from this day forward, Mrs. Raign, you are going to move out of the upstairs bedroom and into mine with me! Besides that, you and I are going to tell Leesie all about our marriage and who her mother really is as soon as we get home. And that's that!"* He stared into her startled eyes, picked up the reins, and unset the brake.

Mama grabbed Papa's hand and pressed it against her cheek; she looked sorrowful. *"No,"* she whispered simply and then dropped both his hand and her eyes at the same time. She turned her head in the opposite direction, folded her hands in her lap, and effectively shut him out.

Just then, I witnessed myself awaken from the lack of motion. I stood behind my parents with my arms stretched out. Papa turned to me and lifted me into his lap as we continued on our way…home.

Papa's mind shifted.

Now, I was standing in front of my home…the orchard. My heart leaped into my throat as I gazed out into the healthy field full of living apple trees in the distance. I turned around, looking up into our *intact* little farmhouse. It had only been a day since it burned, but it seemed like an eternity to me.

I glanced around.

My mother sat on the front porch stoop, watching Papa and me as we ran into the yard. Even though she was smiling, a much-distressed air seemed to surround her.

I sat next to the memory of my mother, watching as she looked out into the yard…at *us*. I knew her mind was troubled. She was torn between letting herself have the man she loved and feeling trapped by the responsibility of keeping her family safe.

I followed her gaze to where Papa was chasing me.

Little-me laughed out loud and squealed with delight every few seconds. Then Papa caught me around the waist. He tossed me up onto his shoulders and spun around in circles. I squealed again just as he lifted me straight up and put my stomach flat on top of his head. He stretched my hands out to both sides and ran through the yard with me bouncing and bumping above him. Abruptly, my father turned. He looked at Mama with a twinkle in his eyes and ran toward her. As we approached the porch stoop, he threw me up into the air, caught me in his strong arms, cradled me against his chest, and then sat me down next to her.

Little Leesie giggled with delight, but Papa's full attention and his eyes were on my mother. He smirked and then dropped down to his knees, took Mama's hands into his, and threw her over his shoulder. Then he jumped up and started running and spinning around in circles. All the while, Mama screamed, pretending to protest, but her laughter gave her away.

I glanced over at my younger self, who was sitting beside me. She was laughing and clapping, clearly enjoying the way our parents were playing.

"I remember this," I laughed to myself and smiled. *"I remember how much I enjoyed watching them play together."*

But then a sudden sense of anger swept through me, anger at that horrible man. *If not for Charles Marshal, not to mention my so-called grandfather, they'd never have had to hide.*

As I continued to watch, Papa spun around faster and faster, chuckling as Mama lay draped over his shoulder. She was also laughing and spanking his bottom as he spun.

"Tell me you love me, and I'll stop," he breathlessly chuckled.

"All right…I love you," my mother laughed, but he continued to spin.

"Say it again. Say my name."

"I love you. I love you, Asa. I love you, Asa Raign!"

Papa set her back down onto her feet. She swayed, stumbled dizzily, and nearly fell to the ground, but he caught her in his arms just before she fell. He wound his arms around her waist and lifted her up until their eyes were parallel. He pressed his forehead against hers. Both were gasping and trying to catch their breath.

"Let's tell her now, sweetheart," Papa whispered, breathless, and then turned to look at my happy little face. *"Look at her, Ali. Just look at how happy our daughter is when we're together."*

I turned to my seven-year-old self, my mouth gaping. *"How can you not see this? I know you're just a little child, but…seriously?"* I asked me, gesturing out toward where our obviously enamored parents stood clutching one another. Papa had his hands around my mother's waist, his forehead pressed against hers, her feet dangling more than a foot off the ground.

"Kiss me," he urged, licking his lips, enticing her. *"Kiss me in front of her. Let's end this now, sweetheart, please."* His voice was beseeching.

Just then, Little Leesie jumped up, ran off the porch, and skipped to where our still-entangled parents stood in the yard. She bounced up and down, took Mama's hand, and gave it a hard yank, attempting to pull her away from Papa. *"Play with meeee, Grandma!"* she squealed, tugging her arm.

I flinched. Seeing myself call her Grandma seemed so wrong to me, and clearly, I wasn't the *only* one that was disturbed by it.

My father winced and angrily shook his head when I spoke those words to my *mother*. He set Mama's feet on the ground, and stepped back. Mama glanced at him as little-me pulled her out into the yard.

I watched her and my little-self running and skipping together, gleefully playing. At least little Leesie was happy. My mother's eyes kept darting toward my father, who was looking quite crestfallen just then.

I sat down on the porch next to him and watched the scene unfold in front of me. He had an angry, distressed expression, almost as if he were truly at the end of his tether, as if unprepared to accept their long-suffering relationship for what it was. He was in dire need of his *wife's* love. That was clear. It was a love that, if denied, threatened to tear him apart. I knew he was about to do something drastic, maybe even impetuous, to convince her. I *also* knew that whatever it was he was about to do wasn't going to work.

He and I sat on the porch watching Mama and my seven-year-old self playing until the sun set over the orchard. Rather, he watched them as I watched *him*. I could almost see the wheels of his mind sweeping one desperate idea around his imagination after the next. By the look on his face, he had decided what he was going to do about it.

I glanced away from him for a moment just as my mother and little Leesie ran back to the house, still giggling with each other as they reached the porch.

Leesie grabbed hold of the front door, opened it, and ran inside with Mama right behind her. But in an instant, Papa swept in front of Mama and slammed the door as little-me stepped across the threshold. At the same time, he turned my mother around, thrust her against the door, and blocked her exit.

He pressed his body against her, *seizing* her wrists with one hand and pinning them above her head. He wrapped his free arm around her waist, bowing his physique into her willowy curves. He bent her backward against the closed door. His free hand moved down to her hip and then down to her thigh. He grabbed hold of one leg, cinched it up around his waist, and wound her body around his, all the while running his hand over the shape of her slight form.

Papa bent over my mother and freed her wrists. He pushed her figure backward, bracing it against the crook of both arms. He took her face between his hands and tilted her chin up until it was angled so he could see into her eyes. *"I love you—wife!"* He urgently, almost angrily, hissed, his body quaking with emotion. He lifted her off the ground and then hitched up her skirt and wrapped both of her legs around his waist.

At that moment, a look of passion fell over my mother's face. She leaned in, slanted her lips over his, and frantically kissed him.

It was obvious to me as I witnessed that display of love between my parents that even though Papa had overpowered her, giving her no choice but to acquiesce to his demands, she wouldn't have objected if given a choice. Clearly, she was just as determined to have him as he was to have her. She had her hands buried in his wavy blond hair, eagerly twisting her fingers through it, allowing her hungry body to have the love that her heart so urgently ached for.

I smiled, watching their dance of passion with a fluttering heart.

Then the feel of the kiss shifted. It was crazed, devoid of control, each soul giving in to its endless appetite for the other, each body feverishly moving against the other's overheated skin.

My mother opened her eyes, gazing straight into Papa's icy blue orbs. She slid her hands around his chest and wrapped her cinched-up legs around his hips—urging him on.

Feeling her desire, my father shifted his hand from her face down to the buttons of her dress. He undid the top three and slipped his long fingers into the opening, exposing her breasts and caressing each one in turn.

Mama gasped just as he plunged his face down to her bosoms, her mouth gaping open, her chest heaving with each flutter of Papa's tongue over her puckering skin. Then in a frenzy of uncontrolled passion, she cried out his name; she cried for more. She threw her glowing strawberry head backward, gasping as he touched her, showing him her readiness for the end result.

Papa, sensing that her heart as well as her body was ablaze with an all-consuming desire for him, abruptly stopped, set her down on the porch, and took a purposeful step back.

My mother stared at him, her eyes wide and bewildered. She was trying to catch her breath as well as her mind and was attempting to regain some semblance of the decorum and poise that she usually maintained.

My father's breath was ragged, nearly gasping; he bent down until their eyes met. "*That, my darling wife, was a kiss from your husband. Now if you would like to finish this, then you and I will go inside and have a little chat with our daughter. Otherwise, you may sleep upstairs alone tonight.*" He smirked, opened the front door, and walked into the house, shutting the door behind him.

From inside the house, I heard my little-self curiously speaking. *"I couldn't get the door open, Papa,"* Little Leesie questioned. *"Was it stuck?"*

"Yes, something like that, angel," he chuckled.

My mother's lustful eyes blazed with red-hot fury, realizing at once what her husband had done to her. She wrenched open the door, slammed it behind her with her mind, and glared at Papa as if she wished to incinerate him where he stood. Clearly, she found it unfathomable that he could partake in such an underhanded and devious plot against her. Her hands shook with ill-concealed anger, her mind seeking a proper punishment for such a sin.

She took one ireful step toward him; her eyes illuminated with rage, carefully considering what kind of pain to inflict upon him. But her wrath soon turned to sorrow as she looked into my confused and frightened little face.

Little Leesie stepped forward. *"What's wrong, Grandma? Did I do something bad? Are you angry with me?"* my little-self asked, her innocent eyes full of tears and her little pink cheeks flushed with fear.

Guilt for his action bloomed in my father's eyes as he stood staring at us both. Obviously, it hadn't dawned on him that his daughter could be affected by his actions against her mother. As a result, guilt ran up his spine and into his head, gnawing at him, corroding and etching its way into his heart and through his brain.

Papa bowed his head in shame, realizing that he had inflicted pain upon the two people that he loved most in the world while also bringing about such anger to his wife that it had frightened his innocent child.

Appearing both confused and tortured by the decision, he shook his head. His distressed eyes were fixed on Mama, who was suffering as much as he was from the ordeal. *"I can't do this anymore. I just can't. It's eating me alive. You win…"* The words were spoken so softly that they were almost inaudible, and his body both stiffened and seemed to weaken in the same moment. Finally, resigned to the sorrowful fate of his crumbling marriage, my father dropped his head, solidifying a decision that came from somewhere deep inside of him, and walked into his bedroom, his head hung in shame.

Mama's face dropped while massive waves of both guilt and grief ran through her eyes. Although she said nothing, neither did she follow Papa. Silently, she picked up Little Leesie and walked up the stairs.

I gasped and threw my hands over my mouth. *This, I remember, too!* Although, before I could react, the scene shifted again…

We were now in Papa's bedroom. I assumed it was later that same night by his sullen and distraught demeanor. He sat alone on the side of the bed, his head downcast. It seemed as if he were going out of his mind with worry. He agitatedly wrung his hands, and distressed tears ran the length of his face. The tears dripped from his cheeks onto his bare chest and then fell into a small puddle on the floor beneath him. The wetness on his chest glistened in the dim light of the single lamp lit in the room. His wavy sandy blond hair flopped artfully over his forehead, partially hiding just one of his striking steel-blue eyes.

The sight of him hit me like a ton of bricks. Never in my life had I *noticed* just how absolutely beautiful my father was until that moment.

His rippled chest heaved. He was trying without success to stop himself from crying. I hated to see him like that, in tears. He didn't just seem upset; he seemed wounded, his emotions mutilated, his heart *maimed* by my mother's rejection.

Hot tears ran down my face as well. *It'll be all right. They'll be together,* I tried to reassure myself, reminding myself that this was merely a memory, and all would be fine…*eventually.*

Suddenly, there was a gentle knock at the door, and then, slowly, it opened.

It was *Mama.*

She stepped through the threshold and shut the door behind her. Her eyes were red and swollen, and she had a flustered, almost panic-stricken expression on her face. She stood perfectly still, looking as if she were about to cry at any moment.

Without even glancing up, Papa reached his hand out to her.

She didn't take it. Instead, she flew into his arms, almost knocking him backward. She wrapped her arms around his neck, sobbing into his chest while running her lips across his bare skin. She dragged her lips up the contour of his throat and then up his stubbly chin to his mouth. She grasped both sides of his face between her palms, urgently kissing him, her tongue flicking in and around his mouth. Then she straddled one of his legs between her own and slipped out of her robe, exposing both her body and her soul to him.

Papa's hands slipped around her naked back and then made their way down. They cupped her bare bottom, his long fingers kneading the smooth flesh as she sat astride him.

My mother groaned and arched her back, heaving her breasts toward Papa's hungry mouth, her hair swishing over his hands, partially hiding them as they worked their way around every curve of her figure. After a moment, she pushed him down onto his back and climbed over his outstretched legs. She slinked over him, straddling him with her milky, unclothed body, and hungrily, fiercely moaned into his open mouth—swallowing his groans while spreading soft licks across his lips with the tip of her tongue.

Then her mouth left his as she inched down and then stretched across his taut torso. She traced the firm lines of his body with her lips and tongue. The tip of her tongue skimmed across his sweat-and-tear-glistening skin.

I watched in shock as she slid her hands as well as her mouth down his muscular abdomen until they encountered the waist of his trousers. As her tongue slid across his flesh, a low, guttural groan derived from unhindered passion arose from Papa's throat, egging her on. He stretched his arms out, caressing both her breasts at once.

Mama sat up. She straddled my father's thighs and took firm hold of the waistband of his trousers. With one pull, she tore them apart, sending buttons flying in all directions around them.

Finally, licking her lips in anticipation, she dropped to the floor on her knees. She bent forward, both her hands and her lips leading her in the search for what she wanted.

I gasped! My eyes drew wide, and my mouth gaped. *Mama?!*

I looked at the ground…*embarrassed*, realizing that this was a scene I should definitely *not* be witnessing. I turned around, my knees quaking. I didn't know what to do next. I was shocked by what I saw my mother doing. My head spun, and my mouth and eyes both gaped open. I wanted to see for *myself* how the story ended, but at the same time, I didn't want to see any more of that *particular* scene at all! But before I could decide, I heard Papa's voice. It didn't sound at all happy, not like I *imagined* it should. It sounded angry and hurt.

"We need to tell her!"

"No. Just let me love you, Asa!"

There was a pause. Then…

"So is this all that I am to you?" my father sternly growled. *"Am I simply flesh? Am I merely the means to satisfy your witchy lusts? Is that what I am to you, Ali? Because if I'm not your husband, then what? What sinful, ungodly purpose do I afford you?"*

I turned back around just as he picked up her robe and flung it at her.

She was frozen, half-sitting, half-lying on the floor at his feet, her robe clutched to her chest. *"I-I don't understand,"* she tearfully murmured.

My father leaned over and righted his trousers, and his eyes flashed into hers. *"If I am your husband, then be my wife. Be a mother to our child! Do you have any idea how much it kills me to make love to you and then to have you leave me because you're afraid that our daughter will find you in my bed? I feel as if my soul dies a bit each time you leave my bed to sleep upstairs in yours."* Furious tears streamed down his face as he sobbed.

"Asa, please!" My mother stood up. *"Please, please don't make me choose between your love and the safety of my child, please!"* she cried, grabbing his arm, pleading with him.

Papa pulled away. He was incensed. It was *frightening* to watch. *"How dare you accuse me of such a thing?!"* he bellowed, his face contorted with livid rage. He grabbed her around the waist, lifted her up, wrenched open his bedroom door, and tossed her out of his room, his teeth gnashing. *"You stay away from me…witch!"* he spat, pointing at her and staring her dead in his sights. *"Or, so help me, I'll deliver you to Charles Marshal myself!"*

I gasped. Mama gasped. *"No, Papa!"* I cried.

I could tell by the look on his face, as soon as those awful words passed over his lips that he regretted them. Unfortunately, Mama was too distraught to notice his remorse. She turned away. *"I think it would be best if Leesie and I moved back to the cabin. You and I obviously can't live here together any longer,"* she choked, pulled the robe around her, hiding her nakedness, and then ran into the front room.

"You are not taking my child away from me!" he bellowed, hurrying after her.

She swung back around, obviously quite angry herself. *"Well, you can't have it both ways,"* she tearfully snapped, her emerald eyes blazing with the hurt he had inflicted upon her. *"You either want me, or you don't!"* She stepped forward. *"And if you don't want me, then let me assure you of one thing…"* She stared him squarely in the eyes. *"You, Asa Raign, are not the only man in the world. If you don't want me, then some other man will!"*

Papa gritted his teeth and took a single menacing step toward her as if he were about to strike her. He stopped himself at the last moment and then turned away, walked back to his bedroom, and shut the door.

Mama gasped, and my body sagged with exhaustion. I hadn't noticed until that moment that I'd been holding my breath throughout the entire horrifying exchange between my parents.

My mother ran upstairs into her bedroom just as Papa ran out of his. He, too, ran up the stairs, wrenched open her bedroom door, and fell at her feet, sobbing. He looked up into her shocked eyes. *"Please forgive me for what I said to you, please, and please don't leave!"* He stood to face his wife, his *love.* *"I've made a decision,"* he whispered. *"From now on, you are nothing more than Leesie's grandmother, to me and, to her."* He sighed. *"And as God as my witness, I will never touch you again, not until the day comes that you tell our daughter the truth about yourself, Alice."* With that, he resolutely nodded, turned away, and left Mama alone in her room.

The scene faded, and my consciousness returned to the strawberry patch, where I was sitting with both my parents. They were kissing and holding each other. Papa let his lips slip away from Mama for a moment. He opened his eyes; his face was somber. *"So do you forgive me for those awful things I said to you that night, sweetheart?"*

My mother smiled and put the back of her hand to his cheek. *"I told you. There's nothing to forgive. It was a horrible night that we both regret. I should've listened to you in the first place. I don't blame you for what happened."* She tearfully smiled. *"Ultimately, Asa, your decision brought us back together. I just wish that it hadn't taken me five years to realize what you knew all along—what my heart knew all along. The three of us belong together as a family."*

Papa sighed. *"Still, I should've realized one thing…"* He took her face between his hands. *"Nothing can come between a mother and the safety of her child. You would've given up anything to keep Leesie safe—even me."*

What? Papa's words shocked me. *Mama would do that for me?*

While my head still reeled, they both turned to look at me. I smiled back a bit cowardly, recalling what I saw my mother doing.

My thoughts drifted…

In my life, I had collected opinions about certain things, one being that there were specific behaviors in which a lady did and did *not* participate, matters that, if shocking or inappropriate enough, would render a woman unfit to be thought of as a proper *lady*.

A lady possessed modesty, correctness, and above all, *restraint*— qualities my beautiful, genteel mother maintained at all times. Those *ideas* had gone unchallenged until a few moments before when I saw my mother conduct herself in a way which until then I would have thought ill-mannered, *unfitting* of a lady.

A picture of my mother dominated my mind as I gazed at her. If ever there were a woman who could be called a true *lady* in every sense of the word, surely it was *my* mama. She was as poised and elegant a woman as was ever created. Yet in a few brief memories of the past, she had changed the idea of what it meant to be a lady and also how a lady was permitted to behave.

Maybe it was the way Papa touched her or the love he made her feel inside. Whatever the reason, one thing was clear: *My* papa had the ability to unhinge my mother so deeply that she let herself become uninhibited, holding back nothing when it came to loving and pleasing him as well as herself. He possessed the power to take her from a demure, soft-spoken, dignified *lady* straight to an unrestrained, uncontrolled, unrestricted, wild, feral *tigress* and then back again once freed from her hungers.

I peeked at my parents. *I guess Mama isn't the only one with intoxicating powers.* I giggled to myself as I looked at her. *I hope to be a lady just like her someday, and I hope that my love with Kristofer turns out to be every bit as passionate as theirs. And above all…* My cheeks flushed. *I hope Kristofer attains Papa's skill.*

As I sat gazing at my beautiful mother, I realized that within a few minutes' time, I had grown an entirely new respect for her. She was a strong woman. Since the day of my birthday when she first explained acts of love to me, I assumed women were mere observers in the deeds of the flesh, but through a few memories from the past, she had shown me that that was a false notion. She wasn't merely a willing participant in her encounters with my father, but at times, she even dominated them. *With* her love, she took it upon herself to let go of her insecurities and to boldly assume responsibility for giving the love of her existence *exactly* what he wanted without hesitation. I knew she loved Papa in a way that was not only satisfying for him but also for her. And considering what she had been through with Charles Marshal—I shuddered at the thought—she was even more amazing than I had ever imagined. I only wished that at the time of their awful breakup, she would have had the courage to stand against the evil that haunted her memories and to reclaim her family.

Papa reached out and took my hand, jolting me from my daydream. I lurched as he spoke to me. *"So I suppose you think that your mama and I are completely mad. Don't you, angel?"*

I laughed. *"No, Papa, I don't think you're mad. I think you're both marvelous. And I love you, everything about you."* I eyed my mother. *"Both of you."* I threw myself into their arms. After a moment, I let go and gazed at the beauty that was my father's eyes. *"When did you decide to try to convince Mama to tell me the truth again? What happened?"* I glanced over at the pensive face of my mother. I didn't wish to rouse hurtful memories for her, but I *had* to know.

Papa squeezed my hand. Once again, I delved into his mind instead of relying on his voice for the answer.

I was transported back to the orchard. It was the same day that I accidentally came across the old root cellar…

Papa, Mama, and I were walking out to the trees. I had to stifle a snicker when my eyes fell upon my mother. She was wearing Papa's clothes. It seemed so ridiculous to me that she did that only a few short days before.

My other-self ran ahead of them as we made our way out to the field.

I walked next to my father, listening to their conversation. *"I came across Jake today,"* said Papa with a bit of a knowing snicker in his tone.

Mama stopped short. *"What do you mean…came across?"* she frightfully whispered, her emerald eyes wide and staring.

Papa seemed a bit taken aback by her upsetting reaction. *"Jake, Molly, and our godson have moved to town…Ali,"* he whispered her name slowly—a name that he hadn't called her in nearly five years. Then he tried to take her hand, but she pulled away, and her hands shook with obvious fright.

"How can that be?" she whispered more to herself than to him.

"Jake's the new minister in town. He and I had a nice long chat. He's invited us to their house. You and I, I mean." He hesitated for a moment. *"We'll bring Lees the next time."*

Mama gasped and threw her hands up over her mouth, stifling either a scream or a sob. I wasn't sure, but it was heartbreaking to see her so frightened. She turned away from Papa, gazing at my other-self in the distance. *"If she's around them at all, she'll know. She'll find out that I lied to her. She'll hate me. That can't happen,"* she whispered to herself.

"Ali," Papa murmured from a few feet away.

She jerked and jumped, shaken to the core by that bit of news. Her big, expressive emerald eyes were as big as saucers. She looked like a scared rabbit.

Papa stood right behind her, almost putting his lips to the back of her head. *"It's over, sweetheart,"* he cooed. *"It's over."*

She shook her head, and terrified tears sprang into her eyes. *"I'm dead inside, Asa. I have nothing to offer you…or to her. I'm dead."*

It pained me to see how deep her fears ran. She seemed so weak, so vulnerable.

Papa, on the other hand, seemed so *alive* again, as if a long-extinguished light had just reignited from somewhere inside his soul. He closed his eyes and inhaled, taking in her sweet scent, which was something that he hadn't done in a long time. *"It's going to be all right."* He breathed deeper as he spoke. *"I'll show you. We'll all get through this together. You and I will rekindle the flames of our marriage together, my beautiful wife."* He leaned down and kissed the top of her head.

Mama's eyes flew open wide. She took a half-sobbing, unsteady breath in and then ran away.

Papa bolted forward and then twisted around to face her, halting her escape. *"No! You're not running away from me anymore, Ali, not ever again,"* he whispered, holding her in his arms, his tone tender yet firm.

She gaped at him, and her big emerald green eyes brimmed with horrified tears. It seemed as if her emotions were about to get the better of her, but I noticed that she didn't struggle.

The sight moved me, touched me in a way that I could feel all the way to my heart. *She was terrified because she thought that I was going hate her. I never realized that I meant that much to her.*

Papa released her and bent down until their eyes met. *"I'll give you a few days to prepare yourself—to give up this fight…"* He pulled her chin up, and his eyes flashed with determination. *"Ali, you will give it up,"* he definitively whispered and then kissed her forehead.

Without another word, he turned and walked a few steps away.

My mother balled up her fist and put it to her heart. *"He still wants me…"* She sounded wistful; she shook her head, as if in wonder, and an agonized smile crept across her lips. *"My God, he still wants me,"* she said again although the wonder in her eyes melted into an expression of panic.

"Oh dear, he WANTS me!" She gulped hard and threw her hands up over her mouth.

The memory of my Papa chuckled from where he stood a few yards away, and then the image in his head changed again.

This time, my parents were in the wagon, just arriving at Mr. and Mrs. Coles' house.

This was the day I was left alone. The day I met…my boy, I thought to myself, peering deeper.

Papa stopped the wagon in front of the Coles' front porch. He jumped down and put his hand out to Mama. *"Come on, Ali."*

My eyes drifted to Kristofer, who was watching the exchange between my parents with a curious expression.

My mother appeared to be beside herself. She hemmed and hawed as Papa tried to take her hand, pulling it away and then giving it back to him several times before letting him help her out of the wagon.

From somewhere in the distance, I heard both Mr. Cole and Molly's joyful voices. They both rushed toward my parents.

Molly grabbed hold of Mama like she had the intention of never letting her go again. Happy tears ran down her face as she looked into my mother's eyes. Mama was also crying. *"Oh, Ali, how I've missed you!"* Molly cried.

Mr. Cole bent down to Mama and gave her a quick peck on the cheek. *"Hello, dear. It sure is nice to see you,"* he muttered just as Molly squealed with delight and threw herself into Papa's arms.

Papa laughed out loud at the spectacle and hugged Molly.

"Well, come inside!" laughed Mr. Cole, spotting Kristofer standing beside them. *"And here's my boy!"* He ruffled Kristofer's hair. *"Say hello to your godparents, Kris. This is Mr. and Mrs. Raign—Asa and Ali to your ma and me."*

Without a second's hesitation, Mama ran to Kristofer and held him to her bosom. *"It's nice to see you again, baby,"* she whispered.

"The last time I saw you, you were just a tiny thing. And now just look at how handsome you are!"

She stood back and touched his cheek, her face beaming. *"You know, you look just like your mama did when she was your age."*

Kristofer nodded. *"Yes, ma'am. She tells me the same thing all the time,"* he politely answered. Then his head dropped down, his expression morose. *"And you look just like your mama, too,"* he muttered under his breath, but Mama didn't hear him.

Just before they went inside, Papa stopped Kristofer. He took him by the arm and pulled him aside. *"Ali's very pretty, isn't she, Kris?"*

Kristofer nodded and his eyes drifted to Mama.

"Well, I have a little girl just about your age who's every bit as lovely as her Mama over there..." Papa pointed his chin toward where my mother stood talking with Molly. *"Her name is Leesie. She's as pretty as a sun-kissed daffodil, just—like—her—mama."* Papa winked at Kristofer.

Hearing the whispered conversation, Mr. Cole snickered under his breath and shook his head. *"Let's all go inside!"* he announced, still laughing, and joyfully gestured toward the house.

My father strode up to my mother. Without faltering, he took her by the hand, and then pulled her to his side. *"No more sitting on the fence. As of right now, the fight is officially over."* He bent down and nuzzled her ear with the tip of his nose. *"Come to my bed tonight, Ali. I promise not to toss you out of my room, and we'll tell Lees together in the morning."* He turned her face toward his, kissed her nose, and then, taking her hand, tugged her into their best friends' house.

Mama's nervous eyes swept between their laced fingers and the sweet face of her *husband* as they walked.

From just inside the house, I heard Molly's voice ring out. *"Bring Leesie by tomorrow, Ali. We'll have tea and get to know each other!"*

As the memory began to fade, I noticed something that my father hadn't at the time: Kristofer, who was running away from his house straight toward the orchard and *me.*

I gasped just as my mind was sucked back to the strawberry field.

Papa was twisting Mama's hair in his hands and gazing with a hypnotic grin into her eyes. *"That night, when you were sleeping with Leesie, I bent down and told you that I loved you and kissed your forehead."* Tears rolled down his cheeks. *"That's when I saw your light again."*

Mama gasped. *"You had stopped seeing it?"*

He nodded. *"After our horrible fight, I willed myself to stop seeing it. For my own sanity, I needed to stop seeing it."* He kissed the tip of her nose. *"Then after it went away, I prayed to the Lord that I would only see it again if ever a time came that we never parted. I prayed that I would only see your light if it became not only something of this world but something eternal."*

The words took my mother's breath away; she gasped and sobbed into Papa's chest.

"I told you I loved you that night, and it blazed for me!" He put his hand on her heart, laughing. *"We did have that one small argument early the next morning, but I knew you were coming back to me. I'm sorry I teased you so shamelessly that day,"* he whispered into her ear and then nibbled it with his front teeth.

Mama shivered, and goose bumps erupted over every inch of exposed skin.

Papa leaned in and skimmed the shell of her ear with his tongue and then made his way up to her waiting mouth. Just as his lips touched hers, she fisted her hands into his hair, pulled him nearer, and devoured his lips.

I cleared my throat. Obviously, they forgot that I was sitting there. *"Umm…should I leave?"* I giggled. *"You know,"* I poked my father in the arm. *"Being around the two of you is sort of like sharing a house with a couple of love-struck rabbits. Did you know that?"*

Papa choked on my words, and they both laughed.

Mama shook her head, still laughing. *"Why don't you go inside? Jake and Kris are probably wondering what happened to us. Your papa and I will be there in a few minutes, all right, my wonderful daughter?"* She bent over and kissed my lips.

"All right, Mama," I laughed, then jumped to my feet.

Papa stopped me before I ran; he clasped my hand. *"You did see the point of our story, right, Lees?"*

"That married people are crazy. Therefore, I should never get married?"

He shook his head. *"No, the point is, darling daughter, I shouldn't have spoken to your mother like I did, no matter how upset I was. It was disrespectful, and that was wrong."*

"And I should've had more trust and faith in your father," Mama chimed in.

"All right, no bad words, and trust and faith—got it," I answered, giggling. *"I'm just happy that you're happy."*

I let go of my father's hand and ran toward the cabin. As I approached, I saw smoke rising from the chimney of our new home. *"Mr. Cole must've made us a fire."* I ran faster, remembering that Kristofer was also waiting for me.

Just as I passed by our horses in the yard, I stopped and looked behind me across the vast strawberry field toward my parents. They were kissing again. *"I'll never get tired of seeing them kiss,"* I whispered just as Papa pushed Mama down amidst the tall grass and covered her with his body. *Hmm. I might just get a little sister after all.*

Just then, a strange rush of emotion spread through me. It was a strangled mix of both grief and joy, all mixed up with a bittersweet feeling of contentment.

20. *Truth and Power*

I trampled through the grass toward the cabin with thoughts of my parents running through my mind. I was grateful to God for bringing them back together and also for delivering us from Charles Marshal: the predator and his huntsmen. My parents and I belonged together, and I knew that it was nothing short of a miracle that we had survived such a heinous attack.

I stepped up onto the porch, thinking. I wasn't sure what Charles Marshal meant by what he said to his men, but one thing was clear: He wanted Papa and me dead, and he wanted to own my mama. I shuddered, determined never to allow that to happen. Even if I had to sacrifice myself, she would be spared, and so would Papa.

I thought again about Charles's cryptic words to his men. Papa was vague in his explanation when I asked him about it. *Hmm. Maybe I'll ask Kristofer what it means.*

Then I thought about that evil monster again and what he had planned for Mama and me *and* for Papa. *"If that evil bastard comes here, then Papa and I will have to kill him. I will help. I'm more powerful than Mama. I'll protect her. I'll always protect her."*

I nodded, opened the front door to my new home, and stepped inside, not at all prepared for the sight that met my eyes.

It was absolute perfection!

It reminded me of a miniature version of our farmhouse. It even had the same furnishings, but being a bit smaller, it was even cozier and warmer than our house was.

Oh…was.

My heart sank, but I sucked back the dark cloud forming in my head and stepped across the threshold.

I closed the wooden door and looked around, taking it all in. First, I noticed that there was no kitchen or staircase, but there was a stove sitting in the corner of the room. Next to the stove sat a dark wood china cabinet, and a small oak table and four chairs sat in the middle of the room. Under the table lay a beautiful, brightly-colored braided rug. I turned to the right, where a gray stone fireplace blazed with a warm fire and where a large oak mantel hung just above the gray stone. I took a closer look at the mantel, squinting. I canted my head and stepped forward, noticing that there was something carved into the wood.

Asa-Ali-Rebecca-Alyce. *"Proof that I actually did live here once,"* I muttered and then turned to admire the rest of my home. Across from where I stood, in between the wall with the stove and the china cabinet and the wall with the fireplace, stood two closed doors. *Those must be the bedrooms. I wonder which one is mine.*

I smiled, and my eyes swept around the entire space as if drinking in the sight of my new and surprisingly beautiful little home. That's when I realized there was something missing, something that I didn't wish to be without…

There was no *piano.*

My heart sank, along with my world. The cavernous hole in my chest reared its ominous head. It sliced through me, threatening to reopen. *No more piano. No more music.* The hole in my chest throbbed, but then a thought lifted my spirits, just a little—my mama. *She runs Papa's music through her mind.* The ominous darkness drifted back and pulled its claws away from my chest. *I'll have to ask her to keep her mind window open to me while she's listening to him play. I imagine she won't object to letting me hear it with her.* That notion made me feel less sad, less lonely for our beloved piano. *Just one more victim of the unspeakable wickedness that depraved monster has thrust upon us.*

As I stood gazing at our almost perfect little cabin, Kristofer stepped up to me. He threw his arms around me and held me tight. *"Your new home is really nice,"* he whispered into my ear, trying to sound cheerful.

I smiled back at him and gazed into his beautiful face. He was trying to seem happy for me, but what I saw just beneath the surface was pain. I took both of his hands, trying not to think about being away from him, trying to relish each and every second I had left to be with him. My mind wasn't there, though; I was still worried about losing him.

It was early autumn, and the weather was turning cold. Soon it would be much too cold to go traveling very far, and *we* couldn't go back to that town until the threat was gone. *After today, I might not see my boy for months.*

Kristofer seemed to sense my pain. His beautiful hazel eyes clouded over with worried tears. *"Shh. No, no, Sita, let's just enjoy one another while we can,"* he whispered and wrapped his arms around my waist. He looked into my eyes. Kristofer's gaze was hypnotic to me, very much like Mama's was. He stroked my face with the back of his hand. *"Don't worry, love, we'll see each other all the time."* He spoke the words, but even as they left his lips, he didn't seem convinced. His hazel eyes shined into my emerald eyes, but instead of joy, only agony and wounds burned through.

Oh, why? Why the wounds?

He reached up and rested his forehead against mine. *"We've been through worse than this, love."*

Have we? I don't remember…

I frowned as thoughts of the night before crept into my mind. Like a dense fog, the horrific memories clouded everything around me in a murky, ominous haze.

I stared into Kristofer's worried face; he seemed to be studying me. *"Kristofer?"* I spoke softly. *"May I ask you something?"*

"Of course, Sita, anything."

"Last night that horrible man, the sheriff." My voice cracked. *"He said something about me. Actually, he told his men to do something to me. Papa tried vaguely to explain, but I still don't understand what it means. I think Papa was trying to protect me from the truth."*

"What did Marshal say?" Kristofer asked, his voice low. He seemed anxious.

I leaned in and whispered Charles Marshal's words into his ear.

He winced and then balled up his fists. His bright hazel eyes drew dark and clouded with rage.

"What does it mean?" I took a deep breath, struck by Kristofer's sudden anger. *"What does that word mean?"* I qualified.

The knuckles of Kristofer's balled-up fists were white as a sheet, almost as white as his face, which had suddenly paled. He shook his head. *"It means that he wanted his men to hurt you in the same way that he did Ali, but he wanted them to take your life while doing it."* His voice was still low—too low and wavering.

"I know that. That's what Papa told me, but what does that word mean?" I still didn't understand.

"It's a vulgar word, Lees, one that you don't need roaming around in your pure, sinless mind. Let's just say that it's not a word spoken in polite society. Your pa was trying to protect your innocence, and I'll do the same."

"Oh," I mumbled just as thoughts of my papa's explanation of the difference between his and Mama's love and the hurt inflicted upon her by Charles drifted through my mind. The sudden image of Papa slapping his hands together made me flinch.

I didn't need to ask again. Abruptly, I understood.

I cocked my head in that same puppy sort of way that Kristofer did to me. *"And what's a cherry?"* I asked, just as a bit more of my childhood innocence slipped away from me.

Kristofer snorted and shook his head. *"It's an offensive name for a young girl."*

Oh…

Kristofer laced his fingers and pressed them against the small of my back, pulling me into him. His sweet lips moved to my ear. *"You are not a cherry, and I would never allow anyone to harm you, not ever, my Sita. And from what I remember, it's not the first time that Charles Marshal has used that word, which just goes to show what a heinous bastard he really is. Don't worry, I'll protect you,"* he whispered, sending shivers and shudders down my spine.

His fingers unlaced. Then he grasped the side of my face with one hand. He kissed my neck just under my chin and then moved down and around to my nape. With the other hand, he moved the collar of my dress to one side. His sweet lips ran along my collarbone. His kiss was soft at first, but gradually he applied more pressure, more force, though he was careful not to upset my injuries.

His sweet touch made my mind blur. *Oh, I like this. I want this…*

After a moment of sheer ecstasy, Kristofer lifted his head until his mouth was at my ear once again. *"You've always liked this. You've always wanted this from me,"* he murmured, skimming his tongue across my earlobe.

I couldn't breathe. I couldn't even *think.* That's when I noticed that I had butterflies fluttering in a place where butterflies weren't *supposed* to be. My core blazed with pristine passion, and I silently moaned. The feeling was primal, intense. It was a feeling that I had never experienced before, not in *that* lifetime, at least.

Oh, but it's so familiar….

Kristofer bewitched me. The web he spun around me was too much for me to refuse. It entwined me, heart and soul, taking my essence and making me forever his. I couldn't deny him anything—that, I knew. In a manner of days, I was at the mercy of the beautiful boy at my side.

Suddenly remembering Reverend Cole, I peeked at him. Thankfully, he was sitting at the table with his back turned to us, peacefully praying, entirely unaware of the bewitching mischief his son was making with me right behind him. I bit my lip, feeling naughty—deliciously naughty—and bashfully giggled.

Meanwhile, Kristofer's lips slid up and down the contours of my neck. *"I can't wait to marry you, Sita,"* he crooned, his sweet breath hitting my neck again, sending goose bumps skating across my overheated skin. *"And don't you worry about the distance between us. I'll always find you, and you'll always be mine."*

He raised his head and gazed into my eyes, trying to reassure me. Then, taking my hand, he pulled me to the fireplace hearth. We sat down, and I laid my head on his shoulder. *"I love you, Kristofer,"* I whispered to him.

He kissed the top of my head. *"I love you, too—Goddess."*

"Huh? Goddess?" I snorted, shaking my head. *"I'm not a goddess."*

"If not a goddess, then what?" he muttered, cocking his head.

I thought for a moment. *"I'm just a peculiar girl with strange tendencies; that's all."*

Kristofer shook his head. *"No. You're a goddess. You've lived thousands of years. You've lived across the globe. You have amazing powers."*

I frowned and sat up. *"We've lived for thousands of years with amazing powers in every corner of the globe, but now we're stuck here hiding in the woods. I don't feel much like a goddess."* My eyes dropped. *"Perhaps I am Atlas, with the weight of the world crashing down on my head!"*

Kristofer's face fell. *"You've always felt that way—responsible for the world. Or your world, at least. But you're not alone anymore, Sita. I'm here, and so is Ali."*

"I'm still not a goddess, though."

"You think that only because you don't remember the power of your light, love."

"I wish I could remember like you do."

He took my face between his hands. *"You'll remember when it's time for you to remember, and when you do, nothing will stop me from loving you as I did then..."* His eyes dropped. *"Like I want to now."* He shook his head. *"We knew this was going to be hard before we came back again, but I promise you, my beautiful wife, the wait as well as the pain will be well worth it."*

"Wife?"

"I know you hate to hear this, Lees, but..." He chuckled. *"You'll see..."*

"See what?"

"Something that not even our Ali knows."

"Does Papa know?" I asked.

Kristofer gritted his teeth. *"Well, he might remember what I mean, if not for the fact that he's so weak!"* he hissed under his breath and shook his head. *"I thought it before, but now, I see his ineptitude in person!"*

"Weak? Inept? My papa is not inept!" I snapped, and a wave of fury swept down my spine.

Kristofer pushed his face closer to mine. *"Really? Well, it took my father and me to stop you from going after Marshal yesterday, and it also took my father and me to protect Ali and you from Marshal the other day! Where was Asa?"* he asked, gritting his teeth again. "Nowhere!" He threw his hands in the air.

"Papa protected us last night!" I snapped. I wanted to smack him!

But before I could say any more, my parents walked through the door. Papa's eyes darted to the hearth where Kristofer and I sat together. He threw a disconcerted look between us. In return, I flashed him an innocent smile, thankful that he hadn't come through the door a few minutes earlier.

Mama smiled sweetly. Then as she walked past, she grabbed my hand and tugged me to the closed bedroom door that was on the left. She opened the door, and I gasped! It was the single prettiest room that I had ever seen. A large ornately decorated wrought-iron bed sat in the middle of the room. Meadow green, burnished copper, and sunny golden leaves were woven into the tapestry of wrought-iron in the bed, moving all the way up each of the four posters. Then finishing the bed was a lacy canopy and a white eyelet coverlet.

I looked around to where an oak wardrobe stood on the right side next to a small white dressing table, complete with a mirror. The walls were a soft shade of butter, with multi-colored cerise and violet wildflowers painted on every surface. There was even a large picture window looking out toward the strawberry patch, and I could see the oak tree standing out back in the distance.

Oh, Pamela! I can see her through my window!

Around the window hung white lace curtains that matched the canopy and the coverlet of the bed, and next to the bed was a small nightstand made from the same wrought iron as the bed.

I couldn't speak. It was just too beautiful for words, so much more than a disobedient girl like me deserved.

A strong twinge of guilt hit my stomach as I thought about my disobedience. I also thought about what Molly said to me, about how Papa was going to punish me for what I did. Suddenly, I was ill at ease.

Mama smiled and stretched her arms around my shoulders from behind. *"Do you like it?"* she whispered into my ear.

"I love it!" I beamed and then turned around and hugged her. *"Who painted the flowers?"* I asked, attempting to push the thoughts of Papa's *punishment* out of my mind.

She laughed, a bright bursting laugh, and she smiled. *"Your papa did, Lees, and he painted them just for you. This is where he went while you and I were having tea at Molly's house the other day."*

My eyes swept the room. *"I didn't know he could paint like this, did you?"* I asked, feeling remorseful for my actions again and also quite perturbed with Kristofer.

She patted my hand. *"Your papa has many talents, baby. He is quite the artist. I'll show you what else he painted later."*

I stepped past my mother and closed the door behind me while thoughts of my father's punishment trampled my nerves.

She threw me a confused look. *"What is it, baby?"*

I took her hand and led her to my new bed. We both sat down. *"What?"* She asked.

I drew a rattled breath, trying not to cry. *"Papa is going to punish me for disobeying him yesterday."* My eyes dropped down to my lap. *"Do you know what he's planning to do? He told me that he was going to turn me over and beat me black and blue when we got…here."* As I spoke, my eyes focused on the eyelet pattern of the bed coverlet. I wanted them to focus on anything, anything *except* for Mama's eyes.

"You terrified him!" Her answering voice was stern, not at all what I had hoped to hear. *"You terrified us both!"* She reached out and grasped my chin, pulled it up, and forced me to look at her. Her intense emerald eyes blazed. *"We need to know that you won't do anything to put yourself in danger again!"* Her mighty gaze bored straight into mine.

Tears welled in both our eyes. I wanted to look away from her, but the hold she had on me was too strong. I couldn't move my sight away from hers. I couldn't even speak. I had hoped that she was going to tell me that Papa was just putting me on, like always before.

But it's different this time. This time, I defied him. My knees shook with fright.

"Reverend Cole and Kristofer are still here," I mumbled to her, finally finding my voice amidst her powerful hold. *"If Papa is going to punish me, I hope he'll wait for them to leave, for…the boy…to leave."*

She pushed up from the bed, breaking the visual hold she had on me, and then crouched down in front of me. She looked into my eyes. This time, though, she didn't force my gaze; her eyes were soft, cajoling. *"He's not going to do anything to you, Lees. You should know that by now. How many times has he threatened you?"* She laughed and shook her head. *"My goodness, how many times have I?"*

"Loads."

"And how many times have either of us actually done anything to you?"

"None. But I think this time was different. You didn't see how angry he was when I ran away from him. I think…" I took a shuddered breath and winced. *"I think I've finally crossed a line with him."* I laid my head forward onto her shoulder and cried.

"It'll be all right, my baby," she cooed and stroked the back of my head. *"You're sorry for what you did. You just need to let him know that. That is all he wants, just reassurance. Tell him how sorry you are."*

I nodded and hyperventilated at the same time.

All of a sudden, the door swung open, startling us both. Mama jumped up just as Papa looked into the room. *"We were wondering where you two went."*

"The two of us were having a little talk about yesterday." She threw him a knowing look and then reached out and took his hand.

Papa looked straight at me. *"Come here,"* he said, holding out his other hand.

My heart fluttered, and my feet felt like they weighed a ton. Slowly, I shuffled forward, the obedient daughter once again, my legs hardly moving though steadily inching toward him. *Please, not in front of the boy. Please, not now.* I took his outstretched hand while my mind raced and my eyes brimmed with tears.

"How do you like your new room, angel?" he inquired. His brilliant, light-blue eyes danced in the sunlight, and he donned the same crooked smile he had as a boy.

Oh, wow, my beautiful, gentle Papa!

My heart leaped, and I giggled through my hands. *"I just love it, Papa!"* I threw myself into his arms, giggling and clinging to his neck like a small child—which, obviously, due to my new bosom as well as my deep love for Kristofer, I wasn't!

"Thank you for painting it for me! Mama says you've painted other things, too." I smiled, peering up into his beautiful blue eyes, all the while continuing to chatter. *"I sure would like to see some of it!"*

Papa slyly chuckled and then peeked over my shoulder toward my mother, who blushed and looked away. His sly smile melted into a worried frown as he peered down at me. He put his hand flat against my cheek. *"Molly sent along some things for you,"* he muttered, taking a long sorrowful breath. *"I hung them in the wardrobe."*

He seems to have forgiven me. I was relieved but bewildered by his sullen expression.

His eyes dropped as he stroked my face. *"Jake and Kris have to go all the way into the city before sunset, so they'll have to be on their way."* He nodded toward them. *"You'll have to say goodbye now."*

Oh, that's why…

Just then, I thought about the many times he was forced to say goodbye to my mother during the fifteen years she lived without him by her side. It was slightly comforting to know that my parents actually *did* understand how hard it is to see the one you love *leave* you.

The bottom fell out of my world. I moved to where Kristofer and Mr. Cole stood in the front room; both were staring at me. *"Thank you, Mr. Cole. Please thank Molly for me, too."* Tears choked my voice.

I glanced at Kristofer, and my heart stung. I couldn't stand to look at him, but I couldn't stand to say goodbye even more. I pushed down the anger I felt for him earlier and turned to him. His hazel eyes were full of tears, and his beautiful soul was bursting with the colors of me. I put my lips to his ear, yearning to kiss him, aching to blend. *"Hello, boy, my Kristofer,"* I whispered, instead of goodbye.

He grinned, showing all of his perfectly straight teeth, his tear-filled eyes alight with love. I didn't think it was possible for him to be any more beautiful, but at that moment, that glorious moment, his beauty nearly stopped my heart, and it *did* stop my breath.

I closed my eyes and let the image of his beautiful face etch its way into my memory.

"Hello, Sita, my wife," he whispered, blushing on his ears. *"I'll see you soon."*

Then he leaned in. The sensation of his breath washed the pangs of pain away. *"The next time I see you, I'm going to kiss you for real,"* he purred into my ear, so my papa couldn't hear. He took my hand, kissed it, and closed his eyes. *"It'll be all right. We won't be apart for long."*

I nodded and tried not to cry.

"Just try to remember," he mouthed as he turned and walked away from me.

I followed him out the front door to where his father's buggy sat in the yard. I didn't know how long it would be until I saw him again, and I didn't know what I was going to do without him. *Five years is much too long.* Then I watched the buggy pull away—the buggy with my Kristofer inside.

Mama stepped up behind me. She placed her small hands on my shoulders and kissed the back of my head. *"Seventeen, Lees, that was the deal,"* she whispered.

"Romeo and Juliet were only thirteen," I petulantly muttered, crossing my arms over my new bosoms.

Mama laughed her beautiful, bursting laugh, and she sighed. *"Romeo and Juliet were two spoiled little children who defied their parents and then died!"*

I peeked over my shoulder at her.

"Remember that!" She curtly nodded, and her brilliant eyes flared with righteous parental indignation.

Mama and I watched as the buggy holding my boy got smaller and smaller in the distance.

"I knew I shouldn't have let you read that book!" she scolded herself from behind me.

"You didn't let me," I answered and grinned over my shoulder at her.

She threw her head back, laughed for a moment, and then laid her forehead against the back of my head. She shook it back and forth. *"Lord, help me!"* she exclaimed.

Just then, Papa stood next to us. He bent down to Mama, smoothed her hair, and put a few strands behind her ear. *"Go inside,"* he whispered.

She smiled, took his hand, and started to walk away, but he let go. *"What?"* she asked.

He glanced from me to her and then back before letting his eyes peer intensely into *just* hers.

I didn't know what to make of it…*yet.*

"Our daughter and I have something to take care of now. Please go inside and wait for us. We won't be long," he nervously muttered, sounding both determined and a bit frightened at once. His voice shook.

My sights bolted to Mama, whose eyes flew open wide, as if trying to comprehend what he meant. I knew in an instant. My knees began to quake.

"No, Asa!" she stammered and took his shaking hands. *"You said you weren't angry anymore."*

My father bent down and gazed into my mother's pained eyes. *"I'm not angry anymore, sweetheart,"* he whispered to her. And I could plainly see that it was true. He wasn't angry, his eyes were soft—soft and sorrowful yet resolved. *"But, I must do this. We had an agreement. Our daughter decided not to obey me."* He wiped a few scattered tears from Mama's eyes as well as his own. *"If I don't punish her this time, then what's to stop her from disobeying us again? And perhaps, next time the outcome may be far worse."*

My father turned to me. *"Go,"* he commanded, pointing to a large fir tree just outside the yard. *"There are some small branches on the ground by that tree. Get one and wait for me there."* His voice was strong and determined although he averted his eyes while he spoke to me.

He walked past my mother, clasped her hand, and pulled her into the house with him.

I stood in place for a moment, numbly thinking. *I finally did it,* I thought to myself, blinking rapidly, desperately wishing that it was all just a bad dream. *I knew I had pushed him too far this time, and I was right...* The whole of my being shook with fright. *I thought this might happen someday although I always felt that Mama would be the one to finally give me a lickin'. But I was wrong. It's gonna be Papa!* I was shaken to the core by that thought.

As I walked toward the tree to find a switch, I heard Mama in my head, and to my surprise, I could also hear Papa's voice from inside her mind, as well. *"You are not doing this, Asa!"* she tearfully hollered.

"We had an agreement, Ali. She was the one who decided! You know what they say. Spare the rod..."

"Leesie is not a spoiled child! She's probably the least spoiled child I've ever met, besides myself!" Mama cried. *"She was protecting me! That's the only reason she disobeyed you! Please, Asa, she's lost so much already. Do you also want her to fear you?"*

Oh, Mama—my savior! My heart leaped. *Maybe it won't happen after all…* I listened closer.

"It matters not why she disobeyed me, sweetheart. The matter is that she did disobey. She nearly got herself killed yesterday, three times!" Papa paused. His breath was heavy. *"If I hadn't come when I did, Marshal would have hurt her. He would have killed her. Damn it, Ali, I had to injure her myself to get her to stop! And even then, she still disobeyed me!"* His voice cracked. *"If this is what I have to do to keep her in line—to keep her alive—then so be it."*

My mother said nothing.

Oh no, that's not good. My heart was in my throat!

"That girl needs a good amount of fear put into her," my father whispered. His voice was soft and hoarse from yelling and crying.

"So you're going to put the fear of God into her?" Mama tearfully retorted.

"No, Ali, I'm not. I am going to put the fear of ME into her."

"She'll be afraid of you."

Papa didn't answer for a few moments. I heard the door open. They stepped out onto the porch. Then he turned to her and put his hand to her worried face. *"I'd rather she lived in fear than not at all."* My father's words were final, decisive, and irrevocable. His head hung down for a moment; he was crying. After a moment, he lifted his head. He sighed and stroked Mama's tear-stained face. *"Please, go back inside, so I may do what needs to be done."*

She shook her head. *"If you're going to do this, then you're going to do it in front of me!"* She shut the door behind her using only her mind and determinedly crossed her arms.

"Please don't try to stop me," he whispered.

She shook her head. *"I won't. You are Leesie's father. You have the right to discipline her in whatever way you deem fit. You're right, the two of you had an agreement. She disobeyed you. So you must…whip her,"* she whispered. The last two words came in an emotional sob. It seemed as if the words she spoke stung as they escaped her lips. She shivered, and large tears fell from her eyes.

Papa nodded once, turned away from her, and headed out into the yard—toward me.

Oh, no! Oh, no! Oh, no! Here goes…

I wanted to run, but the small branch that I held in my hand was the only thing that I could actually *feel*. The rest of my body seemed to be numb. I couldn't move.

My terrified sights were set on the face of my father as he strode closer. I looked into his steel-blue eyes as he approached. He seemed as terrified of what he was about to do as I was.

His hands shook as he stepped up to me. He took the switch from my hand with no preamble whatsoever. Then he grabbed me around the middle, propped his leg against the tree, bent me over his knee, and pulled up the back of my dress until the hem laid over my shoulders.

Please leave my bloomers up. Please leave my bloomers up. I frantically squeezed my thighs together. I screwed my eyes shut, preparing for the inevitable. Frightened tears ran the length of my face. I held my breath. Never in my life had he whipped me, so I was entirely unprepared for the pain that was about to come.

The air around us whistled as the switch rushed backward in my father's clenched fist, preparing to fulfill our agreement. I flinched, and my body went rigid as I imagined the sting of the wood against my backside. I squeezed my eyes tighter, whimpering softly; my legs stiffened. I couldn't breathe. *Molly was right, I shouldn't have stepped outta line.* My body trembled and shook. My untouched bottom didn't know what to expect.

But then a final desperate idea came to mind. *Cry! Molly told me to cry. She said that sometimes works!* Without a beat, I sobbed—loud. "*I'm sorry, Papa!*" I bawled, as if screeching for my life. It was almost pathetic. *"Please! I'm sorry! I love you!"* I wailed, feigning remorse, attempting to pull on his already fraying heartstrings.

There was a pause. Then his body fell limp as he let me out of his grasp. He threw the switch to one side and then fell against the tree with his hands over his face. After a moment, he sat down, all the while shaking and crying. *"I can't do it,"* he whispered to himself. *"I just can't!"*

IT WORKED! I CAN'T BELIEVE IT ACTUALLY WORKED!

Papa looked up at me, grabbed my hands, and pulled me into his lap. At the same time, Mama ran to us. She threw her arms around my father at the same time that I did.

"I don't know what to do with you! You frighten the hell outta me! What am I to do with you?" Papa sobbed, holding me against his chest as if I were about to disappear. *"I can't lose you. I can't lose you! What am I going to do?"*

I hugged him tighter. *"And I can't lose Mama. I just found her. Please understand!"* I sobbed into his neck.

Mama had his face in her hands, and she was kissing him all over his cheeks, comforting him.

"You nearly got yourself killed yesterday! Do you understand that?" He bared his teeth and pushed his face against mine; his weary eyes flashed with a mixture of worry and the panic that I had inflicted upon him.

I nodded, eyeing the switch lying only inches from where we sat.

"Why in the name of God did you attack him after I was already there?" he demanded.

I peeked at my mother. I didn't want to say it.

She nodded, reassuring to me tell him.

"He called Mama a bad name," I muttered.

"A name? What name?"

"I don't want to tell you." I bit my lip and glanced the other way.

"Please, baby." My father took my face into his hands, commanding my sights back to his. *"Help me to understand why you behaved like you did yesterday."*

I took a rattled breath, my scattered wits sent racing. *"He called Mama…a lady of the evening,"* I whispered, using his words from one of the visions and trying not to look at either of my parents.

Papa stood up and then pulled Mama and me off the ground. He took one each of our hands and led us back to the cabin. When we reached the house, he opened the door and took us both inside. He sat down at the table and gestured for us to join him.

I sat across from him, staring at the wood grain of the table. All the while he looked at me, his eyebrows pulled together, considering me for a few minutes. *"Angel,"* he said, staring me in the eyes as I tentatively looked up. *"I know a thing or two about that…"* He sighed. *"About Charles Marshal's personality. He is a vulgar monster who knows no respect and who would never say such a thing to you. Well, not in that manner, at least."* He placed his hand over mine. *"Tell me, please, what horrid name did that man call your mama that you are afraid to say?"*

My ears burned with anger. I shook my head and stared down at the table again.

Reaching over, he pulled my chin up, so he could see into my eyes. *"What did he really call her?"*

"That's not what Charles called me? That was what you showed me in the buggy. What then?" Mama asked.

I shook my head. *No, I won't! I won't let his words hurt her!*

My mother gazed at me. Guilt and sadness ran through her eyes. She felt responsible. *"Please say it."* Her voice came in a soft murmur, beseeching me. *"Charles has been calling me ghastly names, Lees, for many years. So please, baby, please tell us. It can't harm me. Not anymore."*

I looked away as I spoke the dreadful words of a monster. *"He called you…a…ten-cent… whore. He claims that he owns you. He said that he paid for you."*

Papa flinched, and a sudden sense of rage flashed in his eyes. He balled up his fist, and it seemed as if he were about to pound the table, but at the last second, he pulled his anger back. Then he took a slow, gasping breath. He turned his eyes toward mine, taking both Mama and me by our hands, his shaking with fury. He remained composed for us. *"Do you know what that means?"* he asked me. He was forcing himself to remain calm.

"Yes!" I hollered. *"I do know what it means! That's why I wished to destroy him! And I'm not sorry for what I did yesterday! None of it! I blew him straight into a tree with my powers! I'm strong, and I don't care what you say or what Mama says. You can whip me if you want to! You both can! But I wouldn't change anything I did yesterday! Not anything!"* I threw my head onto the table, dramatically sobbing.

Papa stroked my hair and laid his head against the back of mine. *"It's not so, Lees."* His voice was soft. *"It's not the truth. What he told you about your mama. It's not true, angel."*

I nodded and peeked up into his pained face.

At the same time, my mother pushed up from her seat and walked a few paces away.

Oh, but why?

She stared out the window for a few minutes. Her breath was harsh, and she was wringing her hands. She was worried. Finally, she turned back around and stared my father in the eyes. She breathed in deeply. *"Are you sure, Asa?"* she whispered.

Papa peered at her for a moment, nonplussed. His face drew palled. *"Come again?"* he breathed, and then… *"What?"* he asked her.

She threw him a piercing look and then repeated the question. *"Are you sure? The things Charles told Leesie about me. Are you certain they're not the truth?"* Her sights withered and then dropped down to the ground. She seemed shamed. *"In twenty-eight years, you have never once asked me."*

Papa shook his head while clear disbelief raged in his eyes. Obviously, he had no desire to discuss what she was attempting to bring to light. *"I didn't care!"* He stood up, still shaking his head, his eyes beseeching. *"Hell, Ali, I DON'T care! That's why I've never questioned you about it!"* He stepped forward and attempted to take her hand.

"Or…" Mama hissed and pulled away from him. *"You were afraid to broach the subject because you knew I'd tell you the truth. Or perhaps because you thought you already knew the answer."*

Angry tears flowed down her face.

Papa glanced at me, his mouth gaping with obvious shock.

"I already know," I angelically whispered and batted my eyes at him.

He seemed puzzled by my response. *"How do you already know? Did you have a vision?"*

I shook my head and took Mama's hand as she stood beside me. *"No, Papa,"* I answered, feeling a bit exasperated with him. *"I asked her!"*

"You asked your mother about that?" He was shocked.

I nodded. *"Mama told me that I could ask her anything—anything at all—and she would always tell me the truth. So, I did. I asked her."* I glanced into my mother's wary eyes and smiled, attempting to reassure her. *"How else would I know?"* I frowned at my father. *"You don't know. Why don't you know? If anyone should know the truth about this, it should be you."*

"Well," he muttered. He took Mama's hands and pulled her into his lap as he sat down. *"I'd like to know."* He gazed into her hurt eyes. *"Will you please tell me?"* He stared into them for a moment. *"Were you what he said you were? There were rumors at the time about the orphanage headmistress—Miss Kenly. Rumors about her selling a girl, namely, you…"* He paused and took in a lungful of air. *"This*

is probably why she was replaced eventually. Were you that girl, Ali? Were you a lady of the evening?"

Mama's apprehensive gaze held, the hurt in her eyes still present. *"And what if I said yes, Asa? What then? How will you look upon me then?*

Papa's beautiful, clear blue eyes shined into hers, and the torturous expression melted. Only love, only adoration shone through. *"I've never questioned you about this, Ali, because if it happened to be the truth, then what could I do about it? Could I change the past? Could I make it untrue?"* He shook his head. *"No. I could not. Do I feel it's possible that you were in such desperation at the time that you could have done such a harmful thing to yourself?"* He glanced down for a moment before answering. *"Yes, I've always felt that it was, indeed, a possibility. But I didn't ask because I didn't care to know. And I didn't want to cause you any more pain than you'd already endured at the hands of that monster, not to mention at the hands of my own father!"*

He paused and took a deep breath before attempting to go on. *"And I didn't want to embarrass you. I knew how shamed you were by what Marshal did to you. Besides, after that night, you showed no interest in matters of the flesh. So had it been a behavior of yours before, became a moot point, for it surely wasn't to be after. Your spirit seemed to be broken, as was your body. I didn't wish to add insult to your injuries, by doing what? Chastising you? I think NOT!"*

A weak smile loomed. *"I mean, my God, Ali, it was fifteen years before you could bring yourself to the point where you could be with me again."*

He grabbed Mama's chin and pulled it up, persuading her gaze. Then he smiled and placed his lips against her ear. *"I love you so much, Alice Raign. You are in all honesty everything to me."*

He pulled back and stared into her eyes. *"You once told me that you didn't know how to love me, but that is exactly what you've done for me every single day, even when we were apart. You still loved me. I've never questioned that."*

He kissed her lips. *"You told me that you didn't know how to be a wife, but you are my wife, my beautiful wife. You said you didn't know how to be a mother, but just look at this incredible girl!"* They both glanced at me. *"She is who she is today because of you!"*

He hugged her to his chest. *"Through all of your difficulties, through all of the pain, you've not only recovered, my love, but you've flourished! You, baby, have the kind of strength within you that most can merely imagine. You simply outshine every other woman whom I've ever come across in my life, not only with your beauty but with your ability to love, with your immense kindness, your compassion, and your vast humility."* He kissed her lips again. *"Not to mention that you are the most elegantly poised, incredibly refined, graceful creature that I have ever laid eyes on."*

Papa turned to me and winked. *"Excluding our equally incredible daughter, that is."* Then he sat her up and pressed his nose against hers. *"And I, for one, am not simply proud of the strong woman who you've become, but I am in awe of you!"*

He pressed his lips to her forehead as she cried. *"So you see, baby, I don't care what the answer is. Truly, I don't. But if you'd like to tell me, then I would be more than happy to know."*

Mama sucked back a sob and smiled. Then she blushed crimson and wrung her hands. *"What I was, Asa,"* she stammered, *"was a virgin."* She bit her lip and looked away. *"And entirely too innocent for my own good."*

She blushed an even deeper shade of red. *"That was why it was so important to me that I talk to Leesie about becoming a woman. I didn't want her to have to find out the facts of life from…a boy."* She turned and smiled into Papa's shocked expression. *"The way I did."*

My father sat back in his chair, his arms crossed. *"Do you mean to tell me that day in the stable was…the first?"* He tilted his head and raised his brow.

She bashfully nodded.

His eyes sparkled. *"Me, too."*

My mother's answering laugh was electrifying. Her static energy raged around the room as her joy filled the air. Her elation was exhilarating. Papa and I both followed her lead and laughed with her.

Mama coyly smiled, attempting to catch her breath, and a pink flush rushed across the bridge of her nose. *"That afternoon in the stable, when you first told me that you loved me. When you asked me to marry you…"* She stroked Papa's face. *"I got so swept away by you, Asa. I never imagined things between us would get so out of hand, but I'm glad they did."* She blushed again.

Papa laughed. *"Well, that time hardly counted anyway!"*

"It counted for me, Asa! It was the only good memory I had for so long."

"It would've been better had Molly not barged in on us and ruined the whole thing!" He stroked her face. *"Why didn't you tell me you were a virgin?"*

She let out an embarrassed titter. *"Simple. I didn't realize I was one!"*

He threw her a confused look.

"I had no mother, Asa! I knew nothing!" She put her face closer to his, bashfully laughing. *"Nothing!"* she repeated, smiling and kissing his lips. *"Until a very handsome, very sweet stable boy showed me how to make love to him."*

Papa chuckled. *"Then why, may I ask, did that evil devil think he owned you?"*

"Because he sort of did. I mean, he did pay for me, so to speak."

Papa canted his head to the left and frowned.

My mother nodded at his expression. *"Like I said, I was entirely too innocent for my own good."* She mindlessly played with Papa's fingers. *"Charles came to the orphanage one day soon after I'd turned fifteen. He offered the headmistress, Miss Kenly, a great deal of money if she'd allow me to work for him as one of his servants."* She heaved a great sigh. *"Not realizing how mistaken I was about his offer, I agreed. When I arrived at his home, I was given a large room and expensive clothing, and I even had my own servants."* She drew in a deep, almost self-incriminated breath. *"I failed to differentiate between the man who represented himself to the headmistress as a gentleman and the abhorrent monster who dwelled within him—a mistake which would've cost me my life had I not been blessed with your love, not to mention Maggie, Jake, and Molly's love. That was something Charles hadn't counted on. He was under the impression that I was completely and utterly alone in the world."*

I stood up, putting my arms around my mother. *"Was that evil man mean to you the whole time?"* I asked, grimacing at the thought.

She kissed me sweetly and continued. *"Charles was kind to me at first, but soon after I'd arrived at his house, he became possessive and disturbingly interested in my talents, most of which I was entirely unaware of at the time."*

She squeezed my hand as I took my seat across from them.

I frowned. *"You were unaware?"*

"It wasn't until I was expecting you, Lees, that I realized most of what I can do. I've always felt that you actually found a way to show me my talents before you were even born."

We smiled at each other.

"Anyway," she said. *"Charles insisted on knowing all about my powers even though I tried to explain to him that I was uncomfortable with showing him anything and, besides that, I was limited. But he didn't believe me. He told me that he had prior knowledge of my powers, and if I wouldn't voluntarily share them with him, then he would take them from me."*

She shuddered. *"Meaning, he got a notion in his mind that I could transfer my powers to him through…"* Her eyes swept between my father and me. *"Physical contact. So I ran from him! At the time, I had no idea what he meant by physical contact."* She took Papa's hand. *"Well, not until you, that is.*

The night we met, Asa, I tried to get away from him. I ran as far as your parents' house before he saw me, which was why I ducked into the stable."

I gasped and smiled just as a sudden memory surged through my mind. *You ducked into the stable, Mama, because I was right behind you telling you where to hide. I knew Young Asa was waiting for you there...* I looked into her eyes, but she didn't hear my thought. Her attention was trained on Papa.

"I wish you'd told me the story that night—the night we met. I would have stopped Marshal then," he replied.

"Charles had a lot of friends in the city, Asa. He still does. I couldn't be sure who I could trust at first." Mama shook her head. *"I even told Miss Kenly, the headmistress, but she told me that Charles was a rich man, and if I had to endure a few bumps and bruises to be taken care of, then so be it. I explained to her that he'd beaten me unconscious quite a few times, but her advice to me was to give him exactly what he wanted and not to make him angry."*

Mama paused for a moment and closed her eyes. I could see how difficult it was for her to talk openly about that time in her life, even after so many years. She took a ragged breath. *"After you and I began courting, Asa, I did get away from him for a while."* She gazed into his eyes, and hers welled with tears. *"You know the rest,"* she whispered, clearly not wanting to discuss the attack. *"Once I met you, my love, there was no going back...not ever. Even if it did take us a long time to get to this point, it was all worth it."* She threw her arms around Papa's neck. After a few moments, she pulled back. *"I do feel guilty about lying to your mother. I told Maggie that nothing happened between us."*

Papa laughed. *"My mother didn't need to know about that. Besides, sweetheart, you and I are married, and we have a child now. None of that matters anymore."* He wrapped himself around her, holding her tight.

After a moment, Mama sat up. She looked into his eyes and nodded. *"Yes, our child,"* she anxiously, almost distractedly, murmured. Then she turned to me. *"Lees…"* She spoke softly, and as a sense of concern showed in her brilliant eyes. *"What did you mean when you said that you wouldn't change anything you did yesterday? I was under the impression when we spoke of this earlier that you were sorry for disobeying your papa."* She leaned in closer. *"You do realize that disobeying your father was wrong, don't you? If either of us tells you to be still, then you must!"*

I didn't answer her with spoken words. Instead, I sent my response into her mind as an equal or perhaps as a superior. *I will not be still!* My words were demanding and unyielding. *I am stronger than you are! Therefore, I will do whatever I deem necessary to protect you. Even if it means risking my own life!*

I glared at her, my eyes narrowed. *"And, you can't stop me!"* The last words I muttered aloud and my eyes flashed. They blared straight into hers. I didn't even blink.

My mother nodded and then sat in silent contemplation for a few moments.

She blankly stared at me, but finally, she stood. *"All right, then. I guess this is up to me."* She turned to Papa and patted him on the hand.

Having not heard our silent conversation, he seemed confused. *"What?"* he asked.

My mother bent down and looked him squarely in the eyes. *"This is between Leesie and me, Asa, but I will need your assistance if you don't mind."*

She turned to face me, and her eyes glowed with an intensity that I had never witnessed from her before.

I sat indignantly—ignorantly—glaring at her. As I looked at her, a virtually invisible veil lifted from over and around her, almost as if she were removing a cloak, but instead of cloth, it was made entirely of golden static. She took a deep breath and inhaled with so much force that the breath seemed to absorb every bit of energy in the room. The atmosphere around us drew cold and shadowy, almost as if her power had caused the sunlight around us to grow dim. Everything seemed unclear and indistinct. Then the temperature in the room plummeted, becoming cold enough that I could see my breath.

I gaped at the spectacle, foolishly unaware of the grief that my snarky words were about to cause me.

Mama peered at me, and I gawked back at her in amazement. My mouth hung open.

Her beautiful sphinxlike eyes sparkled, flashed, and glistened with the sheer force behind them, making the striking beauty her eyes usually held seem opaque and murky in comparison. Not even in my visions of her had they seem so mesmerizing. The sight was almost incomprehensibly beautiful yet entirely frightening at the same time.

My mind reeled with questions, but naively, I hadn't yet thought of running.

Then a sudden howling wind blew through the room causing the fire in the fireplace to burst forth and go out for a moment before reigniting into a fiercely golden blaze. The cyclonic wind swirled around me. It blew my hair all over the place, causing it to match the fire emblazoned a few feet away. As much as my hair blew, Mama was untouched by the fierce wind. She stood motionless, her chest heaving.

"Mama?" I barely breathed. She didn't answer.

Without a word, she stepped toward me, and as she moved, the windows and the furniture in the room shook, threatening to burst with the sheer strength of her *will* alone.

Uh oh…

Her impenetrable eyes flared, and the mighty emerald pools reached out, grabbing hold of my brain and unwittingly twisting it as I involuntarily gawked at her.

Her flawless face was mere inches from mine. My mind swam, and my body trembled with fear as my mother laid herself bare for the first time in my life. Her previously hidden might was stretched out before me, the reality of her power irrevocably unveiled.

I began to panic.

"The thing is, child!" she whispered, her tone calm—terrifyingly calm. *"You never questioned my strength before because I demanded your respect."* Her hands shook, and a glowing fog comprised of pure energy flowed in all directions around her body. *"And because you gave it, I've never had to show myself as I really am. I've never had to wield my strength over you…before."* She shook her head. *"You gave me respect, perhaps even a little fear, but lately, things have changed. And, if there's one thing that I must demand of you besides obedience it is respect. Respect for myself as well as for your father."*

She turned to Papa. *"Our daughter thinks that I'm weak, Asa. I can't have that."* With those words her head dropped, and a look of deep sadness bloomed in her mighty eyes.

"So, I must show her," she whispered.

Quickly composing herself, she turned to face me again. *"You will obey us. YOU—WILL—OBEY—ME!"* Her voice was harsh, unlike anything that I had ever heard from her before. It echoed throughout the room, reverberating and booming off the walls.

She took a deep breath and pulled her massive power back a bit, which sent the static cloud floating around her body unsteadily soaring. *"So for things to be right again, I must put the fear of ME back into you. But before that can happen, I must first demonstrate to you your flawed perception of my might!"*

My mother took a graceful step back, and with a vast amount of composure and decorum, she raised just one hand. Immediately, the door to the cabin flew open. Then she lowered her hand, wove her elegant fingers together, and folded them in front of her.

I peered, dumfounded, between the open door and my mother. *Run!*

"Go ahead," she whispered, airily gesturing toward the door with one hand. *"Run past me, please…try."*

My eyes shot to the open door as I prepared to bolt, but before I could even twitch a muscle, my feet bonded to the floor, causing me to wobble and fall forward. Papa caught me around the waist just before I hit the ground. He grabbed hold of both of my arms and stood behind me, holding me in place.

Angry tears streamed down my cheeks as I glared at my mother. *"LET ME GO!"* I demanded.

"Strike at me, Leesie," she commanded, raising her arms above her head and turning her back to me. *"Go ahead. Throw me. Throw me like you did Charles."*

Before I could react, she turned. I only saw her eyes for a moment before something cold wrapped around my head. It squeezed, boring into my brain, causing me to shiver, and making every muscle in my body fall limp. The snake-like vise wound around my neck, coiled down to my torso, and then slid all the way down to where my feet stuck to the floor. Finally, the coldness slithered up and around my whole body, enveloping me entirely. It wasn't at all painful, and I was aware of my surroundings, but I couldn't move.

I couldn't even scream.

Her power had incapacitated me.

In one final frantic attempt to escape her, I tried to throw my explosive force out, to release myself from her hold, but her power was too overwhelming. My head flopped forward. I felt like a scarecrow hanging on a stake. I was completely and utterly at my mother's mercy.

Mama glided toward me and then with her index finger lifted my chin until I could see into her mesmerizing eyes. They were amazingly docile considering our present circumstances. But even as tranquil as the emerald green pools that stared at me were, the immeasurable power behind them still pulsed throughout my body.

My mother raised her hand and without looking away from me caught the switch my father had been about to use on me earlier into her hand without even glancing in its direction. She grasped it, her eyes determined yet worried, maybe even a bit frightened.

She bent in and kissed my forehead.

"Mama, please!" I weakly croaked, using every bit of strength I could amass and compelling a few tears from my eyes. *"Please, Mama, I'm sorry. I love you!"*

She held my face between her palms and bent in toward my ear. *"That doesn't work on me,"* she conspiratorially whispered.

Holy cow. Checkmate. I'm finished. A moment of realization set in, sending an icy chill throughout my limp body.

As a final point, my almighty mother stood upright, and her luminous eyes flashed into mine, forcing me to look at her. She was power personified though her voice was soft. *"I am doing this because I love you and because it's my job, as well as my privilege, as your mother to teach you, especially when you are wrong. Leesie, you were horribly wrong yesterday."*

With those words, she pulled herself up further, growing taller, commanding even, her shoulders squared, her might unyielding. *"I am taking back the power, and I will show you, let's call it, an example of my power. So maybe you'll think twice about disobeying your parents the next time. If ever there is a next time."*

Never, there'll never be a next time. I promise!

With that, and with her hands still on either side of my face, she kissed my lips and pushed her forehead against mine. *"I told you the other day that never again will I tell you an untrue thing, so you can be certain that what I'm about to say is correct."* A few more tears fell. *"I vow to you, Leesie, if you ever—and I don't care how old you are—if you ever do anything to put yourself in danger in any way again…"* Tears rolled down her face, and I could see the pain in her eyes. *"Then I will whip you again just like I am going to whip you now!"*

Looking up, she nodded toward my father. In response, he, too, nodded, propped his foot against a chair, and bent me over his knee.

Instantly, the atmosphere in the room stabilized, and the howling wind stopped as my mother pulled the massive power back into herself, returning it to the depths of her light. Simultaneously, the hold she had on me ceased.

I felt her walk behind me. She lifted up the hem of my dress and bent down to my ear. *"We'll leave the bloomers up. It's not my intention to humiliate you or to make you feel exposed in front of your papa."*

Tears ran down my face. They dropped to the floor as I lay over my father's knee, but they were silent tears. I knew crying wasn't going to save me from her. Nothing was going to save me from her. *This is going to happen!*

I braced myself for the inevitable punishment that I surely deserved, a fact I understood well at that moment.

I felt Papa flinch. His body tensed under me, and I knew it was coming.

I tried to brace myself, but it was too late. The sting of wood against my bottom seared through me.

I was right; I was unprepared for the lashing.

I writhed and flailed in agony as Papa held me tighter. My backside burned and stung where she hit me. Before I could catch my breath or even cry out in pain, the switch hit me again…that time harder. I heard myself gasp and wail and plead for it to stop, but it persisted. My mother gave me one more agonizing blow, one swat of the switch for each time I had endangered myself. The third blow was so strong that I saw stars before my eyes. I screamed and cried out. My rear pulsated.

When it was over, my father stood me on my feet. *"Baby?"* he whispered.

I turned to answer him but realized at once that he wasn't talking to me. He was talking to Mama, who was walking toward their room, stopping only to throw the switch into the fireplace. She had her hands cupped over her face, and she was sobbing.

The sight of my sweet mother in tears because of my disrespect caused me immeasurably more pain than the whipping had.

Papa turned to face me. *"You stay right there until I tell you otherwise!"* he snapped.

"Yesss, s-s-sir," I stammered and hyperventilated.

He ran after her. He put his arms around her shoulders and led her away from their bedroom and then out the cabin door. After a few seconds, he hurried back in, ran into their room, and then ran back out with clean clothes, soap, and a towel in his grasp. My father threw me a stern look as he passed and then pointed toward the chair that I was sitting in before. *"Sit!"* he barked.

Immediately, I obeyed and sat down in the chair even though my spanked bottom throbbed wildly from under me. I sat quietly for what seemed like hours, afraid to move. The idea that it was Mama who had punished me gave me a feeling of great pride for her, considering how uneasy she felt about showing her powers to anyone but especially to me. It also gave me a sense of shame. Not to mention how humbling the experience was for me. I couldn't believe that I had thought my powers were stronger than hers.

That, and I'd broken the golden rule of our household, a rule that I had spent my entire life knowing and, above all, respecting.

All my life I had understood just how powerful my mother was, yet in a mere few days, I had all but forgotten the one lesson that I'd learned as a very young child:

Don't—cross—the—witch!

I giggled to myself. *That's one lesson I'll never forget again!*

The movements of the chair as I laughed made my bottom ache a bit. *"Ow!"* I whispered to myself, still chuckling.

I got the feeling just then that things were as they were supposed to be. Still, I couldn't help but wonder what I would do if Mama were threatened by Charles Marshal again. I shook my head. *No. I don't care how much strength she has. I will stand in front of her. I will protect her and Papa, too, if it comes to that.*

At that moment, I was thankful she had her mind window closed to me, and so was my bottom.

I sat for a while longer. Finally, the door opened, and my mother came into the house. Her hair was wet, and she had on different clothes. She swept past me, smelling of fresh soap and lilacs, carrying a small pile of soiled clothes clutched in her arms. *Hmm.* I inhaled as she went into her room.

After a moment, she came back out with a towel and soap in her grasp. *"Here, my baby,"* she whispered, handing me the towel and setting the soap beside me on the tabletop. *"There's a creek down there."* She pointed out the window. *"Just past the tree line. Go clean up."* She sighed and ran the back of her hand down the length of my tear-stained face. *"After that, I'd like for us to have a talk, all right?"*

Before I could answer, she grabbed me and threw her arms around my shoulders. *"I'm not sorry,"* she determinedly choked and squeezed me tight.

"I am," I answered as she let go and looked into my sorrowful eyes.

Thoughts of her immense power surged through my mind. *"Why didn't you do that to the sheriff? Why didn't you just conquer him, put him down? Surely, he couldn't have overtaken you? He's mortal! Why?"* I asked.

Mama put her hands on either side of my face and peered into my eyes. That time, though, they were soft, the intensity used merely to explain, not to intimidate. *"There's one thing you must understand about Charles, Lees."* She sighed and took the seat beside me. *"He is not an unintelligent man. A coward, yes, but he is sly and cunning, and usually never alone."* She shuddered. *"This is why he wishes to destroy your papa. You see, baby, most men seem to possess one of two attributes, brain or brawn."* I frowned. *"Meaning that they are either lovers or fighters, smart or strong. Understand?"*

I nodded.

"Charles is smart, but that is all. He is a coward, which is why he prefers to victimize women and also why he opts never to be caught alone. He chooses a few men whose attributes don't include much thought. Then he manipulates their underfed minds until they perform whatever heinous tasks he commands of them." She patted my hand. *"You witnessed that for yourself yesterday."*

Again, I nodded.

"Your papa, on the other hand, is one of only a very few men, along with Jacob Cole, who just happened to be born…with both. He has a brilliantly talented mind, and he is also gentle, quite large, and exceedingly strong." Her eyes danced as she mentioned my father, and goosebumps erupted on her hands and arms as she spoke of him. *"Charles loathes him for his strengths. That, and he knows that I am deeply in love with your papa. He also knows that as long as your father has a beating heart, his very existence is in jeopardy. But of course, he isn't willing to risk his life to end your father's life. He'd prefer to have one of his men perform the task."*

A few tears ran down her worried face. *"Your papa was smart enough to recognize a trap when he saw one and to get us out of harm's way before tragedy struck."* She stared me in the eyes. *"Charles wasn't alone when he came to see us that first day at Molly's house, and he wasn't alone yesterday either, Lees. There were witnesses. He was* hoping to get me to strike at him in some way to prove to the others that I am a witch!"

She shook her head. *"I am strong. I could've probably incapacitated Charles but only him. I couldn't have protected us all. So instead, I chose to stand down. Do you understand now?"*

I vehemently shook my head. *"But I was there, too, Mama! Surely between the both of us and Papa…"*

She cut me off. *"It was too risky! And after we destroyed Charles and his men, what then, Lees? How many more would we have to kill?"* She grabbed my face between her hands. The intensity of her eyes made my head swim. *"It is not in our nature to harm! You and I came to this earth, with God's will, to protect and to heal, not to maim or to kill!"*

"So you think I was wrong to show the sheriff my powers?"

"I know you were." She shook her head and let go of my face. *"But we can't change what's done. Thank goodness, we escaped. Hopefully, with the Coles' help, the rest of the town will be convinced that the stories about us are merely mad tales told by an insane, power-hungry sheriff and his slightly obtuse and frequently drunken comrades."*

She bent over and kissed my forehead. *"You threw Charles into a tree and exploded a couple of flower pots. Thank goodness, nothing else was revealed. And we did gain quite a few supporters yesterday because of Jake's sermon, so we're not so very hard put. Now, are we?"* She smiled.

I made sure my mind window was shut to her before I thought about what she said. *Nothing else was revealed? I revealed a lot to that awful man. I revealed my past identity to him.*

With that, I reopened the window to my mother's mind and changed the direction of our conversation. *"Papa wasn't at all surprised to see what you're capable of, was he?"*

"*No, Lees, your papa knows just about everything there is to know about me. Well, almost anyway.*" An uncomfortable expression flitted through her eyes.

"*He didn't know about the control you had over the horses, though, did he?*" I snickered.

"*No, he didn't know about that.*" Her ears flushed.

"*How did you do that anyway?*"

"*I controlled them. The same way that I controlled you…mentally.*"

I frowned. "*Huh? But you didn't make them collapse like you did me. They just went where you told them to go.*"

"*Mind control, sweetie. That is in essence what my power is. It is mind control.*"

I frowned again as she went on. "*You are explosive while I am controlling, and because we are innately very similar to one another, at the core, anyway, controlling your mind is quite easy for me. Animals are easy as well.*" She laughed to herself. "*And men! They've always been easy for me to control!*"

Abruptly, she stopped laughing. She looked somber again; her eyes grew dark. "*Except Charles. His mind is like a steel vise. I can't control him, which is why I would have to debilitate him instead. And I couldn't do that and control whoever was with him while protecting you and your papa all at the same time. Truthfully, Lees, the task of undermining Charles would take all of my strength, which would put your papa and you in jeopardy.*"

She looked me straight in the eyes. "*Promise me that you'll never again try to challenge that man, please!*"

"*I promise,*" I muttered, reassuring her, though I crossed my fingers under the chair at the same time.

"*Do you control Papa?*" I asked, again changing the subject.

She shook her head just as he opened the door and walked into the cabin. His hair was wet, and he was wearing different clothes.

"Never!" she whispered and winked. Then she touched my hand, and as she did, something flashed before my eyes. It was something that I didn't understand at all. I saw my mother, but she was different—very different. She was in charge of something important to her. She was in charge, in control, of many men! I also knew that it was in part because of the strength she had exhibited with me that she was able to do whatever this was in the future. She, in fact, had changed her future. It was a positive change.

I smiled, my heart swelled with pride, and I touched my palm to her cheek.

"What?" she asked.

"You've been through so much in your life, but just look at you. Look at how strong you are!" Tears welled in her eyes. *"Papa's right, you are incredible! And I'm so grateful that he and Molly saved your life, so you could grow up to be my mama!"* I threw myself into her arms.

Papa stood behind her chair. He leaned over and kissed the top of her head. *"Your mother saved my life once, too, Lees, and Molly's. Although she's never told me how she saved Molly."* He eyed her. *"Maybe she will now?"*

Mama giggled and pushed one of the chairs out with her foot. He hurriedly sat in it.

My mother sighed as I sat back in my seat. *"Where to begin?"* she asked herself and took both Papa and me by our hands. *"Let's see. Molly and I were five years old, but we weren't friends at that time."* She sighed again at the memory. *"I had no friends. The other children either feared or tormented me. Anyway, one day we were in the woods on a campout, and I saw Molly wander off by herself. As I recall, she was chasing a rather remarkable-looking butterfly. Well, something told me to follow her, and I did."*

Papa and I leaned in.

"Poor Molly was so enthralled by the butterfly that she didn't notice the large grizzly bear standing in her path. By the time I mustered the courage to scream, it was upon her!" Mama closed her eyes, quaking at the memory. *"It all happened so fast, yet I can still see it in my mind. I screamed her name, but at the same time, I mentally commanded the bear to lie down and to leave her unharmed. I remember raising my tiny little hands up and staring it straight in its terrifying eyes."*

She winced at the memory. *"I thought the bear would rip Molly to shreds in front of me, but the bear obeyed. In fact, it lay at my feet and didn't move a muscle until I released it. And I didn't do that until we both were a safe distance away."* She smiled. *"Molly and I have been as close as sisters ever since. She even met Jake through your papa and me, Lees."*

I shook my head in amazement. *"Wow!"*

She leaned over, sweetly kissed my lips, and pushed the towel and soap toward me. *"Now go clean up while I start supper."*

Mama stood up and turned her back to Papa and me. At the same time, I stood, but my father stopped me. I looked at him. *"Did you see the vision?"* he asked. *"About your mama?"*

I nodded. *"Yes, what was that?"*

"I don't know, angel," he answered. *"I guess we'll just have to wait and see."*

Feeling giddy, I ran into my bedroom, grabbed a clean dress from the wardrobe, and then hurried out the door on my way down to the creek. Just as I headed out into the yard, I heard Mama's voice in my head. *"So, you're proud of me for punishing you?"*

I'm proud of you for having the strength to punish me. The actual lashing hurt a lot! I giggled as I ran. *I won't be able to sit properly for a week!*

"So you are going to behave from now on. Am I right?" she asked, laughing back at me.

Yes, ma'am, I answered, but in the very back of my mind, I thought otherwise.

"Alyce Margaret!" she yelled into my mind. *"Do I need to take a switch to you again? Because I will! Right now if I have to! And this time I'll make sure that your bloomers are down around your ankles!"*

No, sorry, old habit! I answered while at the same time pulling off my clothes and jumping into the cool water.

"All right, then," she said, pulling back her temper. *"Enjoy your bath. I'll leave you alone for a while."*

With that, the window to Mama's mind shut, and I dove down into the water.

I soaked in the creek for a good half-hour, washing all the grit and grime off my body from our ghastly ordeal. I couldn't believe how lovely the cool water felt on the many cuts and bruises covering my body. Even my spanked bottom stopped throbbing.

Hmm. Hopefully that'll never happen again.

I stood up and soaped my hair. Then I dove beneath the surface of the water again, reemerging after a few moments. The clean water stripped each strand clean from the dust and ash stuck on it. After that, I ran the soap over the rest of my body and dove under once again. I let the water wash over my skin, soothing and calming me. That was something I needed after the happenings of the past few days—a feeling of calm.

No wonder Papa wanted Mama to swim with him. I'd love it if Kristofer were here with me right now.

I stopped, and bit my lip, contemplating that enticing thought for a moment.

Hmm…

Just then my mind danced with pictures of Kristofer's nude body, and in response my bare body burned from within and flushed with delicious mischief.

The impish little witch in me purred as I envisioned Kristofer swimming with me. I pictured his bare skin against mine and realized with a fluttering heart that if he were with me, we *both* would be naked. I grinned and bit my lip again. That thought made me feel a bit exposed yet a bit *elated* at the same time.

I shook my head, attempting to let the images in my mind fall away, so they couldn't haunt me any more than need be.

All thoughts of Kristofer exorcised from my mind, I left the creek. I picked up the warm towel, ran it over my over-sensitized skin, and then dried my hair. After I had dressed, I grabbed my discarded clothes and my shoes and returned to my new home, feeling refreshed and contented.

I opened the door. Mama was at the stove stirring a pot with Papa standing right behind her, his arms encircling her waist, his head lying on her shoulder, both swaying as she hummed. The sight sent massive shivers up and down my spine. I stood for a moment, silently envisioning Kristofer and me in a similar manner.

Maybe this place won't be so bad.

I padded over to where my parents stood together holding one another. Mama put her arm around me.

All of a sudden, there was a loud knock at the door.

Papa whirled around with his gaze trained on the door, his eyes wide and fearful. He glanced at Mama and me and gestured for us to go into my bedroom.

She and I obeyed his command.

Papa stalked toward the door. "*Who is it?*" he demanded.

Mama's hands quaked, and I clearly heard a prayer arise within her mind.

"*It's Jake, Asa,*" the familiar voice answered.

I tossed the soiled clothes and my shoes on the bed and followed my mother out to the front room.

Papa opened the door with a vastly relieved sigh just as Mama and I both started breathing again.

"We were halfway to the city, my friend," Mr. Cole explained, *"and we came across someone who was looking for you all."* He leaned in toward Papa, grinning, and affectionately clapped him on the shoulder. *"It seems she had a rather disturbing dream about the orchard last night. In fact, she was on her way here to find you. You should've seen the relief in her eyes when I told her you were safely here."*

Mama and I walked to where Papa and Mr. Cole stood and peered out the door.

Then Papa opened the door the rest of the way…

Stepping out from an expensive-looking buggy was Papa's mother, my grandmother, Margaret Raign.

21. *The Other Mrs. Raign*

Just as my grandmother stepped out of her buggy, the first thing that I noticed was how much my papa resembled her. His lovely pale, steel-blue eyes were hers as was the shape of his face. I also noted that although her hair was graying, it still retained remnants of the sandy-blonde color that Papa shared with her. And it was quite wavy, too, just like his…and mine.

The second thing that I noticed about my grandmother was that she looked a lot older than when I saw her in Papa's visions. Even so, she was still a beautiful woman—striking even—and obviously very rich, almost regal in appearance. In fact, she seemed a tad overstated to me. From somewhere deep inside of me, though, I felt a strange twinge of familiarity for her as well.

As this haughty woman emerged from her buggy, her lovely face was etched with worry and even a surprising look of fright.

Grandmother dressed in what appeared to be a rather expensive—and quite showy—midnight blue velvet gown and a matching blue velvet hat with a large gaudy feather sticking out the top. I had to stifle a snicker. It looked to me as if a bird had landed on her head and then decided to either nest or die there.

I bit my lip to stop from laughing as my eyes ran up and down, taking her in. That's when I noticed the somewhat lavish diamond ring on her finger…a gift from my grandfather, no doubt.

Perhaps to make up for the fact that he's a horrid ogre of a man!

Just as that thought crossed my mind, a small, spindly, skeletal man emerged from around my grandmother's horses. He helped her as she stepped down onto the ground. The man held Grandmother's gloved hand in his as if it was fragile as glass, but he was the one who seemed frail. Still, he carefully guided her down onto the ground with absolute care. He had snow-white hair, was clean shaven, and wore a charcoal-gray suit. When the man turned to face us properly, I noticed his striking hazel eyes, also noting that he was the same man who took the apples from Papa during our visits to the city.

I turned to my mother. *"Who's that man with Grandmother?"*

"That's George Kendal, Leesie," she proudly, though quietly, replied. *"He's worked for your papa's—I mean, for our family since your papa was just a baby. He has worked for your grandmother for so many years that he's truly become part of the family."*

My grandmother stepped toward the cabin just as Papa ran toward her with his arms outstretched. *"Mama!"* he exclaimed, rushing toward her.

Grandmother's face erupted into a joyous beam when she laid eyes on her son. A sudden look of relief swept across and erased her previously harried expression. She threw her arms open wide. *"Asa! Baby!"* she cried just as he caught her up into a joyful embrace, her arms clutching him around the neck. She sobbed into his shoulder. *"You're all right!"* she laughed and cried at the same time. *"Thank goodness, you're safe. My baby! My sweet boy! Thank heavens!"* Finally, she let go and looked up into his eyes. *"Alice and Leesie?"* she asked, her expression harried again.

Papa nodded. *"They're fine, Mama. We're all just fine."* He set her back down onto her posh-looking black lace-up boots. *"The house and the orchard are gone, but we're safe. Thank the Lord,"* he said to her. He closed his eyes in veneration, his words like a prayer of gratitude.

Kristofer's pa spoke up. *"I told you everyone was fine, Mrs. Raign,"* he smirked, shook his head, and laughed in Papa's direction. *"She wouldn't believe me. Just had to see it for herself!"*

My grandmother put her palm flat to Papa's face.

Oh, just like Papa does, I thought to myself and smiled a bit.

There were tears in her eyes as she gazed up at him.

Just then I noticed that Papa towered over her almost as much as he did Mama and me though Grandmother was a few inches taller than my mother and me, more curvaceous, and quite busty.

I bit my lip and glanced down at my budding bosoms. *Hmm. Maybe they'll grow a bit more—like Grandmother's!* I inwardly grinned at that thought.

Grandmother's eyes welled with weary tears. *"I had the most horrid vision of you all being killed, Asa,"* she whispered, cupping her shaking hands over her face. She leaned against Papa's chest whimpering. *"I left straight away hoping to find you though I wasn't sure if I would—not alive, anyway!"*

Oh! Grandmother has visions just like Papa and me.

Papa held her in his arms, patting her back as she cried. Suddenly, she began to seem a little less overstated to me.

After a few minutes, she stepped back and wiped her eyes with a white lace handkerchief that Mr. George promptly handed to her. She turned and smiled. *"Thank you, George, dear,"* she sniffled.

Mr. George smiled and nodded. *"Not at all, Mags,"* he whispered and bowed toward her.

Grandmother's eyes passed over Papa until she spotted Mama and me standing in the doorway looking at her.

Without a moment's delay, my father took her by the hand and reached his other hand out in my direction.

Mama was right behind me, pushing me toward him. *"Come on, baby,"* she excitedly muttered. *"Meet your grandmother."*

"She looks…a bit frightening," I whispered and dug my bare toes into the ground.

"No, she's kind, Lees," Mama whispered back to me, all the while pushing me along until I was close enough for Papa to reach out and clasp my hand.

"*Mama…*" my father announced, beaming with pride. "*This is our Leesie.*"

Then he turned to me. "*Angel,*" he said, taking me by the shoulders and pushing me in front of him. "*This is your grandmother, Margaret.*"

I started to say something, but before I could get the words out, my grandmother threw her arms around me, nearly crushing my ribs with her enthusiasm, and held me to her chest.

Following her lead, I timidly put my arms around her, too. *Oh, all right, this is nice.* I breathed in deep. *Hmm. Her perfume smells familiar.*

I felt the love emanating from her heart to mine as she held me in her arms. After a few seconds, she let go. Then she stepped back, put her palm flat against my face, and stared at me with tears in her beautiful light-blue eyes. She smiled and my heart melted.

Now she doesn't seem quite as fear-provoking. Then I noticed her smile. It was also the same as Papa's and mine.

"'*Grandmother Margaret' is much too formal for us, dear,*" she tearfully murmured, dabbing her eyes with the handkerchief. "*Please, darling, call me Grandma Maggie or Peggy, whatever you like. Both are short for Margaret, so it doesn't matter to me. All right, sweet one?*" she asked, canting her head to one side.

I nodded. "*Yes, ma'am…um…Grandma Maggie,*" I murmured.

Grandma Maggie held me at arm's length. "*And just look at how beautiful you are,*" she gushed, beaming, and touched my face just like Papa did again.

After getting a good look at me, she let out a startling gasp. "*Asa!*" she screeched. "*Why is this child injured?*" Her face whipped around to where Papa stood beside us. She glared at my father. "*What happened to her?*"

Papa put his arms around my shoulders as I stared at my toes, chagrined once again.

Jeez! I hope she doesn't wanna whip me, too.

He meant to answer her, but before he could get a word out, Mama spoke first. *"She's an overprotective fool! Just like YOUR son!"* she declared from behind us. *"Leesie nearly got herself killed yesterday. Didn't you, Lees?"*

Grandma Maggie gasped and peered at me and then pulled my chin up with her index finger and thumb though my eyes remained downcast. *"Well, I certainly hope you've learned your lesson, miss!"* she stated rather sternly.

I sheepishly nodded. *"Yes, ma'am, I have,"* I whispered, all the while still studying the contour of my big toe and while realizing that the throbbing ache in my hindquarters had returned.

My mother stood right behind me. *"Has it?"* she spoke into my mind. *"Good!"* Then, rubbing my bottom with the palm of her hand, she bent in toward my ear. *"I certainly hope that you don't forget this feeling any time soon. Because, you know, since I've done it once, I won't hesitate to paddle you again should you give me cause,"* she warned.

I turned my head around and peeked into her mighty eyes. I knew that she meant it.

Grandma Maggie took my hands, and her eyes swept between Mama and me. *"You, child,"* she whispered to me, *"certainly are the image of your beautiful…"* But she stopped short and her eyes widened. Clearly, she didn't know what to say next.

"Her mother," Papa said, wrapping his arm around Mama's waist. He kissed the side of her head. *"Our Leesie is the image of her beautiful mother, Mama."*

Grandma Maggie let out a relieved gasp. *"So you've finally given up on that horrible farce, I see!"* She beamed, her bright light-blue eyes twinkling with joy. *"Well, thank goodness for that!"* she laughed. *"I can't tell you how much sleep I've missed because I was the one who fabricated that travesty of a lie in the first place."*

Shaking her head, she stretched her hands out toward my mother. Once their hands clasped, Grandma Maggie leaned in closer. *"Does this mean that you are being a true wife to my Asa? I hope? Are you giving my son what he needs as a man, dear?"* She winked.

Mama's eyes grew wide for a moment; she was caught off-guard. Obviously, she hadn't expected such a question from Papa's mother. After a moment more, she shyly smiled and nodded though she blushed a bit across her cheeks and the bridge of her nose. *"Yes, yes, I certainly am, Maggie,"* she stammered, averting her eyes.

Grandma threw her arms around my mother. *"Oh, how glorious to hear!"* she exclaimed, clapping her hands together, and then kissed Mama on both cheeks. *"And you are just as beautiful as ever, Alice!"*

I looked over at Papa, who was now hugging Mr. George. When they parted, Mr. George held out a hand toward Mama while peering kindly at me.

Mama took hold of his hand and kissed his cheek.

"It's so good to see your beautiful smile, my dear," Mr. George murmured to her, his eyes twinkling with obvious love. *"It's been far too long."* Then he glanced at her and me again. *"And won't you just behold what a lovely young lady our sweet little one has become!"* he said, gazing at me.

"Tell me, Master Asa," Mr. George asked, turning to Papa. *"How did you get so lucky to have angels such as these to share your life?"*

Papa beamed. *"I am the single most blessed man who ever lived, George. That is how."* Then he walked around Mr. George to Grandma's buggy and picked up their bags. *"Let's all go inside!"* he declared to everyone and then led them all into the cabin.

Everyone but Kristofer and me, that is.

Kristofer stood by his father's buggy, his eyes glued to mine.

Mama winked at us just before she closed the door and mouthed, *"Be good,"* pointing at me as she went into the cabin.

As soon as the door shut and without a moment's hesitation, Kristofer advanced on me. He took both my hands into his. I could hear his breath. It was heavy and unsteady—so was mine. I could also feel that his pulse was racing as he held my hands. He seemed worried, as if he thought I wouldn't understand what was in his heart, or on his mind, for that matter.

"I have to explain something to you, Lees," he said, frowning.
"Explain what?"

He took a deep breath. *"I've become dreadfully tired, sick and tired, actually,"* he barely whispered. *"I'm sick and tired of pretending, of making believe that I still fancy things such as marbles, playing chase with other children, or any other childish games."* He took another deep breath. *"On the surface, I may appear to be a twelve-year-old boy, but that is not who I am anymore. I have vivid memories of our marriage and our child. I remember being your husband and having our beautiful baby daughter with you,"* he whispered, stroking my cheek with the back of his hand.

Just then his eyes darted toward the cabin, and I knew he was thinking of my mother. *"I also remember dying with you, Sita. I am, on the inside, at least, the same man I was at the time of our unfortunate doom."*

He drew nearer, his eyes blazing with such intensity that I knew he could see straight into my soul. *"I love you, Sita, and I need to know that you feel the same way, even if your memories aren't quite as clearly defined as mine."*

My mind raced, and the butterflies I felt earlier returned with a vengeance. All the while, Kristofer gazed into my eyes, waiting for my reply. He looked so worried, so scared that I couldn't stand it. In an impulsive, unexpected moment of courage, I decided not to say it with words but rather with an unspoken act.

A clear image of my mother ran through my mind. It was the memory of her bold and forthright behavior with my father. Then, thinking of her again, summoning the bold part of her in me, and feeling quite daring, I stepped forward and pushed my body against his.

This was a movement that seemed to take him completely by surprise.

Kristofer eagerly smiled and snaked the invisible lasso that he controlled around my waist, answering my siren's call with his body. His hands followed the lasso. He pulled me in even closer. One hand held my neck at the nape while the other grasped my left hip and jerked me against him.

Before I could even think about what was happening, he pressed his lips to my ear. *"I am going to kiss you now,"* he whispered, his voice shaking with a mixture of both excitement and nervousness. *"I am going to kiss you just like I used to, my Sita."*

His sweet breath sent anxious goose pimples soaring through my body while at the same time the butterflies down below fluttered again. I pressed my thighs together. I wished for the aching feeling in my groin to both cease and intensify at the same time.

Kristofer pulled back, impaling me with his powerful gaze. *"This love was our past and is our future, but this moment in time that we are sharing right now is a gift to us, Sita. This is our chance...our fate.*

My beautiful boy leaned in and dragged his lips up the contours of my throat. His expert tongue swept over my racing pulse, skimmed over my jaw bone, then trailed up to my face. He rubbed his cheeks against mine and sighed. His light touch sent both the butterflies and my heart soaring.

"I don't feel twelve anymore, Kristofer," I breathlessly muttered, suppressing the urge to tear off his clothes.

"That's what I'm trying to tell you, love. You aren't—we aren't twelve. Neither of us is, not anymore. So let's not pass on what the fates have returned to us," he whispered. His hands ran down my back, and he twisted the hair that lay against my bottom between his fingers, causing me to shiver and my knees to quake.

He raised his head. His sparkling hazel eyes bored into mine, nearly crippling me with their intensity. My brain swam with desire. I could think of nothing except the wonderful, beautiful boy who had me captivated at the moment. I was a quivering mess, my heart so entwined with his that not even a coherent thought could pass through my mind.

He reached up, angling his slightly parted lips over mine—imploring me.

Silently answering, I tilted my head, mirroring him though I wasn't sure how to kiss him.

Sensing my confusion—and my innocence—he pulled back for a moment and grinned. *"I'll show you, love."* He tilted his head to the right. *"Part your lips and close your eyes…"*

My heart lurched. Part my lips? *Oh, yes! Oh, yes! Oh, yes!* The naughty little witch in me purred with delight and jumped up and down, her black kitty-tail swinging in the wind.

I eagerly obeyed, tilting my head and parting my lips. Then my eyes fluttered closed, and my heart raced.

Just as my eyes closed, I felt Kristofer's soft tongue for the first time. It flicked in and around my mouth, licking, taking in the entire surface of my lips—tasting me along the seam of my mouth.

Following his lead, I returned his movement in kind. My tongue explored his sweet lips. Then, traveling over his mouth, it studied every crevice for the state of bliss that I knew was about to come. Finally, feeling brazen again, I stuck my whole tongue into his mouth, stroking his tongue with my own.

The lasso tightened, and Kristofer groaned. He grabbed my face between his hands and pushed his hungry lips against and around mine, his tongue devouring me, delving deeper and deeper.

All of a sudden, my libido exploded, and my insides liquefied. I was prepared to do anything to keep feeling that way—anything for him.

As we continued to kiss, the lasso wrapped itself around us with such ferocity that I found it difficult to breathe. Idly, I wondered if it was possible to die in such a way, but I didn't care. Dying in his arms was fine with me since I never wished to let go of him anyway.

As I stood in the yard with my arms and my emotions wrapped up tightly within my Kristofer, an unexpected and frightening, albeit intriguing, thought came to mind.

With difficulty, I pulled away from him and gazed into his wondrous eyes.

I thought of my mother again and remembered what she told me about regrets. *I don't want to have regrets. I may not see him for a while after today…*

With my mind focused on what I needed to do, my voice shaking with both excitement and fear, I made the irrevocable decision that would change our relationship and our lives forever.

"Put your hand over my heart," I muttered while at the same time reaching over and placing my trembling hand over his throbbing heart.

With shaking hands, he complied though he hesitated for a moment. His hand hovered just over my left breast as if asking for permission.

A sudden wave of shyness swept over me, shyness that I swiftly quashed. I nodded, took his hand, and placed it over my thumping heart. The sensation of his warm hand on my chest took my breath away. It seemed natural and oh-so familiar.

Kristofer gulped hard and smiled just as I looked him in the eyes. *"Now, kiss me, but don't close your eyes,"* I commanded. *"I'm going to blend with you, all right, my love?"* I whispered to him.

His body shivered, and he nodded while pushing me down until we were both sitting on the ground and facing one another. Then, with our hands still in place, my boy leaned in and pushed his lips to mine. He gazed deeply, dominantly, into my eyes. The fingers of our free hands almost instinctively laced together.

For a moment, I thought I was going to be the one guiding our illicit tryst, but I was wrong. My Kristofer took immediate charge of me, and I obeyed. I submitted my mind as well as my soul to him—forever him, only him. No longer was I my father's possession. Body, mind, heart, and soul, I was his.

I am Kristofer's!

I melted into my boy, offering the whole of my being to him, and he in turn presented me with his sweet essence.

Kristofer's soul grabbed a firm hold of mine. It restrained it and pulled my essence into his. I let go of the power; I let go of the world, my very essence overtaken by my love.

In response, my mortal body fell against him. My limp body surrendered control while also accepting his relinquished spirit into me.

I noted how difficult it was to perform the task of blending while kissing and holding his gaze at the same time, but that thought was fleeting because in an instant, my boy lifted my consciousness up and focused it away from where we sat together on the ground.

It was mesmerizing! Kristofer's every thought and every emotion was bared to me. I felt every physical sensation in his body, and I knew that he, too, felt mine. Then, a wave of ecstasy hit me; it was like nothing I had ever experienced before. My core burst into a blazing inferno.

It was then I realized that our love was instinctual; it was primal. Ours was a love so pure and so ancient that I knew it would never stop or end or die, and it could never be tamed. This love was ours for eternity. It was boundless, limitless, and infinite.

I craved for more.

Feeling my desire, my sweetheart pushed me higher and higher into waves of feverish pleasures. Our hungry souls crashed and mingled in a perfect mixture of both violent-frenzied merges and gentle, almost fluid sways.

Once again, Kristofer pulled my cognizance up, causing me to lose the grasp I had on my mortal body. I closed my spirit eyes and felt the sensation of our connected souls as they floated into another dimension. It was a dimension without margins or confines. It was a place devoid of restrictions such as age or distance from one another. He guided me as we drifted to an atmosphere of sheer bliss.

The trickle of sensations melted into a previously untapped river of warm, soothing energy that in turn flowed into a rush of molten heated desire, a desire that I was positive would at any moment become a passionate explosion from somewhere deep within us...

But, sadly, that was not meant to be.

My perception of reality was suddenly, and quite harshly, brought back to my mortal body by a colossally strong force ripping our souls away from one another.

I opened my eyes and then peered into the livid face of my father just as he lifted me off the ground, away from my boy, and stood me in front of him.

The naughty little witch in me tucked her black kitty-tail up between her legs, chastened by Papa's terrifying eyes. I stood frozen and peeked up into his furious expression. Worse still, my mind wasn't back to Earth quite yet, and the remaining elation caused by our blend made me a bit giddy. I wanted to giggle, but I bit my lip, suppressing the urge. After all, I was in enough trouble at the moment.

My father stood gaping open-mouthed at me. His expression was something between bewildered disbelief and shocked fury. All the while, I heard Kristofer's pa yelling at him from behind Papa.

"We discussed this, boy! I forbade you to kiss Leesie until the two of you are at least seventeen years old and betrothed!"

My papa looked me straight in the eyes and shook his head. *"You weren't just kissing,"* he whispered in a dangerously calm tone. *"You were blending with that boy!"* He tightened the vise-like grip he had around my arm while at the same time turning his head and throwing a terrifying glare toward my boy.

Kristofer stood still, but his eyes swept between my father and his own, and a look of sheer-terror shone in his expression. *"I'm dead. He's gonna kill me!"* I heard him saying. *"And if he doesn't, then MY pa will!"* I heard his voice again, but as I gawked at him, I noticed something strange: his lips weren't moving.

Both Papa and Mr. Cole were yelling at us, but I couldn't hear them. At that moment, I couldn't be upset or unhappy or frightened about anything at all. Only happiness dwelled in my mind, only joy.

I can hear my boy's thoughts!

Just then my mother came rushing out of the house, followed right behind by Mr. George and Grandma Maggie.

Mr. Cole grabbed Kristofer by the scruff of the neck and swatted him several times on his backside.

I darted toward them, pushed Mr. Cole away, and threw myself in front of my boy. *"Don't you touch him!"* I hissed.

Mama ran to me. She pulled me away from the two irate men by my side and peered between Papa and Mr. Cole. *"I think we all need to take a moment and calm down."* She spoke peacefully while also reaching out and grabbing Kristofer's hand, taking him out of harm's reach as well. *"After all, the children were merely kissing,"* she said, looking up into Papa's angry face.

My father almost imperceptibly shook his head as she stood staring at him and then inaudibly mouthed to her, *"They were blending."*

Mama gasped, and her eyes grew wide with shock. After a moment, she sighed. *"Well, we did show her how it's done, Asa,"* she whispered so that no one but he and I could hear.

I peeked up at him.

"You also told her about the facts of life," he hissed, glaring down into my frightened eyes. *"Are you going to try that next?"*

I shook my head. *"No, sir,"* I whispered, but in my head, I heard Kristofer's voice answer with a resounding *"Yes!"*

His answer took my breath away. I gasped and threw my hand up over my mouth, attempting to regain control of myself. I was thankful that Kristofer's answer was discernable to me and no one else, especially not to my father!

Just as I was about to return myself to a more composed state of mind, Mama broke through my thoughts. *"He said yes!"* she blurted into my mind. *"Kris said yes, and you heard him say it. In your mind! You. Heard. Him!"* She glared at me. Her eyes were wide with shock. *"What did you do, Alyce Margaret Raign?!"*

I wrung my hands. *He kissed me, and then…we blended. And now, I can hear his thoughts,* I stammered into her mind just as she pulled her power back.

I peeked into her worried eyes. Then they drifted to where Kristofer stood next to us, looking fearful. At the same time, I pulled myself away from her, making my way, calmly, to where Mr. Cole stood.

"I'm sorry, Mr. Cole, I didn't mean to be disrespectful to you," I politely muttered, feigning sorrow. *"Please, don't blame Kristofer. It was my fault. I kissed him. That was out of line, and I'm sorry."* My eyes dropped to the ground.

"You little liar!" Mama hollered into my head.

I turned to her. *I can't allow his father to punish him for this,* I thought back to her. *I cannot allow him to take the blame because I love him. I love him in the same way that you love Papa. I love him with all my heart and all my soul, and sometime soon, I may even love him with my body.*

My mother's jaw dropped. She stood glancing between Kristofer and me. Then she looked at Papa and gasped!

She grabbed my hand, making sure not to look at my father, and tugged me into the cabin until we were in my new room.

As we entered the room, I realized that I hadn't appreciated how lovely it was. But then again, the whole world was beautiful at the moment. In fact, if we had to live in a hollowed-out tree in the middle of the forest, with nothing but the leaves to keep the rain off our heads, I wouldn't care. I sighed. *Because I can hear my Kristofer!*

"*Leesie!*" Mama yelled, shaking me, and forcing me to look at her.

"*I wonder if he can hear me now, too,*" I dreamily muttered.

She seemed panicked. "*Well, I certainly hope not!*"

Finally, my mind came down from its euphoric high, and I noticed my irate mother who was sitting next to me. "*You seem upset. Why are you upset? Can't you hear Papa?*"

"*No, I can't! That's not the point. YOU ARE TWELVE!*" she yelled and threw her hands in the air. Then, shoving to her feet, she walked a few paces away and stared, unseeing, out the window, attempting to rein in her emotions.

"*Don't you find it a bit odd that I can hear Kristofer after only a single blend, but you can't hear Papa?*" I asked.

Mama whirled around, and her eyes flashed. "*No, I don't find it odd. I find it horrifying!*" she snapped. Then she closed her eyes and took a deep breath. After a moment, she returned to me. She crouched down in front of me. Her voice was no longer scolding. "*Lees, sweetie, I know you love Kris. I know he's your match; he is your soul mate. But right now, you both are just too young for this. You are twelve years old. I don't know why you can hear his thoughts, but I'll try to figure it out.*"

I shook my head, and tears flowed down my face. "*But I don't feel twelve, and I don't look twelve, either,*" I whispered, silently praying for some understanding. "*Kristofer and I used to be married, and I remember how that felt. Why should we be punished for dying?*"

Mama wiped my tears away with her fingertips. "*Oh, sweetie, you're not being punished. Your love isn't being denied; it's being postponed for a few years. That is all.*"

Just then Papa came into the room. He sat down next to me on my lovely new bed. He was silent for a few moments. He glanced from my mother to me.

Please don't tell him that I can hear Kristofer, I whispered into Mama's mind. *Please, oh please, he'd never understand.* I wrung my hands.

Papa sighed. *"Kris takes complete responsibility for what happened between the two of you. And I don't know which of you is being truthful…"* He shook his head. *"I don't think it matters."* He stood up and turned to face me. *"The only thing that matters right now is this…"* He paused and leaned in, his eyes angrily flashing. *"You are never going to see THAT BOY again! NOT EVER!"*

Mama went to retort, but before she could Grandma Maggie breezed into my room and shut the door behind her. *"Asa Josiah Raign, Junior!"* she snapped just as he cringed at his mother's use of 'Junior' in his name. *"Please, tell me, son, what good will that do?"*

She sat between Mama and me on the bed and smiled into Papa's eyes as he stood in front of her. *"I seem to remember a young boy once,"* she said, taking him by the hand, *"whose father disapproved of his love and, in fact, forbade him to see her."* Grandma leaned in closer, peering up into his eyes. *"Tell me, what became of that father-son relationship, huh?"* she asked, inclining her head to one side.

Papa glanced between her and me with worry in his eyes though he said nothing.

"Do you want your daughter to quit speaking to you, Asa?" she asked. *"Or worse, do you want her to journey through life without her love? Is that what you want for your daughter?"* She took a deep breath. *"Especially when both Alice and I told you that this was going to happen. We warned you that the children would someday be lovers."*

Papa squirmed and then blanched at his mother's words.

She leaned in closer to him, her eyes twinkling. *"They are each other's destiny, son. My goodness, you of all people should know that love such as theirs won't be stopped. It's simple, dear."* She winked at me and patted Papa's hand. *"The children won't be left unsupervised until the time comes that they have reached a respectable age, Fifteen, I think."* She winked at my mother. *"After all, that is how old your soulmate and you were when you became lovers? Isn't it, son?"*

My father said nothing, but Mama closed her eyes and blushed. Then Papa snickered a bit, squeezed my grandmother's hand, and then nodded.

Grandma, feeling satisfied with herself, stood up, smoothed the front of her dress down, and sighed. *"There, problem solved. Now what's for supper?"* she asked and swept from my room.

I like her! I hope she stays. I mean, heck, with her living here, I might be married when I'm thirteen after all!

"Over my dead body!" my mother snapped into my mind while at the same time forcing me to look into her eyes. *"I'm not going to forbid Kris from visiting with you just yet. However, should you so much as step a toe out of line again, I will! And rest assured, young lady, I will be watching you, and the window will stay wide open while he's around. Thank goodness Kris won't be here much at all over the next few months. His absence will give your papa time to forget, somewhat anyway,"*

My mother leaned in, and her mighty eyes flashed into mine again. *"Understand, you are not getting married until you are seventeen years old, at least, maybe eighteen!"* she said aloud.

Papa nodded in agreement.

Chastised, I nodded while Mama grabbed one each of my father's and my hands and led us out into the front room.

•   •   •

We ate supper that night in virtual silence. Kristofer and I sat obediently next to each other on the fireplace hearth. Papa had placed three large jugs of cider between us, but I didn't care. I sat marveling over my boy's thoughts while we ate. He thought about how his pa might punish him and what his ma was going to say to him when he got home, but mostly he thought about the kiss that we had shared and how we'd blended our souls together so completely and quite effortlessly.

I realized that he and I must have blended many times for us to be able to perform the act so thoroughly on the very first try. I also knew that he was always in charge during such trysts, and I looked forward to our next encounter with a great deal of eagerness in my heart.

I peeked at my sweet boy, opened his mind just a bit, and tiptoed in. Just as quickly, though, I slammed it shut. Kristofer was no longer thinking about our blend but rather having a few vivid and surprisingly naked thoughts about me.

My mouth popped open, and I deeply blushed just as Mr. George's soft timbre pulled my wayward mind back to reality.

Just as we were all finishing supper, he rose from his seat, yawning. *"Dear me. I know it's still quite early in the afternoon, but I seem to be worn out from our trip."* He yawned again and winked at Grandma. *"If you'll excuse me, I will now take my leave for the evening. I wish you all a very good night,"* he said, nodding toward the adults. Then he turned to me. *"Goodnight to you, too, my sweet."*

He turned to my boy. *"And not to overlook you as well, young Master Kristofer. I wish you both bonne nuit et beaux reves!"* he said to us and then ambled toward the front door.

I giggled. *"Goodnight and sweet dreams to you, too, Mr. George!"*

He turned to me, laughing, and then glanced at Papa. *"I should've known that the child would understand what I said with you as her father,"* he told Papa with a proud gleam in his eyes. Then he reached for the door.

Papa jumped up at the same time that Mama did. They hurried to Mr. George and closed the door behind him. *"Where are you going?"* my father asked.

"Well, to the buggy, of course," Mr. George answered. *"I have a warm blanket. I assure you, Master Asa, I shall be quite comfortable outside."*

Mama shook her head and took Mr. George by the hand. *"You will not sleep outside, George."* She kissed his cheek. *"You will sleep in Leesie's bedroom tonight with Asa, and Maggie and I will stay in my room with Leesie."*

Mr. George went to protest, but Mama put her hand up. *"No argument!"* she said while pointedly glaring at him and gesturing toward my bedroom door.

Mr. George snickered and smiled. *"Much obliged, darling girl,"* he said to her, kissing her hand, and then his eyes darted to Grandma Maggie.

As if on cue, my grandmother rose from her seat and glided toward him. *"I want to thank you, George, dear, for assisting me today without any prior notice."* She leaned in and looked straight into his sparkling hazel eyes. *"Once again, I am grateful to have you as have I always been. I hope you know that."*

Mr. George beamed and kissed Grandma's hand. *"I do know, and have me, you certainly do, Mags. However, it is still—as always—quite gratifying to hear you speak the words."* His eyes twinkled with affection.

My grandmother drew an unsteady breath, and her voice wavered. *"Yes, well, I just wanted to express my appreciation to you for all you've done for me and for my Asa. I am forever indebted to you for indulging my many whims over the years. But assisting me in getting to my dear family in such a timely manner today... Well, that was above and beyond the realm of your duties, George,"* she whispered, her voice trailing off, her hand warmly stroking his.

Mr. George sighed. *"They are my family as well, and I assure you, my lovely,"* he muttered, running the back of his hand down the length of her face, *"duty has no significance in the endeavors which I satisfy for you."* He gave Grandma a beaming smile. Then, turning on his heel, he let go of her hand, walked into my bedroom, and shut the door behind him.

Grandma Maggie said nothing. She swept across the room and back to her seat with a simpering smile stretched across her face.

I glanced over at Papa, who was grinning from ear to ear at his mother. I also noticed that Mama was smiling almost bashfully at her as well.

Grandma glanced between them. *"Yes?"* she inquired, her eyes wide and bemused.

My father snickered under his breath. *"Tell me something, mother,"* he snickered again, still grinning. *"Just how long are you two little bugs going to flitter around the flame? I mean, my goodness, that fire has been burning for over forty years now. Don't you think that it's just about time for the two of you to put it out, so to speak?"* He winked at her.

Grandma Maggie appeared shocked by his question although I did see a slight glint in her eyes. *"Whatever are you talking about, Asa?"* she asked, still feigning innocence, putting her hand against her chest.

Papa threw his head back, laughing open-mouthed at her. *"That man is shamelessly in love with you, Mama, and has been for many years!"* He wagged his finger at her. *"The way he pines for you. Well, it's almost embarrassing!"*

Grandma blushed all the way to her sandy-blonde roots. *"I am a married woman, Asa!"*

Papa nodded. *"Yes, Mama, you are married to a man who ignores your existence. Hell, the man ignores everything that doesn't have to do with his business!"*

She pointed her finger. *"He is your father!"* she snapped.

"Yes, well," Papa snorted, *"and if I didn't resemble the man as much as I do, I'd really have to wonder."*

"Asa Raign!" Grandma retorted, obviously offended. *"I have never! I would never!"* She turned her back to him. *"I am not an adulteress!"* she cried, crossing her arms over her chest.

Papa seemed guilt-ridden. He got up from his seat and knelt in front of her. *"I know you're not an adulteress, Mama,"* he whispered and stroked her cheek. *"Nevertheless, in your heart, are you going to tell me that George is simply a doting servant to you?"*

She shook her head. *"No, I'm not telling you that,"* she whispered, all the while still refusing to look at him. *"But your father is a good man, Asa, regardless of what you choose to think about him. He loves you, and he misses you very much."*

"Father loves me?" he scoffed. *"He didn't even raise me. You and George raised me. I never even saw the man unless he was coming or going to work at his office!"* Papa shook his head. *"And as far as Mr. 'Senior Raign' being a good man, do you happen to know why we are here? Do you know why our orchard and our home are destroyed?!"* he shouted.

Grandma seemed afraid to ask. *"Why?"* she stammered. Her eyes widened with dread.

Papa's hands shook. *"We are hiding because my loving, devoted FATHER told that evil monster where to find us. That is why! My wife and child were nearly slaughtered because of that man, and you wish me to respect him?"* He rose and then started pacing the floor.

After a few tense minutes, my angry father stopped pacing and returned to where Grandma sat gawking, teary-eyed, at him. He bent down and clutched her shoulders. *"That monster, Charles Marshal, wishes to destroy Leesie, Mama. He wishes to harm her. He wants to kill her simply because she is mine! Besides that, he wants to own my wife! He wants to chain Ali to a bedpost! That is, after Leesie and I are both dead!"* Overcome by the thought, he sobbed into his hands.

My mother and I both ran to Papa and threw our arms around him while my grandmother wept. *"Baby, please listen to me. I can explain,"* Grandma whispered.

Papa looked up. *"There is no possible way for you to explain away the near annihilation of my family!"* he tearfully snapped.

She took his face between her hands just as he knelt down before her. *"Your father realizes how wrong he was about Charles and his father. He knows what they are now. He sees how foolish he has been in the past, and he regrets ever trusting them. He didn't intend to give away your hiding place, Asa."* She stroked the tears from his face. *"It was a mistake, a horrible, ghastly mistake,"* she whispered through sobs.

"A mistake? How?" he snapped.

She turned to Mama. She took her hand and sighed, but she was still speaking to my father. *"An acquaintance of your father's happened to mention Alice to him one evening, in a derogatory manner, I should add."* Grandma squeezed Mama's hand. *"Your father was defending her. He told the man that she was staying with you and your daughter, her granddaughter, and that she had grown into a respectable young woman."* She sighed again. *"Of course, he knows the truth about Alice. He is aware that she is your wife, Asa, and Leesie's mother. But he felt that it was, perhaps, unsafe and unwise to mention those facts to the man. Nonetheless, Charles's father overheard, and he told Charles."* She gazed into Papa's eyes. *"Your father misses you, son. He was wracked with worry this morning when I left the house. He wanted more than anything to accompany me instead of George, but he is ashamed of himself, and quite frankly, he is afraid to face you."*

"He should be afraid to face me!" growled Papa. Then he sucked back his anger with a deep breath. *"But how did he learn of my marriage?"*

Grandma shook her head. *"He has always known, dear. He saw the love you had for Alice. It's not unlike the love he has for me,"* she tearfully whispered.

Papa looked into his mother's eyes. *"And how do you feel about him, Mama?"*

"I am devoted to him."

"But whom do you love?" he retorted.

My grandmother seemed taken aback by his question and didn't quite know how to respond. Her face flushed, and she seemed flustered. *"I am a respectable woman, Asa. I don't live my life according to hopes and fancies. Such things have no relevance in my life and would make no difference even if they did hold some degree of importance to me. Your father is my husband,"* she curtly muttered. *"The matter is closed."*

Papa nodded and kissed her forehead. Then he eyed Mama, and I noticed that they both seemed sad for Grandma.

I just couldn't imagine being married to a man I didn't love while loving a man I couldn't marry.

My eyes swept to Papa. *She had a child with a man she doesn't love…* That thought made me shudder. As thankful as I was for Papa's existence, I could help but feel sorry for her. Suddenly, sorrowful tears welled up in my eyes for my grandmother.

I walked around Papa to where Grandma sat and pulled her into a tender embrace. *"I'm glad you're here, Grandma,"* I whispered into her ear.

"I am, too, my sweet," she whispered and kissed the side of my head.

Just then, Mr. Cole stood and glanced around the room. *"Well,"* he said while taking Kristofer by the hand. *"If Kris and I are going to make it home before nightfall, then we'd best be on our way."*

Mama looked at him, puzzled. *"Home? I thought you were heading into the city?"*

Reverend Cole peeked toward my father. *"Well, we were,"* he stammered, still looking at Papa. *"But the 'individual' whom I was asked to retrieve from the city seems to have met us halfway instead,"* he vaguely answered.

Grandma Maggie turned to him. *"Jacob Cole, are you referring to me?"*

Papa laughed and stood up. *"Yes, Mama, I asked Jake to fetch you."*

"Whatever for?" she asked, cocking her head. *"Because you feared that I would be worried about you all?"*

Papa seemed nervous. *"Well, that and…"* He took a deep breath. *"And because I wanted you to be present to witness something,"* he stammered, his eyes darting between my grandmother and my mother. *"Considering…"*

"Considering what?" Grandma asked, tipping her head again.

Papa stepped closer to Mama and gestured to one of the chairs at the table. *"Considering you weren't here for my wedding,"* he answered my grandmother, yet his eyes never left my mother.

Mama seemed perplexed though she followed his instruction without question. She sat down.

Papa knelt on one knee before my mother and gazed into her bewildered eyes. Then, taking a deep breath, he clasped her hands between his own. *"To say that I love you, my beauty, just isn't enough anymore. To say that I want to spend my life with you seems too short a time. To tell you that I want to share my soul as well as every bit of my mortal body with you seems to me to be nothing more than a silly human frivolity—as does the notion of what we call a marriage."*

With those words, my mother frowned.

"Our marriage, as it stands now, represents our love and devotion for one another. Am I correct?" Papa asked her.

Mama nodded. *"Why, yes, of course, it does, baby."*

"Till death do us part, right?" he asked.

She nodded again.

My father gazed into her eyes. *"Well then, I ask you, sweetheart, how many times must you and I part by death? How many times do we each have to be reborn and grow up only to meet and marry all over again, till deaths do we part, and so on?"* he asked, dismissively twirling his long-fingered hand in the air.

Mama frowned again and shook her head.

"Foolish mortal symbolism, Ali. It is all simple, unimportant triviality," he said and then pushed closer. *"You and I, sweetheart, have married and parted hundreds of times before, perhaps even thousands."* He shook his head. *"I don't wish to uphold these silly human customs any longer!"*

He placed his hands on either side of her face, gazing into her lovely eyes. His voice cracked with emotion. *"I am asking that you agree to marry me one last time, permanently and without fail and without even the most inconsequential chance that we may ever be parted from one another again."*

He leaned in, and his light-blue eyes dazzled into hers. *"Meld with me, my darling,"* he whispered. *"You, Ali, are my life, both mortal and immortal. You are my lover; you are my dearest friend, my confidant. You are everything to me. Therefore, I want you also to be one with my soul, so that we may be joined for all of eternity."* He pressed his forehead against hers. *"We both understand that our love is infinite, so let us bond ourselves forever. Please, my glorious, divine, beacon of light from the Lord, please."*

Mama stroked Papa's face. Then she smiled and took a deep steadying breath. *"Before I answer you, Asa, I need to know that you have a realistic understanding of what this will mean for us. I mean, true, it is giddiness and merriment, not to mention vast amounts of pleasure and joyous gaiety, but there are also risks and consequences involved in this decision."*

My mother paused for a moment, her emerald eyes clouded with concern. She shook her head, seeming a tad bit overwhelmed. *"And there are responsibilities. There are vast responsibilities accompanying this, Asa. One, in particular, comes to mind,"* she muttered more to herself than to him.

Papa's brilliant smile shined into her worried eyes. He leaned closer, stroking the worry away from her brow with his fingertips. *"I understand your concern, believe me. I understand it all, sweetheart. I understand that from the moment you and I meld, we won't age a single day. I also understand that our hearts will beat in unison as will our lungs rise and fall together."*

Mama interrupted. *"Yes, and if one of our hearts quits beating or if one set of lungs quits breathing, then do both! We both live, or we both die!"*

Papa shook his head. *"I wouldn't wish to live one moment without you anyway,"* he whispered. *"I also understand that when we do decide to leave this world, whenever that may be, we will leave it together. And it will also mean that you and I will never again have to endure another painful childhood apart."*

My mother peered into my father's eyes, hers wrought with concern. *"And what of my powers, Asa?"* She barely breathed the question, her sights downtrodden. *"If we do this, then you may very well acquire some or all of them."*

She appeared anxious, peeking up into his beaming face. *"Are you prepared to gain such a responsibility? Are you ready to have my naturally inborn idiosyncrasies thrust upon you?"*

Papa pressed his forehead to hers again. *"A twist of fate that would only bring me closer to you,"* he whispered.

Mama raised her head, surprised by his answer. She laughed her beautiful bursting laugh and then kissed Papa's lips, and a torrent of tears flowed down her face. *"Then, I say: yes, my love,"* she tearfully vowed. *"Yes!"*

Having gotten the answer he desired, Papa threw himself around her. He pressed his lips to hers. They both ecstatically sobbed at once.

The rest of us stood gaping at them as they celebrated their love by nearly climbing each other.

Grandma Maggie gasped and blushed as my father pulled Mama's body still closer in a deep-down instinctual sort of way. *"Oh my, how very lovely!"* she exclaimed. I had to admit that I was surprised by her reaction. I thought she would be shocked by my parents' display of affection, but she wasn't. If anything, she seemed elated.

As my parents continued to celebrate their love, I glanced at Kristofer and Mr. Cole, neither of whom seemed bothered by the display either. I smiled and then inwardly hugged myself.

Hmm. I closed my eyes and envisioned myself entwined with Kristofer.

Shaking that thought from my head, I reached over and hugged my grandmother around her shoulders. *"Don't worry, Grandma. I'll make them stop. Recently, I've become quite accustomed to their displays of affection,"* I told her, giggling.

I'd become more than accustomed to it. I loved their displays of affection. I loved watching it, thinking about it, knowing that their love was true. It warmed my soul. Grandma was right; it was lovely.

With that thought and while inwardly smiling and hugging myself again, I stepped toward my still-entangled parents and cleared my throat.

"EXCUSE ME!" I hollered and poked Papa in the arm. *"YOU ARE AWARE THAT THERE ARE OTHERS PRESENT, RIGHT?"*

Everyone in the room, including my parents, laughed just as he let my mother out of his grasp. He pulled her out of the chair and then returned to it and sat her in his lap. He eyed me evilly. *"Maybe that's what I should've done to YOU today, young lady!"* he retorted.

I snickered. *"Save that for the next time, Papa."*

Mama gasped and whacked my already tender bottom with her hand.

"*Ow!*" I complained. Nevertheless, I cleared my throat again, even though I already had everyone's full attention. "*There's something I wish to say to my parents about their up-and-coming melding.*"

Mama's playful demeanor turned to worry. "*What is it, my baby?*" she asked, and I could feel her mind tensing with sudden apprehension.

"*Well,*" I said and then paused. I took one each of my parents' hands. "*As one of your naturally inborn idiosyncrasies, as you put it…*" I rolled my eyes as they laughed, and Mama's tension eased. "*I'd like to say that I love you both, and…*" I choked up. "*I'm very happy.*" I barely got the last word out before becoming hopelessly emotional.

My father pulled me into his lap next to my mother.

With that, Mr. Cole clapped Papa on the shoulder. "*Well, my friend, if I'm to get back here with Molly by early afternoon tomorrow, then we'd best be off.*"

Mama jumped up. "*Molly's coming?*"

Mr. Cole laughed and took her hand. "*Of course!*" he beamed down at her. "*She wouldn't miss her only sister's wedding, now, would she?*"

Mama threw her arms around Reverend Cole's middle. "*Thank you so much for everything, Jake. We're so lucky to have you and Molly as part of our family.*"

Mr. Cole smiled. "*Good thing Asa and you love us,*" he answered while also glancing at Kristofer and me. "*Because I have a feeling that we'll all be blood relatives someday.*"

My heart leaped. *Family!*

Mama nodded, laughing. "*You know, Jake, when Molly and I were children, we used to wish to be family. Wouldn't it be a wondrous surprise if our childhood desire was to come true?*"

Kristofer grasped my hand, pulling me from both my thoughts and out the door.

"You aren't going to punish Kris? Are you, Jake?" I heard Mama ask just as they passed us in the yard.

"No. What good will it do to punish him?" he answered as he climbed into the buggy. He looked down into her eyes. *"Although, Asa and I have devised a plan to deter the children,"* he said and then winked.

Mama nodded, and I inwardly cringed. *Plan? What plan? That doesn't sound good.*

Just before he climbed in and sat next to his father, Kristofer leaned up on his toes. He kissed my cheek and gazed into my eyes. *"Just remember what I told you,"* he whispered, all the while eyeing my father.

I nodded, trying to hold back not only tears but also the longings and cravings I felt for him. *"I know. I'll try."*

Kristofer turned from me and joined his father in the buggy.

Then the buggy pulled away from us—away from me.

Mama put her arms around me as we both watched my boy move further and further away from the cabin for the second time that day. *"It's all right, my baby,"* she whispered, but I wasn't listening to her. I was listening to my Kristofer's thoughts for what could be the last time for quite a while.

I closed my eyes, and his thoughts joined mine. *"I love you, Sita,"* he crooned directly into my mind. *"I can't wait to taste your lips again and to smell the sweet apple blossoms and the strawberry scent of you. My love, my beautiful, divine Beacon."*

His velvety words were like music to my heart. I sighed and smiled, not realizing that Mama could hear the sweet words of my boy from my mind to hers.

"You didn't tell Kris that you can hear his thoughts?" she asked.

"No. I feared it might frighten him away." I peeped over my shoulder at her. *"I'm sorry you don't understand."*

She laughed. *"You don't think I understand what it's like to get swept away by the one you love? Were you not paying attention to your Papa and me just a few minutes ago?"* she asked while still laughing. *"We're no different than the two of you, Lees. Our love is quite the same, which, incidentally, is what terrifies your father."* She took my hand and pulled me to the porch. *"We've felt this way since we were only fifteen. Granted, we weren't twelve…"*

Before she could finish the sentence, my grandma stepped out onto the porch to join us. *"No, you're quite right, Alice. Asa wasn't twelve years old when he fell hopelessly in love with you. He was ten!"*

Mama gaped at her. *"Ten? Whatever do you mean, Maggie?"*

Grandma Maggie nodded. *"My Asa first laid eyes on you when I brought food to the orphanage when he was just ten years old. He took one look at you, and that was it. For the next five years, you were all that boy would talk about."* She took my mother's hand. *"Asa even asked me to continue with his music lessons because someone from the orphanage mentioned to him that 'Alice liked the piano.'"*

Mama's jaw dropped at that unexpected bit of information.

"Then," Grandma went on with a wry smile. *"He sketched you from memory. On every spare piece of parchment he could get his hands on, Asa drew your image."*

She leaned into my mother. *"By the way, Alice,"* she whispered. *"I saw the painting of you that's hanging in your bedroom. It's just lovely, albeit a bit revealing,"* she said and then winked at me. *"I think my Asa was upset not because he doesn't understand Leesie's feelings but because he does understand."*

She turned to me. *"And I, too, understand how you feel, child. Just as I've always understood and have always championed your parents' relationship."*

I was confused. *"What do you mean? How can you understand?"*

Mama shook her head. *"Don't pry, Leesie."*

"No, it's quite all right, Alice. *The child asked me a question. I will answer her.*" Grandma gestured for us to sit down on the front porch swing with her.

My grandmother sighed and grasped my hand. "*When I was just a girl of sixteen years old, a sweet young boy caught my eye. He was the same age as me, and oh-so beautiful.*"

She turned to Mama. "*He had at one time years before I met him, lived at the same orphanage where you grew up, dear. Anyway, I was smitten with that boy, and he was in love with me, too, but my father did not approve of him. You see, my boy was not from the right kind of family.*" She frowned. "*Goodness, he had no parents at all, but I didn't care about such things. I loved him, and I wished to marry him. So one night he and I snuck off and attempted to elope.*"

She closed her eyes for a moment; her face paled, shrouded in the recollection of old wounds. "*I was prepared to leave my father and his wealth far behind me. Unfortunately, my father got wind of our plans, and he stopped us. My father and his men nearly beat my sweet boy to death that night. Then the very next day, I was shipped off to my great aunt's house in Vermont. I stayed there for the next two years. And when I returned, my father had a young man picked out for me to marry. I protested at first, but in the end, I agreed,*" she whispered. "*The man my father chose for me to marry was a decent young man. He still is a decent man, and he has always been good to me. I've never regretted my decision to marry him. I'm content. My husband and I have a comfortable relationship, and I'm really quite fond of him.*"

"*But what happened to your boy, Grandma?*" I asked.

"*That beautiful man came to work for me, Lees.*" She winked and smiled. "*Your grandfather and I hired him as our butler a few years after we were married. No one but I recognized him, thank goodness. My father and I were no longer speaking to one another, so that wasn't a problem. Besides, Father made it a point not to pay any mind to*" *people who weren't of his station in life, especially not servants, like my boy.*" She sighed. "*And my love has been with me ever since.*"

I gasped, and my eyes wandered toward the house—to where Mr. George lay sleeping.

Simultaneously, Mama, too, gasped and threw her hand up over her mouth. "*No wonder Maggie has always been so accepting of me,*" she thought to herself. "*George is a poor orphan, just like I am!*"

I grabbed my mother's hand. *That's not the only reason. Grandma Maggie loves you. And you're not an orphan, not anymore,* I whispered into her mind and then smiled at my grandma, who suddenly meant a whole lot more to me.

Grandma smiled at my comprehension and went on. "*I am fortunate enough to see George every day of my life,*" she said, her expression wistful. "*He and I sit each morning and enjoy coffee together. We spend endless hours talking to each other. He is my dearest friend in all the world. He brings a certain joie-de-vivre to me that I wouldn't otherwise have. And even though our love never quite came to fruition, our friendship has. So, c'est la vie!*" she hoarsely whispered and twirled her hands in the air.

I spoke up—I had to! "*Mama once told me that my papa is her dearest friend,*" I interjected and then grinned like the Cheshire Cat.

Grandma patted my hand. "*Yes, well, my love, when your dearest friend is also your lover, then that is true fortune. But like I told you before, your grandfather and I have a nice relationship. He and I are comfortable with one another, and I am content.*"

With that said, she nodded to herself, rose, and walked to the cabin door. But just before she stepped in, I huffed.

Grandma spun around. "*Was that obnoxious noise directed at me, child?*" she inquired, canted her head to one side, and glared at me.

"*Yes, it was!*" I answered. I then leaped up from the swing and fisted my hands on my hips—just like Mama always did.

Grandma stepped away from the door and glided gracefully back to me. Then she took my hand and sat me back down next to her on the swing. As she held my hand, a vision flashed into my mind. First, I saw her with Mr. George as they were when they met. Then a set of visions unfolded before my mind's eye. It was a story, a complete story. It was the story of my life with my soulmate. Only, it was the lifetime that I spent with him as Lusita.

At first, I was uncertain how the two visions related to one another, but it dawned on me as I stared at my grandmother's lovely steel-blue eyes.

Oh, my goodness!

Grandma and Mama sat in silence just as Papa joined us on the swing.

My mind was sent reeling. *"How is it, Grandma, that you can bear to live each and every day while being so very unhappy?"*

She seemed taken aback by my boldfaced question. *"I am not unhappy, child,"* she snapped.

"All right," I challenged. *"But are you happy?"*

Grandma glared at Papa. *"Overprotective and opinionated. Your daughter certainly is her father's child, now, isn't she, son?"*

"She sure is, Mama!" he laughed and leaned in toward me. *"Leave your grandmother to her unhappiness, Leesie."*

Grandma scoffed and then turned to me again. *"No, please, Leesie, ask anything you like!"* She threw Papa another scathing glare.

"I just have something to say." I didn't mean to upset her.

She crossed her arms over her bosoms in a petulant, childish sort of way.

"Well, I've always wondered how my father got to be the wonderful man that he is," I paused for a moment, attempting to articulate my feelings. *"He is an artist, and he's a musician, not to mention he has great appreciation for things such as the ballet, literature, and the opera..."* My voice trailed off just as my thoughts ran rampant.

I shook the confusion from my head. *"And my goodness, my papa speaks French and Italian as well as he speaks English! So I have frequently been perplexed by these facts, especially considering that he is a farmer."*

Grandma turned and smiled at Papa just a little though she still seemed perturbed with him.

I continued. *"But now that I've met you, Grandma, and Mr. George, I can see why my father is the beautiful, talented man that Mama and I love so much."* I took her hand. *"You and Mr. George may not have ever had a child together, but you certainly did raise one together. And frankly, I don't think he'd have grown up to be half the man he is today had he been raised by Grandfather instead of by Mr. George. Do you?"*

"No," she barely breathed.

I gazed into her eyes. *"I also see why my papa loves my mother so much."* I smiled again as she cocked her head. I drew in closer. *"My mother is poised, kind-hearted, and gentle and very much…like you,"* I choked, attempting not to cry.

Tears flowed from Grandma's eyes as I went on. *"Still, as lovely as you are, I also see a great deal of pain in your eyes. And it is the very same kind of pain that, just a few days ago, my mama had in her eyes, too."* I took a deep breath. *"It was the pain of denying her feeling for her husband."*

Grandma pulled away from me. *"What are you saying, child? I know exactly how I feel about my husband!"*

I put my hands up. *"Please, listen!"*

She huffed and threw my father another scathing glare. *"All right, proceed!"*

"Kristofer told me something today." My words her hesitant. *"He told me something that I didn't understand, not until I touched your hand, at least."* I peeked at my father, all the while knowing that I was about to get myself into a great deal of trouble. Still, I pushed

on. I had to! Grandma needed to know! *"Let me ask you something, Grandma. And keep in mind that I saw a vision of it when I touched your hand."*

She nodded.

"When Mr. George and you were young, did he take—your—hand?" I asked, slowly drawing out the last three words.

"Take…my…hand?" she muttered the question. I knew my question had a double meaning, particularly for her, and I was trying to gauge her reaction. By her nervous demeanor, my suspicions, as well as the accuracy of my memories, were confirmed. Grandma nodded again. She seemed bewildered. *"Yes, of course, he did. He held my hand."*

I glanced at my parents and then looked into my grandmother's confused face. *"Well, that's not exactly what I asked, but all right. Now let me ask you something else."*

Again, she nodded.

"The first time that Mr. George took your hand, did you see a light streak from your fingers to his chest?"

Mama gasped, and Grandma's eyes widened. *"Yes, it happened. But it was simple static. That is all."*

My father spoke up. *"What did Kris tell you, Lees?"*

I peeked at him. *"It's not really what Kristofer told me that matters, Papa. It's what you told me…before. You explained something to me in my last life. Something about the link. It was something that I didn't remember but that Kristofer did. In fact, Kristofer was a bit upset that you didn't remember."*

Papa looked like he was about to vomit; his face paled. *"What? What was it that I explained to you?"*

I took a deep breath. *"You explained to me that the link is as good as a marriage contract and that as soon as your soulmate touches your hand, he quite literally 'takes your hand' in marriage."*

Papa hesitated for a moment before speaking, but when he did, he enunciated every word with extreme clarity. *"What—did—the boy—say—to you—today?"*

I gulped hard, and my hands shook with fright. *"Kristofer told me he couldn't wait to marry me in a proper way. And then he called me..."* I faltered, almost tripping over the last two words. *"His wife,"* I squeaked and then looked down at my feet.

Papa's anger exploded. He leaped from the porch swing, nostrils flaring. Then he grabbed hold of my shoulders and stood me in front of him, a dangerous glint raging in his eyes.

Both Mama and Grandma gasped and rushed forward. My mother clasped Papa's hand and pulled him back and away from me.

"No, no," he said, yanking his hands away and throwing them into the air. *"I'm not going to hurt her. I simply wish to tell her something,"* he muttered in an all-too-calm tone.

He sat back down on the swing and put his hands out in my direction, imploring me nearer. *"Come here,"* he whispered. His voice was dark, and I sensed danger in the depths of his blazing eyes.

My mind swam with images of the day when I had disobeyed him. I could almost feel the stiff leather of his belt pressed against my skin and the vise-like grip of his hand around my arm.

My feet slid like a snail as I moved toward him, my hands stretched out in his direction. I wanted to run, but I knew that I had no choice but to stay and face him.

As I neared, he clasped my hands a little too tightly. He pulled me in front of him and glared into my frightened eyes. His voice was calm, but I knew otherwise. I knew that just under the surface, he was seething. *"Jake and I have discussed this quite thoroughly, sweetheart,"* he growled, taking deep, steadying breaths. *"He and I have decided that if you and that boy behave inappropriately again..."* He hesitated a moment, reining in his growing wrath.

"You'll punish me?" I timidly whispered.

He shook his head. *"No, I won't. But what I will do—and like I said before, Reverend Cole and I have already discussed this—what I'll do is: I will whip the boy in front of you."*

I gasped and threw my hands over my mouth.

My father pulled my face up until our eyes met. *"And I promise you, Lees. I won't do to him what your mama did to you today,"* he said, clasping my cheeks between his hands, and pulled my face nearer. Our eyes were mere inches apart. *"If that boy touches you again, Leesie."* He hesitated while my knees quaked with fear and rage. *"If he puts his hands on you again, then I will horsewhip him, and I will make him bleed. And just to be fair about it, I gave Mr. Cole permission to do the same to you in front of Kris."*

Hot, angry—no, not angry—outraged tears poured down my cheeks. I glared at my father.

"So unless you want to see Kris hurt, I would keep my distance from him, if I were you," Papa hissed.

Then he let go of me. He sank back in the swing with his arms folded and with a smug grin stretched across his face. *"And,"* he said, arrogantly raising his chin up, adding salt to my already bleeding soul. *"I have decided that you will not marry that boy until you're at least eighteen years old, either, possibly twenty-one! I don't know. I haven't decided which just yet!"* he declared and then nodded to himself.

That was it; it was all just too much, too overwhelming. I threw myself into my mother's arms and sobbed.

Papa, obviously feeling guilty all of a sudden, stroked my hair as I cried. *"I'm sorry if you feel that I'm harsh, Lees,"* he whispered, his voice no longer mocking or angry. *"Even so, the simple truth is that you don't have to agree with me, but you do have to obey. Anything less will have dire consequences."*

I peeked up at him from my mother's arms. *"But Kristofer and I are already married, Papa!"* I cried. *"Just like you and Mama were when you touched her hand in the stable and like Grandma and Mr. George were when he took her hand,"* I stammered-sobbed.

Papa's angry expression returned. *"Except that you are twelve years old, and you must obey ME! And I don't care if you feel that the two of you are married! You, Leesie, are my child! You will do as I say! And I say NO!"* he spat and then stood up and stomped out into the yard.

I sat up between Mama and Grandma and ditched the tears from my eyes. Grandma seemed both shocked and saddened at once. She glanced at Mama and me and shook her head. *"I'm not like the two of you. It didn't mean the same thing for me as it did for you. I am a place-holder. That is all I am, just a place-holder."*

I took her hand. *"You may not be just like us, Grandma,"* I muttered, sniffling a few times. *"But you're somewhat like us."*

"What do you mean, 'somewhat like you'?"

I squeezed her hand. *"Papa and I inherited our visions from you, and we both have a photographic memory that, I'm thinking, is also like yours?"*

She nodded.

"You made the link with Mr. George. He is your husband. Besides, he took your hand…" I smiled, leaving that statement hanging between us.

Grandma shook her head. *"I have been married to your grandfather for forty-five years, Leesie. I am too old to go peering back in time immemorial. Besides, like I said before, I am content with my life just as it is."*

That said, she rose and swept toward the door once again.

"Even if you're living a lie?" I shouted after her.

She whirled around and stared at me for a moment. Tears welled in her pretty light-blue eyes. Nevertheless, she didn't stop but proceeded to the house and then shut the door behind her.

"Poor Grandma. I wish she could be happy and not just content."

Mama nodded. *"So do I, sweetie."*

"Do you think she'll tell Mr. George about our conversation?"

"Well, baby, your Grandma Maggie is a grown woman. If she wanted to be with George, then she would be."

"Like you and Papa." I smiled despite my shattered soul. *"Your desire was to be with him, so now you are."*

"Yes, I am, baby, and this time it will be forever," she beamed.

"Just as I want to be with my husband," I whispered to myself.

My mother's face turned ashen, and her eyes shot daggers at me. *"LEESIE!"* she hollered, exasperated.

I grabbed her hand and gave it a squeeze, placating her. *"Don't worry, I'll try to be good. I'd better, or Papa will whip Kristofer. Do you think he really would do it?"*

She sighed. *"If the two of you step out of line again, yes, I do,"* she answered, and it was with a sense of finality in her voice that made me shudder.

"Still, Kristofer and I are married. Nothing can change that," I retorted.

Mama put her hands over her face. *"My sweet Lord!"* she whispered to herself.

I giggled at her expression and took her hand. *"There's something else, Mama,"* I whispered, gazing into her worried eyes. *"I remember a lot more about my life with my soulmate—the life before this one, which includes a lot about you."*

My mother dropped her hands. She gaped at me. *"You do?"*

I nodded. *"If you want me to, I'll show you in a while. But first, will you show me the portrait that Papa painted of you, please?"*

She smiled though she still she seemed fearful, and she nodded. Then she rose and took my hand. We walked to the door. Mama opened it although we both stopped short just before we stepped over the threshold.

Grandma Maggie was sitting on the fireplace hearth, clutched in the arms of Mr. George, and they were kissing.

I gaped at them; my mouth hung open.

Mama stood, wide-eyed and staring. *"Oh, dear,"* she mumbled.

I nodded while gawking at the pair of lovebirds canoodling on our fireplace hearth. *"I think Grandma Maggie told Mr. George about our talk,"* I whispered back to her and then inclined my head to one side. *"I wonder what Papa's going to say about this."*

"Asa?" Mama gasped. *"Oh, my goodness, me. Where's Asa?"* she asked herself just as Papa stepped across the doorway behind us.

Epilogue

Wilhelm Marshal's shiny, black shoes echoed off the wooden planks as he walked up to the jailhouse door. He did not knock, but then again, he was expected.

Charles Marshal pushed up from his desk just as the door swung open.

Wilhelm walked through the door with the arrogance of a king. He was tall and stout with gray hair, a broad face, and dusky blue eyes, and his attire spoke of a man who had become accustomed to wealth and power.

"Father," Charles muttered, tightlipped, his jaw flexing with tension.

"I'm told that the witch has escaped…yet again," Wilhelm growled.

"My men are searching. They won't get far," Charles retorted.

Wilhelm drew nearer. He stretched across the desk. *"I was lenient with you once, boy. The devils must be slaughtered. That is my order."* He pushed a bit closer, locking his steely gaze with his son's equally unyielding glower. *"Do you understand?"*

"The child and man will be killed, but Alice is mine," Charles replied.

Wilhelm's hands shook with obvious rage though his gaze held. *"We do not give names to demons and abominations!"* he bellowed. *"Asa Raign, Senior gave that witch to me on a silver platter… He presented her to me as a show of his loyalty to my organization, and my own son dares to defy my orders?"*

Charles said nothing.

Wilhelm stood upright and turned to leave. *"Consider this matter out of your hands,"* he snapped.

"Tell me, Father," Charles hollered just as his father turned back around. *"How does Asa, Senior feel about the imminent death of his only son?"*

Wilhelm sneered, and his hazy eyes melded into cold, hard slits. *"The same way that any self-respecting man would feel about having a son who would exhibit such crushing disrespect to his father…relief,"* he growled.

"Alice is my wife!" Charles vehemently roared while his eyes blazed with abhorrence for the man who stood before him. He balled his hands, and his fisted knuckles showed white with rage.

"Not for long," Wilhelm calmly stated, and then turned and walked out the door.